The Barbary Dogs

Also by Cynthia Robinson

The Dog Park Club

The
Barbary Dogs

Cynthia Robinson

Minotaur Books

A Thomas Dunne Book
New York

A THOMAS DUNNE BOOK FOR MINOTAUR BOOKS.
An imprint of St. Martin's Publishing Group.

THE BARBARY DOGS. Copyright © 2011 by Cynthia Robinson. All rights reserved. Printed in the United States of America. For information, address St. Martin's Press, 175 Fifth Avenue, New York, N.Y. 10010.

www.thomasdunnebooks.com
www.minotaurbooks.com

Design by Anna Gorovoy

The Library of Congress has cataloged the hardcover edition as follows:

Robinson, Cynthia, 1958–
    The Barbary dogs / Cynthia Robinson.—1st ed.
        p. cm.
    ISBN 978-0-312-55974-8
    1. San Francisco (Calif.)—Fiction. I. Title.
    PS3618.O3235B37 2011
    813'.6—dc23

                                        2011026216

ISBN 978-1-250-00727-8 (trade paperback)

First Minotaur Books Paperback Edition: August 2012

10 9 8 7 6 5 4 3 2 1

For Harry and Ruth

Part One

1

Frank Kelly dove off the middle span of the Golden Gate Bridge. Like almost all the jumpers who went before him, he leapt facing east—looking toward the city that had tormented him. San Francisco, the city he liked to refer to as the painted whore of the Barbary Coast.

Frank left a suicide note wired to the bridge railing. It said: *Ocean, ocean, I'll beat you in the end.* And in the postscript he wrote, *I'd like Max Bravo to disperse my material possessions.*

Well, I—being the Max Bravo in question—shouldn't like it very much. In fact, when the police showed me the note, my pity for Frank was soon dislodged by outrage, followed by simmering resentment.

I don't care for domestic drudgery. And I believe that recruiting one's friends to help one move is a hallmark of the modern Lumpenproletariat. To hire a truck—or, worse yet, to conscript a friend who owns a truck—and to load it up with one's stained mattresses and oak veneer particleboard dressers, and to ferry down the interstate with your belongings flapping in the wind, is a sad and déclassé spectacle.

So, yes, I was vexed that Frank Kelly asked me to clear the crap out of his apartment.

And, it was awkward. Frank and I had become estranged. There was a time when we were very thick. But, over the years, we'd drifted.

I saw him very seldom, and then only by random chance. At those sporadic intersections where we had met, it was inevitably a disaster.

We'd run into each other in some bar or other—as two errantly piloted oil tankers, colliding, sinking. The aftermath was always a twisted carnage of steaming wreckage. My head would burn for days like oil slicks flaming on salt water.

But outside of those occasional bacchanals, Frank lay buried in my past. During the two years of our active friendship, we saw each other nearly every day. Our converging interests—crapulence and irony—clamped us together. That had been long ago. Wasn't there a statute of limitations on ill-advised friendships, just as there are on other crimes?

The problem was that the local gendarmes had meddled all around San Francisco, showing Frank's suicide note to our mutual friends and acquaintances, and a host of barflies and hangers-on. And because those busybodies at the SFPD involved so many people, I was now bound by public scrutiny to go over to Frank's apartment and do as he'd asked. He probably knew that when he wrote the note.

Three days after Frank jumped, I drove to his place in the outer Richmond. It was a drab Sunday afternoon in June, and the diffuse light made objects look far away. The air smelled dank with frustrated rain.

Frank lived in an Art Deco building near the beach where San Francisco abutted into the Pacific Ocean. His building was a white, towering, Jazz Age monolith that dwarfed the surrounding homes—modest two-bedroom bungalows that sprang up like mushrooms all around it after World War II. The older building stood apart, on a grassy knoll like a lonely oaf. The Pacific roared in the background. The tower was shrouded in salty mists. Foghorns lowed like cattle.

This was the borscht belt. Little Russia. Frank was probably one of the only guys in his building that couldn't read Cyrillic. The Slavs don't seem to mind the moody microclimate—the cold wind lashing off the ocean, the fog curling around your ankles, the sky muffled with leaded clouds. Maybe it appeals to their sense of fatalism. Apparently, the Celts can be pretty fatalistic too.

I moved inefficiently around Frank's hollow apartment, boxing his books, sorting out his clothes, piling up items for donation. I searched for one or two personal effects that I could send to his mother in Canada—some keepsake that carried a whiff of her son, without freighting the stench of his tragedy. But everything Frank had was flotsam: chipped plates and busted radios and ghastly acrylic sweaters in every shade of gray.

In one of his books, something by Tom Wolfe, I found a photo of him on the beach. It was taken on a sunny day and his uncombed black hair lifted in the breeze. He was smiling, showing off his false teeth. He looked happy. I put the photo in my jacket pocket. I'd send that to her.

The donation people arrived, a charity organization that provided work for mentally disabled adults. The crew was comprised of two stout Down's Syndrome men and their attendant, who drove the truck.

I, rather grandly, told them they could take everything, the whole lot of it. The mongoloid fellows tactfully informed me that some of the stuff was usable, but most of it was simply landfill. They volunteered to take the junk to the dump for free. I offered them a tip. They found this awkward and informed me that they didn't accept gratuities.

They were just lugging Kelly's desk out when I stopped them. I'd forgotten to check the drawer. I opened it and discovered his personal journal.

It had a black leather cover, soft and pliant. It felt oddly warm.

I riffled through the pages. They were scabbed over with a minute handwriting as tight as Breton lace. The journal seemed to be a living thing, like a heart beating in my hand.

2

I woke up at 4 A.M. My grandmother was sitting on the edge of my bed, Frank Kelly's journal in her hand. She had it open, somewhere near the end. She ran her tongue across the page, smacked her lips, ruminating on the resonant bouquet of the page as though it were a finely aged wine poured from a dusty, cobwebbed bottle.

"Damn it," I said.

I rolled my head back on the pillow, glared at the ceiling.

"Your dilo friend," she announced. "He is in hell."

"I am in hell," I told the ceiling.

"Maximo, why you say such bad things?"

"I am in hell," I said, propping myself up on my elbows, "because you're here."

"You hurt my feelings," she said, smiling brightly.

I reached across my bedside table for the half-smoked cheroot in the ashtray.

I lit it, blew a gust of white smoke across the bed. I watched as the tobacco cloud passed through Baba—it drifted into her indigo skirt, her scarlet blouse, and it fogged through the gold necklaces that hung across her chest in a grill thick enough to stop bullets. A conspiratorial grin torqued her face. And when she looked at me like that, the miles of the long road etched in the lines around her eyes, I knew that I would follow her wherever the caravan led.

"Why are you here this time?" I asked, casually because I don't like her thinking she's overly welcome.

You have to be careful with Gypsies, even the dead ones. Actually, especially the dead ones. Make them feel too much at home, and pretty soon they're wearing all your cologne—at once—and eating your pork rinds and licking the pages of your dead friend's personal journal.

"Put that book down," I told her. "Frank Kelly is dead. Suicide. You'll probably catch some nasty mahrime off of it."

"I fixed it for you," she said, closing the journal. "I cleansed it. No more mahrime. But, I must talk to you about this book."

"Read it, did you?" I cocked my head to side and affected a pert, rather Anthony Newley interrogative expression.

Baba Lumenesta couldn't read. Not words on a page, at any rate.

"This book is alive." She turned toward me, leaning across the bed-covers to bring her shrewd, wizened face close to mine.

I shuddered. I had had the same sense about the book. But I had tried to ignore it.

Baba rose from the bed, placed the book on the table next to the window. The full moon was high in the sky now, swollen and milky. Its light poured through the mullioned glass, casting a grid shadow over the journal, like bars of a prison.

"Max, you're gonna need to listen to me," she rasped. "You could be in danger. This book is not average."

"It's not a book," I told her. "It's a personal journal. They're all the rage now. People codifying the steady drip of their every inane thought. It helps you organize your self-obsession."

"The men who wrote in this book are being held captive," Baba said.

"That's Frank's book, Baba," I told her. "One man. One man wrote the book."

She snatched the book up off the table, tossed it onto my lap. It fell open to the page she'd been slavering. It was still damp.

"Look," she said. "The hand is different."

I switched on the bedside lamp, inspected the handwriting. It was elegant, flowing. The letters were beautifully formed, the spacing was even and the pen had moved across the page gracefully.

Baba told me, "Compare to the other hand."

I flipped to the beginning. Frank Kelly's crabbed, tortured scratch-ing blackened the pages.

"The other writing," I said to Baba. "Maybe it is a woman's?"

"No," she shouted.

"Then who?"

"It is not a woman. But!" She stabbed one gnarled digit into the air, her coin bracelets shook like a tambourine. "Nor is it a man."

Oh God, I thought, here we go. Showtime. Pull out the tarot cards. Put the cap on the monkey. And pass the tin cup.

"Fine. It's not a woman," I said. "Not a man. I can name a dozen nightclubs full of people who match that description."

"It's no joke, Max!"

She swiped the journal out of my hands and once again set it carefully in the pool of pearly moonlight, the shadows now forming a cross on its cover.

"It is the writing of a dead man," she said. "But not Frank Kelly. Another."

"Dead men telling tales?" I chilled at the thought, in spite of my smart-assery.

"He drove your friend mad," she admonished me. "This dead man with the beautiful hand sent Frank Kelly to the bridge. And now, he comes for you."

3

There wasn't much sleeping after Baba's little visit. I would have liked to dismiss her as a crank. But, history wouldn't allow that. She'd been right about these sorts of things too many times. And, her very existence—the fact that, despite her death, she was still popping in and out of the ether, smoking my cigarettes and drinking my Calvados—yes, Baba's very presence lent an insistent gravitas to her warnings about this dead guy. I believed her.

I knew I could deal with Frank Kelly. If he wanted to come slogging out of the bay, a ghostly specter, half decayed, covered in crabs and kelp, fine. I'd seen Frank in bad shape before. It couldn't be any worse than all those times I'd had to bring him menudo and Valiums after he'd crashed from three-day speed and bourbon benders. No, I wasn't afraid of Frank.

But, it was this other chap I was bit worried about: the one that had somehow driven Frank Kelly to his final, desperate act.

My dog, Dixie—pugs being the highly coiled watchdogs that they are—had slept through Baba's entire visit. She was buried under the covers, snoring.

"You bark at the skateboarders," I said to her as soon as I was sure Baba had left. "And you don't even wake up when an intruder comes into the bedroom?"

The little lump beneath the covers stirred, rose, tested a couple of directions, then advanced like a fast-digging mole to the top of the bed. Dixie's flat face emerged, followed by the rest of her stubby body.

She stood, yawned broadly. She pitched herself off the bed.

She headed for the kitchen. She knew I'd follow.

I made coffee and prepared a mash of leftover rice and pork in Dixie's bowl. She anxiously watched as I stirred the pug potluck, standing on her hind legs, front legs splayed across the cupboard door, flat face upraised, intent on my every gastronomic ministration.

I put her dish on the floor and she face-planted into it. I watched her for a moment, the horror of her table manners striking me afresh, despite the countless meals I've set before her. She doesn't eat her food. She augurs it. There's a sense of urgency, as though she'd grown up in a concentration camp.

"I'll just leave you to it, then," I said to her. "Shall I?"

She was plowing into her bowl, sending it skidding across the floor.

"Need anything else?" I said.

She hit the bowl against the wall, and her back legs popped up into a brief handstand.

"Mayo? Steak sauce?" I asked. "Molasses?"

She'd pushed the bowl, now empty, into the corner and was licking and biting the enamel.

"Perhaps you'd like a water pick to blast the food particles out of your face folds?" I suggested.

She started working her way back and forth across the kitchen floor, in search of any errant food particles that may have flown out of the bowl in the melee. She looked like a crackhead picking white lint out of a shag carpet.

I took my coffee and my battered, marked-up *Faust* libretto. I went out onto the back deck. The sun was just topping the roofline of my house. I positioned the chaise lounge so I could see it searing silver through the early morning fog.

The *Faust* engagement was convenient. I didn't have to travel for it. We were playing in Oakland, just across the bay. We'd nearly completed rehearsals, so at least the whole wretched business with Frank Kelly didn't disrupt my work schedule. Not that I'd let it.

I was rather enjoying this production. I was Méphistophélès. Naturally.

I nearly always get to play the villain, being a bass baritone. But it's not often that I get to play Satan several times in one year. And that year, the year of Frank's suicide, I was literally a Satan for all seasons.

I was Méphistophélès in the spring. And, in the fall, I was scheduled to play Nick Shadow in *The Rake's Progress*.

The question that troubled me that morning was how to make Margarethe's Satan different from Stravinsky's. The two operas would be performed in different cities, at different times. It wasn't as though the audiences would notice if I replicated any traits from one diablo to the next. But I would know. And so I wrestled with the two devils, straining as much as any man can to differentiate one from the other.

In both operas, Satan is simply showing up to fulfill the wishes of the main character.

Faust is a decrepit and despairing bookworm who yearns to be young again so he can chase women. He, apparently, frittered away his youth studying.

Tom Rakewell, on the other hand, makes a pact with the devil for wealth. Both men are greedy, manic, wanting the things they don't have.

That's what undoes them. The wanting.

In the first days after his suicide, I still thought of Frank as nothing more than a minor tragedy. I assumed he'd been driven over the edge by depression. I didn't take Baba's warnings about another man—another dead man—at all seriously.

At least, I didn't worry about it once the sun came up and the light of day pushed the night shadows into the past.

At precisely 9:01 my phone rang. It was Claudia Fantini.

"I gave your number to Blashky," she told me.

"My private number?" I raged. "Who's Blashky?"

"He's going to call you," she continued. "You know Stan. Stan Blashky. He worked with Frank for years. He was Frank's partner. Art director."

"What's that got to do with me?"

"You're going to help him organize the funeral."

"What?"

"I can't spend all morning gabbing with you," she said. "I've got a shitload on my plate today, Max."

She hung up, leaving me with a mental image of Claudia sitting at her desk—in her corner office, which she'd elbowed so many people aside to get—with a big pile of shit on her keyboard. I found that gratifying.

This amusing thought bubble soon popped. I reflected on why Claudia called me in the first place.

It was all converging—the irritants were mounting. I felt myself becoming mildly furious.

First, I considered Frank Kelly. Then, his annoying suicide. And his annoying suicide note containing his annoying request.

Then, Baba got involved, and that's always an escalation of pesterments.

Now, Claudia Fantini, with her usual invasive bluster, giving out my telephone number to strangers, dragooning me into orchestrating that most odious of public spectacles: the obligatory funeral for a person of dubious popularity.

I wrote some notes in the margin of my libretto. Opposite the line where I sing to Faust, "Very well! I can gratify your whim," I jotted down the word *funeral*.

The funeral would be the next scene in the Grand Guignol of Frank's showy suicide.

Apparently, the funeral was this Blashky's idea. He had called Claudia, floated the notion past her, and, characteristically, she tipped the entire mess over to me.

Funerals are spectacular on an opera stage, but they're almost always unsatisfying in real life.

In these sterile, modern times—in the absence of belief in the afterlife, and even in the absence of irony—funerals have become like a stage play in which all the actors have forgotten their lines.

It's amateur playhouse.

We show up on cue. We recite rote speeches. Make the prescribed gestures. We heft and hoist the set pieces—the fripperies and contraptions of carcass disposal. And we hope that if we do all this, if we follow the script, then death will take the person we're offering up and somehow pass us by. Immortality will open before us like a toll-free road.

It never works. Death is not negotiable.

4

I got dressed. I stuffed Frank's journal into my overcoat pocket. I leashed the dog, and set out.

Dixie and I clamored down a range of vertiginous streets, crossed Market, and struck a course through the gay rangelands of the Castro. Then, we broached another ascent, into the yuppie baby stroller habitat of Noe Valley.

I sat down on the sidewalk halfway up Diamond. To scale that particular street one needed the legs of a speed skater and the mind-set of a drayage beast. I had neither, of course, just a general restlessness and lack of direction.

Dixie sat down beside me, flat on her little attenuated bum, with her back drumstick legs dangling down the slope. She looked like a potbellied old lady at the seashore.

Together, we surveyed the view to the east—the long-nosed freighters, their decks stacked with red and blue and yellow containers, glissaded across the waters of the bay into the awaiting embrace of Oakland's docks.

Dixie panted noisily through her wide grin. The edges of her mouth filliped in rakish curls and her deep wrinkles rived across her face like Maori war paint.

I caught my breath. Then lit a cigarette.

"This is my reward," I mentioned to Dixie. She swiveled her head, owl-like, and regarded me, still panting.

"I spend a full day carting crap out of Frank's apartment," I elaborated, "and now, those bastardos expect me to organize his funeral."

Dixie smacked her tongue as though she could taste my disgust.

"I haven't even seen Frank Kelly in years," I said, louder now. "No. Actually. Months. I saw him at Octoberfest. But that was it."

I was railing. Only mildly. For me, that is. It's relative.

Dixie was used to my outbursts. She blinked, turned her attention east, to the sun suspended above the Oakland hills, its light hammering sharp glints off the waves of the bay.

"First I have to shovel all that rubbish out of his hovel," I told her. "Hovel shoveler! That's my new title."

Dixie was distracted. A moth fluttered in front of her face. She followed its airborne antics by describing circle eights with her head.

"Now," I continued, "the world is insisting that I'm Frank's one great, good friend. Next I'll be asked to deliver a funeral oration and sing 'Ava Fucking Maria'!"

My telephone rang.

"Max!"

I held the phone away from my ear. Claudia shouted as though she were calling from a bullfighting match.

"Did that guy call you yet?"

"That guy?"

I loosened the scarf around my neck and looked out to the view of the bay. The water looked so placid from that distance, benign.

"That guy," she said. "Frank's friend."

"No."

I took a long drag off my cigarette, blew a few smoke rings and watched them contort in the breeze.

"Nobody called?" she cross-examined.

"No."

Another drag. Another set of smoke rings.

"His partner," Claudia yelled. "Did he call? Stan."

"What man?"

"Stan. His name is Stan Blashky. We talked about this yesterday."

"He didn't call me, Claudia. What do you want me to do?"

"Be proactive, you asshole."

Across the bay, a Japanese freighter settled into the dock. Tall white loading cranes, poised on their steel girder legs, waited to pluck the cargo off of it. They were like primordial birds, fey and fierce, alert to the sea that brought them their prey.

"Are you listening to me, Max?"

"Yes."

"You could call him. He's still at Grey. Or, maybe it's Y and R. I'll ask somebody here at the shop and let you know."

"Yes, ask around," I said. "Somebody over there will know. You advertising thugs keep it pretty thick."

"We gotta stick together, Max. Everybody else hates us."

She hung up. I said good-bye to the dead, buzzing line, closed the phone.

A woman wearing khakis and a baseball cap came slapping down the hill on pink rubber sling-back clogs. She was commandeering a double-wide stroller. She hoved up alongside Dixie and I, lurched the vehicle around, cranked the wheel brake down with her rubber toe.

I stared at the shoe. It was nothing more than a slab of livid, pink rubber that somebody had run over with a lawn aerator. I supposed that was for ventilation—the holes—to prevent the feet from putrefying in that rubber casing.

"Crocs," I said.

"Excuse me?" she said.

"That's what you call them," I said. "The things on your feet."

I looked back toward the vista, playing like I hadn't noticed her there. The woman paused. She decided to forge ahead with what she'd originally stopped to tell me.

"Oh my God. She is sooo cute!" she pealed. Then she demanded, "How old?"

She swiped at Dixie's head, trying to cluck her under the chin. The dog ducked.

"Excuse me?" I said, looking up at the woman.

I remained seated on the sidewalk, which put me face-to-face with a pair of identical toddlers in the stroller. They wore expensive jumpers and dull expressions. They watched me with incurious eyes as they each gnawed on half-unwrapped PowerBars.

"How old?" the woman persisted.

"What?"

"Your dog. How old is she?"

"I'm not sure."

"Can the children pet her?" she commanded.

"No."

"No?"

"No," I said. "She's in training."

"Oh."

"I'm training her to be a bait dog," I said. "We use her to get pit bulls and Rottweilers in shape for fighting. You know, for the betting."

She regarded me blankly.

"Betting?"

"We film it too," I said.

"You're a monster," she said, kicking the brake off the stroller.

"Oh, you'd be surprised," I called out to her wide backside as she slapped rubber down the hill. "She's small, but she's wiry. She's an eye-gouger."

The woman got out her cell phone, looking back at me.

It occurred to me that she was, just maybe, calling the authorities. She did look like the tattling type.

I raked the cigarette nub across the sidewalk, put the butt in my coat pocket. I rousted Dixie to her feet and the two of us hustled down a detour, a shaded walkway between the houses.

We wound our way through a sly series of tree-covered paths, up and down several steep and crumbly old cement stairways. The terrain was far too rugged for strollers, or the Animal Control trucks.

Once I was sure that we'd given Mrs. Croc the slip, we emerged again onto a street and made our way downhill toward the Mission.

The sun was directly overhead now. It struck the dark waters of the bay in direct shafts. The sea crystallized, shimmering beneath the celestial flames.

Frank Kelly was in there, somewhere below. He was no longer a man. He was a secret. He was a sphinx lurking beneath the shroud of iron gray water.

Uncannily, Frank wasn't my only familiar to end up in San Francisco Bay—that handy local repository for people with bad luck, or bad judgment.

It hadn't even been two years since Amy Carter had disappeared, without a trace. We had all thought she was dead. Murdered, actually.

That's how Dixie had come to live with me. She'd been Amy's dog and she was orphaned by her mistress's disappearance.

I kept telling myself that I was just dog-sitting her until Amy came back. Maybe she'd show up one day after having recovered from amnesia, just like in the soap operas. She'd tell us some story about how she'd worked as a waitress in a diner in Gallup, New Mexico. She'd relate how she often had a puzzling sense, while refilling the ketchup bottles, that her name wasn't really Carly Jean and she wasn't really married to this truck driver named Garth who'd found her sitting in front of an In-N-Out Burger in Bakersfield. Then we'd all laugh at the unpredictability of life.

But Amy didn't come back. Not yet. And Dixie was still with me.

And the longer she was gone, the more it looked like she was at the bottom of the bay. Maybe now, Frank Kelly lingered down there with her.

Lots of inconvenient people went into that bay. Lost people. Swallowed up in the indifferent waters.

In the bay, skeletons of great white sharks lay alongside long-dead sailors. Barbary Coast thugs who'd run afoul of their confederates bobbed, tethered to sandbags. Colonies of hermit crabs scuttled over rotting sturgeons long as canoes and old as redwoods. And ghostly

flat halibuts glided over discarded wedding bands bonded into black
spongy beds of creosote.

San Francisco Bay was where three centuries of detritus and secrets sank down to sleep.

5

I descended the Noe peak and walked to the Mission. There was a
bookstore there, on Valencia Street. It was an antiquarian affair with
plank floors and dusty volumes stacked every which way on sagging
shelves. A large gray cat slept on a velvet cushion in the window.

I remembered that I had seen a sign in the window: GRAPHOLOGY
SERVICES—EXPERT INTERPRETATION OF HANDWRITING. REASONABLE RATES!

When I got there, I inspected the sign a little closer. It was hand-
lettered with a brush. The script furled across the board in controlled
abandon.

The transom bell rang. I stepped inside, closed the door behind me,
and I was submersed in an echoing tide of silence. The gray cat lifted
his head, regarded Dixie, green eyes glinting under half-mast lids. He
laid his head back down on the velvet and was instantly asleep.

The carpet marked my footsteps through the store with damp im-
prints. I could smell mold, and that very specific mustiness that lichens
onto old linen-bound books.

"*Bonjour*," a man said from behind a standing desk that was off in
a corner.

He was wearing a houndstooth jacket and an expertly arranged
maroon ascot, and he was scratching away at a piece of vellum with
what appeared to be a quill pen. I was with him all the way up to the
quill pen.

"I saw the sign," I said. "I'm here to inquire about the services."

"The calligraphy?" he asked, laying down his instrument.

"No," I said, suddenly unable to recall what I had come in for.

"You need something notarized?"

I blinked. Dixie cranked her head to the side.

"Well, perhaps you'd like to browse the books?" he suggested.

He came around from behind his writing desk, treading lightly on soft-soled slippers. They were velvet, like the cat's cushion, and they had the letters EB elaborately embossed on the uppers in gold thread.

"Occasionally people still do," he said.

"Do, what?"

"Read books."

"I came about the graphology," I told him. I pulled Frank Kelly's journal out of my pocket, handed it to him. "It's this. I'd like an expert opinion on the writing in this notebook."

He took the journal, made a crisp quarter turn toward his writing desk, and snatched up a pair of reading glasses. He signaled me to follow him.

We marched to the front counter. He waved to a tall swivel stool. I sat. He took up his post on the merchant's side of the heavy wooden counter. It was the color of honey, broad, and polished to a high gleam.

A brandy snifter stood on the counter. Inside it, a lone Siamese fighting fish writhed and twitched, its iridescent scales flickering blue and green ferocity.

"I am Emile Balzac," he announced. He offered me his hand.

"Max Bravo," I told him, returning his brisk handshake. "And this is Dixie."

He smiled perfunctory indulgence toward the dog and, perhaps, me.

"Who does the calligraphy?" I asked.

"*Moi.*"

"And the notary service."

"*Moi, aussi.*"

"And you are the graphologist?"

"Correct."

"But, this is a bookstore. Yes?"

"Of course," he said.

He slid his reading glasses on. The arms of his spectacles strained wide to circumnavigate his temples. I now noticed his head was extraordinarily round and large, nearly hydrocephalic.

"This book," he remarked, flicking deftly through the pages. "It is someone's private journal. Not yours. Do you have permission to analyze it?"

"How do you know it's not mine?"

"It's obvious," he said, looking up at me, a pair of magnified pale eyes, like citrine-speckled koi, swimming around in those black-rimmed glasses.

"Did the writer give you permission?" he asked again.

"The writer is dead," I said.

And for the first time, I felt deeply sorrowful.

Saying the words, pronouncing him dead in my own voice, suddenly made Frank's death concrete. I could picture him, and I felt a surge of that welcome familiarity that I always felt when I'd run into Frank in a bar, or at some street fair, or, most recently, rummaging through a box of old clothes that someone had set out on the sidewalk for giveaway.

Only now, that sense of having come across Frank, the compatible feeling, was tinctured with the metallic taste of loss and regret.

Frank was a drunk. He was a brawler. He was a writer of bad poetry and a quipper of great hilarity. He was my friend. And his loss opened a great chasm at my feet and the very permanence of its darkness enveloped me.

Emile Balzac plucked a tissue from a box under the counter and handed it to me. I dabbed my eyes, blew my nose. He closed the book, laced his fingers over the cover.

"Sorry," I said. I stuffed the tissue into my pocket. "It's just that. Well, that's the first time I said it out loud."

"I understand," Emile Balzac said.

And the way he said it—quiet, dispassionate—I was sure that Balzac did understand.

"This journal actually contains the writing of two distinct persons," he continued. "You know this, do you?"

I told him I had a suspicion that was the case. Baba was right. Again.

Emile explained his pricing for the graphology service. He'd have to charge me for examining two sets of handwriting. But that didn't concern me. His rates were low.

"It will take me several days," Balzac said. "I have to study the material. I have to analyze it. It's very complex. The palette. The flavors. The nuances."

He picked up a small canister of fish food, took out a pinch, and sprinkled it onto the surface of the water in the brandy snifter. The solitary Siamese fighting fish thrashed in the glass, gobbling the food flakes as if he were competing for them.

"I'll need to photocopy it," Balzac said, watching the fish.

He clarified that the photocopying would be an additional charge. I told him that was fine. He took the journal and we went across the store, to a copy machine—a bulky, puce-colored monster that idled against the back wall, alongside a set of shallow shelves crammed with swollen, water-stained paperbacks. A strip of curled-up paper, taped to the wall, announced in futuristic sans serif: BEACH READING.

Another sign—this one hand-lettered in a 1960s retail script that always made me nostalgic for the shopping centers of my youth—was taped above the copy machine. It indicated that photocopies were ten cents a page. Balzac saw me looking at the sign. He assured me that he'd just charge me a flat rate for the photocopies. Forty dollars.

I started to quibble. He informed me this wasn't the Bangkok night market. He wasn't here to barter. He told me to look around. Browse the books. The machine was slow and the copies would take a while.

I wandered to the front of the store, to the display table featuring new releases. The books were piled high in a pyramid. At its apex was, I supposed, the runaway hit of the season; a book entitled *Smashed to Bits*. The cover illustration was a distracted female face peering out from between stormy clouds. The sell copy exclaimed, rather breathlessly, that this book was the follow-up to the bestselling hit *Shattered to Pieces*, by Betty Ann Thibideaux.

I knew her.

I picked up *Smashed to Bits* and opened it to the back flap. There was her photo. Betty Ann. She was twenty years older, but still recognizable. Lunatic moon face. Wide-set bovine eyes. Pupils dilated in vacuous intensity.

Balzac materialized at my elbow. He startled me.

"Did you see her?" he asked.

"What?"

"The author," he said. "She was just here. She comes in and signs the books."

"No. I didn't see her."

"I heard the transom bell when I was in the back," Balzac said. "She must have left."

"Betty Ann Thibideaux was here?"

"*Oui*," he said. "She lives here in the city."

"I knew her," I said. "Years ago. Actually, she knew the man whose handwriting you're analyzing."

"The dead man?"

Yes. The dead man. Frank. That's how I knew Betty Ann—through Frank. I hadn't thought of her in years. She belonged to my wasted youth, eons before my wasted middle age. It was an epoch of continuous night, streaking neon, smoky clubs, and prowling sex. At that time, we thought we'd live forever, and we had nothing to live for. We were artists. Frank. Me. Even this ridiculous Betty Ann.

"She's made a fortune with her memoirs," Balzac said.

"It's an odd coincidence," I said. "To see her book here, when I've come about Frank's journal."

Balzac took off his glasses, tucked them inside his jacket. He said, "I don't believe in coincidences."

6

I left the bookshop with Frank's journal back in my pocket.

I was in the mood for Turkish. It must have been suggested to me by the ambiance at Emile's bookshop; the dank air, the palette drained down to watery grays, Monsieur Balzac's perfectly fluffed ascot. My subconscious surely filled in the rest; the clarinet rilling some vaguely Dalmatian background music, and hint of gardenia on the breeze.

I walked across Market Street and up Larkin, skirting the oily edges of the Tenderloin. A couple of blocks east lay the end of the world, a postapocalyptic veldt of free-range crack smoking, back-alley blow jobs, and unmedicated schizophrenics.

I snapped up Dixie's leash and she smartly pranced past a lumpy, stained ski parka piled on the sidewalk. The hood of the parka was up, its ties sphinctered tight around a swollen, bruised face. The face was immersed in a puddle of vomit.

I stopped. I turned and looked. I couldn't tell whether he was breathing.

There was another junkie beside the downed skier. But that one, being a better planner, had managed to nod off with his air supply unobstructed. He was slumped against the side of the building. He was serene, his eyes closed and his face angled up to the sky. He could have been an angel, or a martyred saint, if it weren't for the brown nimbus, a splatter of human fecal matter on the wall behind his head.

Mr. Upright had two certainties in his future; he'd wake up with bad hair, and some kind of a loopy hangover. But the other one, the drowning skier, maybe he wouldn't wake up at all.

I was, yet again, toggling between the conflicting impulses of compassion and revulsion. These are the freeze-dried emotions served up daily to the native San Franciscan. The city is, in many precincts, a great big outdoor psych ward.

I gripped the phone in my pocket. Then I realized that was stupid. There wasn't time to call 911.

A Good Samaritan wandered by. The gentleman stopped, bent down to inspect the vomit depth, and without hesitation, swung his plastic sack full of malt liquor at the junkie's head. This stirred the dreamer. He shifted and rolled onto his back, basking his vomit-streaked face in the warm rays of the afternoon sun.

I was relieved. I wouldn't have to get involved.

"I was thinking I'd have to call the ski patrol," I said to the man who'd saved a human life with a six-pack of King Cobra.

"Thinking?" he said, and emitted a rumbling "Huh," thereby once again confirming that I was nothing more than an effete white man.

"Let's go eat," I said to Dixie.

We got to Geary Street, rounded the corner, stopped to look at the window of Alex's Gift Shop—a display of bolt-cutters and switch-blades.

"That's a great Mother's Day gift," I said to Dixie, nodding at a butterfly knife with a pink handle.

A zombie floated by. She was wearing a stretched and stained Lycra minidress and laceless boots. She carried a lunch bucket, its lid hung open, bouncing like a fractured jaw as she walked. The bucket was empty.

Her eyes were blacked with smeared mascara and she had painted clown-sized lips on the bottom half of her face. She looked at me and saw straight through to some distant Elysian hell field where poppies grew in self-seeded abandon.

I tried to remember the date. Maybe it was check day. You could usually tell just by the vibe. The meager payments arrived at the P.O. boxes, so the post office lit up first. Then the check-cashing rip-off joints were overrun, then the dealers. The little windfalls riffled through the Tenderloin and the place buzzed and frazzled in an amplified crank and heroin frisson.

"Max," the Turkish cook greeted me from behind the counter. He was slicing wafers of lamb off the giant meat spindle in the window. "Sit anywhere."

The place was empty, save for the two waitresses sitting in the back banquette, chatting over coffee. I smelled fresh bread, and curry, and Windex.

"Max." Lale got up and came sparkling to me—long legs striding in denim jeans and the black T-shirt with *Turca Delight* dashed in cursive over her heart. She extended her arm and her fingers opened like flower petals. I placed Dixie's leash in her palm.

"Sit where you want," she said over her shoulder.

She led Dixie out to the back porch, to her shady spot where she'd be put to work on a lamb hock.

I slid into my usual banquette seat in the corner, glanced over at the daily special on the whiteboard. The top half of the minidress zombie drifted across the picture window. Her big clown face bobbled on her stick figure shoulders.

She was working. It made me angry. Not at her, but at the bastards trolling the neighborhood in their cars. They'd pull up to the curb, and she'd run to them like a carhop.

San Francisco had always been filled with these tragic, shipwrecked people. From its earliest beginnings, hopeful underachievers had left their homes in Ohio and Missouri and other such dull places, and come here to make new beginnings. But, of course, if you're a loser at home, you won't do any better here, clinging to a crumbling shoreline at the edge of the continent.

In the Gold Rush days, they arrived by the shipload. Most went broke. Many lost their motivation, and their minds, as well as all their money. They say that in the 1850s, bums lay all over the muddy streets, comatose on cheap booze and opium, oozing into the rivers of muck.

Lale came back with a bottle of Yakut and a wineglass.

"Nothing ever changes in this town," I told her.

She ignored my comment. Lale isn't one to be snared into pointless polemics. Before I could stop her she pulled out the Windex and laid down a burst of it onto the glass tabletop. And, with that, Windex became the dominant scent in the universe.

I told Lale I'd have the daily special.

"Like normal, Max."

"Yes," I said. "I like it normal."

I waited for the Windex to dry, then set the spine of Frank's journal down in between my wine and my knife. I let it fall open. It settled at a page near the beginning. The page was dated recently, but Frank was writing about the past, back to 1989 when he first moved into Claudia's basement suite.

I found a great place to live and work. A small basement apartment in a big, old Victorian. The ceilings were low, and so was the rent. Time of day never registered down there. Sunlight didn't either. It was always dim. I could feel the weight of the building over me. I liked it. I'd work for hours without stopping, like I was buried in a crypt with nothing but my typewriter.

It was the second paragraph where Frank Kelly began to run amok:

There were no distractions, except this friend of my landlady's. His name was Max Bravo. He was an opera singer. Pretty much B league, I figured. He was always dropping by looking for Claudia, but she wasn't around much because the agency she was at worked them like assholes. Max should have known that she wasn't around. But he still came over just about every day. I could always tell when it was him. He'd stomp up the stairs and lay on the doorbell. Then he'd come banging around the side of the house, let himself into the backyard. I could hear him in the garden, muttering some shit to himself, looking in Claudia and Larry's windows. Then he'd stick his head in my doorway, literally, my fingers would be on my typewriter keys. And he'd ask me the same thing every time. What am I doing? And I'd be like, typing, dude. Once he had you cornered, there was no getting rid of him.

"Bastard," I said. I fortified myself with a deep drink of Yakut and read on:

> *At first I thought maybe Max was hitting on me. Then I realized, he's just a lonely guy. He's going through a divorce, even though he's a total fag.*

"Slander!" I yelled.

"No," said Lale. "Is the special. Lamb with vegetables."

I picked up the journal so she could set the plate down.

"Did I just say that out loud?" I asked.

"No," she told me. "You said it inside your head. But I still heard it."

I plucked up the serviette and snapped it open flamboyantly, as though I were signaling a ship.

"I don't recall having ordered a side of impertinence with my meal," I said.

"Is free," she retorted. "For preferential customers."

She slid back into the far banquette with her coworker. I heard a spirited volley of Turkish, then a shell-burst of laughter.

I stabbed at my lamb, and fumed about Frank Kelly's scunnering remarks. That bastard could write whatever he wanted in his journal and convince himself that it was reportage. But I still had a living memory of those events, of that time and place and who we were back then.

I, being the last man standing, was in a position to write the definitive history. I would Mommie Dearest his ass into eternal infamy if I had to.

And, I thought, pouring myself a second glass of Yakut, it was Claudia Fantini who brought Frank Kelly into our sphere to begin with. She's the one who should be organizing his damn funeral. He didn't write any maledictions about her.

Frank was always solicitous with Claudia, always playing Uriah Heap to her. It was a dynamic they'd developed when she was his landlady, and they never really broke out of it.

She met Frank sometime soon after the 1989 earthquake. That was in October. Frank had showed up a few months later—the weather was grim and overcast, so it was probably June. Maybe the earthquake tore open some vent to hell and Frank Kelly came fluttering out on leathery wings.

He moved into Claudia and Larry's—into that dismal subterranean slum in their basement. Claudia whimsically referred to it in her classified ad as a "garden apartment."

Frank Kelly took the apartment on sight. I remember Claudia agonizing immediately afterward. She sat at her kitchen table, mewling into her martini, demanding that I inspect his signature on the lease.

"I'm not a graphologist," I said.

"But can't you tell anything by his handwriting?" she demanded.

"If you'd wanted to know about him, you should have called his references. Where's your due diligence?"

"Max, do you have any idea how many people I've showed that dump to? At least sixteen. They walk in, take one look, and walk out."

"But this Frank Kelly?" I said. "He fell in love with it. Like it was perfect for him. Maybe he's a serial killer. Or a writer."

"He didn't even look in the closets," she said.

"Maybe he doesn't have many clothes. Just dead bodies," I suggested. "Did he ask how big the crawl space is?"

"Oh God," she protested. "Do you know what something like that would do to our resale value?"

We never did resolve what it was about the apartment that attracted Frank. When Claudia showed it to him, they entered through the galley kitchen—a low-ceilinged bare-bones facility that had taken on a gray patina after seven decades of unventilated fry cooking. Every surface was a potential flash point for a grease fire.

Frank tried to shut one of the cabinet doors hanging open on its hinges. It wouldn't close. "Warped," was all he said.

They walked through the living room—on sculpted carpet moldering with seeping groundwater—and Frank reached up and grazed the nicotine-stained acoustic ceiling tiles with his knuckles. Claudia showed him the bedroom, blue and faded, the kind of bedroom that held out scant hopes of ever attracting romance. And she directed his attention to the bathroom with its beige faux porcelain sink on the oak veneer cabinet, and the rusty towel rack that was long enough for just the one towel—which had, appropriately, been stolen from a Motel 6.

Frank didn't comment.

He came back into the living room. He thrust his hands into the pockets of his jeans, stared out the neck-high window at the rotting underbrush of Claudia's neglected nasturtium beds.

"I'll take it," he said.

He left her with a check for first and last months' rent. She told him she didn't need a damage deposit.

Larry and I had both urged Claudia not to rent out the basement. Just leave it empty, we told her. It was never meant for human habitation. It was originally a coal cellar. It wasn't until the dark nadir of the Great Depression, in fact, that the previous owner converted it into a rental.

It was a desperate place, leased out by desperate homeowners to even more desperate renters.

But Claudia and Larry weren't desperate. They made plenty of money.

And they had bought the house at fire-sale prices. In the aftermath of the 1989 earthquake and the recession brought on by the smug policies of trickle-down economics, they swooped in and picked up the regal Victorian pile at a bargain.

Yet, Claudia insisted on wringing revenue from the basement. She put it up for rent before she and Larry had even unpacked their own moving boxes. She was a manic hoarder of pennies, always imagining the world would take a vile turn and she and Larry would be down to their last handful of kopeks.

"The suite is all set up and ready to rent," she argued, actually she yelled at us. "It has a kitchen. And it's semifurnished."

I thought of the furnishings. The rusty-legged dining set in the kitchen, with the peeling walnut veneer table, the tall-backed chairs upholstered in stubbly plastic stamped with green and yellow flowers. There were only three chairs; the fourth chair broke. And there was an extension for the table, but it got wet and melted. The living room was appointed with a sagging ruffle-skirted sofa and a dark-stained oak coffee table that looked like a piece of an old ship—the kind of thing that survivors cling to in the tossing sea. And the bed seemed to be made from the same flotsam; a heavily shellacked oak headboard with shelves and compartments for stowing your bong and your condoms.

"Who?" I quizzed Claudia. "Who in their right mind wouldn't want to live there?"

It didn't matter what I said, or what Larry said. Claudia couldn't let the apartment sit empty, "just dumping" as she put it. Three generations out of Calabria—and Claudia couldn't escape her DNA. She was destined to be, at heart, the same hardscrabble, lira-pinching peasant housewife that her grandmother was.

But even Claudia had her moments of lucidity, her doubts. She called me on the day that Frank was due to move in. She was worried.

She couldn't admit it to Larry, but she knew she could haul me into her daytime soap opera.

Claudia and I set up in her kitchen with a fifth of tequila and a bottle of grenadine. We positioned ourselves behind the drawn blinds. We heard a car pull up out front. We hustled to the living room and spied the new tenant getting out of a cab.

Frank Kelly brought one hard-cased Samsonite suitcase, a sleeping bag, a plastic mesh lawn chair, and a potted cactus.

"Now I'm worried," Claudia whispered.

"Me too," I said. "There's not enough light down there for that cactus."

"Go tell him he can't move in," she said, the shadows of the louvered blinds ruling thin black lines across her face.

"On what pretext?" I said.

"Say that my mother is dying and she has to move in," she said.

"You wouldn't put your mother down there," I said. "Unless she was already dead."

After some wrangling and another couple of tequila sunrises, Claudia finally got me to agree to go downstairs and meet Frank Kelly. I told her to phone the police if she heard power tools.

"Halloo," I called through the doorway at the bottom of the steep cement steps. "Hello there. Max Bravo here."

The door was standing open, but it wasn't an invitation. I could smell the mold from outside. I assumed the new tenant was airing the place out.

"Friend of Claudia's," I called again. "Her roommate, in every sense but the rooming, and the mating bits—I'm over here so much. Well, maybe more of a fixture, really. Hah. Just thought I'd introduce myself."

"Frank Kelly," he said, appearing in the kitchen from somewhere farther back in the burrow.

He was of average height, but muscular in a tightly coiled way. His face was angular—a tad on the ferrety side—and his jaw joints pro-truded, undoubtedly from excessive teeth grinding. He had a firm, brisk handshake.

"The cactus brightens the place up," I said.

"Guinness?" he suggested, handing me the can.

Two hours later, Claudia clacked downstairs in her slingbacks. She demanded to know what the hell was going on. It should have been obvious.

"Darling," I hailed her, embellishing the greeting with an expan-sive arm sweep. "Frank Kelly and I have decided that this isn't a gar-den apartment at all. It's a rathskeller."

"Can I offer you a drink, Claudia?" Frank asked. He got up and pulled out a chair for her at the table.

"Sure," she said. "But we gotta sit outside. In the garden. There isn't enough oxygen for three people down here."

Another two hours passed and Larry arrived home from work. We heard him wandering around upstairs, calling Claudia's name and turning on lights. He must have heard us giggling because he pitched open the window and thrust his head out and saw us down there, in the garden, in the dark.

"I'll start dinner," he said to Claudia. I'm sure he knew then that he'd be starting dinner for many more evenings to come.

I finished up the last of my lamb, smeared a tear of bread around my plate to sop up the sauce. Lale cleared away my place setting and the empty wine bottle. I put on my coat, stuffed Frank Kelly's journal in the pocket, and wound my scarf around my neck.

"Not so fast." Lale appeared at the table again.

She delivered a Turkish coffee and a dessert plate with a healthy slice of baklava.

"I didn't order this," I told her.

"No," she said. "Is free. For preferential customer."

7

I walked home. It took a couple of hours, all uphill. But I had time.

The fog was coming in from the ocean. A heavy bank of white cloud was already smothering Twin Peaks. The three sharp red needles at the top of the Spiny Norman radio tower poked out of it like the futile fingers of a shipwrecked man going under for the third time.

At the end of his life, Frank Kelly lived in that thick fog. Out in the avenues where he'd chosen to reside, it didn't just creep up over you in the evenings, as it did in my part of town. It was there. Always. Frank was submersed in fog, skimming the deep underside of it like some walleyed bottom feeder. It must have been suffocating. His life didn't just end with an abrupt leap over the bridge railing. It was a long, slow, breathless kind of death.

When I had cleaned out his apartment a few days earlier, I started to get that feeling myself. Like I was drowning. I emptied the place. I took one last look out his window. It was thirteen stories up and faced west, to the sea. The Pacific Ocean roared from somewhere behind a scrim of gray mist gathering against the windowpane. The fog seemed to seep through the thin glass, infusing salt water into the tired beige walls, into the ruts and crevices and roots of the rust-colored carpet.

This was the dim view that Frank Kelly faced every day. I wondered why the fog and the bellowing ocean hadn't goaded him into jumping from there. It would have been simple, just a moment of despair. An impulse. Slide the window open. Step up onto the ledge. One more step. And then, nothing.

I suppose Frank had to make an event of it. He was a show-off that way. He was excessively understated in his personal appearance— the drab clothes, the absence of decoration or color. He rendered himself unremarkable, essentially invisible. But, behind his subdued appearance, Frank Kelly harbored an impulse for spectacle. His personal life was ornate with melodrama.

Dixie and I walked back up Market Street, climbing again. The sun started to go down, extinguishing itself in the fog.

We reached the summit only after the fog had rolled on, leaving outcroppings of puffy clouds. The clouds caught the last rays of sunlight, turning radiant coral in the purple sky.

An ethereal light, close and shimmering and captured, embraced the hillside by the time I reached my house. In the moist evening light, my three-story Queen Anne looked like a big white wedding cake, its domes and arches took on a matte patina like crisp, hardening meringue.

This home was my one great piece of good fortune, my inheritance handed to me by my mother. It was grand and stately, and far too valuable for me to have ever been able to afford by my own means.

My grandparents had given Mother the house as a sort of signing bonus when she divorced my father, whom they despised. That's the way grotesquely wealthy families operate—like corporations, only with slightly less personality.

None of the Lydeckers would have ever used the word *bribe*.

Incentive, maybe.

Or: *assistance*. As in, We have to assist Sylvia and the baby.

Assistance came in an envelope containing a title for the 140-year-old mansion on Pluto Street, and the pink slip for a sporty convertible MGB in British racing green. There was also the monthly trust fund check, and the continuous stream of portrait commissions of the city's estimable personages. They wanted to give Mother more than just moral support; they wanted to abet in her artistic pursuits. And that was fine, as long as she didn't consort with the seedier bohemian types she'd picked up in the coffee shops in North Beach. Poets. And painters. And jazz musicians—my father.

More than forty years later, and they were all dead, all except me.

And the irony was that I grew up to be very much like the man they were trying to excise from their family's life. Undisciplined. Unprincipled. Ethically bereft and ethnically muddled. A squanderer of money (theirs), and of talent (mine).

My only regret was that my grandparents hadn't lived long enough to see how I became the very image and essence of my father.

I climbed the front stairs, pausing to watch the sun's finale—flickering garnet and carmine, silhouetting the attic-story onion dome. One of my tenants was up there on his computer. He waved. I waved back, not sure if it was Glen or his boyfriend, Glenda. Eighteen years on, and I still interchanged their names and identities. They looked nothing alike.

I poured a hefty tumbler of Malbec and dropped into my Eames recliner. I opened Frank Kelly's journal again.

Emile Balzac's card fell out. I examined it, wondering what he'd have to tell me about Frank's handwriting. I hoped that the pages he'd photocopied did not contain any references to me. But I knew that they did. I'd just spent my dinner hour reading the original.

I fanned through the journal. This time, not reading for content, but looking for a general impression.

The pages were ruled meanly by black lines just a quarter-inch apart. There were twenty-eight lines to a page. Frank's deliberate cursive imprinted the pages, bruising and embossing them. The paper teemed with ink. It looked like hundreds of black, newborn spiders scrabbling for survival.

At the top of each page was a serration for neatly tearing away the corner as a way of finding one's place. On the pages on which he'd written, which was all of them, Frank had removed the corner. It was such a grimly deliberate way to mark progress.

Write. Tear. Turn the page.

At the last quarter of the journal, the second set of handwriting appeared. It flowed on for twenty pages in an elegant, assured script.

There was something picturesque about the style. It was so beautifully formed. And yet, it wasn't mannered.

I noticed a slip of handwriting running up the margin, the tops of the letters skimming the book's gutter. I turned the journal sideways. I still couldn't read it. I fetched my magnifying glass, held it up to the tiny lettering.

It was a signature: Duffield Waverly Fallon. And it was dated: 1906/2006.

I wrote the name on the back of Emile's card. I assumed the dates were Fallon's birth and death dates.

Maybe this Duffield Fallon was a friend of Frank's, someone I didn't know. He could have been a neighbor at that gloomy apartment house; some ancient widower that lived next door and whiled away his days watching Mexican wrestling and drinking Grand Marnier with Frank.

After the Duffield Fallon signature, the journal went on for only a few more pages.

The last few pages were missing.

It looked as though Frank, or someone, had taken a sharp blade and sliced away the pages at the end—like unwanted fingers cleaved off at the knuckles. I held the magnifying glass up to the nub of amputated pages and tried to count them.

"Ten pages," a woman's voice said. "They are missing."

I screamed.

"Baba," I cried. "For godsakes, must you always creep up on me?"

"Is my nature, Max. Is not like I have footsteps for you to hear me."

She had materialized on my fainting couch, cloaked in a red shawl, her head wrapped in two scarves, purple and yellow. Her army boots lolled around on the expensive pony hair upholstery. She held one of my roaches. The red ember burned into her thumb and forefinger.

"I like smoking these Mary Anns of yours, Max."

"Mary Jane. The phrase is Mary Jane. And we don't use it. We say marijuana. The substance you are pilfering is referred to as marijuana. And why do you persist in haunting me?"

"Haunting? Such language! I'm visiting. You are my grandson. Is normal."

The roach burned down to a pinch of paper. She popped the ember into her mouth and swallowed it.

"You don't know what I've been through today," I told her. "I've been dealing with pink Crocs, vomiting junkies, and Frank Kelly. Suicide dude. I'm dealing with his shit."

I waved the journal at her. Baba ignored me.

"Say, Baba," I thought to ask her. "Do you know who Duffield Fallon is?"

She picked up the television clicker and aimed it at the set.

Jeanette MacDonald came onto the screen looking like a white taffeta dream. She was standing on the curvaceous balcony of a baroque palace. The air was powdered with mist and you could feel it, taste it—it was thick with the scent of fresh fallen rain and sweet honeysuckle.

Stars sparkled high up in a velvet sky. They were twinkling just for her, Jeanette, smiling because she was a radiant princess. She was blooming, opening up like a night flower, glittering eyes and milky moon skin, drops of perfumed rain on soft petals. She was singing in her crystal soprano voice so pure that it made you feel like love was the most powerful force in the universe. Her voice made you feel like love was real.

"If it weren't for the dead, Max," Baba said to me, "you'd be lonely."

8

Stan Blashky telephoned me a couple of days later. He wanted to meet in person. He was insistent. I danced around the suggestion and finally relented. I told him he could find me on a bar stool in the Sans Souci that afternoon.

Dixie and I got to the bar just as the ship's clock on the wall marked four P.M. Happy Hour. Johnny Miranda greeted me with his standard level of effusiveness. He looked up from his crossword puzzle and said, "Usual?"

We took our customary seats, the two stools at the very center of the massive gleaming mahogany bar. Johnny slid a crisp martini in front of me, and set a bowl of goldfish crackers in front of Dixie, which she demolished in a matter of seconds. Johnny went back to work on his crossword.

"I've come to see a man about a dead guy," I told Johnny.

He ran his manicured fingers over his brilliantined hair, put down his *New York Times,* folded his arms across his chest. He leaned back against his great, mirrored wall of liquor bottles. The rich, jewel-toned potions shone in their glistening glass vessels and lit up around him like an aura, like the high, heavenly host of intoxication.

"You're asking about that jumper?" Johnny said to me.

"How did you know?"

"Claudia."

"They haven't even found the body, and these people want to stage some sort of funerary ritual. Lots of oration and ululating, that sort of thing."

"They may never find the body," Johnny said. "Maybe it's better that way."

"I suppose it would be rather unsightly."

"A body falling from two hundred and fifty feet hits the water at a speed of nearly eighty miles an hour. It's like running into a cement wall."

"They don't actually drown then," I said, draining my martini.

"It's the impact that kills them," Johnny said.

Dixie spotted a bowl of peanuts farther down the bar. She leapt onto three bar stools in quick hops—like a frog traversing a pond on lily pads—and augered her face into the bowl. Johnny coolly snatched it out from under Dixie's maw. He let her hoover up the stray nuts.

"Sit down, you bastard," I told her. She did it, once she was satisfied that she'd gotten every last peanut.

"They've autopsied some of those jumpers," Johnny said.

He pulled a silver toothpick out of his pocket and put it to work on his eyetooth.

"I don't know why they still bother," he continued. "It's always the same damn thing. Just a mess of whirled-up guts. Like somebody got mad with an egg beater."

Being an ex–homicide detective, Johnny was forever offering these cheery factoids. That's one of the things that kept me coming back to the Sans Souci. That, and my drinking problem.

"I suppose they have to rule out foul play," I suggested.

"Pretty hard to prove any kind of play," he said. "Foul. Fair. Whatever. Those jumpers come in fucked up beyond forensics."

Johnny pulled out a clean white towel from underneath the bar. He wiped away the glass rings and handprints from the mahogany. He grimaced at the gleaming, reflective surface with satisfaction.

"How many jumpers do you think they get?" I asked. "Annually."

"Nobody knows for sure. And the parks department doesn't advertise about it. I've heard, on average, about one jumper every two weeks."

"But who knows?"

"Who knows," he agreed. "I figure it's a lot more. Because, think about it, between the tides and the sharks and the ships' propellers, how many can you really expect to find?"

He said he'd heard about survival rates. The accepted figure was 2 percent.

"The most famous survivor was a woman," Johnny said. He put my second martini in front of me. "It was 1958. She had been a competitive diver. When she went over the rail, her muscle memory kicked in. She straightened out into a perfect dive posture. Instinct."

"So she pierced the water surface."

"Like a knife. She had a couple broken fingers. That's all."

"What did she say about it after?"

"Same thing they all say. What the fuck did I do that for?"

A big, beefy man in a brown leather jacket and a porkpie hat came through the door. He moved his heft with remarkable grace onto the barstool next to me, tossed his hat on the bar. His head was shaved bald. He wore a thick gold earring and on his neck, in a flourishing script, was tattooed the word *Immortal*.

"Stan Blashky," he told me, holding out an ursine paw.

My own hand disappeared into his plush grasp. I sensed that, if he felt like it, he could mulch every bone in my metacarpus.

I introduced him to Johnny and Dixie. He ordered a pint.

"I feel like I have to do something for Frankie," he said. "We were partners for seven years."

"You should get a merit badge," I told him, "for patience."

"Yeah." He laughed. "Frank was a pain in the ass. But he was my partner."

"Don't you think this is all a bit premature?" I suggested. "Shouldn't we wait for his body?"

"They might not find it," Blashky said.

I asked him if he and Johnny had been talking. Blashky wasn't surprised that others shared his view. It was the logical conclusion. That current ran straight out to sea. It had probably taken Frank with it, out into the abyss. There was nothing between the Golden Gate and Japan but the rocky outcroppings of the Farallon Islands, where frenzied gangs of great white sharks fed off of fat seals. Frank would have just been another piece of meat to the sleek predators.

"How do we know for sure he jumped?" I said.

Blashky and Johnny looked annoyed.

"Really," I persisted. "How do you know?"

"The bridge cameras caught him," Johnny said. "He was loitering around the middle span at ten thirty-five P.M."

"It was foggy," I said.

"He looked straight up into the camera," Johnny told me, adding, "He looked at it repeatedly."

"How do you know that?" I said.

"I know things," Johnny said.

And it was true. Sometimes it gave me the willies, the things Johnny knew, the sleazy netherworld doings that his sketchy clientele felt at liberty to leak all over the bar.

Johnny knew about everything that crept, and slinked, and slithered around this town.

"And they got his note," Blashky said, drafting onto Johnny's argument with the dunderheadedly obvious.

"I still don't want to say that Frank is dead," I said. "Not definitively."

Blashky ordered another beer. We watched Johnny fill a clean pint glass. The traffic stopped at the light out front. A horn honked. The cars started up again and accelerated past the bar's open door. Their passing sounded like gravelly water running through a sluice.

I felt peevish about the way Blashky and Johnny allied against me. Why couldn't Frank still be alive? Why wasn't I allowed to even suggest it?

Frank could be one of the 2 percenters. He was a tough guy. Maybe he got his bell rung, and he was out there, right now, on the streets, wandering around lost, incoherent. He'd easily blend into the armies of lunatics that roamed the streets, anonymous. Unnoticed.

"The bridge workers swarmed the place," Blashky said out loud, finishing some line of thought he'd been mulling over in his own head.

"Yeah," Johnny agreed. "They would have found him. Those guys know their jumpers."

"Frank jumped," Blashky said.

The sun dropped down in between the tall buildings and crouched onto Bush Street like a fugitive poised to spring down into a dark escape. A flame of golden, red light burst through the open doorway just as the ship's clock hit 6:00 P.M. Johnny lit a few red hurricane lamps and set them along the bar. They cast a scarlet glow—the same color as the velvet flocking on the wallpaper.

"Frankie was so depressed," Blashky told us, staring into the bottom of his third pint. "I should have seen it. I should have done something."

"Didn't he tell you what was wrong?" I asked.

"Frankie didn't talk to people," Blashky said.

And I thought again of Frank Kelly's journal, and the tiny signature of a stranger embedded at the edge of a margin in the final pages: Duffield Fallon.

"I wish Frank had talked to me," Blashky said. "He could have called me if he was depressed."

"I don't know if it was just about depression," I said. "Not the kind of depression that most people get from time to time."

"He must have been so alone," Blashky said.

I looked at my drink, swirled the gin around in my glass. I asked Stan if he'd ever heard of Duffield Fallon.

He hadn't. Stan asked me if Fallon was a friend of Frank's.

I told him I didn't know.

9

I arrived at Neptune's Books just as Emile Balzac was turning over the sign in the front door window. Closed.

I rapped on the glass. Balzac squinted at me standing in the yellow glow of the streetlamp. He pulled the door open just far enough for me to step inside. He quickly shut it behind me and bolted the lock.

"Monsieur Bravo," he started in, as if he'd been expecting me. "I have compiled a brief dossier for you on the subject of Duffield Fallon."

"Dossier?" I bristled. "What about the handwriting analysis? That's what I hired you for."

"Yes, I'm doing that too," he said, and brushed away my outburst with a languid wave of his patrician hand.

"And I take it from your reaction that you know the name," he continued. "Duffield Fallon."

I admitted I did.

"*Bon*," he said. "Then you, no doubt, recognize the importance of identifying Monsieur Fallon."

He pulled a file folder out from beneath the counter, placed it in front of me. I climbed up onto the swivel stool and, I think it was because it felt so much like a barstool, I was immediately mollified.

"Clearly, Frank Kelly was a creative, and troubled, man," Balzac said, stretching the arms of his eyeglasses around his spherical head.

"Monsieur Kelly was concerned with his legacy," he continued. "But lacking in the literary genius to secure it."

"He wanted to be famous," I offered.

"Frank Kelly," he corrected me, "wanted to be immortal."

The name Duffield Fallon flowed across the cover of the file folder in ink the color of dried blood.

Balzac's cat rose up from its velvet cushion, stretched his back into a high arch. He picked his way around the potted plants on the window seat, leapt through the shadows onto the edge of the counter.

"This Fallon fellow," I said. "Why spend time on him? Isn't he just a casual acquaintance? Or, perhaps, a fictional character? Someone Frank was creating?"

"Impossible." Balzac snipped off my suggestion.

The cat sat at Balzac's elbow. He stared at me, and lowered his lids as Balzac said, "The handwriting samples are two distinct persons."

He flipped open the file folder, revealed a photocopy of an old daguerreotype image. It was a portrait of a man. He extracted it from the pile, pincering the paper's edge between his fore and middle fingers.

"This man," he said. "This is Duffield Waverly Fallon. Born, 1858. Died, April 18, 1906."

The man in the photograph was a glittering brute. He wore a diminutive, precisely creased hat tipped down over one eye. His velvet coat was cut close and dandified with shoulder-seams peaked so high they nearly brushed his ears. A cluster of diamonds big as a sea urchin nestled into the crisp white ruffles of his shirtfront.

"This photograph is from the 1880s," Balzac reported. "When Fallon was still beautiful."

"Beautiful like a rattlesnake," I said, taking the picture. I put on my eyeglasses and scrutinized the face.

Fallon's sartorial splendor did not soften his mien. His face was handsome, and he wore it in a slaking leer. He was big. Menacing. And, like a particularly dangerous class of big men, Fallon carried his bulk like a dainty ballistic. He perched on the photographer's spindle-legged chair, one battering ram shoulder thrust forward, waiting for the slightest provocation to which he could respond by cracking a femur or biting off an ear.

"Of course," Balzac said. "This photograph was taken when Fallon was still intact."

"Meaning?"

"He later lost the left hand," Balzac said. "A tavern brawl."

He handed me a sheet of paper. It was a newspaper account of Fallon's hand incident. Duffield Fallon had spent the evening and late-night hours of October 12, 1896, drinking in a succession of dives along Broadway and then Jackson Street in the Barbary Coast neighborhood. He was well lit by the time he reached the Spotted Cockle just after midnight. The bar was relatively quiet that night. A dozen or so elderly sailors, one off-duty whore, and a drunken writer of adventure stories tended quietly to their whiskey shots and their beer mugs. The proprietor, a large man of action known as Angry Dick, was behind the bar.

Fallon entered, ordered a crème de menthe and, reportedly, set in upbraiding the patrons for their lack of festivity. They ignored him. Fallon went into a rage, pulled a narwhale tusk from the display wall and according to witnesses, "ran amok on the premises."

Angry Dick delivered one warning to Fallon. Something to the effect of, "Put down the tusk, Fallon, or I'll whittle it off of you."

Fallon chose to disregard the warning and, in fact, redoubled his mayhem. He drove the lance through an oil painting of a reclining nude that was hung behind the bar. It was while Fallon strove to pull the narwhale tusk out of the wall that Angry Dick unsheathed the Civil War–era cavalry sword that he kept behind the bar for occasions such as these.

Angry Dick brought the sword down on Fallon's wrist, cleanly separating the hand from the rest of him. He then came around the bar, took Fallon by the back of his collar and his belt loop, and ran him out through the front door.

Fallon landed in the street on his face, blood pulsing from his red pulpy stump. He urgently ripped his ascot from around his neck, wrapped it around the blood-spurting wound as best he could.

Fallon staggered to his feet, called out to Angry Dick in the doorway, "Dick, I'm happy to leave as you've asked me. But, before I go, could you flip me back my fin."

Angry Dick obliged. He tossed the severed hand out to Fallon.

Duffield Fallon tucked his severed hand in his coat pocket and staggered away down Jackson Street.

"Of course, they couldn't reconnect the hand," Emile Balzac said when I placed the news story back in Fallon's file. "But I'm sure he found the hook to be, in many ways, more useful."

I picked up the photograph of Fallon, inspected the man.

I set Fallon's image at the feet of the cat. She looked at it, and purred.

Balzac returned the news story to its proper place in the file. Then he methodically worked his way through the dossier, extracting the contents—paper-clipped sheaths of paper. He arranged them in separate piles, lined up neatly in front of me along the counter.

Exhibit A: handwritten notes Balzac had taken down in the library archives. Exhibit B: photocopies of Fallon references from San Francisco history books, mostly chronicles of the city's extraordinarily dense criminal record. Exhibit C: microfilm printouts of newspaper crime stories in *The Call*.

Fallon was a thug. He was born and raised into it, in one of history's most virulent criminal harborages—San Francisco's Barbary Coast.

His mother was an astute prostitute turned madam. Marina Fallon claimed to have been the tarnished scion of a gentile Southern family ruined by the Civil War. Fallon's father was unknown.

From a young age, Duffield Waverly Fallon showed an earnest propensity for the family business. Before he was eighteen years old, he was running a string of his own prostitutes out of the one-room cribs that crammed the back alleys of the Barbary Coast. It was said that the girls loved their rugged nabob, mooning over him like he was a rock star.

In fact, when Fallon made his collection rounds each morning, he would glean extra revenues from working girls along the route by selling photographs of himself. It was not unusual in the late 1880s for a prostitute's patron to glance up at the wall of her crib only to see the bemused visage of Duffield Fallon smirking at him.

During his leisure hours, while his minions plowed lucre in the fields of carnality, Duffield Fallon recreated with his compeers, local toughs known as hoodlums. Here, too, he excelled. Fallon came to be known as the King of the Hoodlums, for he led the way in rolling drunks, bashing Chinamen, and predicting next season's fashion trends.

Despite having a chest the size of a caisson and legs as thick as a ship's masts, young Fallon was the undisputed Beau Brummel of this dandified tribe. His brocade vests were the richest; his velvet jackets were the most jeweled tones of emerald and sapphire; and his boots were buffed to the blackest pitch. But, no matter how fine the cut of his clothes, Fallon didn't worry about getting them dirty. He kept a short, businesslike hickory stick in his boot for cracking skulls, and a set of serrated brass knuckles in his vest for shredding faces.

"Fallon went downhill after he lost his hand," Balzac said. "He lost his strength. His brio. And then his popularity. With the hoodlums. With the prostitutes. He was reduced in stature. He hired himself out as a bodyguard to Chinatown's leading crime boss."

The shop phone rang. Emile asked me to excuse him, picked up the receiver, twirled it a couple times to untwist the cord.

"I have to go," he told me, cradling the receiver in the crook of his shoulder. "I'm tutoring tonight. French conversational."

"Hold on," I said. "I need to know the rest. About Fallon."

"Oh, la, la! First, you make a protest that I do this research. Now you want more!"

He gathered up the piles of documents, stacked them back into the folder. He closed the file, and shoved it into an envelope.

Balzac practically frog-marched me out of the shop. He shut the door behind me; the transom bell signaled my departure.

Valencia Street was swathed in fog. I looked up at the streetlamp and saw rivulets of mist eddying around the amber light.

I got a couple of doors down the street when the transom bell rang again, tinkling brightly on the wet silver air. I looked back. Balzac was on the street in his coat, carrying a bulging and battered briefcase. A thick scarf muffled his neck and a shapeless hat battened down his bulbous, net float of a head.

"Max Bravo," he called. "One more thing. In the library, in the archives room, every time I signed out some material about Fallon, the last name in the ledger was Frank Kelly."

He didn't wait for me to respond. He receded quietly into the fog, the back of his salt-and-pepper overcoat flapping like a torn sail.

10

I was keelhauled out of a deep, black sleep by a great commotion coming from the parlor downstairs. Something, or someone, had gotten into my house, crashed into the baby Liberace, knocked the brace out, and sent the lid slamming down with a sharp bang. The strings inside growled a long, nettled reverberation.

I sat up, ripped off my night blinders, and reached for my cell phone. It was dead. I had, once again, forgotten to charge it.

The candelabra toppled over. I could hear it clatter onto the piano's glossy turquoise finish, topple off, hit the keys, and strike a heavy bass chord.

I gasped and thought of hiding, but Dixie started barking her head off from under the covers.

"Shh," I whispered. "Shut up, you asshole."

Another loud bang. This time, the intruder knocked over the piano bench. I knew that's what it was, because I'd done it myself—a number of times.

"Who the hell is trying to rob me?" I exclaimed. "Helen Fucking Keller?"

Dixie thrashed around under the covers, a barking lump. She did a couple of three sixties, then a figure eight, before she sensed which way was up and burrowed toward the top of the bed.

She popped her head out from under the blanket. Her now unmuffled bark was sharp and cracking like the report from a rifle.

"Shut up, shut up!" I hissed at her.

She pitched off the bed—like a cocktail wienie flicked from a plastic fork—ran to the hallway and stopped. She cocked her head, and listened. She looked back at me, beseeching.

"I'm not going first," I told her.

"Max! Get down there!" It was Baba. She appeared behind Dixie, pointing toward the stairs.

"You go down there," I whispered. "You've got nothing to lose. What could they do to you? Kill you?"

"Don't be a coward," she said.

"Why not?"

"Okay," she exhaled heavily. "I'll tell you why. You can't get hurt. The intruder is a weakling. But if you don't get off your fat ass, you're gonna lose that guy's diary."

"Well, in that case."

I threw on my kimono, fetched the bat that I keep under the bed, and marched out into the hallway.

I hit the top stairs hard, stopped and listened. A floorboard creaked in the parlor. I choked up on the bat and took another step. Silence. Then a pair of heeled shoes skittered down the hallway toward the kitchen. I thundered down the stairs, chased the footfalls.

A cloaked figure hunched at the back door. Fingers struggled with the bolt lock. Seeing the figure was short, and the fingers were tiny, I tackled the individual with what was, arguably, excessive force.

The intruder hit the linoleum. The impact punched a long exhale out of his guts. I sat on the little fella, grabbed his shoulder, rolled him over.

He was a she.

I pulled off her droopy hat and a bale of brassy red hair tumbled out. Her head lay in a pool of limpid moonlight that shone through the kitchen window. On her right cheek, dead center, was a jet black beauty mark big as a sand dab.

"Betty Ann?" I said. "Betty Ann Thibideaux?"

She gasped a desperate rattle. Her eyes rolled madly.

"I haven't seen you in years," I said.

"Get off me, you fat fuck," she rasped.

"Oh, right."

I got off of her. She gulped at the air like a landed grouper. I helped her up, sat her in a chair at the kitchen table.

"You could have just called," I said. "Or friended me on Facebook."

"Here." She reached under her cloak and produced Frank Kelly's journal. She dropped it on the table. "The purloined letter."

"Thanks."

"I'm saving you the trouble of strip-searching me," she said.

I wanted to say "Eeww," but instead said "Thanks" again.

"Bourbon?"

"Please," she said. And she fluffed her brass-works into a Nashvillian bouffant with her poking little fingers.

I hadn't actually seen Betty Ann in years. I hadn't thought of her either, at least not much.

Betty Ann's books weren't the sort of thing I care to read. They were beyond pulpy. More pasty, really. She wrote confessionals, crash-and-burn testimonials that stretched one's credulity, and patience.

"I suppose you've heard about what's been happening with me," she said as I rummaged around in the liquor cabinet. "My books?"

"I've heard," I said, reaching in the back of the cupboard for the fifth of Jim Beam.

"Is it true that you were strung out on crack, Vicodin, and laxatives?" I said, setting a couple shot glasses on the table. "And that you had prison sex with an East L.A. gangbanger who had marbles sewn into the foreskin of his penis?"

"My life story, my journey, touches people," she snarled.

"Yes, it's all very last days of Rome," I said, seating myself. "They say that right before the Visigoths raced through the streets that the Romans enjoyed going to the Coliseum to watch Amazons wearing strap-on dildos sword fighting with dwarfs."

"Mock all you want, little man," she said. "But *Smashed to Bits* sold over a million copies."

"I have no doubt."

"And I just cashed a six-figure advance for my next book."

I opened the bourbon and poured her a shot.

"Keep going," she said.

I added just one more drop, bringing her shot up to three fingers.

"You're not going to get drunk and try to give me a rim job, are you?" I asked, smiling brightly. "Because I don't want you to write about my nether regions, not like you did about that other fellow— the ex–professional football player who got strung out on coke and lived in the back of his mother's garage with his ferret."

"You're getting gray, Max," she informed me.

"Cheers," I said, tapping my shot glass on hers. "Now, tell me why I'm not calling the police."

"Oh, surely, Max," she said, again, adding elevation to her hairdo with those poking digits. "We're old friends. This is like a family matter."

"Yes. If we were the Borgias." I reset the dialectic. "But, we're not. If you've got a point, you better get to it."

"All right," she slammed her empty glass down on the table, and her delivery took on the hard-edged, curiously Brooklynesque accent of the New Orleans larrikin.

"This is a matter of life or death for me," she said. "I need Frankie's diary. I'm sure he wrote about me. And I have to see what he said. My life is my intellectual property. It's copyrighted for godsakes."

"I don't remember Frank complaining about you using his life in your fiction."

"Memoir!"

"Yes. Fiction."

"Frank had nothing to complain about." She heaved out of the chair, and poured herself the refill I wasn't offering.

"You called him abusive," I said. "A misogynist. Alcoholic. And, I don't know why this would bother anybody; sporadically afflicted with erectile dysfunction."

"I look at reality," she said, examining the bourbon in her glass. "And I write about it as it is."

"Yes," I said. "You're a regular Turgenev."

"Can I have the journal?" she asked, her voice modified so it was as treacly as the bourbon.

"Get out." I stood up. "Get out now before I change my mind and have you taken out of here in a squad car."

"I'll call you, Max."

"And if you write about me, I'll unleash my agent, my lawyer, and pug on you."

I heard her knock over my geranium pot as she switchbacked down my front steps. I looked outside to make sure she wasn't driving. She was walking east on Pluto, downhill.

I had met Betty Ann on New Year's Eve, 1989. Frank Kelly and I had started out, and then promptly stalled out, in his rathskeller. Frank had elected to get high on crystal meth that night. It made him extremely tedious. He twiddled around the confines of his basement, rearranging silverware in the drawer and devising a filing system for his poems that was, apparently, modeled on the one used by the Rishikesh government bureaucracy.

"Red folders are for urgent pieces," he told me, writing the word *Immediate* on a sticky-backed label.

"What's yellow?"

"Poems in development," he said, and he stuffed a pile of onionskin sheets into a green folder.

"Green?"

"Good to go to the journals."

"For publication?"

"For rejection."

"And these brown folders?"

"Shit," he said. "Utter excrement."

He crammed a thick sheaf into a brown folder and bound it with a sturdy rubber band, remarking, "But I still can't bring myself to just flush it."

It was close to midnight before Frank finished organizing his paper clips and typewriter ribbons and outfitting all his pencils with eraser heads. He ran out of cigarettes and announced that we should leave to "pick up some smokes, and I need to get laid."

I pointed out that it was almost midnight.

"Shit," he said, looking at his watch. "That means all the good ones will be taken."

He tugged his leather jacket off the back of his chair, punched his arms through the sleeves.

"But don't worry, Max," he said.

"I'm not."

"This can work to our advantage." And he was out the door.

I heard him braying as he strolled across the patio under the neighbor's open windows, "The leftover ones are going to be drunk and desperate."

I smashed out the cigarette he'd left burning in the ashtray on the table. And I plucked up the other cigarette he'd left burning into the edge of the Formica countertop, ran it under the faucet, and dropped it into the sink. I trotted to catch up with him. He was already down the block, on a direct bead for Haight Street.

We planned to drop down Haight, veer south on Fillmore, and dog-leg west to a biker bar in the Mission. But, with closing time drawing near, we decided to pull into the first Haight Street bar that showed promise.

We spotted a bevy of women in front of a dance club. They wore tiny skirts and big hair. We fell into the queue behind them.

The women twitched across the threshold of the nightclub on spiky heels. Each time the bouncer pulled back the heavy velvet curtains to let one in, her form would seem to shimmer in the pounding waves of synthesizer bass. Then the yawing darkness would swallow her.

I followed the women into the concussive strobe lights.

I was just past the curtain. I couldn't make out the bobbing bodies right in front of me, my eyes were still straining to adjust to the murky blue dark, but I could see the performers spotlighted above the crowd. A muscled man in a loincloth loomed large in the center of the stage. His head was sheathed in a large papier-mâché bull's head and he was bellowing into a hand mike. A trio of go-go dancers in minidresses was lined up behind him. They were doing the frug, snapping their arms at the elbows and crimping their torsos in rhythmic, and impossibly cool, jerks. Detached. Louche. Lovely. I was delighted. And hopeful.

I took a step toward the bar and felt a firm tug at my collar. I was pulled back out onto the street.

"Cover charge," the bouncer said, and he let go of my jacket.

He reinstalled himself heavily onto the bar stool in the doorway, a hulking gargoyle with orangutan arms. He was fully armored; wristbands lined with steel spikes, a Mohawk of spikes glued along the center of his shaved head.

"Cover tonight," he said, cocking his head to show me that the spikes weren't simply ornamental. "Fifteen bucks."

I pulled a wad out of my pocket, straightened out a stack of worn small bills, and handed him the fifteen.

"Each," he said.

"It's after midnight, buddy," Frank Kelly told him. "Doesn't it go down after midnight?"

"Yeah. It goes down to fifteen."

"Seems a little steep for two hours," Frank said.

A crowd started to bottleneck behind us. They became quiet, all of them except one drunk broad who was squawking about the holdup.

Frank Kelly removed his trilby, coiled his scarf inside it, and handed it to me.

"Let's go, Frankie," I said, hoping that hearing the familiar version of his name would take the edge off.

Somebody told the mouthy broad to shut up. "What? What the fuck," she slurred. She looked around the crowd, followed their gaze. They were all watching the gathering drama at the doorway. Oh, she said. And she shut up.

"I'm not ready to go yet," Frank said to me, but he looked at the bouncer.

"Get the fuck out of here, you little weasel," the bouncer said.

The crowd behind us fidgeted now. Some of the savvier ones backed up, relinquished their places in the line.

"Keep talkin', buddy," Frank said. "You'll be spittin' Chiclets. In front of all these people."

Frank clicked his tongue across the roof of his mouth and popped out the denture that held his top front teeth. He handed me the porcelains and I displayed them on my palm for the bouncer to see.

"Sir," I said to the bouncer. "I beseech you, do not let my friend's somewhat understated physique lull you into complacency. He's Canadian. Are you familiar with the term *hockey goon*?"

"I'll knock the rest of his fuckin' teeth out," the bouncer said.

He slid off his perch. He landed heavy on his boots.

Frank smashed his fist into the bouncer's ear, dazing him. The bouncer bent over. Frank grabbed the back of his leather jacket, pulled it over the big man's head, stringing up his arms and disarming the points of his steel-tipped Mohawk. In two seconds, he was rendered helpless.

Frank punched an upper cut under his ribs. The air left him in an anguished gust. His legs gave out. Frank backed him up against the wall, and pummeled his face with two quick, purposeful knees to the jaw.

Everyone heard the crack. The bouncer went limp. His legs gave out and Frank released his hold on the man's jacket. We watched the bouncer slide down the wall and puddle onto the sidewalk—his jacket over his head, one leg folded up under him, the other leg sticking straight out.

I turned away. It seemed obscene to look at the inert, beaten man. A pearl shirt button rolled across the sidewalk and stopped at the toe of my boot.

Frank was already walking.

"Here's your teeth," I said as I caught up to him.

"Thanks." He popped them back into his mouth, not breaking his stride.

"Hat."

"Thanks."

Frank wrapped his scarf around his bleeding knuckles.

A clicking sound followed us up the pavement. It got closer.

"Hey. Hey, you guys."

It was a woman's voice.

"Hey, tough guys. Hold up."

We stopped. Turned. She came trotting up to us on four-inch stilettos. Her red hair was teased to a great height and backlit by the streetlamps into a fiery nimbus all around her broad peasant face. Her plain, even features were made exotic by a raccoon mask of black eyeliner painted in a solid bar from temple to temple. Her lips were gloss blue and she'd stuck a black beauty mark onto her cheek.

"I just saw you kick the shit out of that fat asshole," she said.

She smiled, and her cheeks appled up and her teeth were big and flat and her mouth was wide and spacious like an open invitation.

"That wasn't a shit-kicking," Frank told her. "That was just a mild instruction."

She introduced herself as Betty Ann. Betty Ann Thibideaux, lately of New Orleans. New to the area. She shook our hands and locked her elbow with Frank's and fell into step with us.

I heard him say to her, "I could instruct you too."

She laughed. Giddy and wobbling on her spiked heels.

I didn't see it then. Betty Ann Thibideaux just looked like any other club chick; destined to either spiral out on crank, or marry a broker and move to Marin. But looking back on it, I remembered a caginess there, a sense of an agenda beneath all the wild abandon. She was collecting material. And she was never as out of control as she appeared.

11

After Betty Ann Thibideaux's abortive break-in, I slept with Frank's journal under my pillow. It gave me horrific flashback dreams.

The rest of my night was haunted by images of mullet hairdos and an echoing soundtrack—a tinny refraction of Frankie Goes to Hollywood repeating, "Relax, don't do it, when you want to come."

I woke up irritated, sweating. The day broke in hot on still, expectant air. Earthquake weather. I checked the calendar. October 17. It was the twentieth anniversary of the 1989 Loma Prieta quake.

I set up in the backyard, under the sycamore tree. Its pollarded limbs had sprouted fresh green over the summer.

The air shifted. A breeze chattered through the busy bustles of leaves in a frisson of sibilant tones. I positioned the chaise lounge under their dappled shadow. I snuggled a bottle of Sauvignon Blanc down into the ice bucket, placed it within arm's reach, and settled into the chaise.

Dixie hopped up onto my belly and plodded around in circles until she pirouetted herself into a ball. She took one last look at me, smiled, closed her eyes, and fell into unconsciousness as though she'd been chloroformed.

I fortified myself with a drink of wine and opened Frank's journal.

Frank carried his journal everywhere, including the office. So much of it was taken up with the drab marginalia of his workdays at the ad agency.

I've never worked in an office myself. I believe that all organized employment is just an elaborate form of crowd control. Frank's journal confirmed my theory.

He'd taken down the barest possible notes to achieve the minimum possible requirements for keeping his job. He kept track of meeting times, deadline dates, Web site addresses, unremarkable lists of what clients considered to be their products' compelling attributes. And the lists were all the same, no matter what product he was shilling— feature-bloated software updates, oversized vehicles suitable for invading Kabul or making a run to Costco, energy drinks for people who sat all day. Everything was faster. Stronger. More.

As his journal progressed, Frank's interest in his work ebbed. The to-do lists, the headline fragments, the prices and offers and rebate details, became shorter. Then they became scarcer.

Frank gave himself over to fantastical musings, not just at home, but at the office too. It was like he was stoned.

He started drawing cartoons. Doodling. At first, he packed the pages with stick figures and geometric shapes. Then these took on more elaborate forms. He drew baroque sea serpents, their whiskered maws thicketed with lacerating teeth. Octopuses twined their puckered arms around drowning sailors. And, everywhere, enraged waves washed over the pages, whipped on by Frank's urgent pen strokes.

Initially, Frank toggled back and forth between lucidity and fantasia. Then, the two blended.

A woman giving a PowerPoint presentation grew squamous over a series of cartoon frames, until she was a slouching dragon gripping a remote control in her leathery hand. A 4×4 truck lay, overturned, in the belly of a sperm whale, transparent as a jellyfish. Eels wriggled up and down the black ruled lines like they were ladder rungs, and flat skates floated over the pages on caped wings like ghosts of sea angels.

Frank carried the journal to bars. He took notes about the settings, gathering color for various stories and poems. But these interludes, too, became awash in disturbing images out of a mariner's nightmare. Sullen hammerhead sharks slumped on bar stools nursing highballs. Pole dancers with gills in their necks twirled on fin-footed stilettos. And fantailed tropical fish frolicked like Esther Williams in giant pitchers of margaritas.

The pages marked Frank's steady spiral. His dissolution. Madness is a sea. And he was sinking into it.

12

I had heard that Frank got fired a few months before his death. People would surely assume his suicide had something to do with him losing his job. That's a natural conclusion.

But I knew better.

Frank didn't care about advertising. He knew it was all baloney—a bunch of frustrated artists turned commercial. They spent their pointless days in their cubicles, cage-fighting for recognition, desperately trying to goad clients into buying their "concepts" over those of their colleagues.

Left on his own, Frank would have never even thought of working as a copywriter. Betty Ann and Claudia pronged him into it.

When I first knew him, Frank was content. He didn't need much money. And he didn't need regimen. Frank was satisfied with the packet of cash he picked up bartending three nights a week at the Valhalla—a bar frequented by old black men who gathered to drink whiskey sours and Pabst. They drank quietly, convivially, watching baseball on an ancient Zenith television that made everything look oddly green, which sparked a continuous debate as to whether the game was being played on real grass or Astroturf.

His part-time job at the Valhalla paid all of Frank's spartan expenses. Rent on the basement apartment. Beer. Typewriter ribbons.

But Betty Ann and Claudia ganged up on him, as women so often will, and told him he wasn't making enough money. He protested that he wanted for nothing. They said that's just what he had—nothing. He had to think about his future. He had to begin a career. Soon he'd be thirty years old, and after that, no one would give him an entry-level job.

Claudia made some calls and helped Frank get a gig writing for the Sharper Image catalog. He'd never written a line of ad copy in his life, but he had made it through the writing program at Iowa, and that was provenance enough for the marketing guy at Sharper Image who liked to identify himself as a frustrated novelist.

The catalog work didn't impinge on Frank's underachieving lifestyle. It was low gear. Frank would pick up his assignments on Monday morning. He'd spend a few hours during the week, here and there, writing romantic paeans to the life-enhancing joys of electric nose hair trimmers and personal vibrators and air ionizers. He'd drop off the finished copy decks in the corporate office on Fridays.

The editor never wanted to discuss the copy with him. He never even glanced at the decks. He'd just take the stapled pages and throw them in a wire basket on his credenza. Then he'd come around the desk, sit in the guest chair next to Frank's, and talk for an hour.

Frank called these his "writer" chats. The editor often asked Frank about novelists he'd met, or was purported to have met. What is Raymond's process? How is Denis? Tobius?

Frank would occasionally, in bouts of politeness, ask the editor about his book. The answer was always the same. He was working on an idea for a book. It was about a guy who edits a high-end gadget catalog. But, he yearns for more. He really wants to be a novelist.

Frank was writing a lot of poetry then. He was fixated on one theme: the act of forgetting, or being forgotten. It was as if amnesia was the dominant human condition. And he always returned to the same imagery—deep lakes, and labyrinths, and uncharted seas populated with predatory creatures.

He'd work at the kitchen table, stabbing out words on the stiff, heavy keys of his manual Olivetti. It was a hulking gray panzer of a machine. Frank told me that he liked writing on it because you had to hit the keys hard, like you really meant it.

He'd sit bolt upright, his shoulders hitched up to his ears, punching out the pages, so deliberately, one letter at a time. He'd work on one poem for weeks. He'd type the poem over and over, sometimes changing only a single word, but always typing the version complete from beginning to end.

One poem could take as many as five or six boxes of onionskin— forty-five pages in a box. The sheets would arrive pearly white, he'd spend days tattooing them with his iterative verses. Then he'd lay the typed sheets back in their box, tape it shut, and bury them in his closet.

It was in just this pursuit that I'd found him on the evening that Claudia was giving Larry's birthday party. Frank's door was, uncharacteristically, closed. I could hear him inside, banging on the keys.

I knocked. The typing stopped. There was a silence. He called out, asking who was there. Max, I said. He told me to enter.

"Leave it open," he said. "Let the smoke clear out."

"Why was it shut?" I asked. "It's hot. And the smoke! It's like a bloody charnel house in here."

He ratcheted a sheet of onionskin from his typewriter and laid it precisely on his pile of drafts.

He stood up and I saw that he'd been sitting on an inflated rubber cushion.

"What the hell is that?" I asked. "Do you have hemorrhoids?"

"Dude," he said. "That's my Sit-and-Sip."

"Sit and shit? What?"

"No, Max," he said. "My Sit-and-Sip."

A rubber tube sprouted from the side of the cushion. He lifted it to his mouth and sipped on it like it was a straw. He proffered it to me.

"Try it."

I sucked on the tube. My mouth filled with beer.

"Cool, right?" he said.

"I guess so."

The beer tasted kind of rubbery.

"I got it from Sharper Image," Frank said. "I told Editor Guy that I had to test it out. So I could write something really great about it. He let me keep it."

I sat on the cushion and put the tube back in my mouth. I sipped rubbery beer while Frank gathered up his pile of poems. He set the sheets in a shallow box, covered it with the lid, and buried the box under a pile of books on the table.

"Shouldn't you be getting dressed?" I said.

His gray sweatshirt was stained with beer from where the tube had dribbled.

"Why can't I wear this?"

"You'll offend Claudia."

He let out a wearied sigh and trudged back to his bedroom. He reemerged wearing a clean T-shirt, the front of which was silk-screened with the famous photograph of Lee Harvey Oswald in custody, doubled over, at the moment Jack Ruby gut-shot him.

"There," I said. "Now you look nice. Was that so difficult?"

"Claudia invited Betty Ann," he said.

"Perfectly normal."

"Except Betty Ann isn't," he said, one hand on his hip, the other gripping the top of his skull as if to prevent it from flying off. "She's not normal, Max."

"Normal?"

"Not even a little bit."

"What did I tell you?" I said, pointing the tip of the sipper tube at him. "What do you expect when you carry on with a woman who lives within a knife's throw of your door?"

"You were right," he said.

That was the creepy coincidence about Frank and Betty Ann. Well, one of the creepy coincidences. She lived, literally, across his back fence.

Neither of them had even realized it until after they'd been sleeping together for a couple of weeks. One morning, Betty Ann had gotten up out of Frank's bed, slipped on his boxer shorts and prowled around the living room drinking dregs from beer bottles and fishing butts out of the ashtrays.

"Hey, that's the back of my house over there," she remarked, looking up from the living-room window.

"What?" Frank called from the bed.

"I never noticed before," she said. "It was always dark."

She squeaked the window open on its rusted aluminum frame. She blew a lungful of menthol smoke into the exhausted nasturtiums swooning in the dirt.

"I live right behind you," she called to Frank. "Second floor, in the back. My bathroom window looks right into your garden."

Being in the other room, Betty Ann didn't see Frank jackknife up out of bed. She wasn't aware of the panic washing across his face, or the liquefaction he felt deep in his bowels.

She simply smashed her cigarette out in the nasturtiums, sashayed back into the bedroom, and noticed only that Frank was sitting upright.

She said, "Were you getting lonely for me, lover?"

I had told Frank Kelly at the time that he was playing a dangerous game. Betty Ann was clearly eccentric, and possibly a lot more than that.

"She's crazy," I warned him. "And close. Those two things don't mix well."

"What difference does it make?" he asked, knowing exactly what difference it made.

"She can watch you," I pointed out. "She can come over here and boil a bunny on your stove."

"She can't cook," he said.

And then, within four months, it had all come to pass. Frank admitted to me that he had become a hunted man.

He told me that he kept his drapes and door closed. He crouched along the fence line to slip in and out of his apartment. He turned his television down to low volume, listened to his stereo only through his Sharper Image headphones that were as big as bundt cakes.

"So you see, Max," he said, sitting down at the table and taking a hit off the Sit-and-Sip. "I don't know if I should even go upstairs to the party. Betty Ann will be there. I'll be walking right into an ambush."

"What are going to do?" I exhorted him. "Cower in this garret? Like Anne Frank? Choking on your own cigarette smoke, drinking this rubber fart beer through a tube?"

He shrugged.

"Enough, man!" I cried.

I stood up from the beer cushion, yanked the rubber tube from Frank's fingers. I snapped the cap onto the end of the beer tube.

"Let's go," I told him.

Frank stood up, made for the door. And stopped. He told me, again, that he couldn't go upstairs.

"It's time you set this thing straight," I said to him. "Betty Ann isn't going to just disappear."

"She will if I just wait it out long enough," he said. "I stopped calling her."

"Doesn't matter."

"I stopped letting her in when she night-crawls over here after the bars close."

"Doesn't matter."

"Maybe I should move."

"Don't be a wiener," I said. "Just tell her. Put on your big boy pants and tell her in clear English that you don't want to see her anymore."

Frank lifted the typewriter and heaved it to the table edge, up against the wall.

He fell back in his chair, pushed his long black hair away from his face with both hands.

"She's become . . ." he said. "She's decided to be . . . she is . . . more problematic than you can imagine."

We uncapped the rubber sipper hose again and worked on deflating the beer cushion. Time proceeded in the perpetual dusk of the rathskeller. I thought maybe we could take it in stages. I suggested we move to the back porch. Frank balked. He didn't want to sit *out in the open*.

Finally Claudia materialized in the doorway. She brandished a bottle of cheap champagne, insisted we get our *flat asses* upstairs to her party.

Frank could resist me. But nobody could stand up to Claudia Fantini.

We followed her, threading through a throng of smokers on the patio, and up the back steps.

They were mostly advertising types from Claudia's office; men in sharkskin blazers and skinny leather ties, women in shocking pink and electric blue minidresses with plunging backlines and dolman sleeves. Everybody had big hair, teased up into Aztec headdresses. The crowd smelled like Chanel No. 5 and Final Net.

We got inside the kitchen and stopped at the threshold. Betty Ann was leaned up against the sink, talking loudly, without punctuation, and making broad gestures that would have looked overblown on-stage at an amphitheater. She was holding two captives—guys wearing pleat-front Dockers and blue button-down shirts. They had to be Larry's friends from his office, a couple of stockbrokers. Despite their tame appearance, I knew these guys could be pretty aggressive. But Betty Ann had them pinned down like a pair of pinky mice under a cat's paw.

That didn't surprise me. I knew Betty Ann was a relentless and aggressive ear-banger. Nowadays they call it autistic.

But, I was shocked at her appearance.

She had gotten fat, and in a very short time. It was not a generalized fat, not a uniform expansion. Her belly swelled out alarmingly in front of her. Her legs and rear end were still skinny. Betty Ann had the classic boozer's bulge that comes from a swollen liver. And she'd undone the top three buttons of her jeans to accommodate it.

I'd heard she lost her job. She'd been sacked for drinking. And now here she was: drunk, fat, and without a clothing allowance.

She brayed at the stockbrokers, delivering a detailed analysis on Lina Wertmüller's film *Swept Away*. They held tight to their beer bottles. Betty Ann had two drinks—a beer in one hand and a highball of Southern Comfort in the other. She drank them in alternation, in time to the mazurka playing in her head.

The desperate stockbrokers scanned the kitchen for an escape hatch. They both looked at the back door at the same time, just as Frank and I entered. Betty Ann followed their gaze until her eyes stopped on us. She broke off her monologue in midsentence.

"Come over here and give me a kiss, lover," she bawled at Frank.

The room had been buzzing with conversation. I hadn't noticed it, until it stopped, abruptly. The music was playing; "Tainted Love," the instrumental bridge in which the synthesizer runs for about four minutes on nothing but a two-beat, two-key percussion. *Doot doot.* Pause. *Doot doot.* Pause. Repeat. The entire decade of the 1980s sounded just like that.

Every person in the kitchen—and there were probably twenty of them—turned as if they they'd been rehearsing as a chorus. They looked at Betty Ann. Her face had become that of a raptor, fixated on a rodent. Her beak opened in a rictus grin.

The chorus swiveled their heads, again as one, and looked at Frank and me. The captive stockbrokers saw their moment; they stepped lightly away, as if on crepe-soled shoes, walking backwards until they disappeared from the room.

"My friends," I hailed, outstretching my arms and swaggering into the crowded kitchen.

There were scattered calls of Max, Max. The synthesizer break was relieved by lyrics—"Once I ran to you, now I'll run from you." The locust swarm of cocktail chatter swelled up again.

A couple squeezed through the crowd and came over to greet me. I introduced them to Frank. It was Claudia's partner Jeff and his new girlfriend, Ashley, an attractive brunette in a black catsuit.

"Max Bravo," I said, shaking Ashley's hand.

"Max is an opera singer," Jeff told her.

She decided that made me worth looking at. She summarized me with clear green, kohl-encrusted eyes.

"Divorced opera singer," I told her. "Are you an artist?"

"I manage a photocopy shop," she said.

"Don't let her sell herself short," Jeff interjected. "Ashley dances with the San Francisco Ballet."

"I'm just in the corps," she said, and took a drink of white wine.

I watched her place her hand on the sharp jut of her hip bone. Her fingers fluttered there, like elegant little birds.

"I'm not full time with the company," she was saying. "I'm just on call."

"She's remarkable," Jeff piped in. "They love her. She's top of the list for the next open spot."

"That's a very flattering ensemble," I told Ashley, permitting myself to touch her upper arm. "Leather?"

"Pleather," she said.

"Pleasure?" I said.

"Pleather," she corrected me, but she allowed herself to find me amusing.

"I take it you and Jeff are just friends," I pushed it further.

"I think we're on a date."

"Well, no need to get technical," I said, and I wriggled in closer to her, effectively blocking out Jeff.

I was just starting to make some progress. I had guessed correctly that Ashley's favorite fruit was mango. She admitted, with relish, that her feet were permanently mangled, and brutally unsightly, from dancing on pointe. And she'd never dated an opera singer, at least not yet.

And then Betty Ann came crashing in like a block of frozen shit falling from an airplane.

She shouldered Ashley aside, and planted herself in front of Frank Kelly and me.

"Maybe you couldn't hear me from so far away," she yelled in our faces. "I said I want a kiss."

Frank daubed forward like a sandpiper and tapped his lips on Betty Ann's blubbery cheek.

Betty Ann was hectoring—a great long spiel of nonsense. It sounded like a foghorn operated by a deaf lunatic. I felt a thrush of movement in the crowd. I turned to see Ashley's exquisite, pleather-clad buttocks sway out of the room. And I turned back to glare at Betty Ann. She was oblivious of my ire. She was too busy going after Frank Kelly with her raptor spurs.

"What the hell was that?" Betty Ann boomed at Frank, in what was meant to be mock anger, only the mock part didn't quite come off.

"Give Mama a proper kiss," she yelled.

This time he pressed his lips against hers. He jerked back from her and she swiped the palm of her hand across her lips, further smearing the fuchsia lipstick that was only just approximating her lip line.

"That's better," she said, quieter, teetering backward on her mules to counterbalance the forward pull of her prow.

She looked over to me, and scrunched up the side of her face. I thought she was having a petit mal seizure. Then I realized she was winking.

Her face was oddly ductile, like it was made of Plasticine. And it had swelled outward.

She had always been a bit Bouvier in that regard, with the broad face and the eyes set so far apart she bore a distinctly ruminant appearance. But it had been more distinctive than aberrant.

Now, in the wake of her miseries, Betty Ann's face was a swollen and lumpy thing—a dull moon, floating in space without an atmosphere, pocked and pummeled by asteroids.

"Where are you going?" I called out to Ashley, forgetting to suppress the urgency in my voice.

She had come back into the kitchen to fetch her coat. She didn't answer. She just fluttered her long fingers at me as Jeff dragged her away.

I decided to hate Betty Ann Thibideaux.

I turned to glare at her. She was still filibustering. Loudly.

Her lips moved, but her jawline didn't. It was stuck, high-centered, on the pillow of suet formerly known as her neck. I thought of a ship, wrecked, its hull embedded in a sandbar.

I heard her say the word *memoirs* and the phrase *body of work*. In a desperate bid to save my sanity, and to perhaps hijack Ashley away from Jeff, I started to slip away. I pretended I was going to the refrigerator for a beer.

"Got a smoke, Max?" Betty Ann hollered, blocking my egress.

Her mouth hung open as she awaited my response.

I pulled a cigarette out of my case for her. She jammed it into a foot-long black cigarette holder and took several stabs at the flame of my upheld lighter.

"Let's sit down, Betty Ann," Frank said.

He took her elbow in his hand. She shook it off, telling him she didn't want to sit down.

I went over to the three people sitting around the kitchen table and asked them if they could make room. Realizing that Betty Ann was heading their way, they cleared out like evacuees ahead of a tsunami.

"I'm sitting with Max," Betty Ann yelled in the direction of the plate rail.

She struck out for the kitchen table, Frank trailing behind. She spun into one of the chairs. She jabbed her cigarette holder at the chair beside her.

"Sit down, lover," she commanded Frank.

Frank folded himself onto the chair. He crossed his legs and lowered his head. He kept absolutely still.

Betty Ann jammed the cigarette holder between her teeth and clenched it in a jaunty uptilt. She looked disarmingly like FDR.

"I have something to say to you," she said, meaning Frank, although she said it to the entire room.

She paused, waited for a hush to fall, waited for her spotlight.

She slid off her chair. Her knees hit the linoleum with a crack, but she evinced no pain. She crawled on her knees to Frank, her hands clasped in front of her heart. The cigarette holder clamped in her teeth, piping a herald of smoke.

She shifted up onto one knee. She placed her cigarette in an ashtray and took Frank Kelly's hand in both of hers.

The room had gone mute, breathless. Everyone was watching. In another moment of stereophonic irony, Joy Division was playing—"Love, love will tear us apart again."

"Frank James Kelly," she pronounced.

Frank kept his head down. He held still. He was playing dead.

"Frankie. Lover," Betty Ann said. "I want us to always be together like this."

It was horrible. And fantastic. I'd forgotten to be angry.

"Frankie," Betty Ann said, "let's stay together. Always. Will you marry me, Frankie? Say yes. Here. In front of all these people. Will you, lover?"

She held tightly on to his hand. She smiled a big, open smile and, valiantly, she held it there, awaiting his answer. He wouldn't look up.

Betty Ann's cheeks quivered. Her eyes—struck wide in an attitude of mania meant to look like enthusiasm—began to moisten.

The crowd rustled. Someone started to laugh, then altered the outburst into a coughing fit.

I could hear Betty Ann wheezing.

The smile annealed onto her face, as if it were a decorative flourish chosen by someone with very bad taste.

And still, Frank Kelly would not look up from his shoe.

"Betty," a man's voice came on soft and welcome like Demerol through an IV drip.

"Betty Ann. Honey. I need your help with the appetizers."

It was Larry, Claudia's husband. He eased through the crowd, took Betty Ann by the arm and lifted her to her feet.

"Can you help me, Betty?" Larry said. "Can you show me how you wanted to serve your appetizers?"

He squeezed her wrist, waited for her to recognize him.

She turned. She saw him. She pulled herself up straight. Larry let go of her. She stood on her own.

"Is the oven on?" Betty Ann asked. "I smelled something burning."

13

Dixie and I were on Valencia Street at Stan Blashky's front door. I pressed the bell, and spoke into the intercom.

"You got me here," I said. "Now what?"

"Are you alone?" Blashky's voice stippled over the speaker.

Dixie and I looked at each other.

"Open the fucking door," I said.

The buzzer droned and I pushed inside. I let Dixie off her leash and she scrabbled up the stairs ahead of me.

Blashky was on the third floor. The stairs were dark and steep. The building was old and hard-worn. It was Victorian, probably built in the 1870s when the Comstock Silver Strike triggered a boom bigger than the Gold Rush.

I stopped in the hallways of the first, and then the second floor to catch my breath. It smelled of mildew and wood and sustenance living.

Blashky had called me just an hour earlier. He told me he found something. It was important. I had to look at it. He was cryptic, but urgent.

I arrived at the third floor with my heart banging in my chest. I was annoyed to see Stan Blashky standing on the landing dressed in a ratty old smoking jacket and his boxer shorts.

He had slippers on his feet. And, in a bid to assume some semblance of daywear, he'd stuck a porkpie hat on his head.

"Did you just get out of bed?" I asked him.

"No," he said.

I followed Blashky into his flat and down a long dark tunnel of a hallway, his open jacket flapping and swaying like bat wings. Dixie stayed close at my heels.

"What do you call this décor?" I said.

"I call it Planet Man."

Blashky cleared a sweatshirt and a pair of dirt-stiffened socks off of a chair. The chair burst into a mad palsy when he touched it.

I realized that the chair—a faux early Americana monstrosity upholstered in orange and rust plaid—had a rocker mechanism beneath its frilly skirt.

"Where did you get this, um . . . ?" I said. "This. This piece?"

I saw that the earth-toned plaid was covered in rampant stains, clearly marking the mishaps of an underlived life.

"I found it on the street," Stan said. "It had a FREE sign on it."

"It looks like one of those chairs that they find a dead person in."

"Leakers," he said. "They call them leakers because they liquefy. There was a lady who died in her apartment across the street. And they didn't find her for like two weeks. She melted into her chair. And her Pekingese ate her fingers. "

I didn't have a response for this.

Blashky asked me to sit down. He offered me the rocker, which was still in motion, ticking.

I examined the seat cushion. It had turned gray and shiny. Waxen, in fact.

It was clearly Blashky's favorite chair, and I could picture him spending many a blithe evening sunk into it with a cache of tall beer cans. The rocker was positioned to afford a view of both the window, which looked out to a startling blue sky, and the television, which was mounted on the opposite wall by a swing arm, an arrangement typical of hospital rooms.

"Go ahead," Blashky repeated. "Sit down, Max."

I perched on the rocker's arm. It jerked back and forth, bucked me off.

I was forced to sit properly in it, directly on the maculated cushion.

"You wanted to show me something," I said to Stan.

I tried to compose myself against the chair, fighting its backward pitch.

"I couldn't just tell you over the phone," Blashky said.

He went over to the bay window, stood in the center of it. He took off his hat, ran his palm over his smooth, bare head.

He looked undone.

"Something about Frank? Isn't it?" I said to him.

I tried to focus, but it was difficult. I could feel legions of microscopic crabs burrowing up from the plaid upholstery and through the sturdy weave of my wool trousers.

"Yes," Blashky said. "It's about Frank."

The hard light of day battered all about Stan Blashky, standing there in the bay window, in the center of the blue triptych. The sky behind him was so intensely blue, it seemed to swirl and swell. I thought for a moment that the sky would swallow Stan. It was so deep. Miles deep. It looked like it could open up and swallow every living thing.

"Frank lived here," Stan said.

I told him I knew that.

"It was only for about five months," Stan said. "But it felt like five years."

"Frank would be hard to live with," I said.

"Sure," Stan said.

"There was something in his journal about having left his job—"

"Fired," Stan said. "He was shit-canned."

Stan looked out the window, at the bottomless blue. He opened the window, just a crack. The sound of traffic, and a dog barking, came rushing into the room.

Stan lit a cigar, looked down at the parking lot next door. He stepped away from the window and sat on the sofa across from me. The sofa was long and deep, but Blashky seemed to fill it completely.

He invited me to pour myself a drink. He nodded toward the coffee table between us. A half-empty bottle stood on it, flanked by a couple of highball glasses.

One glass had fuchsia lipstick on the rim. Both were dirty.

"Southern Comfort," I said. I picked up the lipstick glass. "How colorful."

Blashky went into the kitchen, came back with a handful of ice cubes. He dropped them into the glasses.

"What did Frank do to get fired?" I asked him. "Assault somebody?"

"Pretty much. Assault," he said. "Yes. Physical assault."

I tipped my glass. Took a drink. Blashky looked at his.

"Frank had an incident," Blashky said. "He went ape shit."

"Is that so unusual? I imagine you see a lot of tantrums in your business."

"Frank threw a number two pencil," Stan said. "It was kind of reckless. He speared some asshole with it. Right in the forehead."

Stan tossed me a pack of matches so I could light my cheroot.

"Someone important?"

"Our boss."

"Intentional?"

"No," said Blashky. "But, it was still pretty spectacular. The pencil stuck right into Ken's forehead. And it just stayed there, sticking straight out for like five seconds, because it was embedded so deep."

"Graphite. That's not good."

"Yeah," Stan said. "Ken had to get shots."

"Lawsuit?"

"Nope," he said. "Just threats. And a pink slip."

I took a sip of the treacly bourbon, tinkled the ice cubes around in my glass, and decided that the lipstick on the glass was definitely fuchsia.

I poured another three fingers of Southern Comfort.

"Help yourself to another drink, Max," Blashky said.

"I recognize this lipstick," I told him.

"She's a busy gal," Blashky said.

"What did she want?"

"She accused me of hiding Frank's notebooks," Stan said. "She wanted me to hand them over to her."

"What did you tell her?"

"I told her that if I caught her breaking into my apartment again, I'd kick her ass. Then I gave her a drink and sent her home."

Stan said that he didn't call me to talk about Betty Ann.

He found something that morning. Something in Frank's old room. He didn't know what to make of it.

We got up. I followed him down the hall, the ice cubes clinking in my glass.

"This place is enormous," I said. "How do you manage it?"

"Rent control," Blashky said. "I've been here twenty-two years. Outlasted all my roommates. Now I don't even need them."

"Why'd they all leave?"

"Oh, you know. They grew up. Got married. Left Neverland. Most of them are divorced now," he said. He raised his glass. "Some got spooked. Ran out of here scared shitless."

"What?"

"Here's Frank's room."

I stepped into the little blue room at the end of the corridor. I felt a shift, like I'd stepped onto the deck of a ship. The carpet was deep—and surely rife with great teeming colonies of mites—but not deep enough to induce the swaying, rolling sensation that made me shuffle to retain my balance.

"Not much of a bed," I said, pointing my glass at the narrow pallet.

"That was all the bed Frank needed," Stan said. "He didn't feel like socializing after he lost his job."

A Christian cross hung on the wall above the bed. It was a rough relic, made out of burned matchsticks. Prisoner art.

"Frank stayed in this room ten, maybe twelve hours a day," Stan said. "Working. Writing."

I went over to the spindly metal table set under the room's only window. The window faced north and, just like the view from the living room, looked out onto an unobstructed sky.

It was a rare luxury in San Francisco, this kind of private sky. Most people had panoramic views of their neighbor's living rooms.

Or they looked out into light wells—the deep chasms in between the hundred-year-old buildings—to see their neighbors' polyester shirts and billowy white underpants drying on clotheslines.

To look out a window in this town and see nothing but clear expanse meant that somebody was very rich. Or, something was very wrong.

Stan ran his hand across the scarred surface of Frank Kelly's desk. "He set up his computer here," Blashky said. "I guess for the light."

"And the view," I said.

I stepped over to the window. The parking lot below was big, bigger than the footprint of Blashky's building.

It was paved with crumbling asphalt. Veins of black tar shot through it where the fissures and cracks had been half-heartedly repaired over the years. Weeds—wild fennel as tall as men, and dandelions, staunch as saplings—shot up in a couple of spots where sinkholes had opened.

The lot was enclosed in an eight-foot-high cyclone fence, topped with concertina wire. Inside the fence, there wasn't much worth stealing. A few junkers: A white Mazda mini-truck. A Camry with the quarter-panel stoved in. A pimped-out pussy wagon—purple-fleck Ambassador, long as a city block.

All the cars looked like they were the vestigial remains of hard-luck stories; loser stories. The cars were probably left to rot in that broken-down parking lot by guys who lost their licenses. Or were doing time in federal penitentiary. Or guys who got themselves killed doing the typical dumb-ass shit like walking drunk on railway tracks, or getting up on the roof to pirate cable TV hookups.

These cars hadn't been driven for years. They weren't parked. They were dead. Only they didn't know it yet. The lot was a kind of automobile purgatory.

"Amazing," I said.

"What?"

"A vacant lot that size, in this neighborhood," I said. "Why doesn't the guy make it into a real parking lot? You know what monthly parking goes for? Or, just sell it. To some developer."

"Nobody wants it," Blashky said. "It's cursed."

"It's prime real estate."

"No, Max, it's not," Stan said. "That site is where the Valencia Hotel stood."

"Do you know how many condos you could put in there?"

"You don't know what happened there, do you?" he said.

No, I didn't. So he told me.

On April 18, 1906, when the big quake hit, and while the rest of the city was crashing down and the fires were kicking up all over hell, the Valencia Hotel sank.

The hotel was built over a swamp.

In the 1860s, San Francisco had started to burgeon west and south. Up until then, the Mission's acres of marshland had discouraged development. But the value of real estate overshot the cost of landfill. And the streets and parks and buildings—like the one that Stan Blashky lived in—went up in just a few years.

Enterprising builders filled in the marshes with dirt. They brought it in from the south of the city, where they were excavating hills to level the streets. And they brought in silt from the bay where they'd dredged the harbor to let in more deep-hulled ships.

The San Francisco developers of the early days thought that just by digging, and blasting, and dumping dirt, they could determine where the land would end, and where the sea would begin.

Their folly was soon exposed. The 1906 earthquake hit, and the ground under the hotel liquefied.

The whole building sank into an artesian pool. At least two hundred people were trapped inside. They drowned on dry land.

I swallowed the rest of my drink. The aftertaste was cloying and I sensed my brief love affair with Southern Comfort was coming to an end.

"Anyway, the Valencia Hotel, that's history," Stan Blashky said. "Here's what I wanted you to see, Max."

Blashky pointed to the wall next to the window.

"I painted this room before Frank moved in here."

He walked over to the wall. He stroked his palm across its surface.

"Frank hung a picture," he said. "Right here. A seascape. He left it when he moved out. I never touched it, not until this morning."

Someone had written on the wall.

The handwriting was cursive. It was sure, precise, and elegant. It had an archaic masterfulness.

Dixie started barking, frenzied and threatened.

I told her to be quiet. She ignored me. She sprang forward and clawed frantically at the floorboards beneath the writing, growling to herself.

"All right," I said, picking her up. "Get out."

I put her in the hallway, closed the door. She stayed on the other side of it, barking and scratching at the frame.

Stan pulled a magnifying glass out of the pocket of his smoking jacket.

He handed me the instrument and I leaned in close. The passage read:

I am cast down from the welkin of the celestial vault. I have landed here on the fires that burn on the forgetful lake. I lie forever drowning in flame, until Ah Ho is restored to me.
D.W.F., April 18, 1906

"You have Frank's journal, right?" Blashky said. "Did he write shit like this?"

"No," I said. "Frank didn't write this."

"And who's Ah Ho?"

I told him I didn't know.

14

I hadn't thought about Frank Kelly in years. But now Frank—and the past that he brought with him—hung over me like a trellis. It dripped with the weedy verdure of his death.

The further I went, the more I tried to get away, the deeper I was led into Frank's hermetic world. And everywhere I turned, Betty Ann Thibideaux was there, a rogue maniac in the funhouse mirror.

She was at the bookstore when I initially went there to hire Emile Balzac to interpret the graphology in Frank's journal. She broke into my home for said journal. Then she showed up at Stan Blashky's.

The pattern was becoming too clear for me to ignore. Betty Ann was connected with Frank's death. She knew something. Some secret. And she was desperate to keep it hidden. Perhaps it was in Betty Ann's memoirs.

I'd have to read her crappy book.

Dixie and I left Stan Blashky's flat and walked down Valencia to Balzac's bookstore. Along the way, I rehearsed how I'd ask for a copy of Betty Ann Thibideaux's first book, *Smashed to Bits*. It would be embarrassing.

I thought I could buy a pile of real books, and tuck hers into the middle of it. That way, it would look as though I were buying *Smashed* as a sort of an anthropological study.

The strategy could get pricey. But, I knew there was a tax on being stupid. Or weak. And I'm used to paying it.

When I got to the bookstore, Emile Balzac glanced up at me, asked me if I was looking for anything in particular. I lied. I said no.

I thought Balzac might try to engage me in a discussion about Frank, or Duffield Fallon. He'd probably been doing further research— for extra credit, damned nerd that he was.

I scuttered quickly to the back of the bookstore, looking for the section that housed outdated bestsellers. I ducked in amid the tall shelves, and found myself lost in a friendly crowd; Melville, and Mann, and George Eliot, and dear old Virginia Woolf. I pulled a copy of *Mrs. Dalloway* off the shelf. Virginia Woolf's photo was on the cover—her long, wise face, so plain. And brilliant. Her gift was her undoing. In the end, she walked into a river, her pockets filled with rocks. Like Frank Kelly, she gave herself up to the water.

I put Virginia back on the shelf. Dixie and I made for the shallow end of the fiction section. I knew we'd find Betty Ann's book there.

Balzac's big gray cat followed, stalking us softly. He kept back several paces, and placed his paws carefully in a straight line as he went, like a tightrope walker.

We got to the popular bestsellers and the big cat circled me, then stood and rubbed his cheek against my knee. I scratched his chin, and noticed his name tag. Pyewacket.

I located *Smashed to Bits*. I was irked that I couldn't find Betty Ann's dizzy trope in paperback. Damned if I was going to pay $25 for that steaming pile of pulp.

I went to the used books and, in a note of unintended hilarity, I found Betty Ann's book shelved under nonfiction. It was a hardback, but Emile had priced it at five dollars. By the looks of the spine, the previous owner had gotten a third of the way through before giving up on it and trading it in.

"This just came in," Emile Balzac appeared from around the corner of the existentialism section.

He was holding a copy of *Paradise Lost*.

"Why would I want that?" I said, rattled that he knew exactly where I was.

"Regard," Balzac said.

The book came in a hardback sleeve box. He slipped it out, and explained that it was in exceptional condition. It was more than a hundred years old.

"And it's illustrated," he said. "With the William Blake watercolors."

"Sublime," I said.

He placed it in my hands. The cover was a deep marine blue. It was sturdy, and elegant. I opened it and turned the pages. They felt like sheaves of papyrus; stiff with a pebbly texture. The papers' edges were ragged, exposing their fibrous composition.

The Blake illustrations were primitive and sophisticated, soft and muscular. The limpid watercolors limned startling, powerful images of angels and devils, and mortals. It was the universe shown naked; its underpinning structures of good and evil fully revealed.

I caressed the book. I wanted it in the same way I'd want a flashy bauble.

"Blake portrayed Satan as a sympathetic character," Emile said.

He pushed his glasses up onto the bridge of his nose. His eyes magnified in the dense lenses.

"Satan," I said. "Yes, he's not all bad."

Pyewacket yowled. I looked down at him. He lifted his face and opened his mouth wide. His eyeteeth were extraordinarily long, saber-toothed in fact, and his eyes were the same chlorophyll green as Emile Balzac's.

"Can you guess why I'm showing you this book, Max?"

"Because you're a bookseller and you want to sell it to me?" I ventured.

Pyewacket purred and leaned into my leg, nearly shoving me off my feet. I shuffled to regain my balance.

Balzac opened the book, turned over the first few pages of front matter. He said, "Voilà," and creased down the flyleaf.

I recognized the handwriting. And the signature: Duffield Waverly Fallon, January 1906.

Emile Balzac watched me, the left side of his face hiked up into one of those uniquely Gallic grimaces that passes in café society as ironic.

"It's an incredible coincidence," I finally managed.

"It's more than that," Balzac said. He took the book back from me, turned another page, smoothed it with his palm, and held it out for me.

It was a second signature: Frank Kelly, January 2006.

Pyewacket pulled away from my leg. He stalked off toward the front of the store.

"How did you come by this book?" I asked.

"One of the local homeless people brought it to me," Emile Balzac said. "She has been bringing me books for years. You've probably seen her. She has a cart, lots of stuffed toys, coloring books."

I could hear Pyewacket. He was at the front of the store, growling full stanzas of gutturals that sounded like some long-dead language.

"The homeless woman," Balzac said. "She described the man who gave her the book. I think the man must have been Frank."

"It could be," I said. "Frank's name is in the book. When did he give it to her."

"Alors," Balzac said; he blew out a gust of breath. "Poor Linda is so completely mad. Delusional. She said he gave it to her this morning."

We heard a sharp bang. Then, a muffled thud.

Dixie ran to the front of the store, barking.

We hurried after her. Pyewacket was sitting on the counter, a puddle of water all around him. He looked at us defiantly.

The Siamese fighting fish was flailing around on the damp carpet, fanning its tail, gasping at the air, drowning.

The brandy snifter was nearby the displaced fish. It rolled back and forth on its round belly, a few drops of water still slogging around inside it.

Balzac dropped to one knee, scooped the fish off the floor, and cupped it in his hands. He returned it to the empty snifter, and ran with it to the back of the store.

Dixie stopped barking. She scurried to my side, sat on my foot, and looked up at me.

Dixie didn't much like the way they did things at Neptune's Books. She was ready to leave.

Pyewacket sat on the counter, the water slowly spreading all around him. He glared at me and opened his mouth to show me his teeth. He threw back his head and I had the distinct impression that he was silently laughing.

15

"Max," Claudia's voice blared over the phone, "wake up. It's Frank's big day."

I looked at the clock. Ten A.M.

Dixie lifted her head from my armpit. I'd been up most of the night, trying to read *Paradise Lost.* It was dawn before I'd finally drifted off from utter exhaustion.

"Frank's funeral," Claudia said. "Let's go."

"When are you coming for me?" I asked.

"We're out front."

"You assholes."

Dixie stretched, pronging her front legs straight. She threw back her head, and yawned.

I got up. Dixie dove off the bed after me. I threw on my kimono. I looked out the window and saw Claudia stalking up the garden steps. Larry was paying the taxi driver.

I couldn't find my slippers. I pounded down the stairs in my bare feet, my night blinders still shoved up on top of my head, fanning up my hair into an impressively tall rack.

"You're wearing antlers," Claudia said, reaching up and patting my hair.

I snatched the blinders off my head.

"Oh," she said. "You spoiled it. I liked it like that."

She barged through the foyer, her chartreuse coat loudly announcing the renaissance of glam rock. A pair of crystal chandeliers dangled from her ears, burying into the deep pile of pink fun fur on her collar. Larry followed in her wake. Dixie ran into his arms.

"Put her down, Larry," Claudia said. "You're getting dog hair on your jacket."

"Can you make coffee," I told her.

She slipped out of her coat, tossed it on the console table. She was wearing a Pucci dress and tall white boots. The print was a tropical tornado in Day-Glo tangerine and pistachio. It rippled and trilled as she moved.

"Why aren't you dressed?" she yelled over her shoulder as she sashayed to the kitchen, trailing clouds of white peony perfume and cigarette smoke.

Larry put his hand on my shoulder. He asked me if I was all right. Yes, I told him. He said I didn't look well.

"You're not wearing black," I said, fingering the yellow silk handkerchief that spluttered from the pocket of Larry's lavender sport coat.

"Claudia wouldn't let me," Larry told me. "She said black is too morbid."

"Right," I said. "We wouldn't want to introduce a somber note at a funeral."

Claudia had dressed herself and her husband in colors of Easter. It was like they expected to bury Frank Kelly and he'd rise up three days later. Not that we were actually burying Frank. The sea had taken care of that for us.

It had been a month, and Frank still hadn't washed up. He was probably mired in a tangle of ship's debris at the bottom of the bay, busy crabs scuttling over his gelatinous remains.

Removing an actual corpse from the agenda leaves a rather awkward gap in a funeral. Without the body to prepare, and showcase, and cart about we had none of the busy practicalities that give ballast to these events.

Fortunately, over the years, and over many drinks, Frank had told Blashky what he expected for a send-off. Blashky listed out these maudlin, late-night grandiosities and used them as a guide for orchestrating the funeral.

The plan was to start out at the Sans Souci. It was Sunday morning, usually a pretty slow shift for Johnny Miranda—just a few dedicated A.M. drinkers, skinny old men with ashen pallor, walking jerky in their soft-soled shoes. Johnny hung a PRIVATE PARTY sign on the door and the old men pegged down the street to the Gang Plank, like a troop of desiccated stick crickets.

Blashky was at the bar with Johnny when we arrived. There were a few funeral bouquets displayed around the place, on the tabletops, and at the ends of the bar. The flowers gave off a sickly sweet odor, as if they were already rotting. I asked Johnny for a tot of brandy. Claudia and Larry joined Blashky in a white wine.

A crew of four elderly Chinese caterers, prim in their black slacks and red vests, arrived. Blashky directed them to the back, where they set up their wheeled trays.

"Frank wanted dim sum," Blashky said when he returned to his bar stool.

"Wasn't he Irish?" Larry asked.

"Yes," I said. "Shouldn't we be having potatoes and boiled meat?"

"Frank was very precise about what he wanted," Blashky said.

Guests started drifting in around noon. Most of them were from the advertising business. That made for a better than average-looking crowd. They were dressed au courant. Subtle sartorial dashes signaled their insider status: the width of a hat brim, the height of a heel, the daring rehabilitation of a 1980s hairstyle that until just months earlier had been the object of jeering ridicule. It was a parade of fops in their finery.

It was odd to see the Sans Souci filled to capacity with so many bright young things. It was usually so vacant and hushed. The regular patrons came there to drink, not mingle.

The noise level ratcheted up, punctuated by raucous laughter. The old Chinese waiters pushed their dim sum carts through the crowd of pretty people, like ducks swimming across a pond covered in lotus blossoms.

Blashky reached for a plate of chicken feet as a cart trolled by. He scooped up the legs, shoved them stub first into his mouth, and turned to us with a half-dozen chicken claws sticking out of his face.

Claudia laughed. It was more of a bark, like a harbor seal. Larry smiled broadly, not sure whether it was okay or not to carry on like a horse's ass at a funeral.

"Do you think Frank Kelly would find that funny?" a woman said.

"I know he would," Blashky told her, the chicken feet tussling around in front of his face as he spoke.

"Me too," the woman said. She pulled the chicken legs out of Blashky's mouth and kissed him with open lips.

She was tall in her heels and her dress was tailored to fit snug over her smooth curves. I wanted to run my hand down the long straight of her back.

"Introduce me to your friends," she said, turning from Blashky to look at me.

She faced me straight on, daring me to react. A brutal scar ran down the center of her forehead and the bridge of her nose. It turned in across her right cheek. The right eye sat a little lower than the left. She looked like a porcelain doll that had been broken, and clumsily glued back together.

"I remember you, Max Bravo," she said, shaking my hand.

"I remember you too," I said, pulling her hand up to my lips. I kissed it.

"Ashley!" It was Claudia.

The two women screamed and threw their arms around each other.

"Remember Ashley, Max?" Claudia said. "She came to our parties when we lived in Cole Valley. Back when Frank lived in the basement."

"I'd know you anywhere," I told Ashley.

"You'd have to," she said, and she smiled—just a half smile, and for a moment her face looked almost even.

"You still have your marvelous sense of style," I told her. "I remember you used to wear the most fetching leather catsuit."

"Pleather," she said.

"Quite," I agreed.

More than twenty years later and Ashley Banks still starstruck me like a *Tiger Beat* teen idol. We were all older. We were, in effect, not even the same people. And, moreover, her scars were horrific. I should have been shocked, repulsed. But I wasn't. And it surprised me.

"Where's Dante?" Blashky broke in.

"I left him with Laura," she said.

"But I wanted him to come," Blashky said peevishly.

"Dante is nine, Stan," she said. "And this is a bar."

"Whatever," Blashky said. "The limo is here. Max, can you give me a hand?"

I took a moment to hate Blashky for extracting me from Ashley's presence. Then I felt Claudia's bossy Calabrian stare fixed on me.

I tossed down the rest of my brandy. Fortified, I followed Stan to a table at the back of the bar where he'd arranged a shrine for Frank Kelly. He'd had a head shot of Frank blown up to poster-size. It had pixilated in the enlargement, so that it almost looked as though Seurat had painted Frank's portrait.

Despite the abstraction, Frank's teeth still looked false. I found that oddly comforting.

The photo was mounted and framed, and around it was hung a bower of red and white carnations in the shape of a giant horseshoe.

"Christ," I said to Blashky, as I helped him lift the hideous portrait off the table, along with the horseshoe flower arrangement. "Did Frank win the Preakness?"

"Watch where you're backing up there, Max."

"Then you bloody well take the front."

"Here's the car," he said.

A stretch limo, ragtop, was parked in the loading zone in front of the bar. The driver opened the door and helped us prop the Frank Kelly portrait up on the middle armrest in the backseat.

"Let's get everybody rounded up," Blashky said, clapping me on the back.

"Did you hire every Chinaman in the city for this thing?" I asked him.

"Just the caterers," he said. "And the driver. And the mourners."

"Aren't we the mourners?"

"No. Those guys are."

He pointed to a group of elderly Chinese women standing on the sidewalk. They were dressed in white.

Blashky stalked back into the bar and stood on a chair. He called for silence. He instructed the crowd to finish their drinks and prepare to leave. The guests began collecting their things and making for the door with all the precision of a corps of Neapolitan militia.

Blashky and I got in the back of the limo, each of us holding on to the Frank Kelly portrait-slash-horseshoe-bouquet monstrosity. Ashley squeezed in next to Blashky, Claudia next to me. Larry sat in the front seat by the driver.

Blashky said, "Let's roll."

The limo driver pulled down his cap, adjusted his aviator sunglasses with his thumb and the tip of his middle finger, and slowly pulled away from the curb. He turned up Grant Street, the main street of Chinatown.

The troupe of mourners fell in directly behind us, proceeding at the speed of moss. As soon as we got moving, they began caterwauling in a most desperate imitation of grief. The guests followed the mourners, picking their way in high heels, many of them openly sloshing drinks that they'd secreted out of the bar. I had the sense that our party was somewhat of a public spectacle.

Chinatown denizens stopped all along the sidewalks, watching our procession creep along amid wailing and heel-clacks. The locals regarded us blandly, as if they were merely dreaming a farang funeral marching through their neighborhood.

"Inscrutable, aren't they?" I said to Blashky.

He told me I was an asshole.

We reached the end of the Chinese sector of Grant Street. If we crossed Broadway, we'd be in North Beach. Little Italy. Blashky declared our procession had achieved its end point.

He stood up on the backseat, turned to face the halted procession. The mourners abruptly stopped wailing. The guests stopped laughing and pushing one another only after Blashky stuck two fingers in his mouth and let loose a piercing whistle. Blashky thanked everyone for coming. He pulled an airline mini-bottle of whiskey out of his pocket, opened it, and raised it aloft. To a man, and woman, the guests pulled drinks out from under their coats and raised their glasses. I noticed Johnny Miranda standing off to the side, his face deeply red, his lips annunciating vigorous expletives.

Blashky said a few words about Frank Kelly. It was mawkish twaddle about Frank having been a poet descended from the finest Gaelic tradition. He leaned over the side of the limo, poured half the whiskey onto Grant Street. Then he slugged down the other half.

The guests, made malleable by daytime drinking, poured their drinks onto the ground, following Blashky's lead. They chanted as one: To Frank Kelly. They brought the glasses to their lips, and drank.

Johnny Miranda began elbowing through the crowd, curtly snatching his bar glasses out of people's hands.

Blashky sat back down and told the driver to *hit it*. We spun out, chirped the tires as we turned onto Columbus Street, and headed south with all eight cylinders thumping and red and white carnations blowing off behind us.

"Are we done?" I asked Blashky.

"One more stop."

We turned west and drove toward the failing sun. After we crossed Van Ness, blocks of tall, spindly Victorian homes—once grand single-family residences, now divided into grandly expensive flats—stood shoulder to shoulder along the street.

These were the buildings that had survived the earthquake and fire of 1906. What the quake hadn't flattened, the fire devoured—from Chinatown west as far as Van Ness. With the exception of a few inexplicably lucky buildings, the structures in that zone were a flock of phoenixes, they arose out of the ash around 1910.

The driver turned south and rumbled down Dolores Street. Behemoth palm trees towered along the center boulevard. They waved their bushy fronds high above us. Blashky reached into his jacket and pulled out a handful of airline booze bottles. Ashley waved him away when he offered her the selection. He didn't look at me. He didn't need to. He tossed an assortment of liquor bottles over his shoulder. They fell into my lap. I rummaged through them, stowed the bottles in my pockets—all of them, except for the tequila. That one, I opened.

"Because we're now in Mexico," I told Claudia, waving the amber bottle at the neighborhood, la Mission.

"Para nos amigos muertos," Claudia told me.

She reached in her purse, produced her own mini-bottle of tequila. We tapped the bottles in a toast. They came together in a dissatisfying plastic *clunk,* rather than a glass *clink.* But we didn't let it deflate the moment. We drank deeply.

The driver pulled up to the old Mission Dolores. Its soaring white plaster walls seemed to billow in the blue sky like the sails of some conquering ship carrying soft-spoken tyrants.

Blashky announced that this was where we were getting out. I asked him if that, too, was part of Frank Kelly's prescription. He didn't answer. He bounded up the stairs leading to the cathedral doors.

The Mission had been there long before San Francisco was even a city. Since 1757, Dolores—Our Lady of Sorrows—had stood as the northernmost pearl on the strand of white-faced missions that ran from Baja up the coast of California. This was Spain.

I heaved up the steep stairs leading to the cathedral doors, tossed on a sea of brandy and tequila. I fell in alongside Ashley. I was short of breath. But made my waning look as though I was slowing down to accommodate her slower, spike-heeled pace.

"Are you and Blashky an item?" I asked.

"Are you quite comfortable asking strangers penetrating questions about their personal lives?"

I was on her left. Her profile was stunning. She still had the china doll features, and the translucent white skin, that had so transfixed me twenty years earlier. The only difference I could detect, from that angle, was a slight softening of the jawline, and a hardening of the laugh line running from the outside of her nose to the edge of her mouth. Delicate spider silk threads radiated from the corner of her eye. She smiled and I saw them deepen. I admired her: the beautiful woman with a broken face, wearing only the traces of mirth.

We followed Blashky through the cathedral, and then outside to the Mission garden. We walked along a colonnade. Hummingbirds plied their nectar trade among the citrus trees—the oranges and lemons blossomed white confections—and I could hear the rumble of fat bumblebees in the tree roses.

We passed through a portico and arrived in the cemetery. It was small, meant only to contain a few dead Spaniards. There was a minority of Americanos among the Californios. That was how old the graveyard was—it predated America.

A stand of tall oaks and eucalyptus shattered the ground with dabs of shade and sunlight. The round-shouldered tombstones teetered in drunken stances, their pocked surfaces lichened and the incised letters worn shallow, now nearly illegible.

Blashky picked his way through the necropolis purposefully. The Archangel Gabriel stood atop a marble plinth, rapt in avenging anger. The furious angel pointed an accusing finger at a stumpy, unkempt headstone against the back wall.

Blashky followed Gabriel's direction, and we followed Blashky. Me and Ashley, and Claudia and Larry, gathered round him and read the epitaph on the stone:

> *Duffield Waverly Fallon*
> *1858–1906*
> *An angel fallen upon the seas of hell.*
> *May he yet shake his wings dry,*
> *And ascend to the welkin of heaven's gate.*

"Well, I'll be dipped," I said. "Did you know about this, Blashky?"

"No," he said. "But Frank had always told me that when he died, he wanted us to come and have a drink here."

A woman screamed.

A sharp elbow knocked me out of the way. I heard crinoline rustling and smelled cheap perfume.

Betty Ann Thibideaux fell onto her knees at Fallon's grave. She pounded her fist onto the moss-covered mound. Her other hand clutched a lacy handkerchief, which she employed in mopping across her dry, tearless cheeks.

"Oh, if only he had reached out to me," she cried. "I could have helped. I would have done anything for Frank."

"Betty Ann," Blashky said, but she couldn't hear him above her own shrieking.

"Now this is worth the price of admission," Claudia said.

She reached into her purse, pulled out another mini-tequila, un-screwed it and took a slug.

"Betty Ann," Blashky repeated, this time clamping his hands around her shoulders. "You have to cut this shit out."

"Frank isn't in there, Betty Ann," Larry said.

He moved in quickly to help Blashky. They got Betty Ann up. She stopped howling.

"Well, then, what the hell?" she demanded, piqued.

Blashky explained that Frank hadn't washed up yet. Then he asked her how she knew to come to Mission Dolores. The invitation had said nothing about it.

"Mine did," Betty Ann insisted. "The second one anyway."

"I only sent out one," Blashky said. "The e-vite, right?"

"Sure," she said. "I got that. Then I got one in the mail. It was hand-written. Beautiful penmanship."

"I don't know where the hell that came from," Blashky said. He turned pale. He grabbed Ashley by the elbow. "Let's go. We're done here."

"We're going with Ashley and Blashky," Claudia said.

I pointed out that their names rhymed. Ashley regarded me with cool detach. Blashky told me I was an imbecile.

Claudia bobbed in close to me and said, "Just because you're jeal-ous of Blashky over that dame doesn't mean you have to act like an asshole."

And with that, they made to depart.

Happily, my revenge on Claudia came instantly. Betty Ann an-nounced that she was sharing a cab with them. Claudia could not mask her horror.

I was left alone, with the dead.

I sat on the small stone bench in front of Fallon's grave. I contem-plated the worn headstone, the cryptic epitaph. I unscrewed a tequila and, for the first time that day, I felt content. My usual aches and pains had been washed away by smooth agave nectar. The sturm und drang of the funeral party had finally ceased. And the sun warmed my face as the tequila warmed my heart.

"You old bastard," I said to Fallon's headstone. "What are you up to?"

A fat robin alighted onto the headstone. He ratcheted his head around to regard me from his profile, his beak parted as if to speak, his obsidian eye affixed onto me. I held still, not wanting to frighten him off. He hopped down onto the grave mound, plunged his beak into the thick, springy moss, and came up with a liver-brown salamander, thin as a worm, stubby arms flailing, spatulate fingers splayed.

"Hell of a shot, old boy," I said, saluting the predator with my tequila.

The robin flew away, the salamander in his beak.

Salamander. I turned the word over several times.

I recalled that *salamander* carries several meanings. In ancient times, it was the name for asbestos, because, according to mythology, the salamander is a fireproof reptile that can pass through flame unharmed. In fact, several medieval noble families throughout what is now Italy and Spain had incorporated salamanders onto their coats of arms to denote the indestructible nature of their houses.

I contemplated herpetology and history, until I noticed the sunlight glinting sharply on the spot where the robin had wrenched his victim from the spongy ground. I got up and went over to it, crouching down to get a better look. It was water.

It was percolating up from the moss. At first, the tequila suggested to me that the underground sprinkler had gone wonky. Then I looked around and realized there was no such modern convenience intruding upon this ancient sanctuary.

I bent down and smelled the water. It was briny. And then, probably because I was just drunk enough, I tasted it. It was salt water.

16

I am alone in Tartarus, the sunless abyss located in the basement of Hell.

I caught myself jotting that line down in my notebook.

In the days following the funeral, the January rains had come, in biblical excess, and I was obliged to batten down the windows, and huddle inside. I immersed myself in solitude so that I could ply my way through *Paradise Lost,* and Frank's ponderous notes, and Betty Ann Thibideaux's hellish memoir.

I wanted to put myself in the same mind-set that Frank had been in before his death. And it was working, maybe a little too well.

One Friday morning, after nearly a week of rain, I waited until it was almost noon before I went into the kitchen to pour my first drink of the day. I was arrested by a shaft of light striking through the window. I opened the back door, looked out at the sky and saw the sun had burst through the dunning pall of bruised rain clouds.

"Dixie," I called. "Let's go."

We strolled along glorious sun-drenched sidewalks and reveled in the light and warmth. People had emerged and they filled the streets en masse, uplifted on the brightness. I heard loud laughter and hailings and the hissing steam of espresso machines pressing out cup after cup of busy-making and commerce.

Dixie and I arrived at Dolores Park and found a relatively dry and unlittered spot on the grass, up on the south embankment. It was the ideal perch from which to observe the multicolored rainbow of denizens frolicking over the lawns and on the play structures and the basketball courts and the drug-dealing enclaves. We could see the spires of Mission Dolores ahead of us, and in the distance, the financial district office towers scraping money out of the empty sky.

I saw the man who sells marijuana truffles, walking among nests of picnic parties. Two big, shiny copper kettles hung low to his knees from a rod that he carried, coolie-style, across the top of his back. I summoned him over. I asked him what flavors he had. Today, he said, he had coconut and Grenache and strawberry. He set down his copper kettles and pulled samples out to show me. I decided on the Grenache. He told me to try eating just half of it. I said, sure, sure. And the moment he walked off, I stuffed the entire truffle into my mouth. Dixie lay down next to me, her chin on her wrists, and watched me doubtfully, anticipating some psychotropic disaster.

After about fifteen minutes I started to feel remarkably relaxed. I entertained myself by watching the truffle man walk up and down the incline, kettle pots swinging on their chains, sunlight stabbing sharp off their polished, curved surfaces.

A group of cute young gays were on a blanket across from me. Dixie bolted to them, jammed her face in their cheese dip. I dashed over, snatched her up, apologized profusely. They laughed it off. They gave me a beer and told me to forget about it.

I settled back down onto my spot, fortified now with TCP and Corona. I leashed Dixie, made her sit next to me. The guys cued up their boom box and I liked their music. It was something ethereal, house music with a tinge of good old-fashioned seventies samba. I was supremely content.

Then I noticed a woman wearing a floppy hat, a short skirt, and a Bolivian serape standing at the base of the hill.

She was staring at me.

Helplessly, and with mounting terror, I watched as she started picking her way up the hill on her bare stick legs, making a trajectory straight for me—swift and prancing like a harpy-footed Fury.

She hauled up on my larboard side, paused and stared directly at me. I was now alarmed, but determined not to show it. I stared straight ahead at the Mission towers, affecting a deep meditation on dolor and martyrdom and other things Catholic. Dixie, the traitorous buffoon, jumped up on the woman's shins and began clawing at her kneecaps in her ever-hopeful quest for dog treats.

"Max Bravo," the woman said.

"Yes," I admitted.

I turned to look at her. She dropped down beside me on the grass. She stretched her scrawny legs out in front of her. She was wearing a pair of ancient Keds sneakers that had once been white. The sneakers had no laces and their tongues hung open, lax and flopping. She removed her hat and shook loose a bouffant of red hair.

"It's me," she said. "Betty Ann Thibideaux."

"How are you?"

"What a coincidence! We don't see each other for years, and now, twice in just a couple of months."

"How are you?" I repeated.

I realized that I probably shouldn't have eaten that damned truffle.

"I'm just taking a break," she informed me. "I've been working like mad since the last time we saw each other."

"When you broke into my house?" I said. "Or, no, wait, it was when you staged that mad scene in the cemetery."

"I'm so inspired!" she continued. "Max! Guess what I'm writing about now!"

"Frank."

"Frank," she said, still fizzing over with enthusiasm she hoped would go viral.

She grinned wide, with big, capped, post–drug addict teeth. She looked like a gavial lurking in the Ganges.

"Huh," I managed.

Betty Ann told me that Frank's death inspired her to write another memoir. She'd already run it by her editor. She said she was getting a fat advance.

"Here's the pitch," she said, fanning her jazz hands as if opening a stage curtain. "A beautiful young woman in love with a tortured artist. He's a poet. She's a sensitive novelist. They have a tumultuous affair. It's a heady mix of genius and raw sexual passion. They are *en fuego* for each other! She goes on to become a successful bestselling author. He's doomed to failure and oblivion. Nonetheless, the spark is still there. She tries to save him. But the downward pull of his anguish is too strong. She's willing to overlook his failure, to love him just as he is. And still, he's emasculated by her success. There's a lot of struggle— addiction, alcoholism, hidden memories of childhood molestation. And more like that. Finally, he kills himself. Then she, battling through grief and shock and abandonment, finds a way to put her life back together and go on—even stronger than she was before."

She smiled brightly.

"I thought you hadn't seen Frank Kelly in, like, twenty years."

She clamped her mouth shut. She considered me for a moment, and decided to curl her lip. Betty Ann informed me, rather tartly, that she didn't appreciate my negativity.

Then she added, "And you still have something that doesn't belong to you."

"If you're talking about Frank's journal, it doesn't belong to you either."

"How can you be so pigheaded? That journal can't be of any value to you."

"It's not as though you need it, do you, Betty Ann?" I said. "After all, your memoirs aren't based on facts, or recollections, or research. They're simply dredged up from that huge reservoir of hyperbolic sludge that sloshes around underneath that ghastly hat of yours."

I felt rather proud of myself. It was the sort of thing that one thinks of saying only in retrospect, when you're brooding over some unsatisfactory encounter. I was inspired to embellish.

"Yes, I'm sure the details of Frank's life and struggles will bloom forth, like algae on an open sewer, quite irrespective of what did or did not happen."

She got onto her feet and fitted the aforementioned ghastly hat back over her hair. She looked down at me, this time with dramatic pity.

"You don't get it, do you, Max?"

"What?"

"I'm an artist," she announced. "NOT a *performer*."

I supposed that the *performer* part was meant to be particularly stinging jab.

"I don't know, Betty Ann. It just sounds like you're writing another implausible memoir. This time you're feasting on poor dead Frank."

"Why don't you focus on singing, Max. And leave the writing to the writers."

"Okay."

She stalked off down the hill. Dixie started to go after her. I caught her leash and yanked her back.

17

I hurried back to the house, poured myself a tankard of tequila. Dixie and I settled into the recliner and resumed our study of *Paradise Lost*. Every time I opened the book, I was struck by how the pages in my hand had been touched by Duffy Fallon, and by Frank Kelly, and even by the poor deranged madwoman who lived in front of Emile's bookstore. Their presence added a collective memory to Milton's work, as if the reading of the words—the knowing of his mind—had become more deeply sonorous.

It was tough slogging at first, like wading through an equatorial bog. Milton is like that. But once I fell into the rhythm of it, I was slithering easily through the lush undergrowth of Milton's florid stanzas. The rococo and the repetition no longer slowed me down, it carried me along, and the story revealed itself in bone-white starkness.

Satan is God's favorite. But he comes to realize that God is running a family business, and he has no chance for career promotion—not with Jesus, the heir apparent, around. Satan is frustrated. He launches a junta. It fails.

God marshals the heavenly host and casts Satan and his followers out. They land upon a boiling sea topped with flames.

The rebel angels lay chained to rocks on the burning lake—like being staked out in a flambé dish. They have three prospects, none of them good.

They could be immolated if "all Her stores were opened, and this firmament of Hell should spout her cataracts of fire."

Or, they could drown, "Each on his rock transfixed, the sport and prey / or racking whirlwinds, or forever sunk / under yon boiling ocean, wrapt in chains, / There to converse with everlasting groans, / Unrespited, unpitied, unreprieved, / Ages of hopeless end?"

Or, worst of all, they could just be left there in a limbo of everlasting torment.

No one, not Milton and not his characters, considers a fourth possibility: that it might turn out okay.

No future.

It was just the sort of thing that would appeal to Frank Kelly's insistent Celtic brooding.

Nonetheless, I couldn't see Frank chewing his way through Milton. He liked his misery soft and premasticated. Frank went in for the more accessible moroseness of Charles Bukowski's drunkard-as-hero screeds.

I closed *Paradise Lost,* felt the heft of it as I slid it back into its sleeve. I realized that the only way Frank would have read it was if he'd been compelled. Surely Duffy Fallon had driven him to search the pages for some key, for some cure to the pestilence that he'd brought into Frank's life.

I got out Frank's journal and turned to the pages attributed to Duffield Fallon. The ink was the same color as what I'd seen on Blashky's wall. And, from what I could remember of the hand, the style was identical.

"It's him," Baba said.

I flinched and tossed the journal into the air, madly, unsuccessfully grabbing for it before it hit the floor, pages splayed.

"Can't you knock?" I cried.

"Be logical, Max," she said, twirling a forelock so the coins braided into her hair clinked against the full set of knuckle-dusters she wore on every finger. "If you can see me, don't you think that your friend could see Duffield Fallon?"

"I'm going to pour myself a pastis," I said.

"Of course you are," she said.

"It settles my stomach," I said. "Not that I have to explain myself to you."

"You should be concerned with settling this business about Fallon."

I scampered to the kitchen. She was there ahead of me, sitting on the countertop, legs crossed, smoking a cheroot. I reached through her, opened the booze cupboard, and poured myself a triple pastis, no water.

"Fallon lies on a burning lake," Baba said. "He is in chains."

"Fine," I said, storming upstairs with my tumbler. "I'm going to go lie in a warm tub."

"Fallon terrorized Frank Kelly," I heard her reciting, as if to herself. "Now he is manipulating the mad redheaded woman. Soon, he will come for you too, Max."

It was a little brighter upstairs, but the light was dampening. Darkness was coming.

I realized that I must have spent several hours, the better part of the day, poring over the writings of Milton, and Frank, and Fallon.

I struck a match. In a deliberate adagio of ritual, I lit the votive candles that stood on the shelves above the bath. I daubed the long match deep into each of the ruby-colored glass cylinders, illuminating the Catholic santos depicted on the labels: Saint Francis, the lover of critters; Genesius, the patron saint of theater people; Jude, whose job was almost the same as Genesius because he's the patron saint of lost causes; Gabriel, the avenging angel; and Jesus, flashing his glowing heart, wrapped in barbed wire and dripping blood.

I had bought them all at my butcher's shop, where he sold votives, bootleg DVDs of Mexican action movies, and metallic party dresses as well as generous cuts of ribs and tripe.

The flames held inside the votives darted like captive birds. They cast red flashes across the wall and drew long shadows from my perfume bottles. Square-shouldered colognes, and swirling atomizers, cast black silhouettes up to the ceiling. They shifted, massing and menacing, like state executioners on a smoke break.

"I'm creeping myself out," I said out loud, trying to break the spell. It didn't work.

I decided that what was needed was a touch of Doris Day. I rummaged around in the cabinet, looking for that bubble bath that smelled like tea roses. But the only bubbles I could find were Jean Naté and damned if I could remember where that came from. I dumped the contents of the bottle under the thundering water—all of it, just to get rid of it—and the bubbles bloomed up like a nuclear mushroom cloud.

I turned on the radio. The classical station was playing Erik Satie, a suitable backdrop for a moody, gray, and dying afternoon. I left the water running, went into the bedroom and changed into my yellow silk kimono. When I came back into the bathroom, the same Satie composition was still playing and I thought that was odd. Perhaps they'd played the same recording twice, back to back.

And despite the radio, I had the sense that the room was quieter than when I'd stepped out of it a few moments earlier.

Then I realized why. The water was turned off. I switched off the radio. The bubbles were thick and bristling over the water's surface to the lip of the tub. I stood very still, listening. The bubbles crackled. The candle flames, deep inside the glass votives, flickered. Their red glow lapped the walls.

I took a drink of the pastis, decided I was being a big girl, and told myself that I had nothing to fear with Dixie in the house. I switched the radio back on. They were playing Mozart and I felt suddenly buoyant. I hung up my kimono and slid into the water.

I lay back, and skimmed my tumbler along the crests of the bubbles to my lips. I repeated that motion until the pastis was gone and I wished I'd had the foresight to bring the bottle upstairs.

The radio DJ switched from Mozart to Carl Orff. It was *Carmina Burana,* the rather spirited part with the chorus bellowing, and one imagines legions of Templars galloping on steeds, big as Humvees, across the Syrian plains.

Then the music abruptly cut out. For a second, I thought that there'd been an electrical short. Maybe it had gone off earlier, and that's what caused the Satie to repeat, or stall—which is ridiculous, because it was the radio—but that's what I thought, and that's also one of the reasons why I'm an opera singer and not an electrician.

The sudden silence was concussive, just as startling as a seismic boom.

A hush whooshed in and sucked all the life out of the room, except for the crackling of the damn Jean Naté bubbles.

I looked up at the shelf above the tub. The candles had stopped flickering. The entire wall was washed over in a deep, clotted red.

The shadows of the bottles now jostled and swayed, like a gang of thugs massing in a dank alley. Their glass bases thumped on the shelf. It sounded like angry knuckles rapping on a door.

One of the atomizers fell over on its side. I watched transfixed as invisible fingers squeezed the spray-ball. A cloud of cologne shot out, and the scented particles hung in the air before fainting onto the foam.

The bottle next to it began to shiver. Its cap slowly turned, spinning upward, revealing the naked threads of the bottleneck. The cap popped off and landed in the tub, sinking into the bubbles.

I screamed and launched out of the tub, as if the cap were a red-hot ingot.

I thrust my arms into my kimono, fumbling to find the sash as the cologne bottles all now started to rattle and tap. Another cap came flying off and landed in the tub. Then a third. Then a volley of tops from several bottles arched off the shelf and into the water.

I screamed again, punched on the bathroom lights. I still couldn't find my sash, but I didn't need it. The kimono's silk stuck to my skin as if it had been melted on, even as I lunged for the votives. I picked them up one by one, held them under my quivering lips, and extinguished the flames with shallow frantic breaths.

I reached into the water, puppy sleeves flapping onto the white foam. I pulled the plug. The water gurgled and gasped down the drain and it sounded like someone being garroted.

The last of the water wheezed and disappeared. I swished a face cloth around in the drifts of bubbles. I could hear the bottle tops tumbling about on the hard glazed surface of the tub.

The radio was still off, but the silence had dissipated. I could hear Glen and Glenda walking around upstairs, and the traffic out on the street. Dixie was barking.

18

I was in shock. I went straight to the kitchen, poured a tumbler of Calvados. I stood at the counter, drinking shots with one hand, repouring brandy with the other.

Someone pounded at my front door. Dixie lost her goddamn mind. She barked and spun in mad pinwheels on the linoleum.

"Shut up," I yelled.

The pounding stopped. My heart thumped. I took a drink. Then the back door rattled on its hinges. A dark form loomed in the glass.

"Max." It was Betty Ann Thibideaux.

I was actually glad to hear her voice.

I swung the door open. She rushed into the kitchen, saw the bottle on the counter and poured herself a drink.

"Max," she said, unpacking herself out of that dreary Bolivian serape. "I'm not going to dick around with you anymore, Max."

"Good news."

"You and Stan Blashky," she said. "How much do you want?"

"Much what?"

"Money. Dinero. Filthy lucre?" She banged her shot glass on the table. "How much do you want for Frank's journal? I'll pay it."

"It's not mine to sell."

I didn't know why I cared. I only knew that I did. I wasn't about to part with Frank's journal, certainly not to hand it over to this insufferable ass pain Betty Ann Thibideaux.

"No," I told her.

"This is just business, Max," she said. "Be reasonable."

She scraped her glass on the table, hoisted up and made for the bottle on the counter. Her serape lay open and empty over the back of the chair like the hide of a rendered beast.

"Maybe you'd better get back on your burro, or whatever contrivance you arrived here on, and vamoose," I told her, the Calvados and her ensemble inspiring a rather spaghetti Western coloration to my delivery.

She ignored me. She was intently pouring out another triple brandy for herself.

Her cell phone rang. She swept into the dining room to answer it. She spoke in whispers, but I could hear the agitation in her tone. The phone snapped closed. The front door opened, and then banged shut.

When I got to the front steps, Betty Ann was scurrying down the street. She hadn't even bothered to retrieve her serape.

———

The telephone woke me from a black, sedated sleep.

I had passed out with the bedside light on, the baseball bat beside me under the covers. It was nearly noon.

I answered. Dixie looked up from the crook of my armpit where she'd been sleeping. She yawned wide and stretched her legs, her paws pressing into my chest.

"Where were you last night?"

It was Stan Blashky.

"Was Betty Ann there?" he demanded.

"Yes."

"The police just left," he said. "They're probably going to show up at your place next."

"Stan, what the hell?"

Betty Ann Thibideaux had just been found—washed up on the rocks at the foot of the Golden Gate Bridge. She was dead.

Part Two

19

I was still standing in the kitchen frantically trying to make coffee and dial Claudia—nothing on but my kimono and my camel slippers—when the police arrived at the door. It was just one guy. And he looked damned bored at having been sent to deal with me.

He showed me his badge, gave me his card. Detective Fung. He was a big block of a man, could have been Stan Blashky's Manchurian cousin.

Fung moved into the parlor, like a refrigerator on a hand truck. He planted himself in the center of the room and, with his hands dangling like grappling hooks at his sides, he stood and turned a slow three hundred and sixty degrees. He blatantly scanned my abode, his face as flat and dull as the business end of a mallet.

I tightened up my kimono sash, ran my fingers through my hair, and decided this Fung person must be the department oddball.

"We're talking to people who saw Ms. Thibideaux yesterday," he said, transferring his underwhelmed gaze from my décor to my person. "She was here with you last night. What time?"

"How do you know she was here?" I said.

I felt ill. I sat down in the window seat, crossed my legs. He continued to stand.

"Her cell phone records," he said, his arms still hanging idle at his sides. "We can locate people by the phone calls."

"Then you know what time she was here," I said.

"Was she in this room?"

"No. She came in the back door. She and I spoke in the kitchen. In fact, she left her coat. Her serape. It's still back there."

I led him down the corridor to the kitchen. He followed me slowly. He held his head back as if dodging a blow. He glanced in the dining room, and then the powder room, before proceeding past the open doorways.

Betty Ann's serape was still draped over the back of a kitchen chair. Fung didn't touch it. He stood and looked at it from a couple arms' lengths away, as though he'd never seen a serape before.

"She rushed out of here so fast," I said. "She didn't even take her coat."

"Why did she run out?" he said, turning to look at me.

"I don't know." I sat at the table. "Please, sit down."

He sat. He kept his spine upright, not touching the back of the chair. He arranged his hands on the table, one on top of the other. They looked like a couple of giant crabs stacked in a tank at a Chinese seafood restaurant.

"We were in here talking," I explained, looking at his hands, fixated on them.

He watched me. He didn't say anything, didn't interrupt or prompt me to continue.

"Betty Ann got a call on her cell phone," I said. "She took it in the other room. Then she ran out the front door. She didn't tell me where she was going. Or even that she was going."

His eyes unnerved me. They were placid, resting on me like I was an object. He reminded me of an octopus I'd seen at the aquarium. They're hunters: trappers, actually. They set up lots of shiny objects in their gardens. Then they squeeze into their lairs and wait for victims to come poking around. They watch from behind those featureless faces of theirs, with those keen eyes.

"Was Ms. Thibideaux distressed?" Fung asked.

"Distressed?" I said, my voice cracking. "She was a fucking manic-depressive. Are you familiar with her books?"

"Did you hear anything she said to the person on the phone?"

"No, no. I already told you. I didn't hear. She was whispering."

"People disappear around you, don't they, Mr. Bravo?"

I thought he leaned in closer to me. But realized he was sitting in the exact same position.

"What?"

"A couple years ago. Amy Carter. She disappeared. She's still missing."

"Amy is not people," I said.

I started to get tunnel vision, my heart was racing and my chest hurt.

"Amy is a person," I heard myself saying. "Singular. One person."

"Your friend Frank Kelly went off the Golden Gate Bridge."

He said "went." He didn't say "jumped." I noticed. Fung knew I'd notice.

"Look," I said. "Do I need to call my lawyer?"

"We're just talking," he said. His face was a placid lake. "But you can call whoever you like."

"You're speaking to me as if I were under suspicion," I said, gathering up the collar of my kimono in my fist, holding it tight to my throat. "You're grilling me. As if I've done something. Well, I haven't. And I will not be harassed and hounded."

"Last night," he said, "sometime after midnight, Ms. Thibideaux, also went off of the Golden Gate Bridge. She, undoubtedly, died when she hit the water. The fact that you knew both her and Mr. Kelly, and that they both went off the bridge, leads us to believe that you could tell us something about their deaths."

I got up and poured myself a glass of water. Fung could see my hand shaking as I brought the glass to my lips.

"I won't say another word to you," I told him.

I set the glass down and clutched at the edge of the sink.

"No need to get queenie about it," he said.

I was startled by this sudden affront. His demeanor hadn't changed. He was still removed, contained. He was experimenting on me.

He continued, "Detectives Sanchez and McGuire in Berkeley told me you can be a bit . . ."

He paused, drummed his crab-leg fingers on the tabletop, and then he said the word "Hysterical."

"That's not true," I cried.

"McGuire thinks you're not very bright." He stopped the finger drumming and patted the table. "An idiot," Fung elaborated. "Oh. No. Wait. He didn't say *idiot*. He said you're a fool. That's right. McGuire said you're a fool."

I folded my arms across my chest to keep them from flailing.

"Sanchez, not so much." He waved his hand over the table. "Sanchez thinks you're about average intelligence. He even said you might be above average. He just figures you're high-strung. And that makes you act like an idiot."

He stood and picked up Betty Ann's serape. He folded it, draped it across his arm, held it in front of him like he was a valet. He let his other arm hang at his side.

"Do you ascribe to Method?" he said.

"What?"

"Method acting," he said. "You know, like Strasberg."

"I don't act," I said. "I'm an opera singer."

"Hmm," he said.

Fung told me he had all he needed, for the moment. He asked me to call him if I thought of anything that might pertain to Betty Ann's death.

I walked him out of the kitchen, back up the corridor. He stopped at the front door, and malingered there.

"I do a little acting," he announced in an arid monotone. "Not professionally. Not like you. Just community theater. But I love it."

"Are you playing a detective?"

He laughed, a single startling bark, and his face quickly resettled into the mask of boredom.

"Maybe we could have coffee sometime," he said. "We could discuss acting."

I said sure. We could discuss anything.

I asked Fung if Betty Ann killed herself. He stepped out onto the porch. He turned his back to me and answered as he walked down the steps.

"She was manic-depressive," he called out. "Remember?"

20

I hadn't, of course, mentioned Duffy Fallon to Detective Fung. That sort of thing can reflect badly on one's credibility.

The gendarmes would have been convinced I was mad. Schizophrenic, most likely. I could well imagine them assembling some theory that, while under the thrall of an imaginary hoodlum, I murdered Frank, and then Betty Ann.

It wasn't just the police. I couldn't talk about Fallon with anyone. And that would have been fine, if it hadn't been for the fact that Duffy Fallon was obsessed with me.

In the wake of the two writer suicides, I found myself thrust into the very spot that they had both vacated. I was the object of Fallon's obsession. It started with the bathtub incident. From that evening forward, Fallon haunted me vigorously.

I soon learned that the ghost of Duffield Waverly Fallon was nothing like my incarnate grandmother. She was a gentle annoyance at worst, a sympathetic ally at best. But Fallon was a villain. He had been a dangerous brute in life, and he was an unrestrained sadist in death.

I could see how he drove Frank and Betty Ann over the railing of the bridge. It would have been the only way to silence the crazy cal-liope music. Fallon was the ringmaster of madness.

He loved water. Every day, at 5:12 A.M.—just as the last dregs of darkness began to wash out of the bedroom—Fallon would turn on all the faucets in the house simultaneously. Dixie would hear it first. She'd bark. It made her angry. And a little afraid.

She'd wake me up, and I'd hear it too—the water. It poured out of the bathroom faucet. It thundered from the tub spout. And it choked and spritzed at the showerhead.

I'd haul myself out of bed, heavy and sleep-sogged, to turn off all the fixtures in the bathroom. Then I'd listen. The water would always be running downstairs too. I'd put on my kimono and trudge along the hall, down the stairs, and into the kitchen to stop the hot water—steaming by this time—scorching into the sink.

I became sleep-deprived, and bumped around the house like a fogbound ship with a broken compass.

It was at least a week before I noticed what Fallon was doing with Frank's journal. Dixie's barking woke me and I looked over to the clock on the bedside table to verify that it was indeed 5:12 A.M. Again. And it was.

But something else caught my attention. Frank's journal—which I remembered having very scrupulously tucked into the back of the bookshelf the night before—was staring at me. It was on the bedside table.

The journal is just an object, I told myself. I wasn't convinced, though.

I couldn't shake the sense that the journal, pouting at me with its slivers of white paper pressed together like impatient lips, had been perched on the bed table all night, watching me as I slept. One of its corners stuck out over the edge of the table, like a foot stepping off a ledge, and it seemed that the thing had been inching toward me.

Then, as if to prove my suspicion, the journal did move. It slid, in a quaking motion, toward me.

I screamed. I sat up, snatched the journal, examined it, and tossed it back on the table. I hauled myself out of bed and made my rounds, turning off the water that was gushing out of every plumbing orifice in the house.

I went to make coffee.

When I opened the kitchen cupboard, the journal was there. It was propped up against the canister of ground coffee, leaning on it like a mugger lurking in a dark doorway.

I screamed again, for the second time before breakfast. I reached in, plucked the loathsome thing with my thumb and forefinger, and flung it into the backyard. While my coffee dripped through the filter, I stood at the kitchen sink, looking out the window at the journal lying in the grass, wet and blue in the morning light.

I took my coffee upstairs, showered, and got dressed. I decided to leave the house. To flee.

I harnessed the dog. I put on a hat and scarf.

As Dixie and I descended the front steps, I thrust my hand in the pocket of my overcoat. My knuckles grazed a cold, pebbled surface. Frank's journal was in my pocket, still soggy from sitting on the damp grass.

I wanted to pitch it as far as I could, but reason tamped down hysteria, and I wiped the cover dry with my scarf. I placed the journal back in my pocket and continued at a brisk pace.

There was no fighting Duffy Fallon. And I, like a man married to a shrew, soon learned that the only way to survive was to do as commanded.

Fallon wanted me up every day at 5:12 A.M. I got up. He wanted me to read Frank's journal. I read it. He wanted me to take the damn thing with me wherever I went. And there it was, my own pocket-sized albatross. I had no choice but to go about with my curse, dead Frank's journal, strung round my neck like a garland of decay.

This went on for weeks.

Duffy Fallon and I were trapped together in my house, in a prison of our own making. I was an opera singer between engagements. And Duffy Fallon was dead. We were on the same schedule. We had the time to be as crazy as we wanted to be.

I didn't phone my agent, Maury, even though I could have, should have. A reasonable man, a sensible man, a man who wasn't a high-strung artist caught in a fabulist net of his own weaving, would have urged his agent to line up something—some engagement, a job, any-thing just to get out of the house.

Christmas was coming. Some opera company, somewhere, would have a production of *The Magic Flute* that needed a last-minute re-placement for Papageno. But I didn't call Maury. I stayed there with Fallon.

I learned, early on, that people's private journals are private for a rea-son. And it's not because they're hiding juicy secrets. It's because they're insanely boring.

Frank's journal was a treasure trove of twaddle. He documented his daily life, mostly petty outrages, and the things he'd remember to say next time. He collected long lists of words—words like *inchoate, diluvian, ossified.*

And, he cataloged book and story ideas. Frank had decided that poetry was not the Silverado he'd imagined it to be, and that fiction was his surest avenue for reaching fame and fortune.

He was right, in a sense. The odds of making any money in poetry are millions to zero. And the odds of making a living writing books are millions to one.

But even that microscopic chance was beyond Frank's reach since, in my opinion, his story ideas were trite, abysmal, deadly dull. Frank was strictly art school.

His plotlines were so shallow you could hear their hulls scraping the bottom of your patience. And the characters were opaque, their speech and actions so hermetic that they behaved like sock puppets, only with less motivation.

There was an idea about a divorced woman who considers answering a personal ad for anonymous sex, but she doesn't. Another featured a small boy with a pica for eating the chalky dirt under his family's front porch. He thinks he should stop eating it. And he does. Frank also considered writing an entire book about a man who loses his hat and this makes him remember what a bastard his father was.

Proust could have pulled off any of these stories. Or Raymond Carver, I suppose. But Frank Kelly couldn't. And it was his imitative impulse, and his rejection of form just for the sake of being formless, that was so very sad.

By the end of the year, I finally finished reading the journal, having only been able to consume small morsels of it at a time, and even that was at the behest of Fallon's constant prodding. After I'd read the last entry, I put the journal away. I stowed it out of sight, high up on the bookshelf.

Fallon seemed satisfied once I'd read it. He stopped tossing it in my path. He closed the book, in every sense.

But the problem was that, by then, I couldn't just shelve the Frank Kelly journal and forget about it. The ending bothered me.

Frank, or someone, had exactingly sliced the last pages from the spine of the book. Why?

It nettled me. I tried to tell myself it was none of my business. And, it didn't matter anymore since Frank was dead. Finally, I got up on a chair, and pulled the journal out of its hiding place.

I got out a paring knife, sat down at the dining-room table, and carefully separated the page stubs with the tip of the blade. I counted them again, as I had done months earlier. There were ten sheets missing, twenty pages of writing because Frank always wrote on both front and back.

On the last page before the excision, Frank had inscribed another of his word lists. This one was unusual in that it was just three words; printed large, and centered on the page, so they assumed some superior significance.

They were obscure words. Unwieldy. They were heavy and clunk-ing with inelegant edges. It wouldn't be easy to force fit them into a story. But I was sure Frank would try.

> *quotidian*
> *frangible*
> *peripeteia*

I knew the first two. *Quotidian* was an adjective describing some-thing that was commonplace, ordinary. *Frangible* meant easily break-able. I wasn't sure about the third word.

I closed the journal. I said the word out loud. *Peripeteia.* I repeated it.

Obviously, it had a Greek origin. I went back to the bookshelf, picked out the dictionary.

Peripeteia. It was a sudden turn of events in drama and literature. It is triggered when the protagonist recognizes a deep truth that has been hidden from him, often in plain view.

He wakes up. Sees things as they really are. And, as a result of his newfound clarity, the character undergoes a complete reversal of for-tune. The dictionary cited two examples: from rags to riches or from contentment to despair.

Neither one of these developments applied to Frank.

Having gone through his belongings after his death, I knew he didn't have two ducats to rub together.

And as for gravitating to despair, that would have been a pretty quick commute. Despair was Frank Kelly's baseline.

It could have gone the other way, though. If Frank was always in a state of muted despair, what would have been the opposite?

Elation? No. Too corny. Even psychotropics couldn't have made Frank feel like that.

Frank indulged in a complex kind of desperation. It was limned out of a philosophy that recognized only the dark matter in the universe. Frank lived in permanent winter. It was always night. For him to leave that place, he'd have to reach its antipode—a land of everlasting light.

Frank, I thought, must have discovered *hope*.

He was hopeful.

But a guy who is hopeful doesn't jump off the Golden Gate Bridge. Does he?

Peripeteia was the last word that Frank Kelly let stand in his written record. After that, the pages were sliced away, the charts destroyed. Frank made some discovery that caused him to sail off the map, over the edge of the known world. He disappeared into a mysterious sea.

21

"I think Fallon pushed Frank Kelly off the bridge," I told Baba. "I don't think Frank jumped. He had too much to live for."

She was sitting at the dining table, her form shimmering gossamer in the diffuse afternoon light. She was casually turning over tarot cards.

I agitated around the room, enacting what had become a frequent ritual—switching the hiding place of the journal.

"Not physically possible," Baba said. "Fallon could not lay hands on Frank."

She shuffled the deck, and dealt six cards onto the table in the shape of a cross.

"Then he tricked him," I said. "He caused Frank to have some sort of hallucination. It's still murder. He killed Frank. And he could do the same to me."

I was down on my knees, trying to wedge the journal under the lip of the tabletop.

"Max, you read too much into things," she said. "Get off the floor."

"It's this damn thing." I waved the journal overhead, still on my knees. "I wish I could just get rid of it."

"Then get rid of it."

"I can't just throw it out." I creaked to my feet, brandishing the journal. "What if Fallon gets pissed off at me!"

"Put it on the bookshelf. Like a normal book. Like you are a normal man."

"Read my fortune," I said, dropping into the chair at the head of the table.

"No."

"Why not?" My voice cracked. "Is it bad? Oh, God. Drowning? I knew it."

"Max, you are not going to die soon," she commanded. "You must first get older. Possibly fatter."

She scooped up the cards, shuffled them.

"Get out of the house, Max. Take a walk."

Dixie heard the word *walk*. She jerked up from a deep sleep, jumped out of the recliner, and stood by the front door waiting for me.

I got my coat from the hall closet, retrieved my hat from the console. And there, beside it on the table, was Fallon's copy of *Paradise Lost*.

"*Bastardo,*" I cursed.

The last time I had seen *Paradise Lost* it was in the bookcase. I had even shelved it precisely in between Melville and Nabokov.

And here it was, uprooted from its proper place, and deliberately set in my path. Milton was obviously next on my required reading list.

"Now this bastard Fallon expects me to read *Paradise Lost*," I yelled.

Baba didn't answer.

She must have slipped off—it was her usual exit mode. She'd slink away, not a word. I never knew where she was when she wasn't with me. But I did suspect she had a regular milk run of relatives that she intruded upon. She was probably in L.A., meddling in the lives of my father's cousins. They ran a used car lot and a palm-reading parlor.

That sort of scene generates plenty of action for an old busybody like Baba.

I picked up *Paradise Lost* and examined it, just as Fallon knew I would. I'd only dipped into it here and there after I'd first bought it, mostly to inspect the plates of the William Blake watercolors. Now, I methodically lifted the cover, creased down the end sheet—a marvelous high-grade cotton paper, swirling with sprite-tailed burgundy paisleys on a sea-blue background.

The first page was the title page. I knew that couldn't have been right. I took the book into the living room, held it up in the light of the window. The first two pages were stuck together. They had probably gotten wet at some point. I worked at the pages' jagged edges with my fingernail. I pried the stuck pages apart to reveal the flyleaf.

There, in the top-right corner, I saw the now familiar reddish-brown ink from Fallon's pen. His hand had inscribed the words, "Given to Ah Ho, with all my heart. The torments we endure will soon end. Yours eternally, DWF. April 17, 1906."

Ah Ho. She was the same woman Fallon referred to when he wrote on Blashky's wall.

I went to my secretary desk, pulled the pile of notes and unopened mail out of the drawer. I riffled through the papers until I found the scrap paper onto which I'd copied Fallon's wall writing.

> *I am cast down from the welkin of the celestial vault. I have landed here on the fires that burn on the forgetful lake. I lie forever drowning in flame, until Ah Ho is restored to me.*
> *D.W.F., April 18, 1906*

Now the gothic floridity of the language made sense. Fallon was smoking the same weed as Milton when he wrote it. Cast down from heaven. Trapped on a burning lake. This was the exact fate of the rebel angels that Milton wrote about in *Paradise Lost*.

And, once again, Fallon refers to this Ah Ho woman. Clearly, she was Chinese. Her non-Anglicized name indicated that she was probably a new immigrant, fresh from Canton, the region from which nearly all of San Francisco's Chinese had emigrated.

Here too, the wall writing seemed to cryptically reference Ah Ho. The Chinese immigrants of Fallon's day were referred to as Celestials. And Fallon wrote that he was cast down from the "celestial vault."

Ah Ho was a bigger piece of all this than I had realized. Fallon was obsessed with her. Finding Ah Ho must have been his great, driving mission at the time of his death. And now, the specter of Fallon was still madly, desperately seeking this woman.

Who was Ah Ho? What did Fallon want with her?

It was high time I found out.

I took up *Paradise Lost* in one hand, Dixie's leash in the other, and headed for the Mission District.

22

Emile Balzac was hunched over the counter, calligraphy pen in hand. Pyewacket was sitting next to him, by the cash register. The feline growled at me.

The transom bell clanged as I closed the door, shutting off the street noise. The shop's familiar hush washed into the room like water in a canal lock. I glanced around. We were alone in the shop.

"How's business?" I said.

"Treading," he said, glancing up at me, his eyes swimming around inside the thick lenses of his horn-rimmed glasses.

He tipped his head down again, concentrated on his work, a white note card. A perfectly plumb line of baroque lettering flowed in the wake of his sure-handed pen.

I picked up a card from the top of his finished pile. It was for Leticia Ramirez's quinceañera.

"You do invitations too?" I said.

Pyewacket opened his mouth and strained a surprisingly human voice over his sandpaper tongue. I distinctly heard him say the word *asshole* as he tipped his head toward a tent-card notice by the cash register. The card said: "Fine-quality invitations for all occasions: Birthdays, Quinceañeras, Weddings, Anniversaries, Funerals. Reasonable rates."

"How can I help you, Max?"

Emile placed the last invitation on the pile. He returned his pen to the marble-base desk set.

He sat on the tall stool, one leg tossed languorously over the other, his elbow resting on the jutting jaw of the ancient cash register. I sat too, opposite him, the counter between us.

"This book," I said.

I put *Paradise Lost* on the counter. Emile Balzac didn't touch it.

The gray cat collapsed next to it, stretching out long and limp, his spine paralleling the spine of the book. He looked like a rabbit on a butcher's table. He fell instantly into a deep, narcoleptic sleep.

"I bought it here," I said, tapping the book's cover.

"I remember," he said.

The air was heavy with the sodden must of old books. Debussy was playing, hypnotic and a little discordant like a jangled opium sedation.

"How are you enjoying it?" Emile asked me.

I'd had the epic poem for more than two months. I noticed that he assumed I hadn't made my way through it in that time.

"*Enjoying* is not a word I'd use," I said.

I leaned on the counter. The cat jerked awake, contorted into a backbend stretch that looked like an opening parenthesis.

"Milton is difficult," the bookseller said to me.

"Duffield Fallon is more difficult," I said.

Emile got up from his chair and carefully removed his glasses. He tucked the spectacles into his shirt pocket. Now he was looking down at me, so I pushed away from the counter and stood to meet him at eye level.

He studied me, and I was aware of how very unstrung I appeared. The circles under my eyes—a permanent fixture shared by all my Romani kin and traceable to our Rhajistani ancestors—had darkened.

They were no longer the soft smudgy smoke color that I liked to think of as sultry, but had deepened to a lush aubergine. My appearance had crossed the line from vampish to vampiric. My hair was a tousle of untended black curls. My overcoat smelled like cigarettes and my shirt cuffs flopped about my knuckles. I'd forgotten to put on my cuff links.

"When you brought Frank Kelly's journal to me—" Emile started.

He looked down. His middle and forefingers were fidgeting, tracing quote marks on the countertop.

"Frank Kelly," he began again. "I recognized the name. You see, Max, I knew Frank."

I felt blood pulsing at my temples. I wanted to smash my fist on those fidgeting, quoting fingers. But I kept still.

"Frank Kelly and I," he said, and restrained his fingers by balling them up into fists. "Frank and I were friends."

"Friends?" I measured the word out carefully. "Exactly how close of friends were you?"

"We shared"—and he paused before he released the word—"confidences."

A thin, tremulous smile leaked across Emile Balzac's face.

I exploded.

"How could you," I said. "How could you not tell me? The deceit!"

"It was not deception, Max. I did not tell you a lie."

"Prevaricator," I roared, pointing at him, my unlinked cuff flopping about my wrist. "Prevarication is lying. It's just a chickenshit form of lying."

"Please, Max," he said. He lifted one hand and, with an upraised palm, unfurled his fingers open in a beckoning gesture. "I see I must now show you something. It is very confidential. But, I think it may afford you some"—he snapped the fingers shut like the petals of a carnivorous plant—". . . it may give you some relief."

He had me follow him. We tramped through the store, over Moroccan rugs, threadbare and flat, dropped overlapping and askew all about the floor, as if they'd been shaken out of the fur of a great wet beast.

We passed the new releases and bestsellers displayed on tables at the front of the store—mostly celebrity memoirs, and aspiring celebrity memoirs, and self-improvement advisories, and cookbooks and diet books. One entire table was devoted to pastiches about vampires—which was ironic, since I could pass for one at that point.

We proceeded into the depths of the store, the deep chasms of shelves where countless books stood entombed like urns in a columbarium. The walls were thick with them. Their spines swallowed the Debussy chords, submersing the music under leather and millboard and words.

We passed by philosophy, and history, and psychiatry. We entered the realm of religion, and New Age, and the occult.

We came to a reading cove, furnished with derelict chairs, all overstuffed, and a paint-by-numbers picture of a sailing ship on the open sea. Emile lifted the painting off the wall, turned the combination of the wall safe behind it. The steel door swung open. Balzac pulled a cardboard box out of the wall. He lifted the lid. The box contained a pile of typewritten pages.

"This is Frank's work," he told me. "It's the original. And it came with this note."

The note was dated a year earlier. The word CONFIDENTIAL was typed in red ink at the top.

I recognized the broken courier type as coming from Frank's

ancient Olivetti. The serif on the lowercase "d" was missing, causing it to drop-step over the page like a crippled beggar.

I remembered how we had even made the typewriter's signature infirmity into a running joke. We called Frank's poems the Clubfooted Despair series.

In his note, Frank had asked Emile Balzac to place the manuscript of his novel in safekeeping. He said he figured it would never see daylight, and he didn't care anymore.

"When Frank died," Emile said, "I removed the manuscript from the safe. I read it. To my surprise, it was good. It was very good."

"Your surprise?"

"*Oui,*" he said. "I had read only Frank's poetry up until then."

"Quite."

"But this book"—he bounced the box in his hand—"this book is not ordinary."

He tipped the manuscript out of the box, showing me the title page. *The Flight of the Singing Bird.* By Frank Kelly.

"You said this is the original," I said. "Are there other copies?"

"I made one photocopy," he said. "I sent it to a publisher I know. I included a note that explained the author was dead. And I stated the nature of his death."

"You told them Frank jumped off the Golden Gate Bridge."

"*Oui.* I questioned myself. Should I reveal this or not?" He did the Gallic shrug, then added, "In the end, I decided, yes. Frank's suicide is also part of the book."

"I think it's a cheap marketing gimmick."

"I won't argue that with you," Emile Balzac said. "It doesn't matter anyhow. The fact remains, the publisher loved the story. Probably, he loved Frank's dramatic suicide story too. His tragedy. *Et,* voilà."

"Voilà what?"

"Frank's book is being published."

I fanned through the manuscript. Two names appeared over and over. Duffield Fallon. And Ah Ho.

Emile Balzac seemed to be taking the narrative of Frank Kelly's personal story at face value. The story ran something like this: Frank entrusted Emile with the manuscript. Frank committed suicide. Emile reveals the manuscript to the world. The world recognizes the book's merit, and Frank's genius. Frank is covered in glory. Albeit, posthumous.

Why not? Life is like that, especially for artists.

It was plausible. Typical, even.

But that's exactly what I didn't like about it. It sounded too much like something I'd heard before.

Frank made himself into a literary device—the martyred artist. It was such a stock character no one would think to question it. His prosaic and bittersweet story would easily gain currency, as though melodrama were the legal tender of the realm.

I told Emile what I thought. I said the whole story was too baroque. It had something counterfeit about it. He responded with some typically existentialist claptrap. Life has no meaning. There is no reward. No punishment. No justice.

I tried to get him to make me a copy of the manuscript.

He flatly refused. It wasn't his to give out, he said. The manuscript now belonged to the publisher.

I tried another tack. I asked what Frank had been reading in the last few months leading up to his suicide.

He considered this request for a moment. Then he said no again. He told me that for a bookseller to reveal what a man reads is like a psychiatrist revealing the contents of a patient's mind. He couldn't betray Frank's privacy.

I told him Frank didn't have a private life anymore. He didn't have a life at all.

"Well," he eventually said. "You were his friend. And it is not unusual for a man to recommend books to his friends."

Frank had returned a cache of used books to Neptune's just days before he jumped off the bridge.

Emile hadn't detected anything unusual in that. Frank was always buying books, then bringing them back and trading them in for more books.

I asked Emile if Frank took that final trade-in as credit toward more book purchases, or if he took the cash. Cash, he said. And as he said it, the significance of that choice struck him too. It was a sign. Subtle, but in retrospect, significant.

"I suppose Frank didn't plan to read any more books," Emile said. "He knew he wouldn't have enough time."

He took Frank's manuscript from my hands, set it back in the wall safe. I watched him turn the dial, and place the painting of the ship back over the door.

"Tell me one thing," I said.

"About Frank's manuscript?"

"Yes," I said. "The story is about Fallon, *oui*?"

"*Oui.*"

"Why would you give me all that information about Fallon and yet you won't let me have a copy of this manuscript?" I demanded. "After all, you prepared that whole dossier. How is this different?"

"Quite simple," Balzac said, motioning me to follow him as he walked to the front of the store.

"You see, Monsieur Bravo," he said, "Frank Kelly left his journal deliberately where he knew you would find it. He, essentially, left it for you when he made his last wish—that you should clean out his apartment."

Emile turned to the stacks of books he kept on the shelves behind the counter. He picked through them, selecting books one by one. He placed them in two piles on the countertop in front of me. He took out his receipt book and methodically printed the name and price of each book on it.

"I am only respecting Frank's wishes," Balzac said. "He wanted you to know the contents of his journal. I assisted with that by providing research materials illuminating Duffield Fallon's presence in the journal."

"Then why not let me read the *Singing Bird* manuscript?" I persisted. "Surely that's the same thing."

"Here, again, Frank was very specific," Balzac said. He pulled a length of butcher's twine from a ball, wrapped it around one stack of books, then the other, trussing them together.

"Frank wanted you to discover the contents of the journal," he said. "And he wanted me to steward the manuscript."

Balzac tore the completed invoice off the pad, handed it to me.

"Two friends," he said. "Two separate bequests."

I asked Balzac if these were all the books that Frank returned before his death. Yes, it was, he said.

I bought the lot of them. I came home from Neptune's and sorted the books in piles on the living-room floor.

The tallest pile was several histories of San Francisco. Frank had surely used these books for reference and fact checking as he wrote *Singing Bird.*

Frank also had a fine copy of *Don Quixote.* This I placed with Fallon's *Paradise Lost.*

The other two books didn't seem to fit a category. They were *A Confederacy of Dunces* and *The Electric Kool-Aid Acid Test.*

I put them together. I didn't know quite why. But I was certain there was a connection.

Balzac's words came back to me. *Two friends. Two bequests.*

I meditated on Frank's intention. These things he'd left behind— he meant for them to be found. And they were. The manuscript and the journal had both lived on after his death.

The manuscript was being published. He left it to Balzac knowing that the bookseller would try to see to its publication.

But why leave the journal to me? Posterity, I supposed. Frank aspired to celebrity. He wanted the journal preserved, to represent him.

He'd selected Balzac to attend to his literary legacy. And he'd appointed me as the unwilling trustee of his persona. It pissed me off. Frank had leapt to his death, certain that he was to become a much greater literary sensation than his meager talent merited.

23

I spent several days trying to read *A Confederacy of Dunces* and *The Electric Kool-Aid Acid Test*. The first was dense and ponderous and dull. The second was tedious and cringe-inducing with all its nerdy, precious 1960s hippie polemics.

I decided Frank couldn't have read either of those books. Why had he bought them in the first place?

I became bored with the books, and depressed by the whole venture. I stopped reading entirely. I watched a lot of Dirk Bogarde movies, and listened to a heavy rotation of the Smiths. I took long baths in the afternoons.

Maury, my agent, called occasionally, always before noon, in the hopes of finding me completely sober. He was ever the dewy-eyed optimist.

He wanted to arrange my engagement calendar for the summer and fall seasons. He aimed to get me the role of Nick Shadow, né Satan, in *The Rake's Progress* scheduled for the Santa Fe opera. We thought it was an easy bid, given my commendable performance as Satan in *Faust* the previous fall.

Unfortunately, the casting director was a certain high-strung Lithuanian whom I'd had a bit of a chafe with five years earlier. I vaguely recalled being goaded into rampaging the dressing room. One of the backstage volunteers caught a few stray cubes from the flying ice bucket.

And now this fellow, whose memory of the event was apparently much more vivid than mine, was carrying a fatwa for me.

He told Maury he would sooner give the Shadow part to a goat. Maury responded with his usual supplicating and slavering. The Lithuanian softened, offered me a choice of two parts: The elderly mother. Or the bald, fat keeper of the madhouse.

"It could be fun," Maury told me. "You could camp it up."

I told Maury to cut off all discussions with that imperious potato farmer. But Maury, being the inveterate toady that he is, went back one more time. The Lithuanian offered me the part of Mother Goose, the whore. And with that, our negotiations came to an end.

"Don't worry, Max," Maury told me over the phone. "I have a lot of other negotiations in the works."

"I'm finished," I bawled into the receiver, bumping around the kitchen, my kimono sash dragging on the floor. "I'm old, and I'm washed-up. There's no future."

"Max, perhaps—and only perhaps—we might be seeing the conclusion of one phase of your career," Maury said. "But the next phase is opening up. You're a mature artist now. This is the time for you to get the most colorful parts."

"Colorful," I screamed. "Now I'm fucking colorful! I am Max fucking Bravo, Maury! I am powerful, and riveting, and simmering with overt sexuality! Remember?"

"Okay, Max. I wasn't going to tell you this," he said. "I was waiting until I had it dialed in, but, okay. I'm working on a deal for you with the L.A. Opera. They're doing *L'Orfeo*. You, Max, are in line to play Pluto—god of the Underworld!"

"I know who Pluto is," I yelled. Paused. "Which *L'Orfeo*?"

"The good one."

"Monteverdi?" I said, wiping my tear-soaked cheek with the back of my hand.

"Yes."

"Monteverdi, right?" I said. "Not Gluck."

"Not Gluck," he said. "I promise, Monteverdi."

"Because if I get there, and it's Gluck, I'm walking."

"I know."

24

I got the call from Maury on a bright, blue, sunny morning. He said he was sending the L.A. Opera contract right over to me. I got the Pluto part.

"Dixie," I called. "Come on. Let's get out of here."

The doldrums of winter, artistic mediocrity, and the stench redolent of the two tantrum suicides were all swept behind me.

We'd begin rehearsals in Los Angeles in May, just about five weeks away. I had a lot to do.

I'd played Pluto once before, but it had been nearly fifteen years, so I'd need every single day to prepare. I still had notes on style and language, but I would probably want to evolve them. I was, after all, a more mature Max Bravo than I'd been the first time I stepped on stage to rule Hell.

I began forming a list of what I had to do. I would reread the libretto, memorize all the parts, not just my own. I'd go over my old notes, create a fresh set. I'd play the music on my piano. And I'd start to formulate how I'd interpret my character. His gestures. His carriage. Expressions.

Pluto, god of the Underworld—I had to give him some serious thought. I had to get out and walk.

Dixie and I strolled along glorious sun-drenched sidewalks and reveled in the light and warmth. It seemed as though the whole city had emerged from the winter's wet sadness.

We walked for miles, through the Castro, along the lower Haight, across Geary, and up into the tony Pacific Heights shopping promenade of Fillmore Street. We sat at an alfresco café table and ordered coffee.

A young couple stopped to pet Dixie. They were on junk, clearly, but the heroin hadn't completely grayed out their appeal.

"We love pugs!" the young man told me. He reached in his pocket, pulled out his cell phone.

"Look." He held up his phone.

On the screen was a close-up portrait of a black pug. It looked like a bat.

"Is that your dog?" I asked.

"No," he said. "But we want a pug."

"I love your pug," his girlfriend said.

She bent her knees, folded down carefully, ladylike in her miniskirt and torn mesh stockings and army boots. Dixie clawed at her leather jacket as the young woman scratched the spot at the small of Dixie's back.

"We'd love a pug," she said, looking up at me, smiling.

She was missing an eyetooth, and her cheeks were sunken, but I was drawn to her, to both of them. They were ragged and frayed, yet there was still a sweetness beneath it. How they would have sparkled if they were clean.

"We were just at Pug Sunday," the fellow said.

"I've heard of that," I said.

"You should totally go," he said. "Your dog would love it."

I'd never been to Pug Sunday. It's one of those San Francisco occurrences that takes root, just because it's fun, and becomes an institution. The first Sunday of every month, pug owners from all over the city meet in Alta Vista Park in Pacific Heights. The humans picnic on the grass, while their pugs roam freely.

"Your dog would love Pug Sunday," the junkie woman said, affirming what her boyfriend had just told me.

I promised them I'd take her. We were close to the park. I thought it would be mean not to go.

As the couple turned to leave, I noticed she had a book in her hand. And on the cover of the book was Betty Ann Thibideaux's face.

Betty Ann was gazing out into the nether distance, as if hearing some clarion call undetectable to the rest of us runty mortals.

The woman saw that I was looking at her book. She handed it to me.

"I just bought it," she told me, smiling again with her rotted and missing heroin teeth. "I've read all her books."

"What do you like about them?" I asked, flipping through the crisp, new pages. The name "Frank" appeared over and over.

"I like how her life is real," the drugged woman said.

I watched the two junkies walk away. They were arm in arm. They went south on Fillmore. I was sure they'd stop at Geary, catch an eastbound bus, get off in the Tenderloin, and within the hour they'd be nodded off on heroin.

I continued up Fillmore Street, dropped in at a bookstore. I bought two books: Betty Ann's. And Frank's first edition of *The Flight of the Singing Bird*.

When Dixie and I got to the park and settled onto the grass, a giant swarm of pugs came swamping over us. A bull pug, big as a Vietnamese potbelly pig, grunted over my shopping bag, looking for food. I pulled out the two books I'd just purchased, and let him sniff them. Once he was satisfied they weren't edible, he trotted off to catch up with the pug herd.

I let Dixie off her leash. She sat next to me for a few moments, not sure whether or not to join the other dogs. The pug swarm was formidable, intimidating. The dogs had bunched into a tight mass, and they thundered over the lawn like a herd of tiny, stampeding buffalo.

Together, Dixie and I watched the pug pack careen up and down the slope. They rolled and whiplashed in violent waves over the slope of the hill, dozens of them in unison, answering to some secret signals that only their collective pug brain could detect.

When Dixie saw the pug gang marauding a woman on a picnic blanket with a bag of tortilla chips, she dropped her natural reserve. She dashed off and fell deep into the pack.

I couldn't look at the cover of Betty Ann's book, at her face. I turned it over. The cover of Frank's book was a collage; old sepia Barbary Coast images of fogbound ships, red lights over alley doorways, and dainty Cantonese maidens with tiny bound feet poking out from beneath silk dresses. Set into the middle of this whirling montage was Duffy Fallon. It was the same portrait that Emile had showed me: Fallon, charismatic and alluring. He leered, his eyes sharp and his muscular mass coiled.

He was seriously terrifying. I thought of how he would have done his work, the journeyman leg-breaker. He must have maimed and dismembered criminal rivals and truculent shopkeepers alike in the same businesslike manner. There would have been no reasoning with him. He wouldn't have broached any discussion. It would have just been the quick, economical movements of a maestro of violence, the sounds of a man at work: the naked threats, the pleading and whimpering, followed by the cracking, the screaming, the groaning. And the crying.

I sensed a crowd swelling. People were getting up from the grass, congregating in a spot down the slope, several meters below me. I looked toward the gathering commotion.

A group of dog owners were pressing in around a woman in khaki pants and bright pink rubber clogs. Beside her was a stroller containing a pair of dull-faced twins.

She pointed. The dog owners, now nearly a dozen of them, followed her treacherous finger. Their eyes came to me.

I stuffed the books back into my bag, looked anxiously about the park for Dixie. All I could see was a roiling sea of pugs. Flat faces. Busty chests. Twitching, curled tails.

I jumped up, began to follow the galloping pug herd. In my

peripheral vision, I detected the woman, the instigator, giving a rousing speech. The rest were drawn in, their faces registering a rising barometer of reactions going from interest, to abhorrence, to rage. I knew bloodlust was next.

I ran into the pug herd, reached for a fawn pug, picked her up, realized it wasn't Dixie, quickly dropped her. I called out Dixie's name. No response, she was still camouflaged in among the scrambling pug pile. I ran with the pugs, feeling like a tourist who, ill-advisedly, finds himself running with the Pamplona bulls.

The pugs took a sharp left. They started down the hill, to the very spot where the lynch party was forming.

Of course, seeing those dim-witted twins and those iridescent pink rubber clogs, I remembered the causal moment—the fluttering butterfly wing moment months earlier—that triggered my current predicament. And I didn't exactly regret having told that fat-assed busybody that I was using Dixie as a bait dog. But I did regret having run into her again.

I especially regretted that I'd encountered her among a posse of virulent dog lovers. Pug lovers. There's no reasoning with them.

Instinct told me to flee. But I'd be damned if I left my dog with those sanctimonious bastards.

I spotted Dixie. She was boxed into the middle of the pug herd, which was galloping en masse toward Croc woman and her lynch mob. To follow them would be suicide.

Inspiration struck. I reached in my pocket, pulled out a dog treat. "Dixie," I called. "Biscuit."

Nineteen pugs stopped, reared up on their hind legs, twirled in midair, and reversed direction. They came thundering toward me. Now their owners followed them.

"Shit," I said.

I turned and ran up the hill, calling Dixie's name as I retreated. The dog owners began to, one by one, catch up with their dogs. They arrested them, leashed them, and led them back to the grassy knoll.

I reached the crest, kept going, pounded down the other side of the hill, ran past the playground, and down the four flights of steep concrete steps. By the time I got to the street, the only dog still chasing me was Dixie.

25

I don't subscribe to physical culture. I prefer to visualize my exercise.

It was a shock to my system—being chased up and over one of the steepest hills in San Francisco by a pack of rabid hound owners. Even after I got home, I was still lathered up, and wishing I'd bought that ambulance defibrillator that guy in Krakow had tried to sell me.

And I was distressed about what happened afterward. I was fleeced like some yokel from Idaho.

I'd flagged down a taxi a block from the park, and had to pay the Somali pirate an extra $35, up front, on an $18 fare. "Vacuum fees," he said. "Because dog has hair."

As soon as we got home, I gave Dixie a plate of beans and sausages, with a dab of sauerkraut. She piled into it, savaging the bowl across the kitchen floor.

I twisted a few cubes out of the ice tray. A couple made it into a highball glass. The rest bounced off the counter and ricocheted around the floor.

I tipped a vermouth bottle over the glass, and counted to four.

Dixie finished her beans, I rinsed off her dish. I poured another vermouth.

I debated having a cigarette; *L'Orfeo* rehearsals were just three weeks off.

I poured another four count of vermouth; no ice this time.

I resolved my cigarette debate with a compromise. I jammed a cigarette into my Swarovski crystal cigarette holder. Much healthier.

I went upstairs, sloshing vermouth onto every other riser, and got in the shower. I stood under the steaming spray, piping smoke from the implement clenched between my teeth. After a few moments, I realized I was smoking in the shower. I pulled the half-spent cigarette out of the holder, dropped it on the shower floor, and watched the pooling water melt the paper and disperse the tobacco flecks until they all swirled down the drain. I turned to set the holder in the shower caddy.

A shadow rippled across the ribbed glass of the shower door.

I screamed.

The shadow crossed again. It was large, the figure of a man. It stopped and faced the shower.

I noticed that the shoulders spanned the width of the door and the neck was about as thick as a pier piling. The big head angled, regarding the shower door, coolly appraising which would render the greatest dramatic effect—smashing the glass or ripping the door off its hinges.

I was blubbering by then, holding a washcloth over my nether region. Desperate, I reached into the shower caddy, picked up a disposable razor, and brandished it.

"Get out," I bellowed.

The shadow did not answer. Instead, the figure raised its meaty hand, and brought it toward me. A dark point, a fingertip, touched the surface of the tempered glass.

Another man, perhaps a braver man—a man who hadn't, as a child, been traumatized by the shower scene in *Psycho*—would have kicked open the door and blunderbussed the intruder with violent, flying fists. Max Bravo was not that man.

The finger glided across the glass, and the glass screamed at its touch. It etched the letter *X* in the steam.

I started to whinny, then worked my way up to a full-throated scream, very Janet Leigh, shaking the disposable razor, with its safety blades ready to inflict a wound every bit as nasty as a paper cut.

Another letter appeared. *A*. Then, the letter *M*.

I thought: *X. A. M.* What the hell does that mean?

There was more writing, faster now. I backed up, knocked into the shower caddy. The cigarette holder fell, clattered onto the ceramic tiles. It bounced a few times, reeled like drunken caravels until it rested on the drain. I shuffled to the back of the shower, pasted myself, naked, against the wall.

The shadow of the fingertip withdrew. The human form wavered just beyond the glass. The other arm lifted. There was a hook at the end of it.

The hook came to the shower door, rapped sharp cold steel on glass. The implement dragged across the door, at neck level, washboarding over the glass ribs like a scabbard scraping a trachea.

Blood swirled around my bare feet. I screamed, again. I realized that some pieces of crystal glass had dislodged from the cigarette holder. I'd stepped on them. The sole of my foot was cut.

On the other side of the glass door, the shadow wavered. It drew in, became faint at the edges and dense at the center. Water freezing into ice. Then it was gone.

I waited, listening. There were no footsteps, no sounds at all.

I opened the shower door, tore my kimono off the hook, and quickly wrapped myself in it. I wiped off the bottom of my bleeding foot, consoled myself that it was just a small, single cut. I fiddled with the box of bandages, sloppily applied one over the wound on my heel.

I ran out into the hallway. There was no one. I retrieved the baseball bat from under my bed and, timidly, poked it into every nook and crevice in the house. Again, no one.

Dixie was lying asleep on the recliner in the living room. The windows were shut tight. The doors were locked, bolted from the inside.

When I was sure that Dixie and I were alone in the house, I grabbed the vermouth bottle, went back upstairs.

The steam had evaporated off of the shower door. The lettering was gone.

"Damn it, Max," I said to myself.

I refreshed my vermouth glass, closed the toilet lid, and sat on the commode, drinking. A thought came to me. I got up, turned on the bath tap, and the shower tap, full blast. Hot water roared out. I closed the bathroom door to accelerate the steam buildup.

I shut the shower stall door, sat back down, and watched the letters slowly reappear:

Max,
Frank Kelly's debt is now yours. Find A.H.

26

Sterling Hayden, John Huston, and Ty Cobb walk into a bar.

There's no punch line. It's not a joke. It's an illustration.

If those three showed up, you'd clear out. You'd leave your drink. Throw down a large bill. And not wait for your change.

This is a metaphor.

Frank Kelly, Betty Ann Thibideaux, and Duffield Fallon had walked into my life.

The problem was, I couldn't just leave. I had to settle the tab. With exact change.

———

Baba had given me the solution months earlier. I should have listened then. But, of course, it was hard to hear anything with all that screaming going on in my head.

Clearly, waiting until Fallon cornered me in my own shower was letting the situation run too far. Had it passed the fail-safe point?

I assured myself that this was nothing that a little Afro-Caribbean witchcraft couldn't cure.

The day after the shower scene, I left the dog at home and walked down the hill toward the Mission. I went to the Santeria shop on Valencia Street.

I'd passed it for years, never once going inside. But I found the shop easily, its perennial window display of martyred saints being a ready marker.

I arrived and loitered on the sidewalk, gawking at the familiar Catholic action figures in the window. They all bore the signs of their martyrdom: bleeding palms, excised noses, bristles of arrows porcupining out of their chests.

The dead saints congregated in a befuddled group. They looked like convention-goers thrown together at a mixer. They'd come for the free cocktails and finger foods, but once they got there, they realized they'd have to pay a price; they'd have to endure the prickly hell of the awkward mingle.

I started for the door, then hesitated. I tried to rehearse how I'd explain myself to the shopkeeper. It was the same self-conscious feeling I get when I go to the hardware store. They always ask penetrating questions. They want to know what it is you're trying to accomplish.

I dread telling a professional handyperson that, for example, I'm fashioning a slotted champagne flute holder to mount on the wall beside the bathtub. It was much the same with these voodoo people. How was I to tell them that I was trying to evict an agitated pimp who had been dead for a hundred years?

I loitered on the sidewalk, feigning interest in the saints display.

They stood collecting dust on their hand-sewn robes piled on in layers of iridescent green sateen, and purple velvet, and silver damask as glittery as disco balls. They were all trimmed in taffeta, yards of it. And I fancied that the rustling would have sounded like an army on the move, if they actually could move.

I soon got the sense that the saints were staring back at me. I knew that couldn't have been, of course. They were plastic. Their stiff little limbs and neutered torsos were nothing more than synthetic shells punched out on presses in Mexican *maquiladoras*.

But, they had a presence.

People had inveighed these plastic figures with certain powers and attributes. And just believing it had made it so.

"Look at my wounds," they seemed to be saying. "Cast your eyes upon the grimoire. For these horrors that I endured, I endured for you. Flaying. Impaling. Garroted breasts. Spooned-out eyeballs."

I turned my back on the saints, and fled. I walked quickly, almost scampering, back the way I came.

I was nearly home before the incline on upper Market Street forced me to slow my pace, and braked the panic that had bolted me. Slowing down settled everything into perspective. My fear of a collection of badly dressed dolls was soon outflanked by the much more concrete threat: Fallon.

"Stupid," I said to myself. I turned and doubled back, walked a couple blocks down the hill to the health food store.

I went straight to the aisle where they keep the aromatic oils and incense.

I found what I was looking for. Sage. It didn't look especially potent. It was just a bundle of twigs wrapped in cellophane and labeled with a sticker that proclaimed its ability to scrub away persistent bad vibes.

The directions said, Use as Needed.

What the hell did that mean? I knew you had to light it. But then what? That's the trouble with these damn hippie wares. Their purvey-

ors assume everyone has lived in communes or ashrams or psychedelic painted school buses where bong-loading, and bread-kneading,
and sage-smudging are all just part of one's daily routine.

I was annoyed.

Now I was forced to talk to one of the hippie store clerks.

I looked around for someone approachable. There were only three
employees on duty. One exasperated woman with pierced lips worked
the cash register as the line lengthened all the way down the aisle,
past the tofu turkey to the bulk kasha bin.

The other two "workers" were in the back, by the cooler. The
young man—his bald head tattooed over with Maori symbols that
could have said, "kick me, I'm a honky asshole" for all he knew—was
restocking bottles of Kombucha while his female colleague watched.

I had the whisk of sage in my hand, and an interrogative expression on my face. I idled near them, trying to muster some story that
would sound casual.

*I had this roommate that moved out and I want to purify his room. My
wife ran off with her yoga instructor, and I want to smudge her closet now
that I've burned all her clothes. There was a suicide in the house. A homicide.
A missed credit card payment.*

No. None of those would do.

It didn't matter. They didn't give me the chance to ask my question
anyway. They ignored me.

The two of them were engrossed in their own conversation. It was
more of a monologue, really. She was doing all the talking, a chronicle of her weekend. She had attended a "sun ritual" in which she
watched a friend get pierced through the pectorals with giant hooks
and then suspended from a tree branch. Upon seeing him dangling
by two hunks of pulled taffy that had formerly been his chest flesh,
she decided she had to do it too.

I couldn't imagine how to interrupt that discourse with my own
rather entry-level inquiries about sage. I decided it couldn't be that
complicated.

I got in the checkout line. Eighteen minutes later, I reached the front of the queue, paid the extremely pissed-off cashier, and walked out with the sage in my pocket.

Once inside my foyer, before I even hung up my coat, I opened the cellophane wrapper. The smell was peaty and strong. It filled the room.

I discovered a slip of paper, cut by hand, the scissor marks uneven. On it was a photocopy of a brief typed instruction.

I had to light the faggot of twigs and walk through the house incanting whatever mantra I felt fit. That sounded rather demanding. So I left the twigs on an occasional table in the living room.

I went upstairs, took a shower, and put on my kimono. Maury called me.

He was anxious, but tried to sound light and airy. Was I ready for *L'Orfeo* rehearsals? They were just a couple weeks off. How was I feeling? My voice? Chest in good shape? No mucous?

I dispatched the correct set of answers. Yes. I know. Fine. Good. No. No. Good-bye.

When I closed the phone, I heard Dixie barking downstairs. I smelled smoke. I hurried down the stairs, lifting my kimono so as not to trip up on it.

I burst into the living room. Dixie was standing up on the chair, barking at the sage I'd left beside her on the table. She was barking so frantically that her two back legs lifted with every shout. I ran to her and gathered her up in my arms.

"Sweetheart," I said, running my hand across her little flat face. "It's all right, baby."

I heard a sharp snap. I looked over at the fireplace. It was ablaze.

The fire roared and burned hot. It wasn't a cozy marshmallow-roasting fire. It was a thuggish gangster fire—the kind of thing that occurs when a couple of guys in sharkskin suits walk into a failing restaurant after hours carrying gasoline cans.

The big logs on the grate cracked and groaned, collapsed under the whipping of angry red flames. The flames flickered up into the chimney, with stabbing spear points.

I screamed. "Jesus God!"

Clutching the dog, I ran to the back porch and tore the fire extinguisher from its brackets. I dashed back into the living room. Dixie leapt from the crook of my arm and, seemingly oblivious to the raging wildfire, she jumped back up on the recliner and again assaulted the sprigs of sage on the table.

I fumbled with the release pin on the fire extinguisher.

I'd never used a fire extinguisher, and had certainly never read the instructions. Operating it was even more complex than the sage.

There must have been some kind of childproof release. But I couldn't find it.

As I struggled, the hasty knot of my sash slithered apart. My kimono opened. I was blubbering, and fumbling with the canister, a long string of spittle suspended from my chin.

I suddenly felt as though I weren't alone.

I looked up, out the window, and saw two young women, and their dog, staring directly at me. They were stopped on the sidewalk—more like struck immobile.

Their mouths were agape. Even their dog's mouth was agape.

I looked down and, for the first time, considered what it meant that my kimono had fallen open. I was, essentially, naked.

Of course, I could appreciate what a jarring sight that must have been. Seeing Max Bravo naked is a treat. But it's a treat best savored by those with sturdy sensibilities and a generous sense of the absurd.

I imagine the fire extinguisher threw them off too.

I dropped to the floor, trying to make the move look as natural as possible. I crawled to the perimeter of the room. Dixie stopped barking and came over to me, trampling my tackle with her little paws, which felt like being stomped by a dominatrix in heels.

I set the fire extinguisher down, rerobed, and crawled to the window. I peered out. The girls and the dog were hustling down the street. They weren't on their cell phone, so I was pretty sure they weren't going to place some tattling call to the local gendarmes.

The fire was still burning. I decided to leave it. I made sure that the flue was open and drew the screen across the front of the firebox.

I searched the house again. I wished Baba would appear. But the old crone never showed up when you actually needed a little assistance from the supernatural side.

I poured a tankard of brandy and settled into the Eames recliner, watched the fire as it burned itself out. Dixie got into my lap, looked at me as if to ask what the hell had I gotten us into. She rested her chin on the backs of her paws and worried her eyebrows until she fell asleep.

I reached for the nearest book. It was *Paradise Lost*. I flipped through it, looking for my bookmark.

It fell open of its own accord to a passage near the beginning. The rebel angels are cast out of Heaven and crash-land onto a burning lake.

27

I decided to dine at my regular vegan restaurant. I had deliberately waited until after the lunch rush because the seating consists of one enormous plank table, and this arrangement requires patrons to all sit and eat together, kibbutz-style. It's not that I mind eating with strangers. I do it all the time when I'm on tour.

It's just that I don't like hoving up to ye olde groaning board with a band of chatty, overly familiar hippies who treat public meals as their express forum for delivering discourses on hydroponics and high colonics and composting toilets.

It puts me off my food.

I had my copy of *The Flight of the Singing Bird* in one coat pocket, and the *L'Orfeo* libretto in the other, and I set out walking toward the Mission. I'd been reading them both over the course of the last few days. And as I progressed through the two works, I saw that Frank's singing bird yarn was very much an Orpheus story.

That's not terribly unusual. Orpheus echoes through many cultures, many millenniums. First, it appeared in ancient Egypt as the Osiris and Isis myth. Osiris is killed and cut to pieces. His sister-lover Isis gathers his scattered bits, aggregates them in a casket, and it sprouts a bountiful crop of wheat. Love. Death. Rebirth.

Orpheus is the later, Greek version. Being Greeks, they add man's own creative regenerative powers to the story—man can create art, art is eternal, therefore eternity is within man's own reach.

Orpheus is a musician so gifted that wild beasts lie down at his feet, tamed by the sounds emanating from his harp. His lover Eurydice dies, bitten by a snake. He pursues her into the Underworld. He presses on through Hell's labyrinth, and along the way, the sound of his music melts the heart of Persephone, Pluto's wife. She implores her husband to let Orpheus take his bride back to the land of the living. Pluto relents. But he sets a condition. Orpheus must not look behind at Eurydice until she is safely back on Earth. He almost makes it. The two young lovers reach the gates of Hell, and Orpheus looks back. Eurydice dissolves like a phantom before his eyes.

The Greeks had concluded the story along the same lines as the Egyptian predecessor; Orpheus was torn to pieces by the wild-ass bacchanates.

The artist pursues his muse into Hell, nearly recaptures her, but in the end fails and is destroyed. Kind of a bummer.

When Monteverdi staged the opera in the seventeenth century, he couldn't follow the original plotline to its desolate ending. He needed to end the opera on an up note because he'd been commissioned to write it as the wedding entertainment for a duke's daughter.

So the composer reached deep into the bag of cheesy dramatic tricks, and pulled out the oldest and ripest: deus ex machina. He put a guy in a gold lamé costume, called him Apollo, and lowered him from the heavens onto the stage—that is, a platform suspended by rope pulleys—at just the moment when Orpheus has lost Eurydice and is about to lose his own life.

The sun god, who is also Orpheus' dad, rescues the young troubadour, takes him to heaven, and shows him how he can see Eurydice for all eternity in the stars twinkling in the firmament.

The implication is that while art can trick death, only love can conquer it.

Frank had sweat blood to write his book, the book that I had in my pocket. He tore himself to pieces with drink, and despair, and self-doubt. Now Frank was gone. The book remained. But for how long? Not eternity, I knew that much.

"Max." Ananda, the restaurant owner, greeted me with a hug that was more heartfelt than gestural, which always makes me uncomfortable. "Let me sit you in the sunlight. Herbal tea to start?"

He showed me to the big table by the window. I was delighted to find it empty. Ananda said that he'd let the staff have the day off. He'd be taking care of me himself.

He handed me a menu, his face swathed in a luminous smile.

"Are we going to go through this again?" I said.

"Yes"—more nodding and idiot grinning—"I am sure we are."

I snatched the menu from him. He floated off, unruffled by my pique.

Me and Ananda—who by the way was not even South Asian but was, in fact, a paunchy little Polack from Cincinnati who had christened himself Ananda, which is the Sanskrit word for eternal bliss—ran these same lines every time I came into the restaurant. It was the naming-of-the-dishes scene. Ananda played it out interminably.

On the Bountiful Harvest menu, all the dishes were named after *affirmations*. So, you were forced to pronounce inanities like "I'll have the I Am Content" or "the I Am Whole and Forgiving."

I always wanted the beet and arugula tartine. But I couldn't bring myself to pronounce: "I Am a Spirit in a Physical Experience."

At any rate, I confined myself to the salad selection since I was under tremendous pressure to drop at least twenty pounds in the next two weeks.

One of my moles at the L.A. Opera had already tipped me off to the wardrobe director's sick and twisted—and so Angelino—scheme for my costume. When I took the role, I assumed that the god of the Underworld would be cloaked in dense draperies, perhaps an ermine muff that I could have some fun with, and capped with a crown the size of an eighteen-point elk rack. Well, no such luck. Not in L.A.

Living in the land of personal trainers and lipo, those mad seam-stresses down there in Lotus Land operate on the premise that per-formers' bodies are routinely starved and sculpted into runway model physiques. Those bitches meant to strip me near naked on stage, to traffic in my flesh. They were nothing more than cheap pornogra-phers, intent on exploiting the Max Bravo sexuality for the express purpose of selling tickets.

My source informed me that Pluto's costume was to be a Diane von Furstenberg sequined miniskirt with a ruched center seam, a set of cobra-skin epaulets, and nothing in between. I was required to prance around the stage in ankle-strap sandals with my entire torso laid bare, like a coochie dancer.

I would be exposed to the world. And the world was peopled with too many individuals—male, female, undecided—with whom I'd had carnal relations, and too many more with whom I'd like to have car-nal relations, for me to not put my best form forward.

As soon as I found out about the costume scheme, I called Maury and had a calculated hissy fit. He, in turn, made calls.

Typically, Maury—squishy, cartilage creature that he is—got no-where. He caved in as soon as they pointed out that if I refused to wear the costume, my engagement, and his commission, were at risk.

I sent a couple e-mails, but was soon silenced. The director forwarded them to Maury and instructed him to "get Max under control."

I was in a huff. But I needed the gig. So I had to play along. And now, I was eating only salads, and drinking only white wine. It was a brutal regimen.

If I didn't get my waist back before I got to L.A., I knew I was in danger of never getting laid in that town again.

Ananda brought me a glass of water and hovered tableside, smiling moonbeams, hands in prayer, strafing me with a full metal jacket of loving-kindness.

"I'll have the squash roulade," I told him.

"And that is?" More beaming, accompanied by Hindi head toggling.

"Number twelve," I said, snapping the menu shut.

"And that is?" He turned up the kilowatts on the smile.

"Must we?"

"Yes, we must."

I opened the menu, traced my finger down the entrée column.

"I'll have the I Am Loving," I said. I snapped the menu shut again and handed it to him.

"That wasn't hard, was it, Max?" he said.

"Yes. It was."

He dialed the smile back down, but kept it there. His affirmation that day must have been "I Am Perversely Patient." He went off to make my usual pot of honeysuckle tea.

I settled into my libretto, scribbling notes in the margins. Since it was just me and Ananda in the place, I read through the piece, softly singing the lyrics out loud.

I was suddenly assaulted by a vision of myself shimmying topless in a miniskirt across the stage. I made a mental note to get my torso waxed, front and back.

I heard a clacking across the plank floor, but didn't look up from my work. A cup appeared by my hand and tea poured into it. The teapot came down gently on the table in front of me. Thanks, Ananda, I said. Again, without looking up.

I was working on the aria where I grant Orpheus his wish. His art has softened the heart of my wife, and she in turn has convinced me to grant compassion. I tell Orpheus that I will return his dead lover, Eurydice, to him. Alive. There is only one condition. He can't look back at her.

I wrote in the margin that I should be holding a sleek, black cat during this interchange. I'd stroke the cat insouciantly; its tail would flick and curl, like a whip.

I'd pitch it by saying that the cat would make the moment rather piquant, the purring cat made a nice counterpoint to the content of my aria; a threat packaged inside an act of compassion.

I knew they'd like this bit, probably even admire my resourcefulness in suggesting it. Of course, my thinking also included the consideration that I'd hold the cat so it would cover a good deal of the Bravo midriff.

I printed, very firmly, in the margin that I wanted the cat declawed.

I heard the chair opposite me scrape along the floor. Surprised, I looked up. Ashley Banks was setting herself down.

"You're welcome," she said.

"Oh, I thought you were Ananda."

"I'm the next best thing," she said, helping herself to a cup of my tea.

"The next best thing to eternal bliss?" I ventured.

I closed the libretto. She asked if she was disturbing me. I told her she was. And I told her I liked it.

"What have you been up to?" she asked. "Since the funeral."

I held up the libretto. She took it from me, lifted her sunglasses to read the opening bits. She was dressed casually, but carefully. Sleek hair. Crisp blouse. Lips lacquered the color of Hawaiian coral. She had always been stunning, but now, she had to be so very groomed and coifed just to assert herself above her startling disfigurement.

She handed the libretto back to me. And, as she did, she tipped her glasses down, back in place like a knight lowering the visor of his helmet.

With the shades, a wall came down. The black squares of her glasses were opaque, impenetrable—as mysterious as the smoked windows of a sultan's limo. She'd chosen them with great precision, and probably, after extensive searching. They were oversized, very Jackie O, not exactly in style, but she needed them that way. They covered both eyes from above the brow to the cheek, even the right eye that sat lower.

The rest of Ashley's mutilation was impossible to mask. In the direct light of midafternoon, the loud scar ripped down her forehead, disappeared into the black pool of her glasses, and then reemerged below them in an angry rift that tore across her cheek.

"You know what I love about this story," she said to me.

I looked at her and felt myself smiling, because I suddenly realized I'd become accustomed to her face, the scar, the way that people became used to the Cubist faces in Picasso's paintings. I thought of Dora Mar, one of Picasso's long-suffering lovers. He painted her to look just like Ashley did now. Sitting in front of me, her face was a broken plate, fitted clumsily back together. And the stutter in the symmetry of those broken faces—the face of the dead artist's dead muse, and the face of this live woman—somehow broke the sequence of time. Dora Mar and Ashley Banks both looked at me from different angles at once, as if all their expressions, all their moments, were compressed into this one eternal moment.

"I love that he follows her into Hell," Ashley said.

"Orpheus?" I pulled my attention back to the libretto she was stroking with her white, soft hand.

"Yes," I said. "He follows her straight into Hell and back. That's love. My ex-wife couldn't even get me to go to her parents' home for Christmas."

Ashley laughed, and I was pleased with myself, because she shifted her handbag from her lap to the empty chair next to her.

She looked at the menu on the wall. She said she'd like to order a second pot of tea. She asked me if I recommended any particular blend. I answered quickly, just so she would turn her attention back to me. And she did.

I discussed tea. I discussed it to beyond the ends of my knowledge of the subject, striking out on an uncharted sea in search of Ceylon, just to fix her on me. And the more I talked, the more I was allowed to watch her face, so white, and clean. It sailed in the clear sunlight beyond the black pools that covered her eyes, and she opened her mouth to speak and her teeth were pretty little pearls and her laughter splashed easily over the conversation.

When we'd said everything there was to say about tea, and the tea trade and mercantilism, and the ever-intriguing question of "What is up with Queen Elizabeth and corgis?" we returned to Orpheus. Ashley, again, said the word *love*. It caught me up even deeper. I wanted to know what Ashley Banks loved.

"Is that what women think?" I asked. "That in order for a man to prove his love he has to go chasing you into Hell and back?"

"If he's in love with me, he's already in a special circle of Hell."

She let her coral lips open for a moment after she said this to me. Then she pulled back and the sun struck through the window like through the surface of the sea and I felt I was descending, diving into clear, warm water and the world had turned brilliant aquamarine.

"All right," I said. "Try it the other way. Would you follow a man into Hell?"

"Yes," she said. "But not again."

She withdrew her smile.

Ananda brought my order. I asked Ashley if she was eating. She waved the suggestion away with a well-manicured hand. I noticed her nails were painted the same coral as her lips, and a diamond bracelet slaked and sparkled around her wrist.

I believe it was the style that they refer to as a tennis bracelet, which I've always found to be an odd, affected premise for a luxury item. But I suppose it's how you start wearing your diamonds when you want to show that you don't think they're all that special. Oh, this old thing? Just a few thousand dollars' worth of diamonds. It's okay for wearing around the house, or running out to Andronico's, or hitting a few tennis balls around down at the club.

I asked her what she did for a living. She reminded me that when I'd met her more than twenty years earlier, she worked at a photocopy shop. She told me how she'd parlayed that job into a sales position— she hustled printing jobs for a commercial printer down in San Mateo. It was mostly corporate stuff; annual reports, brochures, junk mail. Her territory was Silicon Valley. During the fat years she made a nice packet. She started her own agency, specializing in annual reports for high-tech companies.

"That opened up a whole new world for me. I met a lot of those big Silicon Valley guys just as they were coming up," she said. "It was lucky timing. Great connections."

"Your looks couldn't have hurt," I noted.

She agreed. And she smiled, curling up one side of her lip into a feline snarl. She turned her head to face me in three-quarter profile. It was an expression she must have perfected after the accident. It hid most of the broken tectonics of her face. But it also showed off the eyetooth on her left side. It was preternaturally long and sharp.

"Is that what you're still doing?"

"Yes," she said. "But I've scaled back. I don't want to work as much now."

"Oh, yes," I remembered, "you have a son."

"Dante," she said. "From my first marriage."

"His father is local?"

"And loco," she told me.

"It's uncanny," I said. "Since I've started keeping a record on this, I've found that a hundred percent of ex-spouses are crazy. I've developed a spreadsheet. If you came to my place I could show you."

"My ex-husband really was crazy," she said. "But I guess I knew that going in. He was an outlaw biker."

"Was it like Cher's brief marriage to Greg Allman?" I queried. "He'd go out for a pack of cigarettes and come back three days later?"

She turned to look at me straight on. She brushed her fingertip along the scar, at her cheek. I noticed, for the first time, that it ran along a line where a tear would likely flow.

She said, "He gave me this."

"He," I stammered, stupid and embarrassed, "he, was abusive."

"No," she said. "Just reckless. He took chances. He did dangerous things."

"And you did too, I suppose?"

"Yes," she said.

"And you got hurt?" I soft-pedaled it.

"And then he got hurt," she said. "I hope he still hurts."

"Now you're with Blashky," I said.

"Jealous?" she said.

"Yes."

"I need a drink," she told me.

"I'll ask Ananda to bring that pot of tea. Did you decide?"

"I don't want it anymore," she said. "I want a real drink."

I got up and paid Ananda for our lunch. An hour later we were in my living room, drinking gin.

And an hour after that, we were upstairs.

28

The next morning Stan Blashky was on my front porch, pounding on the door with his big, meaty fist. I cowered in my bedroom, in my orange blossom kimono, one bloodshot eyeball peering through the slit in the drapes.

"Max!" Blashky yelled. He pushed his thumb on the doorbell and it rang out like a cannonade.

He looked up and saw my fingertips pinching the edge of the curtain. He tore off his porkpie hat, scrunching it in his paw. His smooth, bald head was as big as a wrecking ball and the muscles in his neck flared.

"Open the door, Max," he called up at the window, shaking his crumpled hat.

I dropped the curtain hem and frantically sashed my kimono. I looked at the bed. It was still askew from when Ashley had left me snoring and sweaty amid a welter of sheets and blankets, twisted and spun up like cotton candy.

I dashed over and tried to untangle the gnarl of bedding. I couldn't get the blankets disengaged from the cover sheet. In desperation I bunched it all together and stuffed it in the laundry hamper. It stuck out the top. I looked over at the stripped bed. The sheet was stained, in several spots. I touched the largest stain. It was still damp.

The bonging accelerated and was accompanied by a hard banging—Blashky's fist hitting the door. Then, it stopped. I heard the door open. That dizzy bitch, I swore out loud. Ashley hadn't locked the front door.

I heard Blashky call out from the foyer, "Max, I saw you up there. Get your ass downstairs."

I sobbed, and felt the hot tears burn my eyeballs. My ass—the part of me that Blashky was shouting for—went numb. I quickly wiped my eyes with the back of my wrists, pulled myself upright, and made my way to the bedroom door.

"Blashky, is that you?" I called down.

"You saw me from the window," he called up.

"Coming," I trilled, sliding into my Moroccan slippers.

My hair was sticking up, and my mascara was smeared under my left eye. I decided to work with it.

I descended the stairs very breezy, and loosely tossled. I patted and mussed my hair. I twilled at my eyelashes.

"Darling," I said. "What are you doing here at this ungodly hour?"

I was adding color and depth to my performance: a sprinkle of nettle, a dash of perplexity.

"What hour?" Blashky said. "It's eleven A.M."

"Follow me to the kitchen." I swept by him, trying not to flinch when I got within swiping distance of those ursine paws of his. "And don't even talk to me until I've had my coffee."

"Rough night?" he growled behind my back as he shadowed me down the hallway.

Now, I've done enough cuckolding in my time to know that the best way to present a lie is to slide it between a couple layers of truth. I willed myself to proceed in a flowy sashay.

"I suppose I did have maybe an extra cordial or two around bedtime," I said. Cue: peal of laughter, hand swish (very limp-wristed) describing curlicues in the air.

I heard Blashky chuckle, deep in his throat, like an amused Komodo dragon. We entered the kitchen and I went over to the sink and filled the kettle. He settled down in a chair that creaked under his mass of muscle and testosterone and granite knuckles.

"Aren't you getting a little old for this, Max?"

"I'm not old," I said, turning on the stove flame. "For what?"

"Alley catting around?"

"I'm an active senior," I said. I spooned coffee into the filter, breathing steadily so as to not shake the grounds all over the counter.

"You should go back to women," Blashky opined. He unbuttoned his leather jacket and his torso expanded forth like an inflatable lifeboat. "They're better for you. Steadier. More monogamous."

I smiled thinly and tightened my sash.

"Toast?" I asked.

"Sure," he said. I set a glass of orange juice in front of him and popped a couple slices of bread in the toaster.

"See, women," he told me, "they don't have the same sex drive as us. They can find one man, one quality man, and stick with him. They're happier that way. Whereas men, we are programmed by nature, by evolution, to spread our genes. So we go for quantity."

"Butter?"

"Yes, please. You fags make it too rough on yourselves," he explained. "Because, instead of one person you can't trust, you got two people who want to fuck everything in sight."

"Jam?"

"Thanks."

I detest being categorized. And I further detest people dictating to me about my own libido. But, in the end, I'm a pragmatist.

"Women?" I told Blashky, raising my eyebrows. "Yes. I must try that sometime."

I sat down at the table and tucked into a hearty breakfast of toast and anchovy spread. The coffee and victuals seemed to soften Blashky. I asked him what he'd come over for.

"I'm about to lose my damn mind," he said, through a mouthful of toast.

"*Pourquoi?*" I asked, gaying it up maybe a bit too much.

"I keep losing shit in the house, then finding it in odd places. My keys. Glasses. Beers. And I was in the shower the other day, and it kept turning ice-cold—the hot water was turning off on its own. And now, for the past week, all the taps in the flat keep turning on every day. Same time. Five o'clock in the goddamn morning. Actually, five twelve. It just happened again this morning. I got so fed up, I had to get out of there."

"How very odd," I said, compressing my eyebrows together in a gesture of concern and wonder.

"Yeah," Blashky said. He took a drink of coffee, set the cup carefully back down on the saucer. "Then I tried to think, when did this shit start?"

"Mmm," I hummed through a mouthful of anchovy paste.

"And there was something I remembered." He pushed his plate away and folded his arms on the table.

Leaning in, he said, "It all started about three weeks ago, when I painted Frank's old room. I painted over that writing I showed you."

I couldn't hold out on Blashky anymore. I could see that he was in this Fallon thing as deeply as I was. And, honestly, I welcomed the subject. It steered us out of the treacherous shoals of betrayal and girlfriend stealing and imminent ass-kicking that we had been coasting through.

I made up my mind right there that I didn't want anything more to do with Ashley Banks. I would banish her from my life, my bed, my mind. I thought that if Stan and I could move on, bond over some shared purpose, the indiscretion would fade into obscurity.

I showed Stan the dossier on Fallon that Emile Balzac had compiled for me. I told him about how Fallon had perished at the Valencia Hotel. He understood the ramifications immediately. He was living on top of the grave of an angry dead man.

As he was leaving, I gave Stan Blashky the copy of *Paradise Lost*. He looked at Fallon's signature on the flyleaf, and the note he had written to Ah Ho. He took it home with him. I was glad to be rid of it.

29

"You stupid peckerhead," Claudia said.

The waiter stopped short and hovered a plate of chicken Caesar salad over our heads.

"Better give her that salad before she gets cranky," I told him.

He landed the plate in front of Claudia and reached for the oversized pepper mill he had tucked under his arm. Claudia waved him off. He looked relieved.

When he left, I noticed that the two women at the table just inches away had stopped talking. They cocked their ears toward us.

"Blashky is going to break your ribs," Claudia said, spearing a halved artichoke heart.

"It's okay." I pushed my polenta around my plate. "He doesn't know."

"Now," she seethed. "He doesn't know now. But he will."

"Who's going to tell him? Ashley?"

"Yes," Claudia raised her voice.

The two women were now frozen in a tableau of rapt eavesdropping—forks arrested, quizzical smiles, staring at each other with raised eyebrows.

We were downtown, at the Poodle Parlor. The place was jittery and frantic with the business district lunch trade. The locust swarm buzz rose, and breached over the décor that was meant to baffle it; a dark dining room with a low ceiling, deep carpets, and drawn sheer curtains that suffused the light until it was almost viscous like melted amber.

Deuce tables lined the walls, barely an elbow width apart, and round tables for larger parties floated over the center expanse of deep carpet.

"I hate this place," I said.

"Well, I have to be back at the office for a two o'clock meeting," Claudia said. "Sorry if you find that inconvenient."

She stabbed at her plate again, this time pulling up a chunk of chicken flesh on the three sharp tines of her fork. She didn't cut her meat. It was a habit that always annoyed me. She brought the hunk of meat to her mouth and savaged pieces of it off with big, lipstick-stained teeth.

I ventured a dab of polenta into my mouth and gummed it morosely. My nerves were shot. I'd barely eaten anything solid since my indiscretion with Ashley Banks a few days earlier. Claudia told me that it was good practice for when Blashky found out and punched my teeth in.

"I'll have another," I called to the waiter, waving my empty gimlet glass aloft.

"What's his name again," I asked Claudia.

She shot me a withering look.

"The waiter," I said. "Do you remember what he said his name was?"

She took a sip of her iced tea.

"Brad," she said.

"What?"

I was staring at a woman coming through the front door of the restaurant. She had sleek black hair, a fitted maroon dress, big sunglasses.

"The waiter's name is Brad," Claudia said.

"Why do I give a fuck what his name is?"

Brad came over. He asked me if I wanted something.

The black-haired woman approached the hostess desk. She took off her glasses. She wasn't Ashley Banks.

"Max," Claudia snapped. "Tell Brad what you want."

"Oh, yes." I remembered when I saw the empty glass in my hand. I passed it to Brad. "Could you get me another of these, please."

"Certainly," he said, allowing a fleeting little smile.

Brad returned promptly. He set a fresh drink down in front of me.

"Thank you," I said, halting. I'd forgotten his name again.

He anchored, waiting for me to regain my thread.

"Gimlet," I said to Brad. "Your eyes are rather gimlet. I think I'll just call you that, if it's okay. I'm not trying to be fresh. Just factual."

He didn't look offended, and off he went.

"He thinks you're shit-faced," Claudia said.

"This is only my second drink."

"This is *lunch*," Claudia said, once again demonstrating her aptitude for recognizing the gross superficialities.

I don't know why I ever even call Claudia for help. She's constitutionally incapable of providing it. From the moment I confided my predicament to her, she showed a marked lack of concern for my well-being.

She'd taken the rather obdurate position that, by sleeping with his girlfriend, I had summoned Blashky's bone-fracturing wrath down upon myself.

A little sympathy would have been nice. But I suppose expecting that was just me chasing rainbows again.

The two eavesdroppers were talking among themselves again. I eavesdropped on them as they dissected their check. It was a complex formula involving who had the side salad and whether or not the tip should be tabulated before or after tax. They got up to leave.

"Bye, girls," I said, toasting them with my gimlet dregs. "Hope you enjoyed the floor show."

The older one—the one who was sausaged into a red knit dress—told me she didn't know what I meant.

"Come back tomorrow," I said, conspicuously looking at the fat bulges over her pantywaist. "We'll be discussing foundation undergarments."

Her colleague, a nervous but amused young woman, snickered. They steamed off and a SWAT team of Mexican busboys moved in and cleared the table, and a young woman talking into a cell phone sat down and started reading the menu out loud to the person on the other end. I stuck my finger in my ear. But she didn't notice. The bitch kept talking.

"Ignore it," Claudia said.

"I can't," I cried. One of the busboys came over and refilled our water glasses. "I'm tired of people behaving badly in public."

"You're the one who fucked your friend's girlfriend," Claudia stated, not angry, but she did project—as though she were giving one of her damn presentations in a conference room.

The busboy left my water glass half empty and hurried off. The cell phone bitch said, "Gotta go. I'll call you later."

She put her phone in her purse and looked around the restaurant. She looked everywhere but to her left, where we were sitting.

"I don't like that language," I said.

Claudia knew that. Fuck is an adjective. Sometimes it's a noun, as in *what-the-fuck*. To use it as a verb is coarse. And ugly. Claudia murmured an apology.

"Max," she said, after some moments of contemplative chewing on her part, and contemplative drinking on mine. "Blashky will find out. Ashley will end up telling him. Or, she'll tell somebody else who will tell him."

"Maybe it won't bother him," I suggested bravely. My glass was empty again. I waved it at the waiter who I thought was my friend, until I distinctly saw him roll his eyes.

"Gimlet, darling," I said when he brought my third cocktail. "Could you please take this away?"

He picked up my plate and looked at it. The polenta chicken lunch special looked barely altered since he'd presented it to me—a little mushed around and rearranged—but volume-wise, it was still pretty much intact.

"I'll box this up for you," he said, rather forcefully. "You'll want to eat it later when you get home."

He marched off with the plate before I could object.

"Gimlet likes you," Claudia said.

"Naturally," I agreed.

Claudia and I went over the Ashley-Blashky debacle a few more times. We worked out a master plan, and a contingency plan. Both were weak.

Our scenarios were grounded in the approach favored by most professional criminals: Deny. Even if they have you on hidden camera, deny.

We deduced that if the story leaked to Blashky, it would not come from me. And it probably wouldn't come from Ashley. Not directly, anyhow.

It would most likely reach Blashky through one person removed; a third column within the Ashley ranks, someone she would have confided in at a weak moment.

If this did happen, and someone squealed to Blashky, I would deny, deflect, and strategically retreat. I'd circle back around to Ashley to concoct a mutual denial.

Gimlet came back with my box of chicken polenta and the check. He set it down, and touched the table with his fingertips, lingered for maybe three seconds.

"Totally cruising you," Claudia said.

"Too bad Blashky's not here to see this," I said, as I swept up the bill, placed my calling card beneath my credit card, and set them out on the check tray. I handed it to Gimlet as he passed carrying a basket of bread.

"You were going to tell me about the books Frank was reading," Claudia said.

"Right," I remembered. "I haven't been able to slog through the damn things. Dreadful. One is *A Confederacy of Dunces*."

"I know it," Claudia said. "That guy killed himself. They published it after his mother found the manuscript in a box under his bed."

"Okay," I said, the back of my neck tingled. "That's a direct parallel with Frank's suicide and Emile Balzac having his manuscript in his vault."

"What's the other book?" she asked.

"It doesn't seem to fit," I said. "At least, it doesn't parallel Frank's situation the way the *Confederacy* book does."

I told her that the other book was *The Electric Kool-Aid Acid Test*. It was Tom Wolfe's 1960s account of the dippy adventures and psycho-dramas aboard Ken Kesey's school bus turned hippie conveyance, domicile, and traveling eyesore.

"Read it yet?" Claudia asked.

"No," I said.

I explained that I'd flipped through it, and then promptly shelved it. Wolfe has his moments, but I found the subject tedious. And I couldn't get past the period journalistic style—that smug heroic realism that passed for revolutionary reportage in the 1960s.

"Read it," Claudia told me.

"No," I said.

"Why?"

"Give me the executive summary."

"All right," she said. "Kesey, after some early literary success at a young age, went off the reservation. Dropped out. Tuned-in. Turned off. As they used to say."

"Loafs around getting high," I suggested.

"Correct," she said. "He inevitably got busted. Just pot, I think, but enough to send you to the pen in those days. The whole thing was a bit of a circus. Lots of courtroom antics and media attention. The judge pronounced him guilty and told him, 'You sir, had so much promise, and now you are nothing but a tarnished Galahad.'"

"The judge should have been the writer."

"Correct. So, instead of sticking around and being thrown in jail, Kesey skipped. He loaded up his bus with a bunch of chicks, assumed a false identity, and hid on a beach in Mexico. Before leaving California, though, he staged his own suicide."

Kesey, apparently, got in his car, drove south from San Francisco along the Pacific Coast Highway. He stopped somewhere near Carmel. He pulled onto an overlook, and abandoned his vehicle.

The authorities later found it, just as he'd hoped they would, parked next to a cliff that cantilevered out over a murderous drop. Thirty feet below, a thin stretch of beach sprouted jagged boulders, and these were washed with furious, torrid tides that rushed in, foamed about, then carried the land's detritus out to the hungry sea.

The investigators found a note inside Kesey's car. The tarnished Galahad, the despondent writer, had penned his last words, "Ocean, ocean, I'll beat you in the end."

"Sound familiar?" Claudia asked me.

"I'm pissed," I said.

Ocean, ocean, I'll beat you in the end.

Those were the exact words Frank Kelly had written in his suicide note before he tied it to the rail of the Golden Gate Bridge.

30

The rest of the day washed away on the torrent of lunchtime gimlets. Claudia went back to work. I went home, too drunk to practice my arias, too drunk to read the libretto.

I poured myself a glass of sauvignon blanc, cold and sharp as steel, and went to the bookshelf in the living room. I stood on a chair so I could peruse the seldom-visited occult section of my library. There were a couple volumes about that fat-assed Satanist, Alistair Crowley, a copy of the Tibetan *Book of the Dead,* and a dense tome about the Rosicrucians, a fin de siècle society of amateur Egyptologists.

I pulled out the Egyptology book. Frank Kelly's memoir, which had been on top of it, fell down onto my head. I took it as an omen.

I settled into the Eames recliner, lit a cheroot, and flipped idly through Frank's journal, looking for some reference to Ken Kesey. He had obviously, deliberately, plagiarized Kesey's fake suicide note in his own. Was this Frank's idea of a joke? Were we to think his suicide was faked too?

These questions led me to read Frank's journal through a different lens. I was wearing gimlet goggles, to be sure, but I also felt that there must be another level to what Frank had done. It almost didn't matter whether he had actually jumped or not. What did matter was why he had staged the entire performance piece.

I thought of something Blashky had said to me when he came over to tell me about the haunting in his apartment.

Blashky had made a rather original observation about Frank and his work. He had proposed that Frank's writing was a sort of incantation meant to evoke immortality. Death terrified Frank Kelly. Not because he would stop living, but because—living as he did, in the vacuum of his spiritual and philosophical agnosticism—he would vanish. There was no afterlife for Frank Kelly. No heaven. No hell. No reincarnation. Nothing. And because The Nothing is beyond comprehension it is more terrifying than all the devils in Hell, and all the Hell's Angels in Vallejo.

I came across a passage that essentially paraphrased Blashky's theory. "Death will come," Frank wrote. "And all my pretty projects, all my grand illusions, will dissolve. Forgotten."

That bleak bastard, I thought. I was glad that I hadn't seen him in those last months. Romantics always become the most turgid of depressives. They generally drink their way to the bottom. And once there, they scuttle across the silty barrens, feeding on decayed hopes and bloated despair.

Years ago, I had watched my mother travel the same downward trajectory. Sylvia painted. She was talented, but not gifted. She could capture a sense of things—the fuzz on a quince, the arching gesture of a snipe's wing. But the essence that pulsed beneath all her subjects

eluded her. It was most obvious in her portraits. She could paint ac-
curate likenesses, but the eyes were empty, the expressions were su-
perficial. The faces were merely oil on canvas, the skin did not breathe,
the minds did not perceive.

Mother was intelligent enough to know it. She knew that she was
skilled, but would never become noteworthy.

It tormented her—not in an obvious way, but in a deep and burrowing affliction. She was an extravagant personality. And my family's
wealth—made, once again, available to her after she divorced my
socially unsuitable father—gave her the means to promote her mytho-
logical avatar, the creature known to the world as Sylvia Lydecker.
Socialite. Bon vivant. Libertine. Most of her creativity went into her
image; her silks and feathers and handsome men.

The general public didn't see, as I did, the soft underbelly of her self-
loathing. She would binge drink, popping Valium and Seconal and
sleeping pills. Glen and Glenda—they were originally her upstairs
tenants—would telephone me, concerned. They'd say that Mother
hadn't left the house in days. She wouldn't answer the door, or the
phone. They could hear her in the flat below, smashing plates and playing Scottish glam rock so loudly that the electric guitars tore the air,
vibrating it like the terrifying bagpipes of an advancing Celtic army.

I would have to come to the house to deal with her. I'd let myself
in and she wouldn't notice me until I turned off the stereo. As soon as
the music stopped, she'd collapse, weeping. It was as if she'd been
buoyed up on the swell of raging guitars that skirled through the
firths of her delirium.

Then she would dump it all on me. She would descant about her
artistic failings in a ritualized series of sophistries. First, there would
be the discussion about critics; they were a rookery of fad followers
who durst not recognize her unfashionable style. Then she'd reel into
the subject of curators and buyers, lashing out against their blunt pal-
ates and prescribed tastes.

She'd segue from there onto my father, who she liked to identify as a pretentious pushcart peddler. This section usually included a eugenics sidebar on the perils of marrying a Gypsy. By this point, she would typically drink herself into a blackout, during which she'd despair against the limits of her abilities.

Finally, she would reach her ultimate destination and—like a mad navigator sailing over the edge of a flat Earth—she would launch into a soliloquy on death and nothingness.

I'd put her to bed, careful to take her pills out of the bedside drawer. In the moments before she slipped into the velvet blackness, she'd call out for my father.

Basically, there was nothing in Frank Kelly's journal that I hadn't heard before. Like Mother, he chewed up everyone in his little world, then he devoured his own heart.

Frank was scared. He equated anonymity with nonexistence. His manias went on for pages in his journal. The tight, strained cursive blanketed the onionskin pages, leaving them more black than white.

I noticed something I hadn't seen in my previous passes through the journal. Frank's handwriting changed. It became more spacious on the page, more elegant, carefully schooled, exact, yet organic and flowing. The descenders and ascenders curled in rococo loops and the Ts were crossed with swirling half swoops.

It was on the last few pages of the journal, the pages that came after Fallon's passage. But it wasn't Fallon's hand.

At first I thought someone else had started writing in Frank Kelly's journal, a third writer. But it was written with the same black ink that Frank used, and the writing still referred to all the familiar touchstones of Frank's life—his work, his anonymity, his concerns about money—all in the "I" sense.

The change began with an entry that I must have drifted over on a punt of sedatives and brandy:

Today I was visited by a muse. Literally. I always thought muses were metaphorical. Or they were hot fantasy babes that are always telling you how brilliant you are while they're peeling you a grape and changing your typewriter ribbon.

Not so. A muse can be real. I know it because mine came to me today.

This morning I woke up and looked at the clock. It was 5:12 A.M. Weird, I'm thinking, because that's the same time I've been waking up for the last few days. And the other thing is, I've had this insane urge to jump out of bed, go right for my typewriter. I'm starting to think I'm in some kind of manic episode.

This morning, same deal. I wake up and I get this powerful sense that somebody else is here in my bedroom. I don't make any sudden moves; I want to figure out who it is before I let them know I'm awake.

It's pretty dark still, but I don't want to turn on the light. I wait a few seconds for my eyes to adjust. And I see him.

There's this guy, and he's lingering in the shadows over by the desk. And he's basically just like a shadow himself, kind of wavering and indistinct. I'm thinking, I've got my hockey stick under the bed. I could reach under there, hook him from across the room, and then tomahawk him if he gives me any crap. But, for some reason, I feel like I shouldn't. Like, he's supposed to be there.

He's staring out the window, down at the parking lot next door. He's suited up pretty debonair in a long coat that hits him at about his knees. The light is dim, but he's so flash I can see the coat is velvet, emerald green. And he's wearing a puffy ascot—the early light from the window keeps catching it, so I figure it's satin. Who wears a fucking ascot?

He looks down at my typewriter, then he lifts his arm and he's got a freakin' meat hook for a hand.

Now I'm worried.

I go for my stick and I'm up out of the bed and I brandish it. I tell him, "Okay, buddy, hit the road, or I'll slap shot yer fuckin' head right off yer shoulders."

He's not even fazed. He looks at me, he taps my typewriter with his hook—I can hear it tapping, metal on metal—and he says to me, "Good morning."

It's starting to get lighter now. Slow at first. Then the sun comes blasting in just as he's looking at me. And the sunshine goes right through him.

He's shimmering, golden, in dapples like sunlight on waves. But his features are still distinctive. Hard face. Big nose, looked like it took a few hits.

He says my name. He says: Francis Kelly.

And I say, "Only my mother is allowed to call me Francis."

And he says, "It's time for you to wake up."

I'm thinking, it's time for me to wake up and kick this guy's ass. I don't care if he's got a freakin' meat hook for a hand, he's getting pummeled. No question. But I don't say that. Instead, I say, "What do you need?"

And I'm thinking, that's a weird thing to be saying to an intruder. But I said it.

Then he just goes off on this tirade, rambling, but still staying perfectly still and in a low voice, which is always more dangerous. If they start yelling, you know they're just shit-scared and blustering and hoping you'll back down. But he's talking real low and calm, like this is just another day at the office for him. Professional. And a guy like that, you know he doesn't give a shit if you take

*a shot at him or not. In fact, he probably would rather you
did.*

*He says to me: "Francis Kelly, your indolent days are
over. Today starts your finer employment in matters of
consequence. Come. Sit down at this contraption of yours
and put a tale of weight and consequence to paper so that
its eternal truth can resound in the minds and hearts of
men down the generations until the sun winks out of the
sky and the endless sea washes over all the Earth and Man
is but a memory in God's infinite mind."*

That was the last episode that Frank recorded about his life.
Reading it actually made me a little jealous. At least Fallon broached
Kelly, had a conversation with him. He didn't toy with Frank the way
he did me.

Frank dated the entry. April 18. A little more than a year later,
Frank jumped off the bridge. Whatever happened in between the
time that he met Fallon and he killed himself was not recorded. Those
pages were lost. I ran my finger down the nub of amputated pages at
the end of Frank's journal.

April 18 sounded like a familiar date, a significant date.

I went to my computer and typed April 18 into the search engine.
On that date, in 1906, the great earthquake struck. It came down from
the north, through Marin, on the San Andreas Fault. At the Golden
Gate, it jagged west, out to sea. It followed the fault south underwater,
then sharply turned back toward the shore, making landfall at Ocean
Beach.

The earthquake hit San Francisco at 5:12 A.M.

31

I promise people all sorts of things. And I do it, mainly, because I'm pretty sure they'll never follow up. This works 99 percent of the time. Detective Fung happened to fall into the 1 percent category.

He mailed me a ticket—third row, center—to the East Bay Players' production of *Crushed Dead,* a new play about greed, intrigue, and murder at a Napa Valley winery.

The ticket was wrapped in a note. Fung explained, in blocky printed lettering, that he was playing two roles: Bacchus in the play's fantasy interludes. And, in the central story, he played Baretta—a reincarnation of the iconic television detective originally played by Robert Blake.

Fung went on to say he hoped he wasn't being presumptuous for inviting me and, encased inside that hope was another, hard-pulsing neutron of a hope—that I would enjoy the play. His "treat!" he added gaily.

Next paragraph: we could/would meet afterwards for coffee to discuss the Kelly/Thibideaux cases.

Postscript: "Thought, since we need to get together anyway, we could mix Business with Pleasure."

"Business with Pleasure?" I raged, waving the ticket in Dixie's face. She rotated her head a couple of notches, trying to gauge the source of my distress.

"More like Torture with Interrogation."

Dixie is accustomed to these scenes.

She sat in the middle of the room, upright like a little man with her legs flopped open on the carpet in front of her. She opened her mouth into a wide grin, and panting, watched the spectacle unfurl.

"The authorities have overstepped," I declaimed. "Do you hear me? Dixie?"

More panting. She heard all right. And I could tell she was with me on this.

"They have gone too far," I said. "Have I not cooperated? Have I not let them into my home? Answered their questions? Have I?"

I threw the missive—envelope, note, ticket—into the fireplace. It fluttered onto the cold iron grate.

"This is intrusive. It's like KGB tactics. It's Kafkaesque. I won't have it. I won't."

The phone rang.

"Did you get the ticket I sent you?"

"Yes," I said, summoning all my skills to answer in a mellifluous tone. "Delightful."

I forced myself to smile. Over the phone, they can hear you smiling.

"It's an honor for me to have you there," Fung told me. "You being such a successful performer."

He paused a beat.

I hung suspended, uncertain whether this was a dilettante's jealous barb, or a flat-footed compliment from a flatfoot.

Fung's pause continued.

"Hello?" I said.

Fung resumed, "I hope that knowing you're in the audience doesn't make me too nervous."

"Oh, I'm sure the Method will see you through."

"Great. Tomorrow night."

"Great."

"This is a good Starbucks," Fung said.

He was drinking a grande half-caf latte. I had a shot of espresso. I looked around the café, trying to figure out how this Starbucks—with its regulation green franchise décor, mermaid logo, and over-packaged sandwiches—was different from the other three Starbucks in the Walnut Creek downtown shopping district.

"I enjoyed the play," I told him.

It was good, in fact. I was entertained. Good script. Clever stage direction. And well performed.

Fung, in particular, was mesmerizing—in a creepy, unsettling way that kept you wondering if he was trying to be weird, or if he just was. His Bacchus was laconic, disengaged. He played the great party god in the opposite register to the usual ribald, raucous character. Fung's Bacchus was distracted, disengaged. In the frenzied bacchanalia scene he stood on a wine barrel, hands limp at his sides, staring ahead like Boo Radley.

Fung played Baretta close to the television original. He went around spouting pseudo-seventies street patois like "that's the name of that tune" and mouthing an unlit cigarette until it must have been as soggy as a squeegee. At the end of the play, when he's solved the crimes, he lit the cigarette in triumph. I found that rewarding.

"I liked that business at the end of act two," I said. "When you were running after the killer and dodging the wine bottles he was throwing at you."

"Thanks. That took a lot of physicality," he said, deadpan.

Then he veered into another lane without a signal.

"When Betty Ann Thibideaux left your home the night she died, what did she say? Where was she going?"

"She didn't say anything. Not to me. I told you that. I was in the kitchen. She was in the living room. She was talking to someone on her cell phone. Then she bolted out the door without even saying good-bye."

He closed his eyes, made a face like he was suppressing a grimace, and tremored his big square head. I wondered if he was using Method, now, on me.

"Is there something wrong?" I asked.

"Did she seem frightened that night?"

"She seemed fanatical. She wanted Frank's journal and she was willing to pay me for it."

"Yes," he said. "Frank."

A barista clanked the metal lid shut on the coffee grinder, turned it on. The cracking and grinding of shredding coffee beans ripped through the air.

"Why do you suppose she wanted Mr. Kelly's journal so badly," Fung asked. "Did he mention her in it?"

I'd wondered the same thing, of course, and had very deliberately gone back over the journal several times trying to glean references to Betty Ann Thibideaux. They were scarce. And neutral. Frank's journal wasn't an historical archive. He was mostly writing in the present—the last year or so of his life—and Betty Ann hadn't been around for nearly two decades. To Frank, she had become only a few faded memories.

I told Fung that. He looked thoughtfully at his grande cup, peeled the plastic lid off of it.

"You said she got the phone call. She didn't dial out."

"Correct."

"And you don't know who called?"

"Correct."

"We looked at the phone record. The call was made from Rod's Hickory Pit in Vallejo. Have you ever been there?"

"I don't think it's in the Michelin Guide, is it?"

"You've never been there?"

I stated that I had not.

"We think someone called Ms. Thibideaux from the Hickory Pit, and she went to meet that person."

"I thought someone had called with bad news," I said. "And that's why she killed herself."

He finished the last of his latte and started to systematically fold in the cardboard cup, closing the opening until the top of it was sealed neatly shut.

"I'm going to tell you something that is classified," Fung said. "We can't have this information getting out. Can you keep a secret?"

I nodded. Fung peeled open one of the cardboard strips at the top of his coffee cup.

"Ms. Thibideaux's body," he said, and this sudden shift to forensics surprised me, "was very badly damaged. They always are when they come off the bridge."

"Yes," I said. "I've heard. The impact."

The barista poured another bag of coffee beans into the grinder. It roared again, shredding the hard little beans in its gargling maw.

"Almost all the bones were fractured," he said. "The organs in the abdominal cavity were like soup."

I felt sick. Betty Ann was a huge pain in the ass, but I was mortified to think of her ending that way.

"There was something odd in the coroner's report, though," Fung said.

"Odd?" I said.

"This is the part you have to keep absolutely confidential, Max."

I nodded, again.

"Ms. Thibideaux had a bullet in her chest."

32

I was in L.A., onstage, playing Pluto. The bastards wouldn't let me have the cat I'd wanted to carry around in front of my exposed torso, so I had to bear it—and bare it. I pretended I was a middle-aged Sicilian man at the beach in a Speedo. I exposed my ample physique with nonchalance. It worked for me.

We played three weeks, twelve performances. On the last night, Duffy Fallon showed up.

I was standing in Hell, surrounded by cumulous banks of dry ice mists and crepe-paper flames. I was watching Orpheus ascend the Styrofoam mountain, winding his way up and out of Hell's gate. Eurydice followed behind him.

As he did every performance, Orpheus blew it. He turned and looked at Eurydice before exiting Hell, thereby breaking my (Pluto's) direct order. One thing. One thing I asked him to do, and it's the exact thing he doesn't do!

So, Eurydice is ticked off too. She sings, "Ah, sight too sweet and too bitter! Thus, then through excess of love you lose me?"

The spirits start singing, informing them both that he has to leave, and she has to return to Hell. Eurydice, stone-faced, starts to descend back down into the sulfur and the flames. She was coming straight back toward me. I held out my arms to her, as I always did, and she stopped.

I was thinking, what now! Perhaps the soprano was having some kind of seizure. Her face froze, in a mask. Silence whirled all around me. It pounded and echoed. The audience fell away, and beyond the lights was only a swirl of black tides, pooling and splashing over the orchestra pit.

The soprano moved closer to me, gliding as if on rollers. Her face was as immobile as those of the plastic saints in the Santeria shop window. And from her sealed lips came a voice.

It was a woman's voice, high and silver. She said, "Find me. Find me, Max."

Eurydice's face cracked. A fissure tore down her forehead, through her right eye, and on down over her right cheek. The two plates of her face then separated, fell apart, and a new face was revealed beneath this sundered mask.

It was dainty, fragile. It was the face of a young Cantonese woman, perfect and symmetrical. A child's face, elaborately made up like a painted doll.

I heard a splashing to my left. I looked over to the footlights. Duffy Fallon, dripping with salt water, walked up out of the orchestra pit.

"Your work is not done, Max Bravo," he said to me.

"You surprise me, sir," I answered him. "I don't recall having offered to do anything for you."

"You didn't offer," Fallon said. "I'm demanding. And you will accede to my wish."

"What do you want?"

"You already know. Find Ah Ho. Find her. Give her the ring that I intended for her. If you don't, I will harry you to Hell, and on into Eternity."

"What ring?" I said. "What do you want?"

The lights flashed, blinding me. A great thundering roar washed over me. I felt hands squeezing mine. I looked to my right. Eurydice was holding my hand. One of the Spirits was on my left.

The audience was on its feet. Applauding.

33

I was back home, asleep in my own bed after nearly two months in Los Angeles. I was awoken by a violent commotion at my front door. Someone was pressing the doorbell so that it bonged in one long sustain.

Dixie barked, muffled under the covers, still half asleep. The bonging continued like shock shelling. Dixie stood up, barked angrily, and twirled in circles trying to find her way out from under the blanket.

Whoever was out front gave up on the doorbell. Now they were smashing the clapper, the iron Chinese dragon, with manic ferocity.

Dixie, furious now, sprang out from under the covers and stood on the bed barking, stamping her front paws.

The clapper smashing stopped. Dixie turned to look at me, dialed her head around in an interrogative.

"God," I said to Dixie. "I thought they'd never leave."

The bedroom window exploded.

Glass shards flew into the room and scattered silently about the carpet. The heavy projectile that accompanied them landed on the carpet with a thud, and rolled several feet before it found its resting place. I recognized it. It was one of the decorative word rocks from my garden display. The phrase on this one was "Be Present." I wished I'd never let the guy at the garden center talk me into buying the goddamn things.

By now, I was sitting up. Dixie, abandoning her offensive stance, scampered around behind me and leaned into my back.

I got out of bed, naked, and crept slow like a lemur across the carpet, careful not to step on the broken glass. I peered out.

Ashley Banks was standing in my flower bed, trampling my zinnias. She had another of my decorative rocks in her hand.

I flung the window open, and yelled, "What the hell are you doing?"

"Why didn't you answer the door?" she yelled back.

I pulled my head in, snatched up my kimono off the floor, and tried to punch my arms into the sleeves. I could only manage one— the damn puppy sleeves were always getting twisted up—and made do by wrapping half the kimono around in a toga-style. I pounded down the stairs.

"You've got a lot of explaining to do," she said.

She careened past my threshold. Stopped. Turned to examine me.

"Why are you wearing your robe like that?" she demanded.

She didn't wait to hear my answer. She charged down the hallway to the kitchen.

She announced, "I need coffee."

"You need a restraining order," I said, padding after her, wrestling my bare arm into the dragging kimono sleeve.

She tossed her heavy handbag on the table, dropped herself onto a chair. She looked haggard. I rinsed yesterday's coffee out of the carafe and put a kettle on the stove.

"That goddamn ghoul you stirred up over at Blashky's is after my kid," she said.

"Don't start," I snapped at her. "Give me a minute, will you."

I pushed the hair out of my eyes, adjusted my sash. I cranked the faucet on hot, ran a cloth under it, wrung it out. I wiped off the countertops. Ashley sat at the kitchen table, lifted her elbows when I came over to wipe that off too.

She started to speak again.

"Ah!" I said, holding up a finger.

She closed her mouth.

"You can get on your phone," I said, my back to her as I worked clearing up some dirty dishes.

"You can call up a window repair service and get them over here *tout de suite*. You're paying for it."

She didn't argue. Within a few minutes she had the repairman arranged.

I handed her a coffee cup. She curled her long fingers around it, impervious to the heat. Her fingernail polish was chipped. No doubt from prying the decorative elements out of my garden display.

"Thanks, Max." She grabbed my hand and squeezed it.

"All right," I said, finally sitting at the table. I took a drink of coffee, sat back in the banquette, and motioned with my hand for her to come forward with her story.

"The ghost," she said. "Or whatever it is. The thing in Stan's apartment—it's been contacting Dante. It's doing something with him."

"Doing something?"

"It's been brainwashing him, or I don't know what. The ghost, it's a man, yes? It has Dante under some sort of influence."

I thought of Quint in Henry James's *The Turn of the Screw*. He was the pervy tutor who "interferes" with his young charges in life, and then comes back to corrupt them further after he's dead. I decided not to mention that to Ashley.

I proceeded softly.

"I know about the presence in Stan's flat," I told her. "And I'm dead certain, so to speak, that I know exactly who it is."

She looked at me, a little more composed now.

"It's a fellow who perished in the 1906 earthquake," I said. "In the vicinity. Near Stan's place."

I very deliberately did not disclose that Fallon's bones would still be interred somewhere beneath the adjoining parking lot. In the mayhem following the initial quake, police and city officials moved quickly to remove bodies, lest cholera break out. In the case of the Valencia Hotel victims, no one knew exactly how many were trapped in the first two floors when the building sank and filled with water. Crews quickly removed the top of the building, and shoveled dirt over the debris resting more than six feet down.

Any of the buried drowning victims that were below the six-foot excavation level were left where they perished. Balzac's research revealed that Fallon lived in the back of the building, on the first floor.

The marker for Fallon's grave in the Mission cemetery stood vigil over nothing but dirt. Fallon was down there, at the site where he died, moldered under the cracked asphalt.

"This Duffield Fallon character," I told Ashley. "He didn't expect to die that morning."

"I don't suppose anyone did," she said.

"There's something he's left undone. And that's why he's here. It's not because he gets a kick out of terrorizing us all."

The last part I wasn't so sure about. I reckoned Fallon did savor the smell of fear, the exertion of elective cruelty. But Ashley didn't need to know that either.

I sketched Fallon's bio for her in only the most salient strokes, rather like a caricature, simplified but narrative. I told her he'd been a bit of man about town, portraying him as more of a boulevardier than of a common thug and a pimp. I said that he was a "bodyguard" for a prominent Chinese businessman, Little Pete. I didn't mention that Pete's business was opium smuggling and sex slavery.

Even the sanitized version didn't convince her that Fallon was benign.

"I'm afraid he's going to hurt Dante," she said simply.

"I don't see how he could," I told her.

"Tell that to Frank Kelly," she shot back at me.

I told her there was nothing to connect Fallon with Frank's death. I couched it as nothing "definitive" at any rate, just to keep marginally within the range of truth.

She stopped arguing the point. It wasn't that she agreed. She was just all tapped out. Her eyes were sunken, red. Her skin was pale, matte. The scar—usually subsumed by the strength of her manner—had grown fierce. It bit across her forehead and under her right eye, raw and enraged.

I asked her to tell me exactly how this communication between Fallon and the boy started. What did they talk about? Was there something specific that Fallon wanted Dante to do for him?

Ashley took a long breath, sat up straight. She started her explanation in a roundabout, as if she couldn't find the actual headwaters of her trauma.

She told me that Dante sometimes stays at Blashky's—whenever she had to work late or go out of town on business. She'd been in Boulder, working on an annual report for a data storage company.

It was a relatively quick trip, just three days. She went straight from the airport to Blashky's to get Dante. It was late. She decided to spend the night.

I flinched.

"Sorry, Max," she said.

"Awkward."

"Yeah. But, you know that I'm with Stan."

"Awkwarder."

She described how Dante seemed fine when she got to Blashky's. He was excited to see her. Dante had a lot of stories he was anxious to tell her. Apparently three days with Stan Blashky is a zestful slice of life for a ten-year-old boy.

Stan and Dante went to the Academy of Sciences and saw the alligators. They had waffles for supper. They bought lotto tickets at the corner liquor store. They watched baseball. They went to the

Laundromat. Stan sent Dante to panhandle a lady for a cup of detergent because they ran out and Stan had spent his last two dollars on the can of beer that he was drinking out of a brown paper bag.

"Yes," I said. "It's easy to see why you wouldn't want to risk losing Stan Blashky for a bum like me."

"This isn't about us," she said.

"There is no us," I sniffed.

"Stan helps me, Max."

"So what's the problem?"

"I woke up really early. Before the sun was up, around five. I heard Dante in the next room, talking. I thought maybe he'd called somebody, on his cell phone. I went in there, and there was a man in the bedroom. He was standing by the window. It was that guy. Fallon."

"Go on," I said.

"I ran in there, pulled Dante out of the bed. I kept screaming for Stan."

"Where was Stan?"

"He woke up. He came running in the room. He saw the guy too. That guy, Max, he just looked at us. And then, the sun came up. The light came through the window. It shot straight through him like he was glass. It seemed to melt him, to make him transparent. Stan and I were completely stunned. And he disappeared. He evaporated."

"Stan told me something was going on over there," I said. I fidgeted, arranged my coffee cup and the sugar bowl, and concentrated on how normal a breakfast table always looks.

"I knew that too," Ashley continued. "Kind of spooky. But that's pretty typical in this town. So many old houses. And this place has always been a magnet for weirdos and eccentrics."

"They don't get any saner when they die, do they?" I said.

"Right," she said. "Every single person I know here has at least one ghost story. So when Stan told me he was starting to notice things moving around the flat—his glasses, the newspaper, whatever—I didn't think anything about it."

"Sure," I said. "And with Stan he could have just been drunk."

"And Fallon never actually showed himself," she said. "Not until we caught him in Dante's room."

"Frank's room originally." I was thinking out loud.

"Fallon had something to do with Frank's suicide," she said, flashing anger. "You knew it. And you didn't tell me."

"I didn't know for sure what was going on." I touched on the subject as light as iodine-soaked cotton balls on an open wound. "Stan was only just noticing things—things that were happening. It wasn't anything worth panicking about."

Ashley opened her mouth as if to speak. Then she closed it again. She stared at me, trying to decide just how angry she should be.

I got up from the table, got away from her. I went over to the sink, looked out the window at the back garden. The neighbor's tomcat—a feral six-toed beast with a head like a Gila monster—was mincing across the top of the fence. He stopped, feeling my eyes on him, and turned his scarred predator face toward me. He pulled back his black lips and his mouth opened wide. His plaintive yowl fell mute against the watery glass of the kitchen window.

Ashley spoke to my turned back, my cowardly back.

"I need you to get rid of Fallon, Max," she said. "I'm afraid that even if Dante stays away from the flat, Fallon will look for him. He'll find him."

I knew she was right. And I knew I wasn't the strong man, the steady captain, she needed me to be. I was nothing but an inept sailor—well, maybe more of a ship's steward, or actually, the piano bar guy—lost, clinging to a piece of flotsam on a turbulent sea. I was grotesquely miscast.

"Let's have a brandy," I said, reaching into the cupboard for the Calvados, the good bottle that I kept at the back hidden behind the Courvoisier.

I set two juice glasses on the table and filled them halfway.

The tragic ballerina, the woman with the broken china doll face, sat slumped in a chair at my kitchen table. Ashley. The Lady of Ashes. She was the woman who had died and was resurrected. And her face bore the mark of the fire she passed through.

That's what I had found in the newspaper clippings anyway—that she'd actually been clinically dead when the ambulance arrived at the scene of the motorcycle accident. They brought her back from death. But when she returned, she no longer had her art. She could still dance. Her body was intact. She still had her instrument, and its power of expression. But what company could put her on stage with that disfigurement? At least, not back then.

She came back as a shadow of what she had been. In a way, she was a ghost herself. She was like Duffield Fallon.

"Is that your answer, Max?" she said.

"I'm sorry," I said, putting the brandy in her hand. "What was the question?"

"What are you going to do to get rid of Fallon," she said, repeating herself in bluntly shaped syllables. "Sitting here drinking brandy isn't going to get rid of that Fallon. That horrible thing."

"No, of course not, darling. But we must take this in baby steps. Cheers!"

She allowed herself to smile, in a grim, cockeyed way. She took a drink. Lowered the glass onto the table, regarded it for a moment, then snatched it back up and finished it off. I poured her another. And, damned if I didn't start to get that warm feeling for her again. Inappropriate. Surely. Especially under the circumstances.

But one can't micromanage these impulses, or even predict them. And there was something distinctly inviting about the way she was knocking back the Calvados—given our history with daytime drinking—and I became acutely aware of the fact that she was here, in my home, and we were alone. And I was rather scantily clad in nothing but my kimono and I reckoned I looked rather rumpled in that "I just rolled out of bed quite satisfied with myself" kind of way.

She smiled again, this time allowing the smile to spread full-wise across her face so that her lips pulled back from her teeth. And I noticed, again, how her face looked more symmetrical when she smiled like this, with unalloyed delight. She looked so much like the beauty she once was.

She had been stunning. I remembered that. Her beauty struck you in flashes, in quick-cut montages. It was in the plane of the cheek, the angle of the hip. There was a flicker of gold in those copper eyes, and the tongue flashed red and pointed and I would have signed over the pink slip on my car to have that tongue lash my bare skin.

Her shattered beauty was now a resonating echo. It rippled like torn tapestries in the breeze blowing through the empty chambers of a ransacked Versailles.

Ashley knew I was studying her. I suppose people had always stared at her. Before the accident, they had stared at her because she was so beautiful. Afterward, because she was so damaged.

She reached in her bag, pulled out her sunglasses. She very matter-of-factly put them on, and then again relaxed with her brandy.

She was fortunate to have that eye—the disturbing eye that she always wanted to keep covered. The doctors went to extraordinary measures to save it. They operated on her nine times, trying to piece the right side of her face back together.

"You're lucky to be alive," I said, continuing the stream of my thoughts into speech.

"I knew you were thinking that," she said. "People often say that when they start looking at the scars. When they let themselves get caught up in the accident. In the violence of it."

"I guess what I was really thinking," I said to her, "is that I'm lucky. I'm the one who's lucky that you're still alive."

The sunlight came through the window, reflecting cold off the white Formica of the kitchen table. Ashley twirled the tawny brandy in her glass, set it down, very exactly, on the ring that her snifter had already left on the tabletop. Brandy eased down the inside of the glass on long sticky legs.

"You don't think about it?" I said. "The accident?"

"It's been too long."

"You're not bitter?"

"I would have lost my looks eventually anyway, Max. At least I was very beautiful once. Most people never even get that."

"What about your career? I suppose it cost you that."

"It did," she said. She lit a cigarette. "But dancers—most of us, the ones who don't go on to choreography—know that our time is short. We don't enjoy the long careers that you opera singers have."

"Quite."

I thought about how, in the course of enjoying my long career, I'd gone from playing dashing, sexy romantic leads to support characters with all manner of physical and mental impediments. I was a king. Now, I was a joker. Endurance does not always deliver sweet rewards.

"Your ex-husband," I said. "Is he Dante's dad?"

She didn't answer the question. She unzipped her sweater. Underneath, she was wearing nothing.

That changed the subject.

"Right," I said.

I set my glass down and slapped my palms onto my knees. I started to stand up. I had made a vow to myself that I wouldn't do this again.

She reached for me, scooped up the lapels of my kimono in her fists and pushed me back down onto my chair. She sat back down in hers and dropped her foot in my lap. She was wearing cowboy boots. They were low-heeled and snub-toed and water stained.

She laughed. She took hold of the heel and pulled off the boot.

Then she pulled the other boot off.

Her feet were bare. And her toenails were painted gray like smoldering coals.

34

"That woman is going to get your nose broken for you."

I opened my eyes. Baba was sitting on the edge of my bed filing her nails.

"What time is it?" I asked.

"Time for you to stop fooling around with that dilo gadja, Max!" She poked me in the forehead with her emery board, then set back into scraping it across those pointed talons of hers.

"Damn you," I cried, throwing my pillow at her. It swept through her and landed on the floor. "You pester me when I sleep with men. Now you pester me about this woman."

"I think you are a mental retard, Max."

Maybe not retarded. But I had to admit, even I noted an absence of prudent judgment on my own part.

I got out of bed. Ashley had crept out in the middle of the night, once again, leaving me behind in a black, dreamless sleep, twisted up in the damp bedding. I made coffee, stood under a hot shower, and contemplated the ferocious libido of the modern middle-aged woman.

I opened my clothes closet. Baba was standing in between my burgundy velvet smoking jacket and my salt-and-pepper sport coat. She was going through my pockets, adding items to her cache of half-empty cheroot packs, BART passes, and crumpled dollar bills that she clutched in her knobby, gnarled phalanges. She whipsawed her head around and regarded me like a startled scrub jay.

"Excuse me," I said.

She vanished. I pulled the houndstooth off the hanger and grabbed a polyester shirt festooned with emerald blue peacocks.

Baba appeared on the divan in the bay window. She was lighting one of the cheroots she'd just looted from my closet. I sat on the edge of the bed and laced up my boots.

"I have to deal with this Duffy Fallon individual," I told her.

"He's becoming a nuisance," she remarked, as if she weren't one herself.

I pulled the sheets off the bed and stuffed them in the hamper. I opened one of the bay windows to draw the cheroot smoke out of the bedroom, and I collected a fresh set of sheets from the armoire. Baba observed me making the bed, her eyelids squinting against the spark with every pull on the cheroot.

"Could he become more than a nuisance?" I asked, punching and plumping the pillows. "Could he become dangerous? To the child, I mean. The boy."

"Little Dante?"

"Yes."

I smoothed the sheets, hospital corners.

"Fallon is becoming angry," Baba said. "Frank Kelly failed him. Now you people are ignoring him."

"What does he want from us?"

"You have to ask him, don't you?" she said.

A direct conversation with Duffy Fallon was the last thing I wanted to initiate. I'd already been living with Baba, the spectral couch-surfer, for nearly a decade. She was forever ransacking my supply of intoxicants and smoking materials. She was an obsessive, querulous meddler into my personal affairs. And her very presence, indeed, her ubiquity, kept the discomfiting polemic about my mental health forever in play. No one else ever saw her, which she claimed was not by her choice. And I could not disclose her presence to anyone, not even my closest confidantes, lest I be carted off to a group home and have some of my distant—corporeal—relatives swoop in to take possession of my much-coveted domicile.

I didn't need another ghost in my life. Those people simply did not recognize the bounds of polite behavior.

Unfortunately, I had promised Ashley that I'd address the Duffy Fallon issue.

"How do I deal with this Fallon?" I sat down next to Baba on the divan. She passed me the cheroot and I took a drag.

"Handle him carefully," she said. "Use the proper methods."

"Can't I just hire somebody to take care of him?"

"No, it's a personal matter. He is angry with Frank Kelly. He believes he was betrayed. And since he can't find Frank Kelly, he holds you responsible for him."

"Oh, this is really too much," I said, smashing the cheroot out in an empty coffee cup. "Why am I always picking up after that loser Frank Kelly? Why don't you tell Frank to talk to Fallon?"

"Frank Kelly hasn't been through yet," she said.

"What?"

"I haven't seen him. He hasn't been through."

That was odd.

"He hasn't been through?" I repeated her words. "What does that mean? How does it work? Is there some processing station?"

"Sure, Max. Is organized. What you think? Everybody just show up! You check in. You get processed. Like Ellis Island."

"No Frank Kelly yet?"

"No. Frank Kelly has not come through."

"No dead Frank Kelly."

"No," she said.

"Then he's not dead!" I announced.

"I didn't say that." She motioned for me to sit back down, settle myself. "Sometimes they get hung up on their way in. They get confused. Should I be dead? Should I be alive? Some of them get all mixed up thinking that crap."

I didn't know which was more disconcerting: the thought of Frank Kelly's spectral soul out there in limbo pacing back and forth, wringing his hands, or Frank Kelly hiding somewhere here on earth, letting us all think he was dead.

"Third possibility," Baba started in.

"Stop reading my damn thoughts!" I snapped.

"Again, I tell you I don't have thought-reading power," she said. "It's just that you are so transparent."

"All right, just go ahead. What is third possibility?"

"Maybe he jumped off bridge. Hit his head. And now he is retarded, living in street covered in filth. No one would recognize him. In San Francisco, no one would even notice him."

No, I told her. I would have seen him. I walked those streets every day, ranging far and wide. I don't just pass by the armies of indigents and abandoned mental patients that crowd the streets. I look at them. I would have recognized Frank Kelly no matter how degraded and deranged he might have become.

It was true that they hadn't yet recovered Frank's body from the bay. And I had had my suspicions as to whether or not he was truly dead, especially since I'd realized he'd stuck that Ken Kesey riff in his suicide note.

But, Frank had been caught on camera at the rail. And surely— when you actuated his chances of surviving a leap off the Golden Gate Bridge—surely, he was dead, and the sea had taken his remains.

"Maybe he's in a waiting room up there somewhere?" I offered. "Or, down there. Purgatory. Some outer circle?"

Baba shrugged, cast the corners of her mouth down, and exhaled gustily over her flapping lips. She nodded her head up and down, the borscht belt gesture signifying no.

Frank could have survived the jump, some jumpers had. But the survivors always came dragging up out of the drink with the same altered worldview. Universally, they report that as soon they left the rail, and hurtled toward the hard, grim sea, one thought screamed through their heads: Why the hell did I do that?

And, if they happen to hit the water at just the right angle, and if a small vessel happens to be within grappling hook distance of their point of impact, they always emerge from the cold, salty waters as a newborn babe from the amniotic fluids: they are, without exception, damned glad to be alive.

If Frank Kelly went through all that and survived, we'd have heard about it.

"You have to talk to Duffy Fallon," Baba said. "You have to help Stan exorcise him from that house on Valencia Street."

"Will you help me?" I was openly begging.

"I love you, Max," she said. "But this you must do on your own. First, get the correct materials. Go to the shop at the corner of Valencia and Twenty-first Street. See the woman named Amarantha."

"Ama what?"

She didn't answer.

She smiled, beneficent. She became translucent. She repeated, I love you, Max. And, for a glowing instant, I could see through her weathered visage to the beautiful young woman she had been.

In the time between the great wars of the twentieth century in Europe, my grandmother was young, a wild Gypsy woman with long forelocks clinking with coins, kohl-smudged eyes, and copper bracelets banding her forearms. She sang, guttural and plaintive, evoking the Vedic chants echoing across the dusty plains of Rajasthan.

She shimmered. Her younger self, the dewy dark woman, came to the fore and the encasement of years and decades melted away. She laughed, tin hammers trilling across taut steel wires. Her form pixilated, slowly. The cells of her body separated and glowed golden. She lit a cheroot, took a deep drag. I could see the smoke fluming down her trachea, it rolled through the bronchia of her lungs, blossoming out of the alveoli. And she was gone, leaving only a puff of smoke where she had been.

I heard her voice echoing from far away. It was crystalline and ringing cold across a north night sky. Striking dulcimers of ice.

"Amarantha. Amarantha. Amarantha."

I had just recently looked up the word *amaranth*. Milton refers to it in *Paradise Lost*. The amaranth is an unfading flower. It never dies.

35

My ex-wife once accused me of being an *anomic* personality. That's how I knew she was having an affair with her psychotherapist.

Beyond that, I didn't actually know what the term meant. Connie explained—with a sigh and a weary pedantry designed to convey how tedious my superficiality had become—that an anomic person was socially unstable. Alienated. Disorganized.

I dismissed the accusation as baseless and went on about my business, attending to my three interests at that time: a macho tango instructor from Buenos Aires who had an "arrangement" with his wife, a pastry chef with large breasts who did interesting things with meringue, and a fragile accountant who was devastated by her own husband's infidelities.

Connie divorced me. Within a year, I couldn't recall her face without the aid of a snapshot or a publicity portrait of her in costume on a playbill. She had ceased to exist. But the memory of her routine personality dissections remained.

Anomic. The word sounded in my head unexpectedly. It did whenever I grew anxious that my impulses had overridden my survival instinct.

Stan Blashky could easily reach out and crack my skull with two swipes of his bear paws. And sleeping with his girlfriend might be just the sort of thing that Blashky would take personally.

That morning, after my second indiscretion with Ashley Banks, I vowed to never again touch the woman. I'd start afresh. Again.

I'd treat her cordially, with respect. It would be as though nothing happened. I would be Stan's trustworthy friend. I would be a better friend to him than I had ever been.

I would start by ridding him of the Duffy Fallon pestilence.

I put on my leather sport coat and my porkpie hat. I fed the dog and left her in the house.

"What's up," Blashky said. He wasn't surprised that I was at his door, unannounced.

He had fishing gear spread out all over his living-room floor. There were three creels, what looked to be six or seven rods all disconnected in a pile of blue and silver lengths, and a round wire crab trap about the size of a beanbag chair.

"I've got a possible solution to your ghost problem," I told him.

"Do you see the other part of this rod?" he asked me. He was screwing together the tip and middle shaft.

I picked up a length of rod with the handle and reel attached. He checked it and found it fit.

"Thanks," he said. "Now let's find one for you, Max."

"Look," I said. "I think we can take care of this Fallon character. Don't you care?"

"Sure, Max. But it's a beautiful day. Let's get down to the pier. I was just about to call you."

A couple hours later we were standing on a derelict concrete pier at the southern foot of the Golden Gate Bridge. I complained of the cold. Blashky explained that the shade made ours the ideal spot for fishing. It provided structure, he said. He outfitted my hook with a live crustacean.

"Ghost shrimp," he said.

"What?"

"That's the name of the brand," Blashky told me. "Ghost shrimp. It's the best for this open-sea pier fishing."

"Thanks," I said.

He offered to cast out my line. I rebuffed him. I wasn't that big a sissy. Blashky was impressed with the grace and distance of my cast.

We sat on the edge of the crumbling concrete pier, drinking a couple cans of beer he'd pulled out of his tackle box.

"Ever meet Dante?" he asked.

I immediately felt a hollow spooned out of my guts, and my palms began sweating onto the cork of my fishing rod handle.

"Who?" I asked, staring at the choppy water.

"Ashley's kid."

"No. Of course not. When would I have met him?"

"You don't have to get snappy, Max. I just couldn't remember if you met him or not."

He lifted his arm and shifted forward. I flinched, but I was pretty sure he didn't notice. He reached around to his back pocket and pulled out his wallet.

"Here," he said, opening the wallet and removing a bright little snapshot. "This is him. He's a little bigger now. This is last year. But he still looks pretty much the same."

I took the photo up by the white border, careful not to smudge the image with my fingertips. It was a school photo, a head shot. The kid in the picture wore a bright red turtleneck that stood out against the marine blue backdrop.

I held the photo up to examine it. Dante looked like a funny kid. A little wise guy. The kind of kid who disrupts the classroom by mimicking the teacher with myna bird accuracy. His ferret-skinny face was strafed with freckles. His mouth was open, the kind of kid that never shuts up.

"He looks familiar," I said.

"I don't think he looks anything like his mom," Blashky said.

"No, nothing like Ashley," I said. "Maybe the father."

I put on my reading glasses. The kid's teeth were narrow, but still jostled to fit into his little, thin-lipped mouth. His eyes were an icy blue and his hair was dark—nearly black—and tousled in careless curls.

"Oh wow," Blashky said. "I forgot I had this in here."

He pulled a tiny Ziploc bag out of his wallet.

"What is that?" I asked.

"It was stuck behind Dante's picture."

"What is it?" I asked again.

"It's acid, dude."

I handed Dante's photo back to Blashky. He returned it carefully to the vellum sleeve. But he kept the baggie pinched tightly in his fingers.

"We should do this," he said.

"What?"

"This acid."

"What are you? Timothy Leary? Fuck off."

An hour later I was starting to feel the first waves of prickly heat, and a pulsing echo chamber of howls buffeted inside my ears. It sounded like wind, only it didn't just blow in one direction. It blasted in, and then withdrew—like waves. And the stern voice intoned in my head. It was that same voice I've heard every time I embarked on an ill-advised acid trip—which was every time I'd done acid.

The voice said, "For the next ten hours, you are mine."

I was at the mercy of that most unmerciful of drugs, LSD.

"I can't believe I let you talk me into this," I said to Stan. "You're a fucking asshole, Blashky."

"Just be mellow, dude," he told me. "Let's enjoy the beautiful ocean waves."

"Fuck you, Blashky," I suggested.

I looked at the ocean waves. They weren't beautiful. They were gunmetal gray, and threatening. They were a sealed hatch door, clamped over the top of a liquid death chamber.

"And don't call me dude," I said to Blashky. "Christ, do you know we're sitting mere meters from where Frank Kelly jumped. What if his body washes up, right here? Or we hook it and reel it in. And we're all fucked-up. We couldn't even call the police. I can't even push the buttons on my cell phone."

Blashky didn't answer me. He was transfixed, reading the label on the ghost shrimp jar.

"Max, listen. Did you know that the guy who makes ghost shrimp tests it himself in his pool?"

"Yes. I'm sure it's all very scientific."

"It says that it's good for tournament fishing and casual anglers."

I took the bait from him, tossed it back in the tackle box, and slammed the lid shut.

"You're definitely a casual angler," Blashky said.

My line tugged and the tip of my rod bowed. It snapped back up. Then tugged again.

"I'm good," Blashky was saying. "But I don't know if I'd qualify as tournament class."

He seemed dejected.

"Can you help me with this?" I said. "There seems to be something on the line. Probably some sea creature."

He brightened.

I looked out to the red bobber riding the water's turbulent surface. Blashky watched the water, his mouth hanging ajar.

"You know what was the biggest prehistoric creature?" he suddenly asked, turning to me with a blank earnestness smudged across his big meaty face.

"Alistair Crowley," I ventured.

He stared at me.

"Megalodon," he said. "The giant shark. It was sixty-six feet long, bigger than a six-story building. You could drive an doolie truck into its mouth, man."

My bobber twitched, then snapped under the water. It stayed under.

"You got something, dude," Blashky said.

"What?"

"A fish, man."

I mechanically began turning the handle on the reel.

"Pull up, pull up," Blashky exhorted. "Pull and hold the rod up, he's got too much slack. Now, ease off. Let him get that hook stuck good in his mouth."

I pulled the rod up. It bowed so sharply I was afraid it would snap. The fish, or perhaps the Megalodon, dove deeper into the water, battling against my pull. I let him run deep, taking out several meters of line. When he stopped running, I again began cranking the reel, pulling him in toward the shore. He was getting tired now. I could feel his strength dissipating.

Blashky grabbed the hand net and slid off the lip of the pier. He held his own rod high above his head as he picked his way to the shoreline, over the piles of broken concrete that looked like the aftermath of a building collapse. He got to the water's edge and wedged his rod between a couple of jagged cement boulders. He waded into the water up to his ankles, brandishing the hand net.

A flash of dark brown broke the surface. Blashky yelled to me to give it a yank. I did and the fish came out of the sea. The creature contorted his long, sleek body into an *S*. The sun, now high in the sky, cast the fish's shadow across the surface of the iron gray sea. The shadow was fleeting. The creature plunged back below the water. This time it seemed harder for him to break into the sea, as if the molecules forming the water's surface had transformed it into a more solid substance—as if the water had turned into glass.

Blashky called to me to reel him in, hard and quick. I stood up, held the pole high, bracing the butt of it against my chest. I cranked the reel, using all my strength. The cars overhead sped across the bridge, the sound of tires droning along the asphalt. A giant freighter—big as a Megalodon, I thought—drifted in from the open sea. It glided under the bridge, entering the Bay nose first, its long open deck stacked high with red, yellow, and blue cargo containers marked with kanji lettering.

The fish flagged. I could feel his strength draining away. Then it abruptly spilled out. He had given up on his life.

The line went slack. I turned the crank and hauled him, inert, up to the water's edge. Blashky scooped him up in the hand net and carried him, with both hands gripping the net's long handle, across the rocks, and back up onto the pier. The fish collapsed deep in the net. He was folded in on himself.

"Max, you got a sturgeon," he told me. He was delighted.

"Oh my God," I said. "He looks prehistoric."

"Yeah. That's your sturgeons. They're pretty much the same as they were back in the Pleistocene. Evolution didn't touch these guys."

Blashky flipped open the lid to his tackle box and riffled through the tangled fishing line and iron weights and rusty hooks. He pulled out a ball-peen hammer.

"What are you doing?" I gasped.

"Max, we gotta kill him. To eat him," Blashky said. "We didn't pull him up here to make him a pet."

Blashky raised the hammer and struck the sturgeon on the side of the head. The fish jolted up. I screamed. It wasn't dead after all.

Blashky struck him again, this time with more force and accuracy. The fish fell still. Blashky lifted up the bowl of the net, upended it, and the dead sturgeon slapped out onto the table of flat cement.

It was a vicious-looking creature. Long and powerful, it wore its hard, knobbed skin like a suit of armor. Fluted spikes raked along its back and sides in three straight lines. Its sharp face jutted querulously. And its narrow mouth gaped, bristling with sharp teeth that filliped into an elaborate underbite at the tip.

"Let's throw it back in the water," I said.

"Max. Don't be such a fag. It's dead."

I was certain I saw the tail flicking, like the tail of a cat watching a goldfish in a bowl.

"How can you be sure?"

Blashky hoisted up the fish in both hands, turned it around to face him as though it were a three-foot submarine sandwich he was about to eat. He brought the fish to his face and kissed it on its hard black lips.

I jumped back. My heart was racing and the sea was pounding

hard against the shore. The sound of the cars skimming the asphalt overhead became louder. Blashky laughed. But his laughter didn't reach my ears until after he'd closed his mouth.

"You know how old this fish is, Max?" he said, and his face was melting, the contours of his cheeks pulsing in and out.

He turned the fish around so it faced me. Its jaw dropped open. It blinked.

"It has eyelids," I heard myself saying. A cold breeze blew through my chest and neck.

"No, he doesn't," Blashky said from very far away.

The sturgeon's jaw lifted and he pulled back his thin black lips and his thicket of thorny teeth closed together, the upper and lower fitting like a zipper.

"He's alive."

"No, Max. I promise. I killed him dead."

I heard Blashky's voice, but now he was standing very far away. The sturgeon came to the fore, floating in midair, as though he were still swimming, only now through the ether instead of the sea.

The fish swam indolently toward me. He got within arm's length, his face in line with mine. Killer and victim, face-to-face. He tilted his head back, exposing his throat to me. He dropped his tail down and became vertical. The cartilage of his tail fins scraped like nails across the rocks. He collapsed, falling in traces, becoming an infinite cadre of serpent-fish as he descended to the hard stone ground.

I gasped and clutched at my chest. Blashky, his voice now echoing from deep beneath the water, called to me.

The sea monster lay flopped across the stained and chipped gray cement. Its distended lower jaw was opening and shutting.

"I won't leave until I get what I want." The voice came from the serpent-fish. It was hard like the hard gray water, and deep like the plunging dark abyss, and eternal like the sea.

"What do you want?" I said. But I couldn't feel my mouth move.

"To be pulled from the water."

"I did that."

"Not me. I'm still in the water, beneath the earth. Beneath the rock."

The sturgeon lifted its head. It looked at me with one round dead eye, opaque yet deep. And at the center of that eye was a small black mirror. I got down on my knees and inched forward. I could see myself reflected in distortion over the convex surface of that black mirror.

"What do you want from me?" I heard myself saying.

"Pull me out from the depths, Max Bravo. Or you shall forever be terrorized in a living hell. I am a fury that will pull the sky down around your head and the earth up over your face until you drown on dry land. I am the Fallon."

Blashky had hold of my shoulders. He pulled me back away from the fish. He grabbed it by its tail and curled it into his wicker creel, closed and latched the lid.

"If you think he's fascinating now," Blashky said, "just wait 'til I fry him up in steaks."

"Oh no," I cried. "Oh no, we can't."

"I'm gonna fillet him, bread him, and fry him," Blashky was gabbling.

He started packing up the gear; reeling in the lines and sticking the hooks into the cork of the rod handles.

"You know how old that fish is?" he said as he crushed our empty beer cans under his boot, then tossed the crumpled aluminum disks back into his tackle box. "I bet he's a hundred years."

"The sturgeon?"

"Yeah. They can live to several hundred years. They can get as big as orca whales. This guy here, about three feet, he probably was around back during the Great Earthquake. Just think of it, Max. 1906."

Blashky walked to the water's edge. He pulled on the heavy blue nylon rope and scraped his crab trap up onto the shore.

"Score!" he said.

I went over the edge of the pier, picked my way across the rocks to the water's edge. I inspected the crab trap. A half-dozen gray crabs, the smallest the size of a mouse, the largest the size of a roof rat, scuttled around inside the modular penitentiary.

Blashky reached into the opening at the top of the trap and, one by one, grabbed the smaller crabs and tossed them out into the bay. They hit the water in muffled plops, and the salt water enveloped them. "Too small," Blashky said. "Don't want the game warden on our ass." He told me the two largest crabs were the only ones big enough to be legal.

"Legal," I said. The word spun around my skull like a ball bearing descending inside a funnel.

Blashky handed me the two poles. He hung the sturgeon-filled creel by a strap over his shoulder. He took up the tackle box in one hand, and the crab trap in the other. The crabs scrambled around inside the trap, making it wobble and bob.

"Let's go," Blashky said, adding jauntily, "It's time for a sumptuous feast."

Then I realized why the concept of legality seemed germane.

"Who's driving?" I said.

"I am," Blashky said.

"But you're tripping on LSD," I pointed out. "And so am I."

We sat in Blashky's car looking at the bridge. It started to rain. We turned on the windshield wipers.

"How long now?" I asked.

Blashky checked his watch.

"It's four P.M. And we dropped at around noon."

I counted the hours on my fingers.

"Christ," I said. "That still gives us another six hours. We can't sit here for six hours."

Blashky's eyes were following the motion of the windshield wipers. I pushed the button to roll my window down. The dead sturgeon on the floor was stinking up the car. I could hear the two big crabs scratching at the aluminum netting of their trap.

"We're running out of gas," Blashky said.

"You have the engine on?" I asked.

Then I heard it. The engine was droning. I looked out the windshield, at the molten pewter sea churning, and it felt like we were on it, in a boat with an outboard motor. I heard the motor droning. I remembered. It was the car.

I said to Blashky, "Turn the damn engine off."

"I switched it on to make the wipers work," he said. "So we could see out the window."

"We don't need to see. We're not going anywhere."

Blashky switched off the engine.

"He jumped from there," Blashky said, pointing toward the middle of the bridge.

"What?"

"Frank. He jumped from the very middle of the bridge."

I told Stan I didn't want to talk about it. The fog was rolling in— fast moving, as if acting with intent, and malice. It shrouded the bridge, then washed away to reveal it again. The bridge quivered in and out of view, antic and clipped like old newsreel footage.

The fog got heavier. It clung to the shoreline, thick as lamb's wool. We could no longer see the spot where we'd been fishing, just a few meters from the car. I imagined Frank Kelly appearing out of that fog, walking toward us decomposed and tattered, his eyes eaten out of the sockets like oysters scraped from their shells. I didn't really expect such a thing would happen, but I did worry that excessive discussion about Frank Kelly could trigger a hysterical LSD hallucination involving his dead, rotting corpse.

"We should get a cab," I said.

"A cabbie wouldn't let us in his car with this fish," Blashky said. "And two live crabs."

"Let's leave them here," I urged. "We'll come back for them tomorrow."

"No way, Max."

"Okay," I said. "Then let's walk."

I took the poles and the tackle box. Blashky carried the crabs in the trap, and the sturgeon in the creel. We walked across the wind-swept dunes of Crissy Field, and through the orderly streets of identical, pricey row houses that is the Marina district. We stopped for a while in front of one house to gape at a soaring juniper in the front yard; its multitude of topiary arms waved green pom-poms in a mesmerizing semaphore.

"Why did you bring all the gear?" Blashky asked me.

I didn't know why.

We decided we'd come too far to double back to the car to stow the rods and tackle box. We marched onward.

The rain tapered off to a drizzle as we rattled down Chestnut Street, past burls of blond sorority girls wearing Stanford sweatshirts and miniskirts. They parted before us, giving wide berth to avoid being speared by our fishing poles and assaulted by our briny stench.

"Have you got any change?" Blashky asked me.

"Yes."

"Good. Let's hop on this bus."

We got on the Fillmore bus and held up the queue as we stood at the fare box fumbling for change. I dropped the poles and they clattered onto the washboard rubber floor with a deafening din. The bus driver—a large, forceful-looking Negro woman with fingernails long as hummingbird beaks and a tall, mahogany fall pinned into the top of her head—eyed us with cool contempt.

"What you got in them baskets?" she asked, tapping her fingernails on the steering wheel.

"Fishing gear," Blashky said, trying to ease a crumpled dollar bill into the maw of the fare box.

"Go get set down and come back with your money," she commanded. "You got these people all piled up waiting behind you."

We gathered up our gear and made for a seat in the middle of the bus.

"Get to the back of the bus with all that mess you're hauling!" she yelled at us. We nodded at her glaring face in the rearview mirror and shambled to the seat at the very back. A couple of people were already back there. They abandoned their seats and moved to the front of the bus.

The bus driver shook her head, her mahogany fall tracing blurs in a shaking cone above her head. The cone rose up high into a beehive and I thought I saw bees crawling all over it. The bees were busy, buzzing all over that mahogany hive. I pointed out the bees to Blashky. He wasn't seeing it.

The bus lurched forward and proceeded up the steep hill. We made a couple of stops, loading more passengers. When we reached the crest of the hill, most of the passengers got off. After they disembarked, the driver remained at the stop, the bus idling loudly like a great boiler in the bowels of an oceangoing ship.

"You forget about something?" she yelled, looking at us in the rearview mirror.

"Is she talking to us?" I asked Blashky.

"Yes, I'm talking to you!" she said. "We are not moving until you pay up the rest of your fare."

"Uh, yes," I said. "I'm sorry, madam. How much was that?"

"You owe me another one dollar and fifty cents."

Blashky and I riffled our pockets. We hastily pooled our change. I rose to my feet and walked—with bent knees in a trajectory that felt vertiginous—to the front of the bus.

"We only have a dollar and thirty-five cents change," I told her.

The news jerked her head sideways. She nodded, as if it confirmed some long-held suspicion.

"Then you both best get off the bus right here, right now."

Her mahogany hair hive shook violently, sending bees flying in every direction. I could hear them buzzing.

"Oh, please, madam."

"If you do not have the correct money, you have to get off the bus."

"Do you have change for a five?"

She clicked the tip of her acrylic fingernail against a sign on the fare box. DRIVER DOES NOT GIVE CHANGE. She sighed.

"Then, can I just pay the five?"

"Suit yourself," she said to me, staring straight ahead through the bus's enormous windshield.

I carefully brushed the wrinkles out of the five-dollar bill and proffered it to the narrow slit of the fare box. The box snatched it up and ratcheted the bill into its jaws. I watched it disappear in a slow, chugging motion.

"It's in there," she said, regarding me from behind a pair of enormous gold-tinted square lenses.

"Excuse me?"

The zirconia gems on the arms of her sunglasses sparkled and I wondered how they could twinkle so in this dampened light.

"The bill is in there," she told me, enunciating each word.

I realized she was telling me to step away from the fare box. I started walking to the back of the bus, and the driver punched the accelerator. The bus lurched forward, sending me trotting.

"Max," Blashky whispered as I seated myself back down next to him.

"What?"

"We had two crabs, right?"

"Oh," I said, looking into the crab trap at the solitary crab languishing there.

"I'm gonna look for him."

"No." I grabbed Blashky by the sleeve. "Don't wander around the bus. That'll only arouse her suspicion."

The bus driver glanced into the rearview mirror at us. The gold squares over her eyes grew bigger and her mahogany hive swirled into an upside-down tornado. She fluttered her large hand, unfurling her pike-line of long fingernails with a grace that nearly broke my heart. She was frightening and magnificent. She affixed a silver telephone device, the size of matchbook, on to the rim of her ear. I thought it quite impressive, quite advanced. It would be years before I would ever adopt such a futuristic model, if ever. The driver spoke with the cool dispatch of an air traffic controller as she maneuvered her enormous vehicle elegantly along the narrow southbound lane of Fillmore Street.

"I think I should give her my card when we get off the bus," I said to Blashky.

"Who?"

"The driver," I said. "The lady driver."

"What for?"

"Maybe she'd like to have dinner," I said. "With me."

"Max," he told me. "She thinks we're assholes."

A chain gang of kindergarten children paraded down the street, marshaled by a pair of young female handlers. They had the children all holding on to a rope to keep them together.

"Have you ever met Dante's father?" I asked Blashky.

"No," he said. "Ashley doesn't have any contact with him."

"That kid must look like his father," I said.

A motorcycle cop stood in front of a Starbucks sipping coffee out of a tall cardboard cup. I thought he stared at us. But he didn't move. We crossed the bridge over Geary Street and entered the Fillmore district. A group of crackheads crowded in a park next to the McDonald's. Two of them were in wheelchairs.

A woman with cornrows, the lower half of her face sunken in to fill the vacuum where her teeth had once been, was pulling off her puffy goose-down jacket. She ripped the parka off with such violence that the sleeves turned inside out. She tossed it onto the sidewalk and strode out into the traffic, windmilling her arms. The bus driver honked at her, flung open her side window, and yelled at her to "Get your self out the road."

"I'm falling in love with the bus driver lady," I told Blashky.

"You know who I think Dante looks like?" Blashky asked me.

I struggled to loosen the scarf around my neck. Hot prickles were running up my throat and I could feel a layer of greasy sweat slathering across my face.

"I've always thought that Dante looks like Frank Kelly."

That was it. I knew I'd seen that face before. The rabbity teeth. The tousled black curls. The sharp blue eyes. And the mouth that's always running.

"Did you ever ask Ashley?" I said. "Did you ever try to pin her down about it?"

"No," he said, shaking his head, defeated by his own reverence for the woman.

Ashley had a way of doing that to men. She made us complicit. I was carrying a secret for her. I wondered what secrets Blashky was smuggling. What secrets did she involve Frank Kelly in? Dante's paternity, I supposed. But she couldn't keep that covered up forever. DNA refuses to encrypt. It surfaces. It was all over that kid's face.

"Why are we stopped here so long?" Blashky asked.

We were at a bus stop at Valencia and Fifteenth Street. I hadn't noticed when we'd left the Fillmore and entered the Mission. No one was at the bus stop.

"Holy shit," Blashky said. "Here she comes."

The bus driver was advancing straight for us down the aisle, swaying wide and looming large. Her mouth—beautiful, plush lips—was set hard. We were reflected in the gold squares of her sunglasses. We looked like a couple of gibbering gibbons dressed up by Gypsies in ill-fitting jackets.

Her arm came out from behind her back a thousand times. The traces of it swung up in an arch like the numerous arms of Kali, goddess of destruction. At the end of it, a crab inflated from her hand. Its one big claw and its one small claw waved in an animatic motion—it was a creature in a Ray Harryhausen *Sinbad* movie. Its pincers opened and shut against some invisible resistance, slowly like they were working a grip exerciser to build up their forearms.

"I believe this is yours," she said, shaking the crab until it swirled into an orb. The two antennae on top of its head probed the atmosphere frenetically.

The driver lady paused, placed two fingers on her telephone, pressing it tighter to her ear.

"Yes," she said to the person on the line. "Of course they are."

She looked down at the crab trap on the floor. She tossed the crab into it.

"You can't bring live animals on this bus," she said.

She towered over us. I felt like her supplicant. I wanted to worship her, burn incense at her feet, and smear her bronze enormity with ghee and lick it off.

"These are pets," Blashky said. "Guide pets. Actually, support pets. For my anxiety attacks."

"Don't you get smart with me," she said. "Pick up all this mess and get off my bus."

We fumbled to scoop up our gear. She stepped aside, making sure to follow us to the bus door, not turning her back on us.

I alighted onto the sidewalk and shifted my feet to find my balance, like a sailor stepping onto dry land after several months at sea. I turned and looked up at the driver through the open accordion doors. She was once again arranged in the driver's seat. Queenly. On her throne. She was just about to pull the handle to close the door. I called up to her.

"Madam," I said. "Would you care to join me some evening for dinner. Perhaps at some cheerful French bistro?"

She looked me, a sphinx behind her reflective gold sunglasses.

"I assure you," I said. "I'm not as I appear. I am, in fact, a well-regarded opera singer. An artist. And a gentleman."

She laughed, rocked with a genuine mirth. She grabbed the door lever to pull it shut.

I flicked one of my calling cards up into the bus. It landed on the floor beside her driver's seat. She pulled the lever and shut the door. The bus eased away from the curb and cruised down Valencia Street.

"Cool," Blashky said, looking around. "We're only a few blocks from my house."

36

I was jittery and agoraphobic for nearly a week after my acid trip with Stan Blashky. Dixie's daily walks were my only segue back into the life of normal humans.

She forced me to get out of the house to trek up and down the hills of my neighborhood. I wore my hat pulled down low and my darkest sunglasses. My eyes, I was sure, were permanently dilated with spirals pinwheeling around where my irises used to be.

"I should sue you for personal injury," I told Blashky. I was talking into my cell phone, walking Dixie down Twenty-second Street. I preferred making my phone calls during these walks. When I feigned absorption in a telephone conversation, it helped discourage the pug groupies.

"I found that psychedelic trip very enlightening," Blashky told me. "I had an insight about Frank Kelly."

"Enlightening? How about disturbing? The Frank Kelly moments were the worst part."

"We have to deal with it," Blashky said. "We have to resolve the unanswered questions about Frank's death. I know that now."

"I prefer suppressing these things. We should have done barbiturates instead of hallucinogens."

"Are you out walking?"

I told him I wasn't. But he heard a large truck drive by, followed by a lowered Chevy full of gangbangers. The driver hit the horn and it sounded with the signature riff from the song "Low Rider."

"Are you in the Mission?" Blashky surmised correctly.

He convinced me to walk over to his place. I said I'd do so, only on the condition that hallucinogenic drugs were not involved. He accused me of having the power of free will. I didn't argue the point.

When I buzzed his flat, he told me to hang on, he'd be right down. He came out his front door dressed in his coat and hat and said, "Walk with me."

"Destination?"

"The Santeria store."

I felt a wave of numbness, the opening salvo of a panic attack. I wanted to bolt. Stan took my elbow and ushered me down Valencia Street.

Perhaps this was the best way. I knew I'd have to go there eventually. Fallon was turning up the heat on everybody. Stan. Ashley. Dante. And, most important, me. Fallon barging into the last act of the last performance of *L'Orfeo* was heightened terrorism. I didn't know how much longer I could dodge Fallon and his demands.

At least now I had the imposing bulk of Stan Blashky to buttress me through.

We arrived at the storefront. It was unchanged; tricked out with incense and saints—all coated in dust so thick it looked like a diorama of Pompeii.

Dixie and I followed Blashky past the threshold.

The inside looked much as it must have when the place was built in the 1880s: transom over the front door; clerestory windows, painted over white and sealed shut, running along the top of the twelve-foot-high walls; rough wood floor, scuffed and unfinished. It smelled of wood and must, like an old dry goods store. Surely, that's what it had been, back when the Mission was an outlying suburb of the main city that hunkered around the harbor.

More than a hundred years earlier, San Franciscans expanded southwest to the Mission. They built a wide plank road to the Spanish outpost, originally occupied by padres and Indian acolytes—or, more precisely, by imperialist stooges and their exploited indigenous slaves.

Large tracts of the Mission were covered in swampland. Early residents built wooden walkways over the marshes so they could walk from one building to the next. Then they filled in the marshes—with dirt from the hills they leveled south of Market Street.

Like much of the waterfront property around the harbor, this land in the Mission was reclaimed. It was land stolen from the jealous sea.

I inspected the shop's wares, sparsely displayed on shelves lining the walls. The items were, I supposed, the essentials of magic. Bags of powdered herbs and leaves. Jars of potions. Ampules of tinctures. And everywhere, votive candles dedicated to a great wide hagiography of saints.

I picked one up and showed it to Blashky.

He examined the label. It said that the candle's light would wash away troublesome ghosts. It was for both home and commercial use.

"All right," I said. "Let's pay for this and go."

"I don't know if this is enough," Blashky said.

I smelled smoke. I looked over my shoulder and standing a few feet away was a man in slippers and an undershirt smoking a cigarette without using his hands, which he employed as pocket-stuffers in his gray slacks.

He was standing in the doorway to what must have been the private living quarters of the shopkeeping family. A pair of crimson curtains were pulled back to reveal an anteroom. It was wide and shallow and painted a vibrant cobalt—the kind of room that made you feel like you were drowning in a wading pool. It contained one piece of furniture: a lumpy sofa draped with a green bedcover. A fat boy of nine or ten sat on the sofa, zombified by the antiquated handheld electronic game that he played with urgent, pecking fingers.

The old man squinted behind the lash of cigarette smoke. He regarded us as though we were inanimate objects, not requiring any gesture or signal of social intercourse.

"We have a bit of a problem with an unwanted guest," I offered.

The old man took a drag on his cigarette. The ember bellowed red. The ash lengthened and curled down.

"Bit of a pest," I slogged ahead. "Of the noncorporeal kind."

I attempted a hale and hearty laugh. But it came out as more of a snorting gasp.

A small woman in a housedress scuttled out from somewhere deep in the private quarters. She brushed past the old man on clacking legs. She too was ancient—slightly stooped, her wrinkled face thrust forward by the widow's hump at the back of her neck. But her eyes were big and alert, magnified inside the thick lenses of her large square eyeglasses.

"You need help." She didn't ask us, she told us.

"There's a ghost in my house," Blashky said.

"This won't work." She snatched the votive out of Blashky's hand and set it back on the shelf.

I wanted to grill her as to why she was selling the votives if they didn't work. But she had such a forceful air of professional competence that I didn't dare.

She turned and started for a table display in the middle of the store, rattled her brittle fingers in the air over her shoulder, beckoning us to follow her.

"This," she said.

She picked up a package of small black disks in cellophane. She placed the disks in my hand. They looked like cookies.

"Burn these," she said. "It's myrrh."

She rummaged around the table and chose another cellophane bag, this one containing what appeared to be a spray of dried weeds.

"This too," she instructed. "Burn it on top of myrrh. Is sage."

"I tried that once," I started to explain. "And it wasn't really—"

"Just burn it," she said.

She jerked her head like a fish pulling down on a hook. Her eyes were rheumy behind the watery lenses of her glasses.

"Do we just burn it? I mean, aren't there some words we have to recite?" I persisted. "Some incantation?"

The eyes rolled up and blinked. The lids lowered under the weight of a repeated weariness.

"Sure, sure," she said. "Say something from your heart. Something you mean. *Con corazón*."

I tried to remember the name Baba had mentioned to me. It was a flower. Lily. Hyacinth? Hydrangea? No, that would be ridiculous.

"Amarantha," I blurted out.

She looked surprised. Then suspicious.

"*Sí*," she allowed.

"That is your name?"

"*Sí*." Her face drew back and the eyes scanned me head to toe. Then she inventoried Blashky. Finally, she studied the dog.

"Someone mentioned you to me," I broke into the uncomfortable silence.

"Who?"

"My grandmother, actually. Lumenesta Inoescu."

"I know her," Amarantha said.

"Quite," I said.

Blashky shifted his chest like a port barrel rolling around in a cargo hold. He unzipped his jacket. I suddenly felt overcome by a close and cloying heat. I opened the buttons of my coat and loosened my scarf.

Amarantha's eyes peeled off of us and traveled toward the old man. I had all but forgotten about him. He had not moved or made a sound. He was still in the doorway. The fat child remained on the couch in the background, working his thumbs over the game controls. It emitted a series of fuzzy beeps and tinny dings.

The old man pulled one hand out of his pocket. He picked the cigarette out of his mouth and a two-inch curl of ash dropped off the end of it. It landed on the toe of his slipper.

Some silent discourse ran between the two ancients. Amarantha turned back to Blashky and me. She told us to wait a moment.

She disappeared back into the family quarters.

The old man pulled the cigarette out of his mouth. He held it between two yellowed fingers and spoke to us. He delivered a lengthy monologue, in Spanish. It was like something out of a Buñuel film—disconnected and solitary.

He finished speaking and turned away.

He retired to the private sanctum, shuffling past the child on the couch, parting the crimson curtains, disappearing.

"What did he say?" Blashky whispered.

"He was speaking in a Central American or perhaps Cuban accent," I said. "I don't know those dialects very well."

The boy on the couch didn't look up from his game.

I confided quietly to Stan, "The old man said that he once had a cat that drowned in a canal. He fished the cat out. It revived. Later, he wished he'd thrown a brick on it to sink it."

"That's fucked-up," Blashky observed.

Amarantha came back. She held a paper sack in front of her, at arm's length.

"In here is everything you need," she said. "You must gather some people. Make a ceremony. Your ghost requires effort. I wrote instructions."

I asked her the price. She quoted a figure that was absurdly low. I offered more. She batted the suggestion away with a wave of her burled knuckles. She rang up the exchange on an old mechanical cash register that had enough metal in it to build a gunboat. She punched in the amount and the cash drawer sprang open.

She pecked the change out of the drawer, dropped it into my palm, and said, "Say hello to your grandmother for me."

"I'm afraid she's dead," I said.

Amarantha said, "I know."

37

Blashky and I needed to regroup, to weigh anchor somewhere and plan the logistics of this event we were about to stage. Neither one of us used the word *séance*.

Blashky steered us into the shelter of a blue grotto three blocks down on Valencia Street.

Minos by Night had been a tiki lounge in the 1940s. Hence the lava rock wall tinkling with sheets of fountain water, the bamboo-clad bar, and the royal blue ceiling punched through with pinhole lights that simulated the night sky over the Pacific.

"I feel like I should sing 'Bali Hai,'" I said to Blashky as we hoved up onto a couple of bar stools. "It's like we came here for a South Sea holiday."

"No," Blashky said, "we came here for her."

He nodded toward the bartender. She was down at the other end with a customer. She was enrapt in conversation, and little else.

"Is that a pignoir set she's wearing?" I wondered aloud, fascinated by her sheer, ice blue bed jacket, trimmed in white poofy fun fur. The jacket fluttered over a blue satin slip that shimmered like glaciers under the midnight sun.

The other patron, the one she was conversing with, was an old man in a checkered jacket and swirling comb-over and a pair of long white loafers that must have fit before he shrunk, back when he probably sat on that same bar stool watching the Watergate hearings. He had his feet perched on the kick rail of the bar, and every time the bartender lady said something to him he'd waggle the tips of his loafers up and down.

She heard us settle in, looked over and raised one finger to let us know she'd be over directly. She winked. It must have been an effort, given the sheer weight of those glue-on lashes.

"I haven't seen hair like that since Prissy and Elvis got married," I said.

"It gets better," Blashky said.

And it did.

She lifted her elbows off the bar, came toward us. She was big and billowing and moved like a Carnival Cruise line. Her bed jacket wafted up and floated behind, the gossamer blue and white fur rippling in her magnificent wake.

Blashky introduced me to Miss Vicky. She leaned her forearms onto the bar, framing her bounteous breasts in the strong embrace of her bare arms. A man could lose his motel keys in that cleavage.

"What can I get you?" she asked.

"I'm not sure," I said, staring into the amplitude of flesh laid before me. I blurted, "Something plush."

Blashky swiveled around on his bar stool. I thought he was going to smack me on the back of the head.

"Two rum and Cokes," Miss Vicky said. "What to eat?"

"Nothing right now, thanks," I said.

"I bring you something," she commanded. "You can't just drink. Not eat. What kind of place you think I run?"

She strode away from us, down the length of the bar, and disappeared into the kitchen, her bed jacket floating behind her. I turned around to survey the premises.

Blashky informed me that the men playing cards beside the rock wall fountain were Miss Vicky's relatives. One of them was her husband, Stavros. I asked Blashky why she went by "Miss" if she was married. He told me to stop asking stupid questions.

I developed an instant, inane, and cowardly jealousy toward Stavros. He was, of course, oblivious to me. Stavros lounged in his chair, examining his pinochle hand, a trilby pushed back on his head in a recreational attitude, and a cigarette affixed permanently to the side of his mouth. He had a detached attitude. Yet I sensed that the slightest impropriety would launch him out of that chair faster than I could duck.

Miss Vicky returned with a plate of Mediterranean victuals. Olives, feta cheese, pita bread, dollops of baba ghanoush and hummus. She interrogated Blashky as to who I was, referring to me in the third person. I busied myself with the appetizer plate and listened to Blashky describe me as "a friend of Frank Kelly's," which caused her to regard me with concern.

"Frank was a troubled man," she instructed me. "Lost. A man lost in a labyrinth of his desires."

"What do you think Frank desired?" I asked her.

"He wanted to never die," she said.

"Funny phobia for a suicide," I said.

"He wanted to live forever," she told me. "Because he couldn't live for today."

"You talk like my grandmother," I told her, and sipped rum through a straw.

"Your grandmother?" she said. "She is a hundred percent Gypsy. Am I right? You are, I don't know, maybe half."

A customer came in, a man with swollen eyes and an air of exhaustion. He seemed to be held erect solely by the stiffness of his caramel-colored leather safari jacket. Miss Vicky went to him. He told her he wanted a rum and Coke and a slice of baklava. Then he darted a spray of Binaca into his mouth.

"Miss Vicky certainly knows her eugenics," Blashky told me.

"All the Europeans do," I said. "Most Americans just think I'm swarthy. But she nailed it."

"Miss Vicky is right about Frank too," Blashky said.

"About wanting to escape death?" I asked.

"Yes," said Blashky, popping a shriveled black olive into his mouth. "Frank was a desperate guy. He wanted to make a mark for himself. Write the great American novel. What an asshole."

"At least he tried," I said.

"Nobody told Frank that the novel is dead," Blashky was saying. "Literacy too, for that matter."

"You encouraged Frank to keep writing," I pointed out.

"I'm a hopeless romantic." He held up his empty glass, signaling Miss Vicky to bring him another.

"Frank was writing to cheat death, I take it," I said. "For posterity. Immortality."

"He was scared of dying," Blashky said.

"Then why did he jump?" I said.

Miss Vicky floated by. Blashky and I both craned forward onto the bar so we could watch her walk away.

We turned to business. We pulled out the materials we'd purchased at the Santeria shop; the myrrh and the sage and the rest of it. We lined it all up on the bar and began making a guest list on a cocktail napkin.

Blashky printed three letters at the top of the napkin.

"What's F.O.F. mean?" I asked him.

"Friends of Frank," he said. "Amarantha told us they all had to be his friends. Six people."

"Did Frank even have six friends?" I asked. "I mean, real friends.

Not that crowd of hyenas that showed up for the free drinks at his funeral."

"Sure he did," Blashky said, defensive.

He held up his bratwurst fingers and began counting, "There's you. Me. That's two right there."

He stared at his extended forefinger and middle finger.

"What about Ashley?" I tried to help.

"Right." He perked up. "Ashley." He named a third finger.

We stared at the three fingers a while.

"What's a matter," Miss Vicky barked. "You got spooks?"

She slammed two rum and Cokes down in front of us, even though only Blashky had ordered another.

"Spook," Blashky said. "Just one."

Miss Vicky smelled the myrrh through the cellophane. "Stinks," she pronounced. She tossed it back on the bar, picked up the package of sage. "Weeds," she said. She selected the tall votive candle, held it at arm's length, read it with silently moving lips. "I don't believe that shit," she said.

"Why did you get the votive?" I asked Blashky. "Amarantha said it wouldn't work."

"Dude," Blashky said. "That son of a bitch is terrorizing me. I'm gonna nuke him with everything I can get my hands on."

"You got instructions for all this?" Miss Vicky demanded.

"Yes." I reached in the bag for the piece of paper Amarantha had given me. It was torn out of a child's school scribbler, folded more times than an origami swan. I unfolded it, set it on the bar, smoothed it over with the palm of my hand.

"What's it say?" Miss Vicky said.

"Yeah," Blashky said. "Read it out loud, Max."

"If you two would stop yapping I could read it," I said.

I put on my spectacles and lifted the paper by its edges as though it were a fragile papyrus exhumed from the crypt of a long-dead

pharaoh. I positioned it under the blue beam of the pendant lamp
overhead. To my surprise, an elastic and supple script had flowed
from the old woman's calcified fingers. In uniform and certain letters
she had formed the following words:

> *First, gather the correct people: a man who lives in the
> house—that is you, the big, bald man. A woman who lives
> in, or often sleeps in, the house. A child who sleeps in the
> house. A second woman—either an artist or a madwoman
> is preferable. A man of letters, a scholar. And a man who
> has access to a daemon—that is you, the Gypsy singer, the
> lustful one.*

I set the paper down on the bar and removed my eyeglasses.
Blashky took up a pen and started writing on the cocktail napkin.

"Okay. We already got most of that figured out," Blashky said.
"Number one. Me." He printed the name Stan.

"Number two, obviously, Ashley. Three, Dante."

"Hold on," I interrupted him. He lifted the pen and stared at me
impatiently.

"How do you know that this won't scare the shit out of Dante," I
said. "He's just a kid."

"Wait 'til you meet him," Blashky said, and returned to his list-
making. "Now, an artist or a madwoman."

"That's me," Miss Vicky interjected.

"Which are you?" Blashky asked, without irony.

"An artist," she asserted. She swept her arms wide all around her
as if gathering up a cornucopia of fragrant flowers. "This place. Minos
by Night. I create it all myself. A masterpiece."

I glanced over at Miss Vicky's husband and his cronies. He picked
out a card, threw it on the table. The other three players groaned,
tossed their losing hands onto the card pile. Stavros scraped the kitty
of matchsticks into his cache.

"Too bad Betty Ann Thibideaux is gone," I said. "She was an artist and a madwoman."

"Betty Ann," Blashky echoed her name ruefully. "You gotta think Fallon had something to do with that too. Both of them jumping. Like it was an epidemic."

I told him I thought it was weird. I didn't tell him what Fung had told me. Neither Blashky nor Miss Vicky needed to know that Betty Ann went off the bridge with a bullet in her chest. Fung told me to keep it quiet, which meant the cops weren't sure who shot her. It could have been anybody.

Stavros picked up the deck and shuffled it. Behind him, the water sheeted over the rocks and I was overcome with an insane fear that the water was seeping through the wall, and that it would soon burst the rocks apart at their cement seams and flood into the room and overtake us all.

"I think," Blashky was saying to Miss Vicky in diplomatic tones, "that this means artist in the absolute technical sense."

"What you mean? Technical?" she fired back at him.

"A painter. A sculptress, perhaps," he said. "We have to follow this list exactly. It's like ingredients for a cake, Miss Vicky. We have to be exact to bake it."

"You're not going to start singing 'MacArthur Park,' are you?" I asked Blashky.

Miss Vicky left us again to attend to her customers. We nursed our drinks. We watched Stavros rake in another couple kitties of matchsticks.

"Betty Ann was a pain in the ass," Blashky said after a while. "But she didn't deserve to die like that."

"Who could have done something like that to her?" I said it before I even thought about it.

"What do you mean?" Blashky looked at me hard.

How many of those damn rum and Cokes had I drunk? Nobody should ever entrust me with a secret. Why did Fung do it? Surely he knew better. Maybe it was a ruse to call me out. Maybe he thought I shot Betty Ann.

"I mean," I said slowly, staring at the ice in my drink. "I mean, Fung, he told me that every bone in her body was broken."

"Of course, dude," Blashky said. "She jumped off the fucking bridge."

"Right."

"Stop thinking about that shit, man." Blashky laid his paw on the side of my head and gave it a shove.

"Right," I said.

We batted around names of candidates for the other woman's spot on the séance team. It was tough. She had to not only be weird enough to want to want to participate in the séance, she also had to be weird enough to be friends with Frank Kelly.

There was a woman who lived in the flat below Blashky's. She'd been on casual speaking terms with Frank. But she hated Blashky because she said he always stomped overhead in his big boots.

There was an art director at the agency, a young pretty thing. But Blashky told me that Frank ruined that by having sex with her in the server closet at the agency Christmas party.

We came up with another couple of candidates. But every woman we mentioned was somehow disqualified either because she'd been alienated by Frank, or by Blashky, or by both.

The only uncontaminated name that kept coming up was Claudia's.

"She is an art director, like me," Blashky allowed. "We like to think of ourselves as artists."

"She does still paint," I reminded him. "Her canvases are good. I have a couple."

"Oh sure, art directors still try to be artists." Blashky was perseverating now. "Even after we go over to the dark side and aspire to actually make a living. I do my installation pieces, my paintings. But it's getting harder. My tank is running low, man. On fumes. All the creativity I have is being sucked out of me, every day in that office. Selling shit. Every goddamned day."

"Yes, Stan," I interjected. "We must have a good talk about that some time."

"Claudia too, I bet." Stan was tearing up his cocktail napkin into strips. "They bleed you dry until you're nothing but an empty, jaded husk."

"Good enough," I said. "Put Claudia's name down."

"What about me?" Miss Vicky whined, pitching her eyebrows into an angry *V.*

This roused Blashky out of his fugue.

"We need you here, Miss Vicky," Blashky told her. "We need someone—a strong, rational person—to observe the effects of the procedure from the outside. Otherwise, if we all get hypnotized or possessed or something, we won't have anyone to step in and take control."

"I'm in control?"

"Yes," Blashky told her. "You're like the ground control when they launch astronauts in space."

"Okay," she said. She reluctantly left us, grabbed her ticket pad, and went over to a booth at the back of the restaurant to attend to a large dinner group that was just settling in.

"Me. Ashley. Dante. Claudia," Blashky read the cocktail napkin.

He paused, examined Amarantha's list.

"Oh yes," he said. "Aaaannnd—lastly, but not leastly—the lustful one."

He printed my name.

"That's libelous," I said, slamming my rum and Coke down on the bar. "Defamatory."

Stavros looked up from his pinochle hand. His stare wasn't precisely stern, but he was clearly the type who didn't brook distractions. I instinctively hunched forward, bent my head over my drink.

"I'm an artist," I whispered hoarsely, punching my finger onto the bar to emphasize the word *artist*. "And a thinker. I am a thinking man."

Another finger punch.

"Why cast me as the lustful one?" I harangued. "What the hell does that mean anyway?"

"Oh, I don't know, Max," Blashky said. "Maybe it means you hop in the sack with anybody on two legs."

I didn't like the way he made that remark. There was an element of bitter menace lurking beneath the words.

I hadn't seen Stan Blashky for a few days, not since the acid trip. A lot could happen in that time. Claudia had already tried to scare me about that. The scenario she'd painted—that old chestnut where the girlfriend gets drunk, feels guilty, and spills her guts—was all too plausible.

Or maybe they'd had a fight. And Ashley decided to smash Stan in the teeth with it. "I slept with your friend." That's got impact.

Whichever way, it didn't matter. The point was, she could have told him.

Women always tell, in the end. Of course, so do I.

"Max." Blashky grabbed my shoulder and squeezed.

He wasn't even making an effort, and I could feel his big thumb indenting my clavicle like a rubber bullet. I thought I was going to faint.

"Buddy," Blashky said. "Relax. I'm just giving you a hard time."

"Uh-huh," I squeaked.

Blashky said, "You're an amorous guy, Max. Okay?"

"Fine."

"It's a compliment." He squeezed a little harder and shook my shoulder in what was meant to be a gesture of manly affinity. I felt like a worm on a hook.

"Now let's see," Blashky said. "We need to go back to the third person on the list. We still don't have the other guy. The scholar."

"Did Frank know a professor?" I asked.

"Emile Balzac," a voice yelled behind us.

I turned and saw Stavros greeting Emile. He'd just come through the door. He walked over to the card table and embraced Stavros. They kissed, both cheeks.

"Go have a drink," Stavros told him. "Your friends are at the bar."

As soon as Miss Vicky settled him down on his bar stool with his rum and Coke, we informed Balzac of our project.

He listened without comment. Then he said simply, "I'm in."

"And, actually," he added, "I have news of Betty Ann Thibideaux."

He pulled a newspaper out of his satchel and opened it on the bar. He pointed to an article on page six. It was the *San Francisco Chronicle*. Book section. Betty Ann Thibideaux's photo was meant to depict her as reflective.

The headline read, HAUNTING TALE FROM THE GRAVE OF SUICIDE NOVELIST.

"It's already started," Balzac said.

Predictably, the article focused on Betty Ann's suicide, and Frank's.

"Betty Ann is going to be bigger dead than alive," Blashky predicted.

Just like Frank, I thought.

38

Dante opened the door.

"Hello, young man," I said. "I'm Max Bravo."

I thrust out my hand. He took it and gave it a loose snap, like he was shaking a trail of ants out of a picnic blanket.

"I know who you are," he said, rather impertinent.

"Marvelous," I said. "Then we needn't waste time with niceties."

He turned and slid away from me on sock feet across the hardwood floor. He was smaller than I'd anticipated—he looked at doorknobs from eye-level and could probably shimmy through a drainpipe. He tossed himself into the crook of the sofa and stared at a cartoon on the television. I closed the front door behind me.

"Where is everyone?" I asked him.

"Kitchen," he said, aiming the remote at the television set.

Ashley was emptying the dishwasher. Blashky was talking on the telephone. She said hello—rather too cool, I thought, and her feline indifference annoyed me.

Blashky nodded at me, pointed at the phone pressed against his meaty face, and rolled his eyes.

Ashley told me that Emile Balzac was on his way and Stan was speaking with Claudia. She was in her car, just blocks away.

"I'm going downstairs," he said to us. "There's an open parking spot right out front. I'm going to hold it for Claudia."

I was alone in the kitchen with Ashley. She told me to help myself to the tortilla chips. She closed the door of the dishwasher, locked it. I sat at the table, watched her work. I thought she was overplaying the charade—she seemed to have convinced even herself that there had never been anything more between us than a casual acquaintance.

A pair of cartoon characters were arguing on the television in the other room. The channel switched and there was a tatter of machine-gun fire. The channel switched again—a rapper singing, "I ain't saying she a gold digger, but she ain't messin' wit no broke niggas."

"Wine?" Ashley offered. She poured me a glass before I answered.

I took it, rolled the stem between my fingers. She ran a dishcloth under the hot water, began wiping down the spotless countertops.

Dante turned the television up louder. He switched the channel again. He stopped at a Mexican soap opera. "You want to know where I've been." A woman angrily spat out the words, and they sounded all the more vituperative in Spanish. "With Don Diego," she said, note of triumph. "Because he can give me more than passion. He can give wealth and comfort. He can protect me. I'll never have to work in the cantina again. Can you do that for me, Miguel?"

I rather thought Miguel couldn't do that. But I fancied they had some pretty satisfying evenings out in back of the cantina after closing time. And once Don Diego's lifestyle lost its luster, our little spitfire would be back at the cantina once again.

"I've been thinking," I said.

"Let's not start, okay, Max."

"No," I said. "Let's not. Look, we only have a few minutes to talk. Let me say this one thing before Stan and Claudia come busting back in here."

She threw the wet dishcloth into the sink, spun around, leaned against the counter, one fist jammed onto her tilted hip bone, the other gripped around the bowl of her wineglass.

"Talk," she said. "Talk fast."

"I've been thinking." I rushed the words together. "We have to discontinue our association."

"We don't have an association."

"For Stan's sake." I was headlong into my speech. "We need to think of Stan's feelings."

She took a drink, rolling her eyes.

"Wait," I said. "What did you say?"

"We're not associated, Max."

"Well, what do you call it then?"

She shook her head. Stared at me. Oddly, she frightened me. She was tired, and when she was haggard like that, the scar looked fresher, the violence of it seemed more immediate.

"What do I call it?" she parroted archly. "I call it nothing, Max. You and me. Nothing. Just one of those things."

"What things?" I was already exasperated, twelve seconds into the conversation.

"Drop it, Max. Jesus. Between you and Stan. You two are bugging the shit out of me."

I felt myself being watched. Not by Ashley. She turned her back on me and started rinsing out the dishcloth under a torrent of hot water.

I looked around. Dante was standing in the kitchen doorway. His skinny face shone white in the shadow. He was studying the scene—a behaviorist observing a pair of white rats negotiating their way through a maze.

"Those guys are all here now," Dante said. "And Fred is still acting weird."

"Weird?" I said, a little too loud, a little too quickly.

I anxiously tried to audit the last several remarks in the exchange between Ashley and I. Would this ten-year-old know what we were talking about? I looked at him, his eyes—bright and blue—and I felt Frank Kelly looking at me. Dante knew exactly what was going on.

"Fred is the cat," Ashley said. "He's been weird all day."

"He sits in the hallway," Dante explained. "Staring at the wall. Then he jumps up like this."

Dante curled up his arms in front of his chest, hands folded in tight like they'd been laced into boxer's gloves. He crouched down, sprang up, punching the air with the boxing kitty paws.

"He jumps like that," Dante said. "Right into the wall."

Voices drifted in from down the hall: Stan's bass booming sounds of welcome. Claudia, braying and honking as she always does to announce her arrival. Emile Balzac, in a low register, asking where to hang his coat.

"Go turn off the TV, Dante," Ashley said.

"Can I light the candles now?" he asked her.

"Yes," she said. "If Max helps you."

I got to my feet. Greeted the guests and joined Dante in the dining room. He showed me an assortment of candles on the sideboard and explained that his mother had let him assemble them, but he wasn't to light them without an adult present. I told him I was a reasonable equivalent. For the first time, he seemed appreciative of my presence.

I congratulated him on his collection. He had short votives and several tall ones embossed with saints' portraits. There were a few column candles in blue and umber, and the ghost-repellant votive that Blashky had purchased, and a tarnished candelabra outfitted with a half-dozen black tapers. There was one black taper for each member of the séance party, Dante explained to me.

We lit the candles and distributed them around the room—on the sideboard, atop the bookshelf. We debated whether to put the candelabra in the center of the dining table, or the ghost votive. In the end, we decided on the candelabra. An antique occasional table stood in front of the room's only window. On it was a vase brimming with lilies. We moved the lilies to the sideboard, and set the ghost votive on the table's leather top. Dante pulled the velvet curtains shut.

The room hushed in the smothering darkness. The candles glowed upward in soft yellow halos on the dark paneling. Dante's and my shadow skimmed the walls, elongated, flickering back and forth over the box beams. High above us, in the center of the ceiling, the filigree curves of the chandelier cast lacy shadows across the plaster rosettes— one of the few original details left intact after years of shabby rental property alterations.

"Totally spooky," Dante said with satisfaction.

"You know this ghost, don't you?"

"Yes," he told me.

"Do you think he'll come when we call him?"

"Yes."

"Do you think he'll leave when we ask him to?"

"Let's get the chairs ready," Dante said.

He went to a chair set against the wall, picked it up by its heavy oak back, and hefted it over to the table. I fetched the other spare chair from its resting place beside the window. I parted the drape and looked out. It was the same view as from Frank's old room—the room that

Dante now slept in. Below was the unattended parking lot. Its chain-link and concertina-wire fence kept vigil over the ragged collection of derelict cars.

The other four members of our party entered the room, marveled at the effect Dante had achieved with his candles.

"One more thing," Dante said. "This is important."

He opened the door of the sideboard and pulled out a metal bowl. He set it in the middle of the table, beneath the flickering light of the candelabra. He went into docent mode, telling us that he'd arranged the myrrh and sage in layers in the metal bowl. He chose this particular bowl because a sea monster was etched around its circumference. He said the sea was important to our ghost.

Dante requested that we all take our seats.

The two women sat across from each other. Ashley was elegant, and eerily spectral. She wore a black turtleneck and combed her black hair straight back so it blended into the darkness. Her white face seemed to float above the table, the candlelight licking the scar that ran down her forehead and across her cheek.

Claudia, in contrast, had decided to camp it up for the occasion. She was overblown and blousy in her white ostrich feather boa. She had her black hair teased up so that it was more topiary than coiffure. And the shock-white streaks that shot from both temples glowed in the dark like reflectors on interstate mileage posts.

It made me feel vaguely grateful to her. Claudia had dampened some of the inherent creepiness of the whole affair by meeting it head-on with sartorial frivolity. I took heart. It gave me the sense that nothing terribly serious, or irreversible, could take place at this table.

Emile sat next to me. Blashky sat across, in between Dante and Ashley.

"Can I have a drink?" Claudia asked.

"Good idea," I said.

"No," Blashky said firmly. "Afterward. Max, do you have the instructions?"

I pulled Amarantha's notes from my pocket.

"First," I read. "Light the incense."

Dante stood up on his chair, leaned across the table on one hand and one knee. He plucked a taper from the candelabra and dabbed it around the stack of myrrh and sage like a Hindu fanatic lighting a settee pyre for an ill-fated widow. The sage crinkled up and turned bright red along the edges. The myrrh reddened, then ashed gray almost immediately. Wires of smoke aspired up from the metal bowl, filling the room with dusty perfume. I noticed that the bowl was turned so that the sea serpent's hoary head was facing me. Its gaping jaws were closing around the tip of its tail, swallowing it—a symbol of eternity, the snake swallowing its own tail.

Dante settled back into his chair. Blashky told him he did a good job. He bade me continue.

I referred back to the sheet of paper. I told the group I was supposed to repeat a phrase three times. Then they were all to join me in it for several minutes.

"How many minutes?" Emile asked.

"It doesn't say," I said, turning the paper over. There were no more instructions on the back.

"Maybe just until it feels right," Ashley said.

"Or, until something happens," said Claudia, and Ashley looked at her, frightened.

I told everyone to settle down. Clear their thoughts. Once the rustling and adjusting had stopped, I began.

"*El tiempo es breve,*" I chanted.

Time is brief. I intoned it twice more.

"*El tiempo es breve,*" they chorused at the fourth repetition.

We chanted together. The words flowed in waves, lashed against the wooden hull of the room. Time is brief. *El tiempo es breve.* The Spanish—its vibrations, its resonance—conjured up epochs. Centuries swept across the floorboards, washed over us in aural waves.

The smoke from the metal bowl thickened and roiled like fog. The candles wavered and snapped, flame persisting against a chill wind. The room seemed to shift, ever so slightly at first. Then it settled into a rolling motion, a ship at sea. It felt eternal, and outside of time— awash in the primordial oceans, in the amniotic fluid of the planet.

El tiempo es breve. El tiempo es breve. El tiempo es breve.

Baba resolved out of the darkness behind Dante. *"El tiempo es breve,"* she said, stepping forward into the candlelight.

"Are you here to help me?" I asked her.

"He sees something," Claudia said to the others.

"Shush," Ashley said. "Let him concentrate."

"I'm here to bring Mammy Pleasant to you," Baba said. "She'll take you to what Fallon wants."

"I'm concerned," I told her.

I was still holding hands with Emile and Claudia. But I could no longer feel the touch of their flesh against mine. The warmth had leaked out of their fingers. I held two bundles of bones in my hands.

"Pay attention to me," Baba said. "Mammy is from Fallon's time. She was there. She knows what to do. Listen to her. She is coming."

I couldn't feel the chair anymore. Nor the table. I was light. I was floating in a viscous liquid. I broke apart, my cells drifted away from one another, shimmering. I was sparkles of golden sunlight cast across the ripples of a pond.

"I'm dying," I said to Baba.

"We should stop this," Emile was saying from very far away.

"Tell them *no!*" Baba said sharply. "Tell them it is okay. It is dangerous only if you stop now."

I told them. A rustling went around the table. I thought, they must be nervous. I looked down at them. Then I realized that I was on the ceiling. I was floating facedown, my back pressed up against the plaster. I could have seeped through it, and kept going. I could have floated above the rooftops, above the bay. I could have drifted across the Pacific.

"Stay here," Baba said.

I felt a tug in my guts. I looked down and saw a silver cord, kinked and curling, tethering my floating self to my corporeal self, which still sat, earthbound, in the chair at the table. Emile was squeezing my hand hard. Claudia regarded me with fear and awe.

"Max," Blashky was saying. "What do you see?"

Fallon was standing in the doorway. His long black hair was streaked with gray. But his frame was still imposing, erect. Water dripped from the hem of his coat and, as he walked into the dining room, wet boot prints marked his steps.

"I'm owed a debt," he said to me, to the Max sitting in the chair. "And I mean to collect it."

"We'll make it right," I heard myself saying. "Who owes you?"

"His father." He pointed at Dante. The boy convulsed. Ashley screamed.

"Tell them not to break the circle!" Baba yelled at me.

I did as she said. Ashley objected. She started to get out of her chair. Blashky pulled her back down, refusing to let her hand go. She cried out, he was hurting her. He told her that if she really wanted to protect Dante, she'd have to collect her wits. A jolt ran through her. She sat down, resolved.

"Frank Kelly owes me," Fallon said. "And if he doesn't pay, I'll take my marker out in kind."

Duffy Fallon appeared behind Dante. He put his hand on the boy's shoulder. He disappeared, slowly, in bits—head first, then his massive torso broke apart. At the end, just the hand lingered, and flickered away.

Someone new came into the room. She was a tall woman, a handsome Negress in a rich costume of aubergine silk cut in the style of the turn of the century.

"Your grandmother sent me to help you," she told me.

"Mammy Pleasant?" I asked.

"Yes, Max," she said with the careful diction of the successful boot-strapper. "Accompany me, and I will help you to find your way free of these troubles you find yourselves in."

She was suddenly close to me, floating high on the ceiling. She took my hand, and we plummeted down, as though we were in a fast-moving elevator. We seeped through the floor like rainwater. Down. Down. Down through the flat below. Down through the cellar. Down into the earth underneath the city.

"Are you taking me to Hell?" I asked her.

She turned her patrician head to look at me. She smiled, her high cheeks glowed bronze, and her eye lit with burning intelligence.

"Oh goodness, no, my dear Max," she said. "I'm taking you to where I hid Fallon's treasure for him."

We advanced through the darkness, through winding caverns and tunnels, like the hard-clawed mines of the old Gold Rush days. Figures, vaguely human, flitted by us. Their forms were transluscent, milky.

"Now we are below Chinatown," Mammy told me.

We came into an expanded chamber, three stories high. It housed a structure, a tenement, cobbled together from salvaged wood and rusted hardware. It was bustling with people—washing clothes in tubs, cooking on oil flame burners, climbing up and down the rickety stairs. Men. Women. Children. All of them Chinese—Cantonese in the traditional costumes of the early 1900s. Many of the women tottered on tiny bound feet. The men wore the long braided queues that signified their subservience to the Manchu overlords who still ruled China before 1912.

"Come quickly," Mammy said, taking my hand. She pulled me past the tenement, explaining that when they first came to San Francisco, many of the Chinese lived underground in these subterranean dwellings because there simply wasn't enough housing on the surface.

We entered a dark alley, then penetrated a closed door. Inside was a low-ceilinged room filled with smoke, and lined with rugged bunk beds hammered together out of old planks. Bodies, desiccated and gray, lay on tattered blankets in the bunks. They held slender, long-stemmed pipes in their brittle, skeletal fingers. At the end of each pipe, resting on a small table, was the pipe bowl—a diminutive cup burning red with each draw on the opium.

"Hopheads," Mammy Pleasant said. "No future in it."

We swept out of the opium den, unnoticed by its denizens. Mammy turned to me and said, "Duffield Fallon came to me for help. He knew, as did everyone, that if you needed someone stole away, I was the woman to do it. There was many a slave I stole away from the clutches of the evil institution back in the days before the war."

"Who was he after?" I asked.

"His precious jade," she said. "His Ah Ho."

We came to an underground alley lighted with red paper lanterns. To the right, and to the left, were tiny structures, each fronted with a door. And at the center of each door, placed just where a man could look in, was a grilled opening.

"May I look?"

Mammy nodded. I looked in the first window. A young Cantonese woman was there, sitting on a chair. She was on display. She'd combed her hair out long, so it hung over her bare breasts. She was wearing a pair of black silk pantaloons and a turquoise cummerbund. She bade me to enter. Ten cents for feelie, she recited, twenty-five cents for doie.

"Ah," I gasped, retracting from the window. I was shocked that these spirits, or hallucinations, or whatever they were, could see me.

Mammy Pleasant laughed. She hooked her arm in mine, swept me along the passage past the rows of doors. The passage telescoped out long before us. The doors shot past us as we flew down the alley, hundreds of them. And the sounds of the girls singing out their prices rose in a cacophonous chorus.

We suddenly halted. We'd come to a door, overhung by a red lantern, just like the others.

"This is where I hid Fallon's treasure," Mammy Pleasant said proudly. "Right under Lil Pete's nose. Right in the middle of his own cribs."

She knocked on the door, rapping out a code. Three quick knocks, and three with long pauses between. I looked in the peep window. An empty chair sat in the display chamber; a colorful calendar on the wall behind it—the year of the red horse—was the room's only decoration. The red curtain behind the chair fluttered. A woman stepped out from behind it.

She stood beside the chair. Unlike the prostitute I'd seen earlier, she was dressed in the respectable attire of a Cantonese wealthy merchant's wife. She wore a long emerald green silk dress, belted with a deep blue sash. Her hair was carefully pinned up in an elaborate dressing that made it look like the waves flowing in a tide pool.

She was a woman of class and stature. It went beyond her costume. I could tell by her feet. They were encased in miniature pointed slippers that poked tiny tips out from the hem of her dress. Her feet were bound.

Unlike the "big-footed" women that were recruited from the poor fishing villages of Szhechuan province to work in San Francisco's brothels, this woman was carefully raised and cultured to marry well, to be the wife of a wealthy man.

"She is Fallon's lost treasure?" I asked.

"Yes," Mammy told me. "She is Ah Ho, his employer's wife. Fallon loved her. The only woman he ever did love. When Lil Pete treated her bad, Fallon resolved to take her away with him. I helped him. It wasn't a great trick—not for me. I had my Negroes everywhere in the town, everywhere that I needed something done. We had her stole away, and hidden here. Then Fallon sent Lil Pete to meet Jesus."

"He killed his employer?" I asked. "This Little Pete?"

"That part was his affair," Mammy said. "My job was to get Ah Ho onto a ship to Mexico. And I did that."

"Fallon was to meet her there? In Mexico?"

"Yes. In the silver country. He had invested in a mine there."

"Where?"

"Guanajuato."

The candelabra jittered on the table. I felt my back hitting the plaster of the ceiling, banging up and down against it. I returned to the dining room. Claudia and the rest of them were still around the table, holding hands. They looked exactly the same, as if no time had passed.

"What does he want?" I asked, looking about wildly for Mammy Pleasant.

She was gone. But I could hear her voice. It was faint, and moving away, like she was on a boat being rowed out to sea.

"He wants to marry her," Mammy said. "He wants to give her his ring."

The chair legs rattled on the floor. A loud boom exploded, like the report of a ship's cannon. The chandelier swayed wildly, tinkling and creaking. I felt suddenly heavy. I crashed down from the ceiling, back into my chair.

A wave rippled across the floor, shuddered our chairs, and bounced the table. The candelabra fell over. We opened our hands and broke the circle.

Lit tapers rolled onto the floor. Blashky ran to the vase that had fallen from the sideboard. He poured the flower water onto the errant tapers. The water smelled of decay.

"Earthquake!" Blashky yelled. "Is everybody okay?"

"Fred, Fred!" Dante was screaming.

"Where is he?" Ashley was frantic.

Fred the cat shot into the room. He was powdered in white dust. He yowled. Dante scooped him up and squeezed him hard against his chest.

"Fred got hit in the head," Dante said. "With that heavy chunk."

Dante pointed down the hall to a piece of plaster that lay on the hardwood.

Ashley dropped onto her knees, wrapped her arms around the boy and Fred. She told Dante that Fred would be fine. He was a hard-headed old cat.

Blashky switched on the hall light. The bare bulb glowed hard against the dirty gray walls. A ragged hole gaped in the center of the hallway where the plaster had been torn away like a scab from a wound.

"Looks like that piece had been a patch job," Blashky said. "I never even noticed it before."

We peered into the newly opened wall. Behind the plaster, yellowing newspapers nested in brittle wads. Blashky pulled out the sheets, straightened them.

"*San Francisco Chronicle,*" he said, "2006."

"Isn't that when Frank lived here?" I asked.

Blashky didn't say anything. His silence was agreement.

Blashky reached deeper into the hole. Ashley told him not to put his hand inside.

"What's it going to do?" he said. "Bite me?"

He reached his hand around in the hole and pulled out a clump of hair.

"Oh my God!" Claudia cried and fell to the floor.

Emile righted her, propped her up against the wall. He ran to the kitchen to pour her a brandy.

"Bring the bottle," I called out to him.

Blashky laughed.

"This is horsehair," he said, shaking the clump of coarse sorrel strands at us. "They used it for insulation. It works good."

He reached his hand back into the hole. Emile returned with the brandy bottle. I took it from him and helped myself to generous swig. We'd forgotten about Claudia hyperventilating on the floor.

"Something else here," Blashky announced.

He reached farther, his arm venturing into the wall all the way to his shoulder.

"Got something here," he said. He carefully pulled it out. In his hand was a manuscript, housed in a soft cover. It was rolled up and held by a thick rubber band.

As Blashky pulled at the rubber band, it broke and flew off down the hall. The manuscript sprung open, leapt out of Stan's hand.

It fell onto the floor, the cover splayed open. It was lined paper, with torn edges. I recognized the handwriting.

It was the missing twenty pages from the back of Frank's journal. At the top of the first page was written the title:

> *The True Life of Duffy Waverly Fallon*
> *As told by Mr. Fallon himself to Frank Kelly*

And taped onto the page, below the title, was a gold ring—a wedding band.

Part Three

39

The relics that we'd pulled out of Blashky's wall went directly into another one. Emile Balzac took the ring and the story that Fallon had dictated to Frank. He locked them both up in the wall safe in his shop, alongside Frank's original typed manuscript of *The Flight of the Singing Bird*.

We decided, as a group, that the ring had to be restored to Ah Ho. Emile set to work researching the silver mine holdings in Guanajuato. If she'd escaped to that distant province set in the arid highlands of central Mexico, Ah Ho had likely lived out her days there, beyond the reach of Lil Pete's avenging hatchet men.

There was a single cemetery in Guanajuato. Perhaps she was in it.

Privately, I told Emile that I would possibly, and very soon, be traveling to that very city to give a performance. Guanajuato hosts the Cervantino every October. It's a monthlong performing arts festival dedicated to the spirit of Cervantes. I'd always wanted to be in it. And I'd had Maury worming around international opera circles for years trying get me a part with any of the guest companies.

This year, he'd been angling for the part of General Horemhab in a production of Philip Glass's *Akhnaten*. The company was small, independent, and gallingly Gallic in the way that only an isolated, and conquered, colonial offshoot of France's dead empire can be. They were Quebecois. From Montreal.

I called Maury up the morning after the séance to see if he'd made
any headway with the Montreal people. He said he was still working
on it. Whatever that means.

I berated him. I told him that if he was half as quick to follow up
on these engagements as he was to skim his cut off my paychecks that
we'd have a signed contract by now.

"You're hurting me, Max," he said.

I told him that was bullshit. Dramatic agents don't feel pain. They,
like all good salespeople, have Asperger's syndrome. The myriad re-
jections and insults they hear in the course of their days don't even
penetrate their force fields.

He told me to give him time. I waited, my obsession mounting. It
was more than wanting the gig. I wanted to be the one to take the
ring to Mexico. I wanted to be the one to find Ah Ho.

Nothing would bring Frank Kelly back. But paying off his debt to
Duffy Fallon would at least finish his business.

Golomlike, I became obsessed with the ring.

I went to Neptune's and told Emile that I was going to Guanajuato
to perform in the Cervantino.

"So, I'll just take the ring," I said. "Now."

Emile folded his arms across his herringbone vest and crinolated
his lips.

"Perhaps you can show me your contract," he said.

"Excuse me?" I exclaimed.

"Your contract," he repeated. "As proof of your engagement."

"You impertinent ass," I roared. "How dare you get officious with
me?"

"You have no more right to the ring than anyone else who was at
that table," he said.

"I have the right," I told him. "I am the man who's been terrorized
by Duffield Fallon for nearly a year. And I will be the man who puts
the issue to rest. I will take the ring and deliver it to Ah Ho."

Emile's cat jumped down from the counter and walked toward the back of the store. Balzac emitted a gust of breath, as if he were doing a little interpretive dance, enacting the wind of circumstance that he, willowlike, was obliged to bend with.

He capped his fountain pen, placed it in his vest pocket with a shrug. He followed the cat, threading through the maze of bookshelves to the reading pit. I followed him.

He removed the ring from the wall safe and tossed it at me. It bounced off my lapel and I had to chase it across Balzac's filthy, mildewed carpets.

"I hope you are not lying about your Guanajuato engagement, Max," he said, watching me, on my knees reaching under the credenza after the rolling ring. "Although, I know you are. Lying."

The transom bell rang. Emile Balzac went swanning off across his marshy wet carpets to greet his customer.

I held the ring up to the light. Inside, Fallon had inscribed the words *Eternal in Love*. I jammed the ring on my pinkie finger. It wouldn't slide past the first knuckle.

Remarkably, my plans for Guanajuato hatched. I wasn't the liar Emile Balzac declared me to be. I was prescient.

Maury called to say that, after a protracted logrolling contest with the Quebecois, he got me the contract. He was exalting in his victory, and expected me to heap coronets onto his shiny pate.

I obliged. I told him he was a champion and I was lucky to have him. He thanked me for the endorsement, even though it sounded like I was reading off a teleprompter.

I'd gotten my way. And as soon as I got it, I didn't want it anymore. I felt as though I'd been lured in. I was the white chick in a horror movie; alone in an isolated cabin on a stormy night, the power goes off, there's a noise in the cellar, and I get a candle and go downstairs to investigate.

To amuse myself, I dialed Emile Balzac. In a show of mock defer-
ence, I told Balzac that I could come by the shop to show him my contract for the Cervantino performance.

"So you just now got it, I suppose," he trilled over the line. "How
remarkable for you."

"You're not surprised?" I asked, because I was surprised.

"Not in the least," Emile said.

"It's uncanny," I insisted. "No?"

"No."

"*Alors*, Emile!" I said. "My agent is good—and I'm magnificent.
But I've been trying to get into the Cervantino for the past twelve years.
Never even a callback. Impenetrable. Now, suddenly, this opens up.
It feels like a trap."

"It's what you wanted," he said. I could hear him shut the front door
of his shop. The transom bell rang.

"But isn't the coincidence too much?" I asked, sounding like a tethered lamb.

"Oh, Max," he said. "This is not a coincidence. There is no such
thing."

I know, I told him. Everybody kept saying that.

40

I went to Montreal. I wore Ah Ho's ring on a gold chain around my
neck. It was my talisman. My scarab. My albatross.

I was soon immersed in the business of integrating with the rest
of the cast. They were generous, welcoming. I was replacing the bass
baritone they'd been working with for a couple of weeks, and we
only had two weeks left to pull the performance together. They ral-

lied around me, often working until midnight, helping me get my bearings.

I liked them all, with one exception. The poncy artistic director—prosaically named Jacques—who I knew would be a nuisance from the first moment I set eyes on his stubby blond ponytail.

He presented me with my costume. It was every bit as revealing as that pole-dancer costume those L.A. bitches had made me wear in *L'Orfeo*. Only now, I was even less prepared for that kind of exposure—I'd gone on a gluten-and-fermented-beverages bender the moment *L'Orfeo* closed. And it showed.

I tried shock and awe. I attacked Jacques, roaring with outrage, in front of the group. I was hoping to incite some sort of Bastille moment. Perhaps the Quebecers would put on their stocking caps and grab their pitchforks and join me in storming Jacques.

I was wrong. I hadn't factored in their very "Canadianness." Everyone went silent at my outburst, I saw a couple of them elbow each other. The rest looked down at their librettos or pretended to find loose threads on their costumes.

"I am not," I bellowed, kicking a Styrofoam pyramid block across the stage, "not, I say, going to prance around the stage in that damned Caspian Sea bikini like Charlton Heston in a sword and sandals movie."

"Perhaps monsieur would care to consult the original friezes depicting persons of the times," Jacques barbed back at me, unfazed. "Clearly this is faithful to the period."

The bystanders—for that's what they were, bystanders unwilling to come to my aid—were by then openly ogling the spectacle. Every one of them had their mouths hitched up in the same wry expression.

I decided not to let Jacques make this into a polemic on historical accuracy. There's no such thing.

"I am not a fucking peeler in some titty bar," I declared, hoping, even yet, to rouse the rest of the cast—my erstwhile confederates—to my cause.

"No," Jacques said, "you are not a *titty* peeler."

And then, in a moment of what I interpreted to be derisive onomatopoeia, he repeated the word. *Titty.* He said *titty,* and then he tittered.

Literally. The guy tittered.

"Titty peeler," Jacques said. "Monsieur would certainly not have the physique for that line of work."

That got the rest of the inbred Gallic colonials tittering too.

He continued, "Monsieur may wish to embark upon a program of fitness to prepare his physicality for this role. The character, after all, is meant to be a powerful general, a man of action."

"*Je ne vais pas être traité comme un imbecile,*" I roared, in a pure Parisian accent meant to ridicule their colonial honking. "*Monsieur* does not require a physical program. *Monsieur* requires a costume design with taste."

And with that I kicked over another boulder but—having not noticed that this was one of the "illuminated" boulders—I neglected to account for its structure: a metal frame covered with a gauzy painted muslin skin. My boot went through the muslin, and caught inside the chicken wire. It stuck. I tried to kick it off my foot. Still, it stuck. I shook my leg furiously. Finally the boulder flung off my boot, spitballed backward, and hit me in the chest.

The tittering exploded into a chorus of snorts and yelps.

I stalked off the stage. Later, I found the costume neatly laid out on my dressing table.

Maury was soon on the telephone, with the usual damage control that he's obliged to perform at this point in just about every production I'm involved in.

"Max." He called me after speaking with the artistic director several times in one day. "Please, for God's sake, just wear the costume. Jacques sent me a photo of it on the other bass baritone. It looks good on him."

"I'm not him."

"There's nothing wrong with it," he said. "Especially when you take it in context of the entire cast's wardrobe."

"It's too revealing."

"Max," he said, firm now. "I'm warning you. Do not pull this stuff."

"It's too revealing," I repeated, louder. "I'd have to wear a damn butt plug."

"Now you're being hysterical," Maury told me. "I've seen the costume. It is more coverage that what you'd wear at the beach. And besides, you got in such great shape for *L'Orfeo*. I'm sure it looks terrific on you."

Maury didn't know, and I didn't tell him, that in the weeks between the final performance of *L'Orfeo* and the beginning of rehearsals for *Akhnaten,* I'd been gorging like a steer in a feedlot. In fact, as we were talking on the telephone, I was plowing through a box of mini-macaroons and washing them down with a tumbler of muscat.

"Max, are you there?" he said.

I was there. I was just chewing.

"Max, will you please cooperate?"

"Yes," I finally said.

I closed the box of macaroons, tossed it in the garbage. I hung up the phone, strode across my hotel room to the lavatory, and stuck my finger down my throat.

41

Jacques and I reached a détente. He discreetly offered to arrange my meals for me—boxed lunches and dinners from a health food restaurant near the theater. I discreetly accepted.

The Montreal performances came off very well, and the kinks were small and easily straightened out. I was enjoying myself. I even began to develop a fancy for King Akh himself, a local luminary with a piercing tenor range and a swimmer's dolphinlike body—long and lean and hairless.

But, following my own rule, I tabled my carnal thoughts regarding Pierre. Overinvolvement with other cast members during a production run was an error I'd committed only once, and at a great price. It had been nearly fifteen years since Connie and I divorced, but the entire episode had left me with an acute case of Irish amnesia: I forgot everything but the grudge.

I kept up with news from San Francisco via Stan, and Claudia, and to a lesser extent, Emile. Fallon had, evidently, left Stan's flat after we removed the manuscript and ring. It was the paranormal equivalent of when your girlfriend throws all your stuff out the window onto the street.

Stan asked me if the ring, which I faithfully wore on the chain around my neck, had attracted Fallon. Was he in Montreal with me?

No, I told him. Not a sign of the old scoundrel. And I did look for him.

My secret truth was, I kind of missed him. Fallon had become part of my life, just as Baba was. He had been dogging me for months—breathing his foul crypt-cold breath down my back, watching me from the shadows, melting into the putrid ether from whence he'd emanated whenever I turned to accost him. Damned nuisance.

But one comes to embrace even the annoyances in life once they are embedded into your daily routine. I remembered how I had missed Connie—for much longer than I ever admitted to anyone.

I didn't miss any particular thing about her. Not her conversation. Not the sex. Certainly not her cooking.

But I did miss her way of being with me. I missed the way we'd make coffee in the morning without having to figure out who was spooning the grounds into the filter and who was putting on the kettle. I missed driving with her and knowing that she'd never run a yellow light. I missed finding there was a certain movie playing on TV and not having to ask her if she wanted to watch it.

Like Connie, I came to miss Fallon only after he was gone. But I think my nostalgia took on a deeper note after I'd read his story, in his own words.

Maybe that was why people tell their stories. Oral histories. Memoirs. Fiction. It's all one. Betty Ann Thibideaux was proof of that. She, and Frank, and Fallon, probably all wanted the same thing. To be remembered is as close as one can get to immortality.

Over time—long after the storyteller is subsumed into the darkness—he becomes his story. He is no longer viewed as the bastard who used women, or borrowed money, or kicked Styrofoam blocks across a stage.

Just look at the colossal dickheads who became saints through art. Gauguin. Hemingway. Fucking Ezra Pound.

So, why not Duffield Fallon? Indeed, why not Frank Kelly?

42

It was my last night in Montreal. I had a late supper with the cast. We celebrated. We shared a big, meaty meal at a cheerful restaurant in one of Montreal's Victorian-era neighborhoods. Plenty of wine. Laughter. We were brothers in arms, a company, a corps.

I told them about Fallon, not the part about my involvement with him, but just about Fallon as a colorful character. He became, for this audience, a delightful figure. He became his story.

I was surprised by how much of Fallon's lore I easily recalled. I even recited whole passages of his lengthy tale, like a medieval troubadour or a Rhajasthani bhoupa. The story, the language, the images flowed.

It made me realize what a masterful, natural storyteller Duffield Fallon had been. And why Frank Kelly sought to ride his coattail to fame.

Talent is nothing more than personality. Fallon had barrels of it.

His story, as he'd told it to Frank, was alive and breathing and its heart was beating. Frank's book, with all its technical proficiencies, could never achieve the same.

But, even diluted through lesser talents, Fallon's story was powerful. The Quebecois were swept up in the daring, the abandon, and the seedy glitter that was the Barbary Coast in its last days, just before the earth shook. That legendary American Sodom stood tallest right before it was knocked onto its knees and the fires roared through and consumed the felled houses of recreational vice.

Channeling Fallon, I was able to make them smell the dank cobblestones, wet with beer and blood and morning mist. They could feel the twitch of the opium addict's urge, and the gambler's compulsion.

They howled at Fallon's leg-breaking escapades, taking on the brooding rage of the street hoodlum. Their expressions turned salacious, even the women's, when I told them about the gilded and perfumed elegance of the finest banjios; the bestiality "circuses" staged in underground dives; and the vast, covered cattle yards filled with hundreds of prostitutes working openly in pens. And they were touched with a genuine grief at the stories of used-up whores, left in back rooms with a candle and a blanket to rot to death, after their market value fell below twenty-five cents.

I realized how right Frank Kelly had been. If he could tell the story of Fallon and Ah Ho with even a glimmer of the animation that Fallon himself had brought to it, he would have achieved a great thing.

———

At the end of the evening, we strayed out onto the empty street. The streetlights wore soft halos, lending their glow down on us from the black sky. I looked up and thought it was raining stars. They fell all around us, on us. Tiny glittering stars.

Someone said it was snowing. And we laughed. It was the first week of October. This was the first snow.

We all embraced and kissed good night. I even kissed Jacques. He vised his arms around the thick padding of my overcoat and wouldn't let go. He stood on his tiptoes and breathed Cabernet Franc into my chin and told me I was a great fearsome moose, crashing through the forest, and he loved me for it.

It doesn't sound like much of a compliment. But I figured Canadians know their wildlife, and Jacques said it with such bonhomie that I could only take the moose analogy as a compliment.

They offered me a ride back to my hotel. I declined. I chose to walk in the still, cold night, the silent snowflakes floating all about me, dusting my shoulders with a diamond mantle.

Back at the hotel, I cranked the window open, pulled the armchair up to it, and sat with a cognac and a cigar. It was my private moment of celebration. I reflected on the Montreal run, the successful launch of the show, and on all the events of the last year that had brought me here, to this hotel room, in this wingback chair, blowing cigar smoke into the black, cold, sparkling night.

It had been a year ago since the past returned to assert itself over the present.

Last October, Frank Kelly came back into my life by taking his own.

Then Betty Ann Thibideaux resurfaced. And died. Whether she was her own victim or someone else's was never clarified. Detective Fung didn't discuss it with me again. I figured there were only two possibilities: either she shot herself, or she didn't. But whatever she was up to on that bridge, no one knew. And they probably never would.

I thought of Ashley, how I'd wanted her those many years ago. Then I got her. Lost her. And it made me more miserable than if I'd never had her at all.

I grieved over Ashley. It was not because I couldn't have her, but because I couldn't be the kind of man that could keep her.

My thoughts swirled around, always eddying back to Duffield Fallon. He, the man standing in the most distant past, was the man at the fore of everything.

I poured a second cognac. The heavy amber draw of it pulled me down into a hollow abyss. I set my cigar carefully in the ashtray and watched as the ash grew a tiny bit thicker, then the ember subsided, and the last wisp of smoke trailed off out the window into the night.

I took another drink of cognac, swirled the remainder around the snifter, and watched its viscous legs descend in gummy tears down the glass.

Shimmering snowflakes whirled white diamonds in the black velvet sky. A ship's deep horn sounded. A tall ship hauled into view. It was a triple-masted schooner, cutting through a bank of fog with its attenuated prow. I was on the pier. A foghorn called out from an island in the distance. The schooner pulled alongside the pier, its ropes furled and looped around the pilings.

Steel-heeled boots echoed across the wooden planks. Duffy Fallon stood in front of me. He wore a dandy's top hat; sheared beaver, crest bowed out wider than the brim. He touched his hat with two fingers, tipped it to a rakish tilt. He grinned. And his eyes were brilliant green emeralds, cut in many facets.

"It's Christmas," he said to me.

The night air was dank. Fog rolled across the bay, seeped up over the pier's edge, and drifted along the splintering wooden planks of the pier. Fallon turned his back. His hobnail footfalls echoed across the wet air and drowned in the sea water.

Fallon stood at the foot of a gangplank, he read aloud the ship's name—the *White Lotus Maiden*.

"Who goes there," a raspy voice called from behind the curtain of fog.

"Fallon," he said.

"Come up," the rasp, now friendly, instructed.

"Captain Shea," Fallon greeted a crooked figure, bearded and gray and grizzled.

The captain stood in the cold night, impervious in his sealskin coat. A meerschaum pipe clinched in the side of his mouth cast a white glow up across his lined face and into the hollows that housed his squinting, sea-gray eyes.

"That's a pretty job they did on your face," the captain said to Fallon.

I looked at Fallon's face. I wondered why I hadn't noticed it before and then, as is so often the case in dreams, I told myself it was because I was dreaming and there was never a linear order of events in a dream. A scar, fresh and vicious, sliced down Fallon's face. It hooked from his right eye, skated across his cheek, crossed both lips, and exited on the right side of his chin.

Fallon said nothing.

"They're clever with their cleavers," the captain persisted.

The scar opened up, bloomed red and wet, parting like lips. Fallon looked at me, daring me to look away from his wound. I knew that if I did he'd smite me for my weakness. The savage lips of his wound again pursed. The scar line faded from raw red to porcine pink, then white as albacore.

"Looks like the Chinaman meant to take yer eye," the captain said.

"He didn't get it."

Fallon scratched the scar with the curve of his hook hand, proud of his wounds and his whittled-off pieces. He was proud of having survived. He was unkillable.

"He got something else instead, I'll wager." The captain smiled grimly, showing nubby teeth stained black with beetlenut. "I know you well enough, Mr. Fallon. You gave that Chinaman a turn for his trouble."

Fallon unbuttoned his coat, took a gold watch out of the pocket of his brocade vest. The watch dangled on a chain of braided hair—long hair, shiny and black.

"Got them Sum Yups under control now, I suppose?" the captain said, eyeing the braid.

Fallon pressed the latch. The watch flipped open. The face of the timepiece glowed like a moon. The hours, marked with diamond studs, flashed like agitated stars.

"Little Pete is anxious about the cargo," Fallon said.

"The box is still sealed," the captain promised. "I do as I'm told. Don't open it 'til Duffy Fallon arrives, the manifest instructs. And so I don't. Just told the lad to put the victuals inside the pass-through cupboard, and take away the chamber pot. Twice daily. As instructed. No man has laid eyes on the contents. That privilege was reserved for you, Mr. Fallon."

The captain led Fallon and I along the croaking boards of the clipper's deck. We descended three steps under the wheelhouse and entered the captain's private quarters.

"I stow the special cargo in a secret compartment," the captain said, grinning black teeth. His walrus mustaches bristled and he raised his thicket of gray eyebrows.

"I must swear you to secrecy about my arrangement," the captain said. "Otherwise I can't guarantee the safekeeping of Little Pete's cargo of this nature. Men being what they are. And seamen being even more of what they are."

"The cargo had best be intact," Fallon said. "Or you'll find yourself at the bottom of the bay looking for your ears."

"Oh, to be sure," the captain said, unfazed by the factuality of Fallon's words. "And that's why I take these here special measures. Canton is two weeks out, Mr. Fallon, and buggery can be a poor substitute for a man's more natural inclinations."

"Little Pete is waiting," Fallon interrupted.

"And he's not a patient man," the captain finished Fallon's thought for him.

Captain Shea got Fallon to help him move a sideboard on which were spread the ship's navigational charts, a sexton, and a heavy flagon of brandy. Shea tapped sharply against an oak panel where it met a mahogany pilaster, and the panel sprung open.

The two men bent down and stepped through the threshold into a small but well-ventilated room. It started out wide, then the two walls arced center and met at the fore. Two mullioned windows, placed high above the waterline, stood open on either wall.

Stacks of barrels lined the floor, lashed against the walls with heavy ropes. I heard Fallon's heart pound hard at the sight of them. I tasted his mouth go dry. I'm Fallon now, I realized. I wanted to pull the hatchet out from Fallon's waistband. I wanted to smash open the top of the first barrel with it, reach inside and snatch out one of the bags. I wanted the tarry opium for myself.

"The dragon is always close enough," Fallon said to me. I was back in my own body now. He smiled conspiratorially. "No need to steal from Pete. Not what he gives freely, anyhow."

"Are you taking these too?" Captain Shea asked, seeing how my interest had been arrested by the opium barrels.

"San Gee will come with a couple coolies for that," Fallon said. "Is this mine here?"

Fallon walked over to a large wooden crate—the size of a Barbary prostitute's crib—wedged into the far end of the room. He tapped the top of the box with the tip of his ivory-handled cane. He swung the cane in an arc, tapped the walls on either side of the box.

"A generous size for a shipping crate," the captain remarked.

"And a tight quarters for a voyage." Fallon swung around, his upper lip curling into a snarl where the scar tore through it.

"Oh, they's used to much worse," Captain Shea said, rummaging around in a wooden bin and coming up with an iron pry bar. "You should see how they live in Canton. Like vermin in a harborage, Mr. Fallon. Packed into stinkin' rooms, squatting around a single cook fire. This is posh by them standards."

"This one ain't of that class," Fallon admonished him. "This one comes of a fine house. A rich merchant man's house."

"They's all monkeys to me," quipped the captain, singsongy now, his head bobbling as he shambled, bow-legged, over to the wooden box.

Shea jimmied the iron teeth of the pry bar into the side of the box and started working it apart, moving down the seam of the seal. It lifted gradually, and then gave open with a loud snap. The box door swung wide on its hinges.

A strong wind, soaked with gardenia, rushed into the room. The inside of the box shimmered emerald green. Its walls were upholstered in shiny green silk. Golden dragons and sapphire fire birds capered across the field of shantung silk. A carved ivory platform, covered in pink silk bedding, stood against the far wall of the box.

A woman sat in the center of the bed. She was exquisite. Small. So small and pale, she looked like she too had been carved out of ivory. She stood up. Her feet were impossibly tiny. She lowered her eyes in a discreet, but imperious, acknowledgment.

"Pretty as a petunia," the captain whispered.

The girl raised her head to regard us. I heard a cascade of sparkling bells—the trickling of green glacier water over ice. A bower of tiny silver bells draped from the ebony sticks in her hair. The clever sticks poked out in all directions; engineering an elaborate series of coiffure flying buttresses. She stepped delicately, but assuredly, from the box on her tiny feet.

Fallon held out his hand to her. I thought she would step right onto his palm. Her feet would fit in it.

She didn't, of course. Instead, she gave him her little hand, and allowed him to steady her as she stepped from the box's carpeted platform and onto the polished planks of the ship's floor. She withdrew her hand from Fallon's gentle grasp, and snuggled it into her muff. She regarded me impassively with obsidian eyes. The eyes slid to the captain. He too elicited no reaction. She turned her gaze onto Fallon. Her face was still a mask, but I thought I detected an undercurrent of expectation.

Fallon lifted his hand to the brim of his hat. He swept it off in a courtly flourish, held it over his heart, and bowed.

"Your future husband sends you his most felicitous and heartfelt welcome," Fallon said to her. "I am Mr. Fallon, his lieutenant. He has entrusted me to escort you to your lodgings."

"Fa Lon," she spoke, her voice as sparkling as the bells she wore in her hair. "Thank you."

"Well, that's the prettiest gift I ever seen come out of a box," the captain said.

"Yes," Fallon said.

He turned and fixed on me. The girl and the captain were now two-dimensional, frozen in a pose. Captured inside a sepia tintype.

Fallon loomed in close to me. His scar throbbed and his eyes became kaleidoscopes filled with jewels—tumbling rubies, diamonds, and emeralds.

"Her name is Ah Ho," he said to me. "I stole her fair and square, Max Bravo. And if it weren't for the bad luck, I'd have kept her. I want her back, Max Bravo. Get her for me."

I woke up in the chair, the window open and the cold air blowing snowflakes into the room. They fell onto the carpet and melted.

I shut the window, got into the bed. In the morning I'd be flying back to San Francisco.

43

I was 30,000 feet above Saskatchewan, that table-flat expanse of northern farmland. The vast wheat fields spread out below in precise patchworks—the labors of four generations of Ukrainians and Lithuanians who had arrived in Canada, and moved west until they found the soil as black, and the terrain as flat, as the breadbasket lands of their origin.

Fittingly, Air Canada served sausages and pierogis for lunch.

We were flying to San Francisco for a one-week engagement of *Akhnaten*. The rest of the cast was languishing back in steerage, dying the long transcontinental death, while I luxuriated in business class. I'd upgraded using my air miles.

It wasn't easy. There had been only one opportunity for the upgrade. We were waiting in the concourse and they announced it, and I had to practically knock over the soprano who made a game dash for the ticket counter. She informed me that I was no gentleman. I informed her that she could stake out her moral high ground back in coach.

I stretched out my legs, brooded over my dream about Fallon. The stewardess startled me when she asked if she could bring me another can of beer. I looked at my hand, and saw that I'd crushed the Molson's Canadian can in my fist. I gave it to her. She went off to fetch me another. They're used to that sort of thing, I told myself. They get a lot of NHL players up here in the pricey seats.

She brought me a fresh beer.

"Right on," I said, addressing her in her native tongue. "Thanks, eh."

The second Molson's stimulated me to an even deeper state of cogitation. There was a direct connection between Fallon and Orpheus. Perhaps even King Akhnaten, or at least there was something there to do with the ancient Egyptian funerary rituals.

Orpheus was an artist who followed his dead lover into Hell to bring her back. His only weapon was his art. Like Orpheus, Fallon was in Hell, looking for his lover, this Ah Ho woman.

Orpheus was the Greeks' interpretation of an Egyptian mythology that traces back to around 6,000 B.C.E., and perhaps even earlier. The Osiris story.

The king, Osiris, is tricked and murdered by his usurping brother—another reason I'm glad I'm an only child. The rotten brother cuts Osiris up into fourteen pieces and scatters them all up and down the Nile. Isis, Osiris's sister-wife, then kicks into action. She retrieves all the pieces, binds Osiris back together. She then transforms herself into a birdlike creature. Isis stands over the top of the Frankensteined Osiris, wafting the breath of life back into him by fanning her wings.

I pulled Frank Kelly's book out of my satchel. *The Flight of the Singing Bird*.

I knew that in the Barbary Coast days, the Chinese prostitutes were known as singing birds because of the way they'd call out their price lists to men who passed their cribs. I had, naturally, assumed that this was the singing bird meaning that Frank referred to in his book's title.

But now, reflecting on the lady Isis and her feathery life-giving dance, I wondered if there was another meaning to Ah Ho being called a bird.

If Fallon was rummaging around in Hell, or purgatory, looking for her, was she perhaps, like Isis, the bird creature who could return him to life?

I turned to the final chapter in Frank's book:

Fallon handed Ah Ho's valise to Captain Shea.

"The same ship," she said to him.

"Yes, but this time you won't be traveling in a box," Fallon told her, his face so close to hers, he could smell the jasmine tea on her breath, he could see the tears welling in her eyes.

"Fa Lon," she whispered. "Don't send me alone."

"You must go now, darling," he told her. "I'll take care of Pete. If I don't he'll hunt us down. And we'll never have a day of peace. I'll end this now. Here, on the Barbary Coast."

The captain swaggered over to the lovers embracing on the ship's deck. He swept his hat off his head, apologized, and told them the ship had to cast off if they were to catch the tide that would carry them out of San Francisco Bay.

Fallon asked for one more moment. Shea agreed, clapped his cap back on his head, and strode off across the deck yelling instructions to the men in the rigging.

Fallon turned his face back to Ah Ho's. The tears had broken over the levee of her black lashes now. They traced down her cheeks and he had to set his chin firm at the sight of them.

"Bierce will meet you at Puerto Vallarta," he told her. "He'll take you to Guanajuato by train and coach."

She steadied herself, nodded, and wiped her cheeks with the long silk sleeves that hung out from below the cuffs of her tweed traveling coat.

"Do you have the documents?" he asked her, urgently now.

She unbuttoned her coat, reached inside the sash that banded her middle in a wide swath of garnet-hued silk. She pulled out a leather-bound secretary's packet.

"Good," he said. "Keep it there. Even when you sleep. When you get to Guanajuato, take the documents to Señor Hector DeSilva. I've already wired him. He knows what to do. Hector will see to it that you're settled comfortably."

"The words on these papers," Ah Ho said. "What do they say, Fa Lon? What exactly?"

"These words protect you," Fallon told the girl. "The letter to Hector entreats him to care for you as carefully as if you were his own daughter. The documents are my shares in the Alvarez mine. A lawyer has transferred them to your name. There's a notarized seal attesting to it."

"I will be alone," she protested.

"No, you won't, Ah Ho," he said, gripping her tightly by her tiny shoulders. "Hector is my partner, and so he is yours too. There's enough silver in that mine to keep us all in fine style for the rest of our days."

The ship's bell rang, a hard clang against the wet, black air. The first mate called out through the fog, ordering the men to prepare to cast off the lines.

Fallon kissed Ah Ho.

"I am afraid for you," the girl said. "Pete is a very bad man. Very dangerous."

"It's Duffield Fallon you're in love with, my pet," he said, the scarred side of his face turning hard in a squint. "The floor of this bay is littered with men who once tried to impress upon me just how dangerous they were."

Two things about that passage struck me. One: Frank Kelly was nowhere near the gifted storyteller that the old barroom raconteur, Duffield Fallon, had been.

And two: Fallon was a man who had been derailed while in pursuit of his life's greatest quest. He never did meet Ah Ho in Mexico. The Great Earthquake of 1906 stopped him.

On the very morning he was set to catch a ship to Mexico to follow after Ah Ho, the earthquake struck. Fallon was trapped in his room in the Valencia Hotel. The burning hotel sank into the artesian pool below its foundation.

Fallon perished in a burning lake. He was still down there, in fact. Emile Balzac's research revealed that no one was in Fallon's grave site at the Mission cemetery. It was empty. Fallon's mother had used her extensive sway—backed up by her knowledge of the sexual perversions and peccadilloes of every powerful man in San Francisco—to secure a proper Christian tombstone for her son in the consecrated tract.

Fallon's body was never recovered. It, like so many others, was still down there, beneath what was now a decrepit parking lot.

But what became of Fallon's eternal soul?

The Egyptians believed that after you died, your soul had to pass through a couple of testing stations before being allowed to proceed to Heaven. First, they weighed your heart on a scale; heart on one side, a feather on the other. If your heart was light as the feather—that is, if you were free of guilt—on you went. If you had anything weighing down your heart, you were summarily devoured by a hideous creature.

Perhaps Fallon could pass the feather test. Sociopaths aren't troubled by guilt.

But he still had to pass through a burning lake. Fallon—like the rebel angels in *Paradise Lost*—had been defeated and cast down into a burning lake.

As Emile Balzac kept reminding me, there are no coincidences. All the disparate pieces were fitting together, in a lattice of meaning.

Duffield Fallon was still languishing in his burning lake, trapped and gnashing at the cruel turn of events that kept him from Ah Ho.

I reached for my throat, pulled the gold chain out from under my scarf. I closed my fingers around Ah Ho's ring.

I counted the number of days until I'd be in Guanajuato. Fallon was lying quietly beneath Valencia Street. But that was only for the moment. I knew he had not been a patient man. And now—now that he was roasting in a watery purgatory—he would be more impatient than ever.

44

I tore down the temples of the sun god, Aten. Ordered my men to raze the city. Executed the royal couple, Akhnaten and Nefertiti. Usurped the throne. Declared myself the son of the bird-head god Horus. And then I called it a night.

It was our last San Francisco performance of *Akhnaten* before decamping for the Guanajuato engagement. I found myself savoring my role as Horemhab with a renewed relish. My villain stole the show.

The *San Francisco Chronicle* wrote: "Max Bravo, thundering bass baritone, rumbles with menace and power as the mighty Egyptian general." And it was all the more savory since I was able to show off in my hometown.

When the lights went up in the house that last night and we trotted onstage for our final bows, I was feeling giddy and buoyant. I bowed—courtly in my knee-high gold sandals—smiled broadly, sure to nod my head in a gesture of oh-I'm-not-really-worthy-it's-the-company-who-deserves-your-adulation, tapped my loose fist to my heart, and smiled at the soprano, who shot me a sour glance—she was still seething over the dustup at the Montreal airport.

I quickly shifted my attention up to the box seats, beaming, and was struck dumb at the sight of Ashley and Dante Banks in the first private balcony. Those tickets cost $385. Each.

Sitting beside them was a well-oiled, middle-aged man looking delighted and comfortably familial. He had his arm around the back of Ashley's seat in a proprietary gesture.

I blinked into the lights, caught myself squinting at them. Ashley handed Dante a bouquet of red roses. The boy stood and tossed them over the balustrade. I was still so dumbfounded at the sight of those two that I didn't raise my arms. The bouquet struck me on my gold breastplate, and fell to the floor. I quickly recouped my presence of mind, scooped up the flowers, and smiled as if I meant it.

Dante cheered and called out to me. I waved at the boy, then had to restrain myself from biting the heads off the roses when the man in the box—the dog in the manger—rose to his feet in ovation and after clapping like a seal, set his hand on Dante's shoulder.

I was fuming in my dressing room when one of the attendants asked if I'd receive my well-wishers.

"No," I said. I stretched my hairnet over my head. I furiously circled a thick layer of cold cream onto my face.

"They say they're friends of yours, Mr. Bravo," the attendant, an elderly woman in orthopedic shoes, pressed on in tremulous strains.

"*No!*" I screamed.

I picked up the rose bouquet from my dressing table and threw it at her.

She scampered out. I was impressed with how quickly the old gal could sprint in those crepe-soled hoppers.

A few moments later there was a brisk knock at my door. The door swung open and the portly form of the stage manager heaved into the room. I refused to turn around in my dressing chair. I regarded him in the wide angle of my dressing mirror from behind a congealing mask of snow-white cold cream. I reached into the ice bucket, pulled out the Moët & Chandon, and topped off my flute.

"Max," he began, even tones, akimbo stance. "The attendants are volunteers. You can't abuse them."

"I suppose not," I said, taking a sip of my champagne, pinky finger in full erection as I daintily raised my flute. "One generally has to pay people for the privilege of abusing them."

I took another sip. Regarded my flute. Downed the rest in a big slug. Repoured until the foam fizzed over the top.

"Or, there are people," I spoke through the bubbles in my nose. "People out there—who think that if they sleep with someone they have the right to abuse them."

"Please keep your voice down, Max," he told me, folding his hands in front of him, in prayer.

"Oh sure," I opined. "Once they've had you—really *had you*—then they think they can treat you however they damn well please. Like you're a doll. A plaything."

"You'll have to apologize," he said.

"To whom?"

"The attendant you just threw the roses at."

"Yes. Good idea," I chirped. "Please tell Valerie I'm sorry."

"Her name is Edith."

"Yes. Tell her, would you?"

He was still standing there, fists jammed into his pear hips.

"Is there something else?" I asked tartly.

I finished toweling off the cold cream. I whipped off my hairnet and started brushing out my hair with vigorous strokes. Deftly wielding my paddle-sized hairbrush, I achieved a lustrous effect. I appraised my coif with open approval.

"Your guests are waiting out here in the hall," he said. "I'm going to tell them to come in."

"Absolutely not," I screeched. I bolted up, knocking my dressing stool over backwards, and threw my hairbrush across the room.

"Absolutely yes," he said. He was unimpressed, as if he'd actually expected my response.

I pincered my champagne flute in an angry lobster grip, and stormed toward him, shoulder-first, rather a sideways crab walk. I thought the oddly crustaceous physicality would throw him. But, again, he retained his composure. He even managed a bemused half smile.

"You're going to see these people, Max," he said. "Because not only are the lady and the boy your personal friends, but their escort—the gentleman who paid for the most expensive box seats in the house— is Teddy Argent."

"I don't care if he's Gary Glitter," I stage-whispered, still loud enough to reach the odious trio hovering just outside my door.

"Teddy Argent," he continued, "is one of the top five contributors to this opera company. Without his kind gifts—without his money, Max—you would not even be here. You would not be performing, either on stage or here in your dressing room."

He finished speaking and watched me as his meaning sank in. I said something like "harrumph," and finished off the last drizzle of champagne. I tossed myself onto my sofa, adjusted the sash of my kimono, and crossed my legs, stared at my gold-sandaled foot kick up and down.

"Are you ready for your guests now?" he asked me.

He bent down, set the stool upright, picked the roses up off the floor, and stuffed them in the waterless vase on my dressing table.

"Hold on," I said. I abandoned the sofa, went over to the dressing table, re-inserted myself onto my tuffet stool, filled my flute.

"Let me get set up," I said. I dabbed off the last traces of face cream, wanded mascara on my lashes, and slid a buff lipstick across my lips.

He fetched my hairbrush off the floor, handed it to me. I replumped and smoothed my coif.

"Ready?" he asked, his hand on the doorknob.

"All right," I said, waved him away.

I hated Teddy Argent the moment he stepped into my mirror. Of course, I didn't do them the honor of standing, or even of facing them. I let them all step awkwardly inside my sanctum and stand by the door, fidgeting, waiting to be offered a seat.

Teddy Argent was dressed expensively, but he still looked like a jackass. His Wilkes Bashford suit was impeccable—charcoal wool cashmere, a long jacket with slim lapels. He wore expensive brown leather boots, Iberian, probably Portuguese. Instead of a tie, he had a paisley scarf draped around his neck. His hair was fashionably cut, short, in a Caesar. It was all a little too perfect. A little too prescribed. If you did the reverse math on it you could see that the sum total was the product of adding Argent's money to Ashley's taste.

Argent smiled winningly, waiting for me to turn around and sashay over to greet them. I lifted my champagne flute, locked on them in the mirror, and tossed off an "Oh, hello there," then washed the words down with a belt of bubbly. Argent played the role I'd maneuvered him into; eager supplicant. He lavished a burble of lapdoggy praise for my performance on me by way of a greeting.

But Ashley was having none of it. She crinkled up the side of her mouth, threw her purse down on a chair, and stormed into my dressing room. She made for the guest flutes, and proceeded to pour herself and Argent drinks.

"Shall we toast Max's marvelous performance," she said. It wasn't a question.

I still refused to turn away from my dressing table. I tipped my glass to her reflection, then his. Argent was all here, here, well done, raising his glass like a rube.

Ashley shot me a withering look, drank her champagne without comment. I wasn't going to let her win. And she didn't. It was the boy who got me to stand up and consort with them.

Dante came running up to me, tossed his arms around my neck, told me I was great.

"You flatter me, sir," I told him. "And I like it. Champagne?"

"Max," Ashley said. "He's ten years old."

"Oh, of course," I said. "Pinot Grigio then?"

Argent brayed like a circus ass. He was one of those parvenus who's always astounded at the social entrees that his money purchases for him.

"How about one of these chocolates?" Dante asked me, smudging his little booger-picking fingers over every truffle in the box.

"How about it, Ashley?" I appealed to her. "Can Dante have a bonbon? Or are you the only one around here who gets everything she wants?"

Argent brayed again. Ashley ignored him.

She fixed on me and said to him, "Teddy, darling, could you take Dante up to get the coats. He's starving. There's a PowerBar in his jacket. I don't want him eating sweets."

Argent complied.

"He hops right to it, doesn't he?" I said as soon as Argent hustled out with Dante.

"Max," she said to me. "You're going to have to get on the other side of this."

"Where is that, exactly?" I said. "I'm not good with geography."

"But you're good with psychology."

"You had no business barging in here with that"—I cast about for the appropriate descriptor—"that, that Silicon Valley bindle stiff."

"Let me edit this scene for you, Max." She set her champagne flute on the dressing table, unbuttoned her coat, and jammed her fists onto her hips. I wondered what it was that encouraged all these people to assume that posture.

"I'm going to marry Ted."

I started to speak. Then I realized what she'd just told me.

I was struck mute. I slowly set my flute down on the dressing table.

"I'm tired, Max. I'm tired of trying to raise Dante by myself. Tired of working like an asshole, worrying about rushing to pick him up from school. I'm tired of wasting my life on men who are drunk, or have no ambition. Men who want to have kids, but don't want to grow up themselves. I'm tired of Blashky. He'll never get anywhere. And I'm tired of you—you'll never think about anybody but yourself."

"I love you," I said.

"I know," she said. "But you won't. Maybe next year. Maybe in two years. Five years. But it'll happen. You're easily distracted, Max. You'll run off and leave me for another woman."

She pressed her mouth shut. Her eyes glittered wet. She winced. She spoke again. "Or you'll leave me for a man. And there's nothing I can do to change that."

I turned away from her. She was right.

From the hallway, footfalls ran along the corridor. A man called out. A snatch of muffled laughter. Women's voices. The cast was going out for drinks. A raucous fist pounded on my door. They asked, in that honking Quebecois French, if I was ready. I called out to go ahead without me. I looked at Ashley.

"Ted is so good with Dante," she said. "I need the help. I need somebody I can count on."

"I know."

She smiled grimly. "He's even going to fix this."

She touched her fingers to the jagged scar on her face.

"He can afford the best surgeons," I allowed.

"It's arranged. We're going to Venezuela. It will take three procedures. But we'll make it into a sort of family holiday."

The word *family* stung me.

"Blashky will be inconsolable," I said.

I whirled around on my stool. I started screwing the lids back on my various cream jars, plucking up greasy spent tissues and dropping them into the wastebasket.

"Stan is okay with it," she said. "We already spoke."

"And Dante? Is he?" I snapped the lid of my eye shadow on tight, "Is Dante okay?"

"He's very happy, Max. He's happy to finally have a dad."

"Dad," I repeated quizzically. I flipped the lid shut on my makeup kit, clipped the latch. "That shadowy figure. That mystery man. Is dear old Dad okay too?"

"Yeah," she said, her hand gripping the doorknob.

She examined me from across the room, like I was a piece of furniture set in an odd arrangement. She swung the door open. The corridor was dark and silent on the other side of the doorframe.

Before she went through it, she said, "Dante's dad is okay with all of it. He's dead."

45

There was only one thing to do. I was already on a bar stool in Minos by Night when Emile Balzac and Blashky arrived.

"I expect you're going to need a drink," I told Blashky.

"She told you too?" he said, throwing a twenty on the bar in advance.

Miss Vicky waved at him and Emile from the end of the bar, the lacy ice-blue sleeve of her dressing jacket fluttering around her forearm. She started pouring two rum and Cokes.

"Ashley told me this morning," he said, and his great ursine body sank down over the bar.

"I'm so sorry, Stan," I said. I slid the twenty across the bar, back to him. "Your money is no good here," I told him.

He folded the bill, dropped it over onto the bar's gutter for Miss Vicky.

"Thanks, Max," he said. "But, I guess I knew it was coming."

"How?" Balzac asked. "How could anybody know? Ashley kept this Argent man such a secret."

Blashky shook his head, slow. Resigned.

"It's not about that guy," Blashky said. "It's about me. If she'd married me, she'd be Ashley Blashky. That's fucked-up."

I thought there was probably more to it. But hoped we could leave it there.

We drank silently. Like men. We faced forward, our eyes scanning the slope-shouldered bottles lining the wall behind the bar.

Blashky tossed down his rum and Coke fast. He signaled for another. The second one went pretty much the same. He shifted around. A hard flicker lit behind his eyes, and he menaced his mustache with taut pulling fingers as thick as rebar.

"She's been seeing somebody," he growled at his fourth rum and Coke. "Somebody other than Argent."

"Oh?" I managed.

I'd been feeling quite light, quite relieved. Because, despite the stinging slight Ashley had dealt me, she had also granted me a sort of absolution. I no longer had to quell my sense of guilt around Blashky—or my sense of fear that he would squeeze my head like it was an overripe Gewurztraminer grape.

By skating off with some hitherto unknown, Ashley had obviated my indiscretions with her. She had erased my error. Or, at least, that was my interpretation according to the Max Bravo Paradigm—a world order filtered through the misty, amber-colored lenses of the rum and Coke goggles.

"But, I don't know," Blashky festered. "I can't be pissed at this rich guy. He has honorable intentions. But I keep thinking there's another guy. Some kind of a don't-give-a-shit guy."

"Who?" Emile chirped.

"Who wants dinner," I laid in. "Stan? Emile? What ho? How's about a nice heaping trencher of moussaka? Come on, men, let's feast."

"Who do you think, Stanley?" Emile perseverated. "Another man, besides this Argent she wants to have marriage with?"

Who did Balzac think he was, Associated Press? Damn nosy little bastard, stirring things up.

"I got him profiled," Blashky said, and he swung his big bald head around like a wrecking ball on a chain. He stared me in the face.

"Huh," I exhaled.

"He's kind of showy," Blashky supplied. "Kind of a showboat."

"Ah." I emitted a guttural sound, my mouth gaped like the un-hinged jaw of a rigored cadaver.

"How do you know all that?" Balzac asked, leaning over the bar, freaking Frenchie Lois Lane. I wanted to punch him.

"I found this," Blashky said. He reached in his pocket and slowly extracted a long silk scarf like he was performing a magic act. "In the drawer beside her bed," he said. "It's a man's scarf. It's like she took it as a souvenir."

Blashky laid the scarf out on the bar, smoothed it with hands big as irons, so the pink and purple paisley pattern flattened under his palms.

I regarded the scarf with horror, and although I knew better, I was sure the paisleys were forming themselves into quote marks. And inside the quotes were sentences.

Phrases like: "Max Bravo slept with your girlfriend. Max Bravo cuckolded you. Kill Max Bravo."

Or statements to that effect.

It was, of course, my scarf. I'd worn it many times around Stan Blashky and Emile Balzac.

"*Merde*," Balzac said softly. "It is a man's scarf. But it looks to me like the scarf of a homosexual?"

"What are you," I jerked around and shot at Emile, "a fucking FBI profiler?"

"Why are you so angry?" Balzac asked. He looked hurt.

"Listen, you guys," Stan said.

He paused, indicating that what he was about to divulge was of great import. He leveled a hard, serious look on us both, raised a platter-sized paw, and stabbed the air in front of him with a finger that seemed to be making for my chest like a stinger missile.

"This motherfucker," he said, bringing his finger down onto the scarf. "What he did, it was unforgivable."

His mouth hardened around the word. Unforgivable. His head bobbed, ever so slightly, as if it were counting off the seconds it would take for us to fully grasp the meaning of living in a world without forgiveness.

"Why?" I finally had to ask.

"Because," Stan said. "This other guy, the rich guy, at least he wants to marry Ashley. He wants to do something for her, and for Dante.

Take care of them. This other guy"—and he stabbed the scarf a couple more times with his finger, for emphasis—"he skulks around, in the dark. He just wants to use her. He's a good-time Charlie. Just out for a good time. No follow-through."

"How do you know?" I said, my voice cracked. "How do you know she isn't using him?"

Blashky looked at me intently. He squinted, as if I were very far away.

Someone started screaming.

"Get the fuck out of here," Miss Vicky yelled.

A gaggle of sorority girls were standing at the end of the bar in such a tight bunch they looked like they were lassoed together. They were stunned at the concussion blast of Greek fury.

Miss Vicky yelled, again, indicating that she meant what she'd said. The sorority girls turned, in a tight parade-ground formation, and penguin-walked out the door.

"They want me to make them Mojitos!" Miss Vicky yelled at us.

She lit a 100-millimeter menthol cigarette and slammed her lighter down on the bar.

"Like I'm some kind of asshole," she appealed to the gods of irony, flicking her arm overhead, describing great lariats of smoke. "Stand here grinding up mint leaves. Like I'm a fucking monkey."

46

I flew into León, Mexico, in a little plane full of casually rich gringos on their way to their sun homes in San Miguel de Allende.

They don't bother with cumbersome contrivances in Mexico, like terminal shoot exits. So when they wheeled the staircase up to the plane's open hatch, and the passengers descended and fanned out across the tarmac, I elbowed past them all and commandeered the only porter in sight to drayage my portmanteau into a cab.

I was glad to be there, glad to be away from San Francisco and the fear of Stan Blashky's jealous rage, and my own jealous rage. Once I was out of range of the Ashley-Blashky psychodrama, I no longer heard the grating ostinato that had been playing nonstop in my head: *Ashley Argent, Ashley Argent, Ashley Argent.*

But the distance didn't mollify my peevish mood. Only time could do that. At least, for now, I wouldn't have to see Blashky or Balzac. I wouldn't have to endure the I-told-you-so hectoring of Claudia Fantini—the one human on earth I had foolishly confided in about Ashley. And I wouldn't have to run into Ashley herself. I wouldn't have to endure her solicitous questions about my work and my dog and my fucking dahlia garden, the details about which I now wished I'd never shared with her. I'd even told her about how I dig up the tubers every fall and carefully sort them and wrap them in newspaper and store them in a cool dark cupboard over winter so I could plant them again in the spring. Damn her.

There were no seat belts in the cab. I relinquished myself to fate. The driver gunned his dented Honda Celica with effortless brio, as though he was accelerating up a ramp from which he intended to launch the car airborne over a half-dozen semitrucks that would, naturally, be on fire.

I endeavored to allow his businesslike demeanor to lull me into a sense of ease. His proper working attire stood as a recommendation. I noted, with approval, that he wore a pressed shirt, with a collar, top button done up. This was offset somewhat by his gangsterish Fu Manchu mustache, which was very nearly overtaken by several days' worth of new beard growth across his cheeks and chin.

We started chatting. The driver spoke with a courtly diction—a charming relic of the argot spoken in this region when Spanish mining barons clawed fortunes out of the ground.

"*Esta aqui para el Cervantino?*" he asked me.

I told him yes, I was here for the festival. He asked if I was a performer. I paused, quickly inventoried my travel mufti. I was wearing a rather expressive yellow ascot, a maroon jacket, umber and pumpkin plaid trousers, and a rust-colored trilby with a saffron hatband. All I needed was a walking stick and a cape and I'd be Oscar Wilde.

"*Sí,*" I admitted.

I told him he was very astute. He asked about my line of work, how was business going for me? Business was good, I said.

He pressed on with more penetrating questions. I answered: Bass baritone. Montreal opera company. *Akhnaten.*

"Philip Glass?" he ventured.

"*Sí,*" I said. "*Muy bien, señor.*"

He pulled into the opposite lane to pass a convoy of speeding trucks, their bumpers so close together they were like train cars. The truck beds brimmed with tall mounds of tomatoes, and corn, and bricks. I rolled up the window.

We passed the lead truck. It was streaming razor-sharp strips of roof flashing from its open flatbed. The aluminum tore like lightning in the headlights, whipsawing through the night air, twisting angry eels.

"*Que peligroso,*" I commented, trying to match his unconcerned attitude.

"*Que tenga suerte,*" he said. He reached up and pinched the crucifix hanging from the rearview mirror.

The lights of an oncoming vehicle thrust up from the crest of the next hill. I dug my fingers into the armrest.

The driver continued to chat, breezily, about Philip Glass. He said he had the film *Mishima* in his home DVD collection.

I could now see the driver of the oncoming vehicle. It was a man. A woman holding a sleeping child was in the passenger seat. Several other passengers cavorted around in the backseat; children, except for one stolid figure in the middle—probably an old woman. The driver of the oncoming car must have gone to the same driving school as the cabbie—both men piloted their vehicles as if they were trying to out-run an oil refinery explosion.

I closed my eyes, and when I opened them the cabbie was easing back into the right-hand lane, steering with one wrist draped over the top of the wheel. The Celica shuddered in the wind shear of the on-coming car as it drafted past us.

"People think Mexico is dangerous now," he said.

"Ha," I croaked. "How silly."

"*Sí.*" He shook his head at the delusions that plague our lives. "They are afraid of the gangsters."

I'd read about the recent incidents, but had soon forgotten the stories, my own personal traumas taking precedence.

Just three weeks earlier, gangsters had set off a bomb in a crowd of festivalgoers in Morelia. A couple dozen people were dead, many more horribly maimed. It was the drug cartels. The new government had been cracking down on them. Now they were fighting back. This wasn't a crime wave. It was a war.

The driver was immediately sorry he'd mentioned it. He and I both stepped carefully around the subject, like two men trying not to leave footprints on a fresh, blood-moist grave.

"The visitors are afraid to come because of Morelia," he said.

"*Los cartels,*" I said. "*Es drogas?*"

"*Sí. Drogas.*"

The moon came up over the mountain ahead of us. It was full and close, dripping over the mountaintop. We drove into its swollen, milky light.

"He was made a mummy." The driver suggested a new topic.

"Who?"

"The pharaoh," he was saying. "They dry him up. They make him a mummy."

"Yes," I said. "I suppose he was mummified."

I didn't think Akhnaten was mummified actually. I figured Horemhab tossed his cadaver onto a dung heap, sans funerary preparation. It was the worst thing you could do to someone, far worse than killing him. He relegated his enemy to an eternity of limbotic Hell.

"We have mummies here too," the driver told me, glowing with civic pride.

He explained that the bodies in the local cemetery were mummified naturally, by the high iron content in the soil. No one ever mined the iron. There was too much silver in the ground to be bothered with the baser metal. In fact, no one ever thought about it, until they moved the cemetery.

The city had beetled through four centuries quite comfortably, nestled as it was along a gentle river hemmed into a temperate valley. It wasn't until the 1930s that Guanajuato needed to stretch its legs and reach the city limit several miles westward. The cemetery was moved to make way. When the bodies were exhumed, much to the locals' fascination, they were not drawn out of the ground as bundles of bones. They had hair and skin. The hair was rather unmanageable and the skin was dry as crepe, but this diminished the Guanajuato corpses' celebrity not one whit.

The bodies were declared mummies, posed in museum dioramas, and set up as an official attraction. State scientists explained the phenomenon as having to do with the iron in the soil. It seeped into the bodies and desiccated them.

The cab driver strenuously urged me to visit the museum, adding that many locals attend regularly. I believed it. There is a peculiar affinity for death built into the Mexican national character. It's not so much about the afterlife, it's about the physical reality of dead things.

I've often wondered if this cohabitation with death was some insistent racial memory that endured from the bloodred Aztec times. In those centuries, the pending apocalypse was the dominant zeitgeist, and the Aztecs believed that only human sacrifice would stave off the end of the world.

In Mexico City, by 1520 when Cortés came and conquered, the

Aztecs were killing 10,000 people a day. The victims were taken to the center of Mexico City, to the top of the great pyramid that loomed over the metropolis. There, at the summit, the priests dispatched death with the chilling efficiency of a Nebraska meatpacking plant. They would force the victims to lie over a stone altar, and they'd cut out their beating hearts. The killing went on day and night, for years, unabated. Blood ran in rivers down the pyramid to its base, soaking into the rhythm of the marketplace below—the people, the chatter and laughter and music, the vibrant flowers, and the colorful finery— that pulsed on in a frenetic din under the shadow of the abattoir.

"The cemetery," I asked the driver, "where is it now?"

It was easy to find, he said. It was right next to the *mumias museo*.

I said that I was curious about a person who may be buried there. A woman. She had left San Francisco in 1906, traveling to Guana- juato. She would, of course, be dead by now. I asked him if foreigners were buried in the local cemetery.

"*Sí, claro,*" he said. "*Gringa?*"

"No," I answered. "*China.*"

"*No importa.*" He told me it was not an issue. "*Todas personas aqui en lo cemetario.*"

Death, he told me, does not discriminate in Guanajuato.

47

The name for natives of Guanajuato is *topos*. Moles. They're called that because the underbelly of the city is shot through with subter- ranean tunnels, old shafts from when the mines were active in the sixteenth through the eighteenth centuries. The silver veins in which the Indians had once slaved are now crosstown arteries—two-lane roads that the wilier local drivers use as expressways, bypassing the tight, twisting aboveground streets that squeeze through the topsy ancient stone warrens, clogged with trucks and taxis and, still, the occasional burro cart.

I arrived more than a week before our performance. I wanted the extra time to myself. I wanted to look around.

I knew I should go to the cemetery. I had a vague idea that I'd find Ah Ho's name on a headstone, plant the ring a few inches down into the dirt, and my obligation to Duffield Fallon would, at last, be at an end.

I rented a house on the east end of town. It was in a compound made up of four separate dwellings barricaded behind a high adobe wall, the top of which brandished sharp broken bottles cemented in place.

The estate had once been the seat of wealthy mining family. It had fallen into disrepair after the revolution had whisked their fortunes away in its downdraft. Now a retired American and his young Filipina wife, her name was Happy, owned the place. Ray beetled about all day in his dungarees, directing bricklayers and plumbers and electricians in his mangled Spanglish.

I'd only glimpse Happy in the very early mornings when she left the compound to walk her dog. Happy, like many Asian women, waged an ongoing war of evasion against the sun. Tanned skin, back in the Philippines, would have marked her as a peasant, a woman obliged to labor in a rice field or on a road crew. Furthermore, she probably knew that the sun would rob her of her youth, her beauty. Happy sheathed herself from her enemy. She wore a smoke-tinted, full-face plastic visor, a pair of cotton gloves, and a turtleneck and sweatpants. Her dog—a permanently puzzled, brindle-haired curiosity—was always pressed against her knee. He walked in a loopy gate, never taking his eyes from her, agitated, obsessed with keeping in close step with his speed-walking mistress.

I'd been there a couple days when Ray mentioned to me that the dog was deaf. He had been a stray. He followed Happy home one morning. They fed him. Bathed him. Didn't notice anything especially odd. Then, their gardener pointed to the dog, and made the universal sign for "plumb loco," a finger circle at the side of his head. No wonder the creature had been cast out on the street. He would be useless as a guard dog. And in Mexico, there's no place for the slobbering sentimentality that Americans slaver all over their pets.

I'd wave to Happy and her dog every morning from my hacienda's little stone garden where I took my coffee. They'd return from their walk just as I'd finish my second cup. They adhered to a precise routine—this woman hiding behind a smoky visor and her deaf dog. I timed my mornings by their comings and goings. When they returned from their walk, and the deaf dog would howl for his breakfast in that flat-noted monotone, I'd step back inside to make my own—a frying pan brimming with chorizo and eggs.

My house was dark and cool. It turned its back on the sun; the dense adobe walls ran solid across the south side. A gallery of arching windows along the opposite wall admitted the only natural light, which was suffuse because it was northern. Ray told me that the north gallery room had once been the house's outdoor portico. But there had been an interfamily feud with the owners of the house to the north. So they bricked in the portico, fenestrated its archways, and hung heavy drapes over the windows. I imagined that the drapes must have always been shut tight.

The furniture was ramshackle, but well staged. And the art was anonymous, abstract, and ingeniously curated for its subtle menace. The painting that hung over the billowing, baroque stone fireplace was particularly striking. It was a beatnik still life; a book, a glass of wine, and a flaming crimson bromeliad blooming from the palm of a severed hand.

During the hottest hours, I went inside. I ran scales and rehearsed my arias. I ate. I napped.

Once the sun left its midday peak, I'd return to the crumbling little terrace where the bricks were slowly turning back into dust. I'd bring the tequila bottle out to the crooked table beneath the ruby bladed bower of a towering poinsettia. To ward off premature agave saturation, I ate crackly sheets of deep-fried pigskin, chicharrón, that I bought from the butcher down the road.

For entertainment, I read through the stack of *New Yorker* magazines I'd brought. Diminishing the pile always made me feel that I'd accomplished something. As I read, Ray hitch-stepped purposefully back and forth across the grounds, in busy stewardship over his estate's slow, elegant decay.

The mood of life amid the ruins suited me. I indulged in self-pity.

Ray would interrupt my fugues. He'd pause at the edge of my terrace, brandish the latest contraption he was cobbling together in his jumbled workshop. He'd explain his projects in telegraphic bursts: *Chair leg. Needs a weld.* Or, *Old door. Makes a good headboard.* Or, *Koi pond. Leaks like hell.*

Then he'd head back into his workshop, swinging a hammer. He never waited for me to reply to his announcements. That was good. Less effort required on my part.

I perseverated about Ashley Banks. I tumbled her over and over in my mind like a particularly hard agate that refused to be polished. She would never have taken me seriously. I knew that. She was far too practical.

And I knew that I would never have wanted her to. I was far too frivolous.

But I enjoyed the feeling, the free fall into a chasm of loss. I dove into it. The sense of disintegration was the only thing that made me feel as though I'd actually ever been whole.

I'd been in Guanajuato for less than a week. It was midday. The sun reigned like a mad prince, straining hot flames through the poinsettia's rickety limbs. Happy was underground, shut up in the compound's coolest rooms, a troglodyte quarters dug out under the terrace. I could hear the deaf dog's off-key howls emanating from the ground below.

Ray had set out for some big-box store. He said something about gypsum and electrician's tape.

I looked across the compound and saw the deaf dog emerge from Ray and Happy's living quarters. He slunk against the mud wall, lying in a strip of shade. The cruel Aztec sun burned white-hot, piercing the azure sky. The deaf dog howled whenever he remembered to—not at trespassers, but at their probability. He'd bawl at his own auditory phantoms, then lower his head in a spiral motion back down so it rested on his outstretched front legs. He lay on his narrow jaw, worrying his eyebrows. The silence that surrounded him palpated with confusion.

It was the time of day I normally retreated to the dark quiet inside my little hacienda. But I was restless. I put on my cap. I left the compound.

I walked down the street, darting from one splotch of shade to the next. When I saw a tunnel opening, I ducked inside it.

Below ground, it was damp and chill. The air stung with the metallic tang of wet, cracked rock. The darkness ruled in unchallenged dominion. It was sharp and black. There was a finality to it. The sun never intruded down here.

Headlights streamed by. They strafed the gray rock walls and struck me at blinding angles. Tires rolled across the rippled asphalt, echoed in the chamber. It was a familiar sound. After a while I recalled where I'd heard it before. It was the day that I'd gone out fishing with Blashky. We took LSD. And the cars driving across the bridge overhead sounded just like that. Only, back in busy San Francisco, the sound of tires tracking into the metropolis hummed a thick, unbroken sustain.

In these tunnels, the cars came seldom, and singly. They'd flash bright and loud, and when they passed, the darkness would drag in their wake. The blackness pulled over me, relieved only by the bare lightbulbs, strung far apart, high up on the rock walls.

I wound through the tunnels, like a lone diver swimming deep and lost in an underwater cave. They broke off into branches, bent back on themselves, crissing and crossing and rejoining. They seemed infinite.

I had a map. It was useless.

I think it was that—the futility—that drew me back into the tunnels the next day. And the day after that. And the next day. And the next.

I would enter the tunnel system at one portal, judge myself to be heading in a certain direction, and emerge from another opening to find I was in the complete opposite end of town from where I had expected to be.

I abandoned all faith in cartography. I left the map at the house and wandered the tunnel system without any particular destination.

I suppose I hoped that I possessed some sort of latent bat sonar and that it would kick in given a little time. It didn't. But I continued to return to the labyrinth.

The day before our first performance, the matinee, I ate a heaping plate of carne and beans, drank a cerveza, and walked downtown. I took the overland route.

I picked my way through torrents of people filling the open-air markets and the cobbled streets. I inspected hand-carved skeletons and hand-painted ceramics and walked through the house that Diego Rivera grew up in.

Down the street from Diego's house, just outside of the university's museum, a small photography exhibit was on display inside a former guard's station set into a wall. Muertos de la Oaxaca. I went in.

I soon realized that the subjects of the unblinking black-and-white portraits were all corpses. I sensed I should leave. But I stayed.

The photographer had gone to the Oaxaca morgue to record the fast-fleeting images of the anonymous dead. They'd been brought to this place—this empty room of old adobe walls, and stone floors, and open-air windows latticed with iron bars. The people of Oaxaca had found them; their bodies washed up on beaches, bleeding in back alleys, lying on dirty carpets in hotel rooms incandescent with the racket coming from three or four clashing radios.

They'd look at the bodies. They didn't know them, these inert people, these leavings. They called the authorities. And the bodies were brought here, to this waiting place.

It hurt to look at them. They were so alone. These dead people had made themselves something of a nuisance with their lack of identity, and their careless solitude. They'd become a burden heaped upon strangers. But, not for long. Their features—their being either this man, or this woman—would soon be erased. The certitude of decay hovered in these last moments when the flesh was dead, but not yet diminished.

The dead were of all ages, but most of them were young—they had likely come to Oaxaca for the beach, for the fiestas. A holiday. And their festivities ended in this. The unthinkable. In the morgue, they were collected and assembled with the others who, like them, had started their day like any other. And ended it unlike any other.

The dead were naked. Some were on pallets, on the floor, in hallways, waiting to be sorted. A few were laid out individually on tables. Most were stacked in mounds several bodies high, their limbs settling together like tree branches piled after a fall pruning.

One young man lay alone on a table, his skull opened at the forehead. The lid of his cranium hung ajar, like the lid of a tin can, dangling over the table edge. His face was beautiful and smooth and timeless, an Aztec face.

Another, a woman, a young woman I imagine, was shown only as a pair of beautiful naked legs, crossed at the ankles. The angle was her own, seen from her eyes—it was as if she were lying on the beach, gazing out, beyond her pretty feet, to the ocean.

I looked at every photograph. I couldn't stop myself. These dead people, these problematic people huddled together in their final anonymity, demanded I look at them. I walked the length of the exhibit, and emerged at the other end feeling chastised and humbled and brokenhearted for the lost—and all the people who loved them and didn't know where they were.

I saw a dark escape, and made for it. I descended into the tunnels at the entrance that ran below the opera house. I had a vague idea that I was heading east, toward my house, where I intended to pour myself a neat tequila and settle down for my siesta.

A small party of Goth kids entered the tunnel just ahead of me. I'd noticed them around town, hanging out in the plazas in small groups, or picking their way over the street cobbles on their platform-heeled boots. I found them charming.

They'd picked up the American Goth style—the vampiric makeup and the black funeral duds—and pushed the look to its furthest, hitherto unimaginable extreme. In rather the same spirit as the Mexican wrestlers who amplified the traditional wrestling costume with full-head masks, these Goth kids had amplified the genre. They weren't just making a street-style statement. This was theater.

They wore shiny black vinyl pants. Skintight. And some of them affected top hats and canes and short, sporty capes. I imagined their dear old mums, patiently sewing their outfits for them, the radio blaring trumpet and accordion music in the background. It must have made sense to the mothers on some level, because their kids were dressing alike, following a prescribed coda. They were wearing uniforms, and the Mexicans love uniforms.

Everyone in Mexico wears uniforms: the legions of *condottiere* prowling the streets with automatic weapons and kerchiefs over their faces. Waitresses. Street cleaners. Even beggars. Once, while staying in Mexico City, I tipped a uniformed man in front of my hotel for three days running until I realized that he didn't even work there. After that, I doubled it.

I started down the steps into the tunnel. Two Goth boys and a girl bounced down the stairs ahead of me. They got to the bottom and turned right, into the darkness. One of the boys looked up at me. His face shone against the subterranean black, a mask of white grease-paint, thick as the icing on a wedding cake. Steel rings pierced his eyebrows and pointed studs bristled out of his cheeks, and he'd hollowed his eyes with black paint so they looked like empty sockets in a bleached skull.

He smiled at me and called out good afternoon. I returned the greeting as he submerged into the dark and disappeared.

I reached the bottom of the stairs and turned left into the tunnel, quite certain that I was heading in the direction of my house, and my afternoon tequila nap.

I heard the wet echo of the Goth kids' metal boot taps on the cement walkway. I turned but couldn't see them, their black leather backs had dissolved into the dark. I heard their chains—thick enough to hoist a ship's anchor—clanking on their jackets. There was some shouting, good-natured banter. The girl shrieked. Then she laughed. Their conversation receded into a muffle. Their footfalls grew faint, distant, until they vanished.

I was alone. And afraid. The kids were long gone. I realized that no one could hear me scream down there, beneath the city. I struggled to bury the hysteria creeping up on me.

Water sheeted down the chiseled stone walls. I stayed to the center of the narrow sidewalk. Rattling cabs and top-heavy trucks blew by me. The trucks were tricked out with extravagant side mirrors big as elephants' ears. One flew by so close, it brushed the hair on the side of my head. I moved in tighter to the rock side of the walkway. The sleeve of my jacket was damp from the trickles spritzing off the rock.

I came around a corner and the rock receded, drawing back into blackness. A car sped by, its cockeyed lights trained across the crevice, revealing where the rock had been hacked and picked into a grotto. A pool of copper-colored water stagnated in its clay floor. A ripple pulsed across the water's surface and I thought I saw a shadow. I jumped and scampered, like a little girl.

I sensed someone was following me. I looked behind me. Nothing.

The road ahead widened to allow a parking shoulder that would accommodate two or three cars. One battered old Rambler was parked in the first spot, and a Chevy LUV truck had pulled in right in front of it. A man was in the driver's seat of the Rambler. He sat in the dark, reading a newspaper. I walked by and a woman's head popped up from his lap.

I had been so frightened that I was actually relieved to stumble across the hooker and her trick. They were human—we were on the same team. That counts for a lot when you suspect you're being stalked by a ghost.

Fallon had followed me to Mexico. I was now sure of it. I could feel him in the tunnel. That was him lurking in the shadows of the grotto, skimming across the fetid waters.

He was checking up on me. Guanajuato was precisely where Duffield Fallon wanted me. And now that he had me there, he was making sure I followed through—that I found Ah Ho.

"I can't be micromanaged like this," I said.

The hooker and the man looked at me. I realized that I'd said it out loud. I quickened my pace and hustled past them, leaving them to their business.

I shoved my hands in my pockets and trudged on through the blue-black tunnel with the sullen determination of the perennially lost.

But Fallon wasn't lost. He was just inconvenienced by his own death. For more than a century, he'd been aiming to come here, to this ancient silver city in the middle of Mexico.

In the dark, early morning hours of April 17, 1906, Duffield Fallon was running. He was aiming to get away with murder.

Fallon worked for Little Pete, the most notorious crime boss in Chinatown. He had escorted Pete to one of his favorite brothels on the night of April 16, a banjio on Maiden Lane, where the Cantonese gangster availed himself of the most prized and costly prostitutes in the city—Jewesses, with their long, cascading hair of burnished copper or black coal, who were reputed to be possessed by insatiable libidos.

After an evening of sport, Fallon accompanied Pete home. The two staggered toward Chinatown, Pete seriously drunk, and Fallon seriously faking it. They were in an empty alley off of Post Street. It was that quietest, darkest hour before the sun starts to glow from the crest of Mount Diablo on the eastern horizon.

Pete stopped to urinate behind a trash barrel. Fallon came up behind him, wrapped his arm around Pete's chest, lifted him off his feet, and dragged his hook across Pete's throat. He sliced him so deep that the sharpened steel scraped the inside of Pete's spinal cord.

Fallon stashed Pete's body behind the trash barrel, his head dangling, held only by a few threads of cartilage and ganglia. Fallon riffled his pockets, took his employer's cash and jewelry. He remembered to also pilfer Pete's jade hair comb, studded with diamonds, which the dandified gangster always kept in his breast pocket.

He knew that even though he'd dragged Pete's body out of sight, it would be only an hour or two before the corpse was discovered. And besides, Fallon had a ship to catch. He hurried back to his room on Valencia Street.

His valise was already packed. He opened the drawer of his desk, pulled out a packet of travel papers. They were in order; his passport, his banknotes, his billet of passage aboard the *Timely Haven,* a clipper ship that plied the route between San Francisco and Valparaiso, Chile. The *Timely Haven* always made a stop in Puerto Vallarta, on the coast of Baja. And, while Fallon's ticket booked him through to South America, his plan was to slip off in Mexico.

At the bottom of the ticket envelope was a gold ring. Fallon took it out, inspected it beneath the one gaslight sconce that lit his barren room. He slid the tiny band onto the first knuckle of his pinky finger, closed his valise, and strapped it shut.

His hand was on the doorknob when a thundering blast tore apart the silence of the early morning. It sounded like an enormous warship had pulled up alongside the port side of the city and fired a cannonade onto its sleeping inhabitants.

Fallon was tossed onto the floor. The chiffonier, heavy as an Andalucian bull, toppled over and blocked the door in front of him. The building timbers screamed and cracked and the north side of the hotel plunged down. Fallon scrambled uphill across the slanted floor on his hands and knees. The whole building continued to sink, the weight of the north end pulling it down. Another boom exploded, the hotel shivered violently. Then it shimmied into the ground. Fallon lunged for the window. Before he could reach it, the view outside of the purple crepuscular sky and the gaslights with their fading yellow halos gave way to black dirt. Fallon's room sunk into the earth. He roared with anger and clawed at the soil, but his digging could make no purchase.

The ring, the tiny ring he'd pushed onto his pinkie finger, came off. It was carried away in the heaving, churning dirt. And the hotel sank deeper.

Above him, Fallon could hear screaming. He smelled smoke.

And still, the hotel sank.

Fallon dug even more furiously now, with hand and hook. He was like an enraged badger. He attacked the window opening, clawing the black dirt until there was no more dirt. The hard wet earth gave way to swampy muck. Then brown, dirty water.

Silt and sledge and acrid water poured into the window. Seams of spray burst through the walls.

And in his last moments, Duffield Fallon—a man who feared his own death as little as he feared inflicting death on others—relished the irony that he was to be drowned on dry land before he was to be burned in hell.

48

I emerged from the tunnel into the stark Mexican sunlight, amid a noisy outdoor market. It was miles from where I reckoned I'd be.

I consulted the map that I kept mashed up in my breast pocket. I struck out on a narrow, serpentine street, tightrope walking along a slender sidewalk.

I was obliged to step off the sidewalk every few feet into the cobbled road to cede the right-of-way to housewives. They were heading for the *mercado,* their arms bent with fists upraised, carrying their big straw shopping bags strung from their elbow crooks.

The housewives were replaced by waves of university students with heavy backpacks, pierced lips, and jeans tight as stockings slung low on their hips, their tattered cuffs dripping over the backs of their black Converse sneakers. One girl, an American, carried a pole hung with beaded bracelets. She asked if I'd buy one. Damned nuisance, these hippies. And, poor business strategists. Why would you go to Mexico—where millions of people make cheap crap by hand—to sell your cheap, handmade crap?

I traversed from the campus district to the main plaza. It was thick with crowds passing through on their way to the many theaters that dotted the neighborhoods around the centro. Late-afternoon diners shaded under the sycamore trees, lingering over coffee and liqueurs. Street performers mimed, and sang, and pulled puppet strings.

I realized I was hungry, but didn't feel like a public meal. I crossed the plaza, picking my way through the mayhem and, incredibly, arrived where I meant to be. I was on a familiar street, not far from my house.

I walked up the street, intending to stop along the way at a *panadería* I'd remembered seeing there. The building was nondescript—another gray, crumbling edifice—but the window display was eye-catching. I stopped to inspect it. Just as I'd recalled, the shop offered a minimal, but essential, selection of traditional Mexican pastries. Dry, crumbly concha cookies; and pink, puffy meringues; and sugary, swizzly churro sticks long enough to stir the devil's chocolate martini.

I entered the shop and realized it must have once been a private home, because I was in a vestibule. The flooring was antique cement pavers, adorned with green and yellow filigrees. Plaster molted off the walls, revealing the dusty adobe bricks beneath. A glass display case laid out evidence that the shop was prepared for all the Hallmark high holy days: a desiccated white cake, covered in dust, conveyed the sentiment "Feliz Día de la Madre" in blue icing. A plastic Santa Claus cake mold stood ready to conjure up the fat man on demand. A troupe of Easter bunnies sat up on their hind legs, proffering their empty chocolate heads to be bitten off. And—strung over the threshold to the heart of the store—a garland of shiny gold letters riveted together to express a reusable, reflective CONGRATULATIONS.

I stepped through the narrow, congratulatory doorway. It contained three glass cases, each bearing two or three large aluminum trays on which were carefully arranged stacks of pastries. The cases looked like the *santo* terrariums I'd seen in the church—the ones where they kept their dead, bleeding saint mannequins laid out on display.

I heard voices coming from around the corner.

"*No te puedo dejar ir,*" a man was saying. I can't let you go.

"It's no use," a woman replied, also in Spanish. "I can't marry you and live in poverty. Like a peasant. Let me go. I have to marry Don Velasquez. I deserve a chance to live a comfortable life."

She sobbed. Then she added, "*Y mi niña.*"

Another man's voice broke in loudly. He spoke rapidly, urgently, about the importance of a good moisturizer, especially if you do a lot of dishes. A gang of demented children began caterwauling a mad allegro about well-hydrated skin.

I called out a hello. The children suddenly stopped singing.

A woman appeared in the doorway.

"I didn't hear you come in," she said. "The television. It was my program."

"Pardon me," I said, as if I'd come barging into her home. Which, in a real sense, I had.

She struck a settled stance behind the counter, like a patient person resigned to waiting in a long line. She folded her hands on the glass countertop.

She was, perhaps, forty or forty-five. And in all her life, she'd apparently never once cut her hair. It was extravagantly long, and black, and thick. The sides were captured and trussed up in a series of flying buttresses that were held in place by cloisonné sticks stabbed into them from different angles. Blunt bangs hung high across her forehead, promoting the precisely plucked arch of her eyebrows.

She watched me without speaking, moving only her eyes, her head steady as a funerary bust.

"So many tasty things," I prattled, unnerved by her cipherlike presence.

"*Por favor,*" she said, "take your time to choose."

Her voice was light, the syllables plinking like notes on a clavichord, metal blades striking catgut strings. I felt nervous in her presence, beneath her cool gaze. I measured her in quick-cast glances. Her eyes; brown, almost black. Heavy eyeliner. Her face—wide, and round—the soft yellow ivory of harmonium keys.

"Two of these," I said, pointing to the Coronets de Luna. I studied the selection another moment. "And these, the marzipan fish."

She reached into the case and pulled out a clean aluminum tray. She laid a fresh sheet of wax paper on it, picked up the tray and a pair of tongs, and came out from around the counter.

She wore a black smock, the sort of thing that a Parisian painter sports while dabbling in the atelier. Despite the puffiness of her costume, I could tell that she was very thin. A hint of a miniskirt poked out from her smock. I took note of her legs. She kept them private in a pair of very thick black tights, but their skinny outlines were on full view and, I suppose, they would have looked rather bandy had she been in flats. But she wasn't.

She stilt-walked around the shop in chunky, high-heeled platforms that gave her another four inches. They made her small feet look impossibly tiny.

The shoes should have been crippling. But she pranced daintily on them, her legs seeming to twine and untwine, like willow branches dangling in a breeze.

She opened the cases, one by one, and reached inside with the tongs. She carefully placed my selection of sweets on the serving tray. When I told her I was done, she took them back to the main counter and loaded them in a bag, pinching each soft pastry with the steel-toothed tongs, observing her own actions from behind an aura of cool detach.

49

I woke up from my tequila siesta with Frank Kelly's book on my chest. A crepuscular light seeped in through the arched windows in the gallery room. The bedside clock reported five o'clock.

I got up and reheated a skillet full of pork, beans, and peppers, and sat at the kitchen table with my hearty viands and robust Bourdeaux, which I drank out of a heavy glass goblet.

It wasn't until I'd nearly finished my meal that I heard the songbirds start up. Outside the kitchen window, the sky was a livid amethyst. I watched it fade to a watery heliotrope, then all the tint seeped away. The sky hung limpid, like a bulging drop of quicksilver. A shaft of sunlight struck the poinsettia tree.

"What the hell?" I said.

I went outside, on to my patio. Ray came around the corner, his face red and gleaming and his wet hair slicked down, the tooth-marks of his comb describing deep striations.

He told me good morning. I saluted him with my wine goblet. He asked me if I wasn't performing that evening.

"Oh, this," I said. "Ha. I was just clearing up the dishes."

I jerked my arm and flung the goblet's contents into the dirt.

"Good for poinsettias," I said. "I read that somewhere. It's the iron. In the tannins."

Ray paused, absorbing my explanation. Then he tilted his head back as if he'd been glanced by an errant tennis ball.

He informed me he had a lot to do that day. There'd been an unfortunate incident with the plumbing in the big rental house across from mine. Apparently—before Ray's tenure—the toilet had been installed without a sewage line. Every time it was flushed, the bowl's contents were whisked underground, and left to percolate into the substrata. Incredibly, the rude apparatus had worked for years. It wasn't until just that week that the system buckled under the heavy usage of a large party of beer-drinking Swiss who spent a fortnight in the hacienda.

"Got a crew coming," Ray said. "Tearing out the patio. Sorry about the noise."

I went back into the kitchen and brewed a strong pot of coffee.

I did the math. I'd slept for roughly fifteen hours in a kind of death trance.

I stood under the shower and, as if I were sleeping still, my mind was overtaken by a flotilla of dream images. Faces. Pieces of conversations. It was Frank Kelly. And Duffy Fallon. Poor dead clown, Betty Ann Thibideaux. And, wisps of the graceful Ah Ho. They persisted, bubbling up from some deep, submerged cityscape. It was an empty place—a reversed-out image of San Francisco—where the landmarks weren't buildings and statues, but desires and frustrations.

I shut off the water, stepped out of the shower, dried myself off. I listened. Ray's crew was already out on the terrace, breaking apart the stones with iron-headed sledgehammers.

I went back into the bedroom to get dressed. Frank's book, *The Flight of the Singing Bird,* was still lying open on the bed.

I shouldn't have been reading it before going to sleep. Now Frank—and the raging lunatics he'd chosen to populate his downfall—was embedded in my subconscious.

I closed the book. Frank's face looked at me from the moody, dark photo on the back cover. I was startled by it, because Frank looked so unfamiliar. His signature features were still there; the fox-thin face, the disarray of black curls, and the ice blue eyes, so blue they shone almost white in the black-and-white photo. But I'd always recalled Frank in motion. Frenetic. Arrested like this in a fractured moment, he wasn't recognizable as the man known as Frank Kelly. Frank in still life was no more an expression of him than if I was looking at his empty jacket hanging in a closet.

That's how it had begun, more than a year ago. It was me, alone, in Frank's dismal apartment, emptying clothes from his closet, packing up books and plates, and throwing away his shaving gear and his toothbrush. There was nothing left of him of any worth. Nothing, except for the manuscript that became this object, this book, I held in my hands.

And still, I didn't know why he'd jumped.

Over the past year, I'd learned more about the context of Frank's suicide. I knew where he was living. I knew that he wrote that book. I even knew something about his private thoughts. It was all in his journal.

But why? Why did he jump?

It seemed the road that led Frank to the bridge had originated long before he was even born. Frank's suicide plunge was, incredibly, the domino outcome of Duffy Fallon falling in love with Little Pete's wife.

Everything started with Ah Ho. She was such an unlikely harbinger of havoc. Petite and precious and reserved. She moved so quietly, mincing on tiny silken slippers, her cruelly bound feet broken and bent into cloven hooves. She was a precious little bird, crippled to prevent her flight. But she slipped her tether, and disappeared.

Her flight called for the murder of her husband. Pete—slick in his Occidental dress, and drawing-room manners—affected the pose of the upright businessman. All the while he steered the great subterranean commercial wheel of gambling and opium and prostitution that turned beneath the dark, teeming streets of Chinatown.

Next, Duffield Fallon died just as he was running to catch up with her. Fallon, the felon—he was a prurient beast of well-slaked vices. Fallon could beat down any man on the Barbary Coast. And in the end he was felled by a delicate, tiny-footed creature.

Frank Kelly should have left them dead and forgotten, as they had been for more than a century. But he had to exhume them. He dug up the whole damn thing because he was so greedy for a story. He didn't have the imagination to invent one himself. But he had the sense to recognize a good tale when someone told it to him. Frank made a deal with the devil, with Fallon. And he got what he asked for.

I couldn't decide how I felt about Betty Ann. She was such an irritant with her vapid books, and her avidity for promoting them. And there was something both pathetic and galling about her willingness to make herself ridiculous for the consumption of the public. How desperate she was. I was still pissed about her breaking into my home, and leaving her damn serape in my kitchen, and bringing the police investigation down on me. All of which, ultimately, forced me to attend an evening of community theater.

But despite all that, I still felt sad for Betty Ann. Poor dead clown.

Whether she jumped off the bridge, or shot herself and jumped. Or whether somebody else shot her and tossed her over the rail—she didn't deserve it.

I had to stop thinking about them. All of them. They were dead. And it was time they were forgotten.

I had a show to put on.

I told myself that tomorrow, after the performance, I'd go to the cemetery and put an end to it all. I'd find Ah Ho's grave, claw out a hole, and drop her ring into it. Fallon would be appeased.

I splashed myself with Tres Flores cologne, and forced Ah Ho's ring past the first knuckle of my pinkie finger. I thought wearing the ring would bring me luck. I didn't bother to consider what kind of luck.

50

I blinked. The spotlights were trained on me, blinding white, and I couldn't see the audience out there, but I could hear them.

They were on their feet. The house echoed with their thunder. Their approval, their adulation, their love, surged over me. It ran warm and sparkling through me like a drug. The clapping swelled to a roar.

I bowed. "Bravo! Bravo!" they called out. The shouts resounded off the lavishly carved and painted Moorish walls and ceiling of the old opera house.

I bowed a second time, and stepped back in line with the rest of the cast. We joined hands. I'd situated myself in what I'd hoped was a becoming facet—between a charming Nubian handmaiden on my left and the beefcake captain of the guards on my right. I tried calculating which one I had the better chance with, now that we'd just finished our final performance and I was free from my self-imposed moratorium on sleeping with cast mates.

The two principals came out—the pharaoh and his queen—and, as they took their bows, the rest of the houselights came up, as did the standing ovation holdouts. All of them came out of their seats. We took three curtain calls.

I looked over the audience. They were a well-turned-out group for the most part. It was easy enough to spot the upper-class Mexicans by their precisely tailored leather jackets and pressed designer jeans. Their armed guards would be waiting for them on the steps of the theater.

Mexico's servantless classes were also represented. They, too, were carefully dressed and groomed and impeccably mannered.

I spotted a few Americans; embarrassing representatives of the wealthiest country on earth. They were dressed for a car camping junket. They wore weatherproof high-altitude jackets in bright, kindergarten colors—navy and red. And when one of them, a gray-headed senior, stepped into the aisle I could see that he was wearing dirty, bulbous cross-trainers and nylon waterproof pants with multiple pockets and knee zippers so that he could, with a quick zip, transform his mufti into an even more inappropriate costume—the dreaded adult in short pants phenomenon.

I wondered if I should start telling people I was from New Zealand.

Just as we were taking our third and final bow, I noticed a tall, thin figure rising from his seat in the second balcony at the back of the house. He clapped a cap on his black, wavy hair and tossed a scarf round his neck. He slid a pair of amber-tinted glasses over his eyes and grinned. And when he did that, he took on a very lapin aspect.

The curtain came down. I ran to the wings, down the stairs at stage left, and quickly needled through the crowd. I was after the man with the rabbit-toothed grin. He saw me coming, and scampered for the lobby. He cut through the crowd, pushing people aside with his fore-arms raised in a bowsprit in front of him.

I burst through the front doors and stopped. I stood at the top of the theater portico, scanned the swarming crowd.

They'd emptied out from the theater and then dammed up on the sweep of stone stairs. They were chatting and lighting cigarettes, and casually signaling their awaiting bodyguards to come and escort them to various parties and meals and general fabulousness that the ruling classes in Third World countries enjoy.

It took a few moments before I realized I was attracting stares. I looked down at my attire. I was bare-chested in a silver miniskirt, gold-lamé boot sandals, and a conical hat that was as tall as a pigeonairre.

One by one, the little groups stopped talking and turned to look at me. The crowd was silent, unsure as to what my presence meant. They were, I dare say, somewhat apprehensive. The big, near-naked man in the Diane von Furstenberg mini and the Mary Quant eyeliner was a ripping good diversion up there on the stage, but now that I'd descended from my thespian promontory—once I'd crossed the thresh-old and invaded their world—I was a bit of a fright.

The crowd fidgeted. No one spoke. One lady—an elderly grande dame, her pure Castilian features framed in the upturned lapel of her sheared lamb coat—slipped off her gloves, draped them over her arm, and, smiling regally, began to clap.

Little knots of applause tatted up all through the crowd. Soon it spread, and they regained their collective ease. Now they were certain what was expected of them. They looked at me, approving smiles, warm applause. I held out my arms, bowed deeply, and edged back into the building, turned, and trotted through the lobby. I ran to my dress-ing room.

I kicked off my sandals, ripped off the skirt, carefully set the cone hat on the wig stand. I stepped into my slacks and boots, pulled my sweater over my head, put on my jacket and scarf. I mounted my trilby low on my head, because I didn't bother removing my makeup. I left through the stage exit, jogging out into the alley.

"Max Bravo," the guards called, their automatic machine guns slung fashionably over their shoulders like expensive handbags. "Max, you want a cigarette?"

"Not tonight, amigos. I have to find someone." I turned and jogged backwards, calling out to them, "An old friend."

51

The streets were full of revelers. All the theaters had just let out, and throngs of people vied amiably for passage along the narrow, cobbled streets. Vendors with pushcarts were selling chorizos and plates of cheesecake and every neighborhood square and billow in the road was occupied by musicians with electric guitars and portable amplifiers, their overturned hats on the sidewalk in front of them.

I saw the Goth kids I'd followed into the tunnel the day before. They were in their standard uniform; black vinyl pants and towering platform boots. The Goths were sitting on the steps of a cathedral listening to a power trio grinding out Jimi Hendrix covers.

I stopped to listen. I lit a cigarette and sat on a stone bench. The band was playing "Purple Haze," in Spanish.

It was useless. I couldn't find anyone in this mob. And certainly not someone who'd become an expert at convincing the world that he was dead.

A contingent of federales prowled through the crowd. They were dressed similarly to the Goth kids; all black, heavy boots. The only difference was they carried automatic weapons.

One of the soldiers stopped in front of me. He wore a balaclava. It made him look menacing, and even more so when you reflected on why he, a cop, was hiding his face. Mexico is a country where the police, not the criminals, are hunted.

The masked federale stared at me for a moment. I smiled weakly. He moved on, falling in behind his comrades.

The crowd surged up onto the sidewalk, making way for a heavy black truck. It rumbled past, yet another cohort of armed police. Their AKs bristling over the top of the truck's wood panels that penned them in like they were heavily armed cattle. Some wore face masks. Others didn't. The federales with exposed faces looked apprehensive.

The band finished their set. The crowd started to drift away, small particles breaking off and reentering the flow of people that surged through the city's narrow arteries.

I joined them, wandering directionless, carried along by the surge. I walked uphill, through the neighborhood by the university. I heard a drum pounding, slow, a steady, funerary beat. There was a line of torches up ahead, lining the perimeter of a courtyard in front of yet another cathedral. A crowd was building. The spectators looked toward a cobbled street that bent around the back of the cathedral. The drumbeat was coming from behind the church.

I stopped and found a spot against the wall of a house. I looked up the street toward the sound of the approaching percussion.

It grew louder, the three-beat rhythm gathering like a storm. Torchlight flickered across the red adobe walls. The light spread in a pool over the street stones. Then, from around the bend, came a procession.

They were skeletons. Dancers in black catsuits painted over with white bones. The bones glowed in the torchlight. They wore heavy skull headpieces. They danced a stilted, hopping three-step matching the three-beat drum dirge. They danced stiff and dry—no flow, no flourish, no liquid grace—just bones knocking on stones. The drum would beat, the dancers would leap, turn a quarter around, and look at the living with their dead skull faces.

One skeleton dancer carried a sign: WHAT I AM, YOU WILL BE.

Another held up a leering, round clock face. The clock arms were set at ten minutes before midnight. He pointed to the time with an arched bone finger.

They passed slowly, intently, as if they had all the time in the world. The crowd hushed as they approached. As the dead dancers passed, the still-living watchers fell in silently behind them.

I stood my ground, waited for them to pass. The dead and their followers filed by. The crowd was silent, subdued by the grim message, but entranced by its allure. Young and old. Men. Women. Some carrying small children.

All of them knew where they were going. And they knew they must go there. There was no resisting it. No buying your way out. No bargaining. They followed the dancing dead.

I started to turn to leave. I noticed a brown cap floating by along the top of the crowd.

I squeezed through the throng aligning the procession route until I got up beside the cap—and the man underneath it.

He must have sensed me looking at him, hunting him.

Frank turned and faced me, his eyes hidden behind the amber-tinted glasses. He wasn't smiling this time. He bolted.

Frank Kelly darted through the crowd, negotiating its clogged narrows and drafting in its torrents like an expert kayaker shooting the rapids. I got bogged down in the nets and snares, reaching across the shoulders of doddering old women, sidestepping tottering children.

I kept my eyes on Frank's cap moving swiftly ahead of me. It veered out of the crowd, then disappeared.

I made for the spot where he'd suddenly winked out of view.

I got there and found it was the top of the stairs leading into the tunnel system. I ran down the steps, my boots scraping on the stones, echoing off the wet rock. I reached the bottom, ran through the tunnel around a curve. I stopped. Listened. Another set of boots was pounding in the distance. I ran toward the sound.

I heard a sharp pop. Then another. A third. *Pop. Pop. Pop.*

The lightbulbs down the tunnel ahead of me went off in steady succession. Frank Kelly was breaking them.

I ran into the darkness, now I was a mad bull charging. Senseless. I entered the black, cursing. A hard blow fell across my chest. I went down to my knees, gasping.

A flame flickered in front of my eyes. Behind it, two brown eyes gleamed from black orbs. A chalk-white face floated.

"*Qué tal?*" the voice said.

Hands lifted me to sitting upright, my back braced against the rock wall. More faces drifted into view. These had flesh on them, and the flesh was elaborated with black eyeliner and blue lipstick.

More lighters clicked on. The Goth kids crouched down on their haunches, settled down all around me, watching me patiently. Lovely fallen angels. I was raised up on their black leather wings.

"I must have slipped," I told them. "I had the wind knocked out of me."

"An old man like you," the skeleton-faced youth said. "You gotta be careful. Slowly. Slowly in the dark, *señor.*"

They lifted me gingerly to my feet. I told them I was all right. They refused to leave me. They asked where I was going. I told them I was going home. I named the neighborhood. They informed me I was heading in the complete opposite direction.

They formed a protective cocoon of black and silver all around me. They walked me through the tunnels, and up out of the earth.

"Now you go down this street," one of the girls said, the metal rings in her cheeks clinking as she spoke. "You want us to walk you to your house?"

"No, darling," I said. I pulled out my money clip, peeled off a couple hundred pesos. "Here, please take this."

They shifted on their platform boots. It was a sizable sum to them. One of boys started to reach out for the money. Then he thought better of it, retracted his hand quickly, and stuffed it into his pants pocket.

"We don't need a tip," the skeleton youth said.

"Oh, it's not a tip," I insisted. "I'd like to buy you all a beer. I'd join you, but I'm too tired. I am old, you know."

The skeleton lad considered this. In that case, he said, it would be rude of them not to accept my hospitality.

The girl with the hardware in her cheeks squeezed my arm, and told me to be careful. They bade me good night, and descended back down the stairs into the netherworld.

I walked uphill, along the main street leading to my house. I started to turn into the street leading to Ray and Happy's compound, to sanctuary, but my impulses wouldn't let me go there. Not yet. I returned to the *carretera*. I proceeded up the hill to the end of the road where the city's deep, still reservoir lay, ringed with public parks, boat rental concerns, and alfresco restaurants.

Lots of people were out, sitting around rusted tin tables at makeshift ice cream and taco stands. Children ran up and down the paved walkways, chasing balls and pushing bright pink and purple scooters, plastic ribbons streaming from the handlebars.

Mariachis played. Their plaintive voices rippled across the shallow waves of the reservoir.

I sat down at a table and ordered a beer. The waiter poured it carefully into a tall glass. I paid him and he bowed and moved off to the next table.

I glanced to my left. There was Frank Kelly, alive and drinking. He was sitting two tables away.

I sprang out of my chair, got to him in two steps.

I grabbed his coat. He wormed. I lost my grip.

A woman screamed. Frank knocked over his chair. He ran through the cluster of tables, and sprinted, full-out, along the path beside the reservoir.

I followed. I could see he was heading for a dead end. I thought for a moment that he'd dive into the water. But, instead, he disappeared into the dark entry of the Byzantine watchtower that stood sentry over the lake.

I reached the watchtower, stopped, remembering what had happened the last time I followed Frank Kelly into the dark. I stood at the threshold, heard him ascending the stairs. Goddamn it, I raged. I rushed in after him.

I ran, spinning up the spiral staircase. The hard white face of the full moon glared over the turrets of the tower's open roof. I reached the top of the stairs, popped up to the surface into the pool of moonlight beaming on the stone-tiled roof.

Frank Kelly stood with his back up against the crenellations.

"You're pretty quick for a dead man, Frank," I told him.

"I wouldn't have been dead for long, Max."

"All this," I said, raising my arms beseechingly. "Everything we all went through. For what? So you could pull some publicity stunt? So you could sell some books?"

"I figured it was my only chance, Max. I tried the honest way. That doesn't work anymore. Too many wannabes. Too many manuscripts in the slush pile. I had to break through. I had to become a story to get somebody to read my story."

"That's pathetic," I said.

"Not as pathetic as working your whole life at something. Only to be ignored."

"Fair enough," I said. "But why are you here?"

"I owe Fallon," he said. "I want to make sure he gets paid. So he'll leave me alone."

"Why didn't you just take the ring yourself?" I said. "Why leave it up to me?"

"That's just it, Max. I never meant to leave it up to you. I thought you'd just clean out my place, and with your knack for drama, you'd help turn the suicide into a big story."

"You played me, Frank."

"I didn't make you do anything you wouldn't do on your own," Frank said.

He was right. Frank knew I had a predilection for drama. Histrionics was, to me, an essential provender, like bread, or brandy.

I asked him about the ring. Why had he not taken it with him and delivered it to Ah Ho himself? His answer was simple enough. He shirked it.

He thought that if he left it behind, he'd leave Fallon behind. He hadn't accounted for Fallon's furious, limitless zeal. Fallon was a skip tracer of the old school. Frank could cross state lines, even flee to Mexico, and Fallon would still pursue him. And apparently he did pursue Frank with extreme prejudice.

Frank had another reason for leaving the ring too, he admitted. He thought that if the ring was later discovered—and he was sure it soon would be—that it would spark off another wave of publicity for his book.

"You are no artist. You are not a writer," I roared at him. "You, Frank, are nothing more than a vile mountebank!"

"Call me what you want, Max." He grinned. "But *Singing Bird* has sold over five hundred thousand copies. And when I reemerge, once I recover from the amnesia, eh, then I'll be collecting some pretty fat stacks."

"You craven prick," I said.

He smiled, satisfied.

"What about Betty Ann?" I veered. "Maybe you'll be collecting those royalties from San Quentin. Don't tell me you had nothing to do with her death."

"She jumped from the bridge, Max. She was—"

"Manic-depressive," I interrupted. "Yes, I know. I also know about the bullet in her chest."

"She must have shot herself before she went over the rail," he said steadily. A little too steadily.

"What?" I mocked him. "Just to be sure? Like the twenty-story drop into shark-infested waters in the middle of the night with the tide rushing out to Japan wouldn't be enough to kill her? Right. She wanted to be sure."

"Okay, Max." He took a step forward, trailing his arms out from his sides, palms forward, in an attitude of calming beseech. "I'll confide in you. Me and Betty Ann. We're old friends."

"You and I were friends too," I said. "Once. Long ago. Now, I don't know what we are."

He told me that Betty Ann had spotted him, early on after his faked suicide. He was hiding in plain sight, filthy and dressed in rags, sleeping in a doorway of an abandoned car dealership on Van Ness Avenue. Dozens, maybe hundreds, of people walked by him, over him, every day. But Betty Ann didn't. She recognized him.

Betty Ann accosted him. She told Frank that she'd blow the whistle on him unless he cooperated with her. She wanted to write a book about him and her, another of her fabricated "memoirs" to cash in on a piece of Frank's momentary notoriety.

They reached a thieves' agreement. Frank decamped and moved to Vallejo to hide. They didn't speak for several months. But then, Betty Ann's book came out. Frank didn't like it.

He didn't like that she painted him as a heavy, a bully. And, worst of all, she turned the truth on its head and made out that it was Frank, not her, who was the obsessive bunny-boiler in the relationship.

Frank was furious. He wanted to set her straight. He called her, from a pay phone at Rod's Hickory Pit. He told her he wanted to meet her. It was a foggy night, they could both drive to the Golden Gate

Bridge. He'd park on the north side. She'd park on the south. They could walk along the east rail, and meet in the middle—where he had left the suicide note. She agreed.

"So it was you who called her that night," I said. "That night she rushed out of my place. Thanks for leaving me as the last guy to see her alive. Asshole."

"Totally unintentional, Max," he said. "You gotta believe me."

"Because you're such an honest guy."

"Max, let me just get this out." He was closer to me now, within reach.

I instinctively started backing up, closer to the short wall that ringed the edge of the tower platform.

"She met me there, on the bridge," he spun. "She was raging, out of control. Screaming about her career. Saying she didn't want to be brought up in front of a *media tribunal*. She didn't want to be like that idiot who wrote the fake book about being strung out on enough dope to kill the entire population of the Tenderloin."

"So you killed her," I said. The small of my back was now scraping against one of the crenellations. Frank inched forward. I could smell the beer on his breath, see the frost in his eye.

"She pulled a gun on me, Max. We struggled. It went off. I was trying to defend myself. It was an accident."

"And what will this be, Frank?" I said to him. "Another *accident*?"

I tried to step to the side so I could get away from the edge. I looked over my shoulder. The drop to the water was about three stories. Survivable. But if I went over with my head bashed in, I'd surely drown.

"This deal here," Frank said, narrating like it was a story. "This will be the tragic end of a marginal opera singer who never accepted the mediocrity of his talent, and his career. He drank too much, and fell to his death in a senseless mishap."

"And then you emerge," I said. "Postamnesia."

"I'll give it 'til the end of the year."

"Still reads like a dime novel," I said. "Do you really think Detective Fung will buy it?"

"He'll have to buy it," Frank Kelly said. He pulled a short, hard hickory stick out of the inside pocket of his coat. "And it's not a tough sell, you being the drunken hack that everybody knows you are."

"No, Frank." I was openly pleading now.

I was bigger than Frank, but I'd seen him work people over. I knew I was no match for him.

"You couldn't possibly," I said. "Not after all our years of friendship. Not after all I've done for you in this past year, what with dealing with Fallon and everything."

"Fallon?" he said. "That's right. I'll need that ring you've got on your necklace. Thanks for reminding me, Max."

He raised the stick, aimed it in a trajectory straight for my temple. I tried to duck, but Frank Kelly, former hockey goon, was too skilled in the art of pain to miss me completely. He glanced the stick across my forehead. It thumped hard and there was a crushing sensation, and the skin burst open.

"For godsakes, Frank," I cried, desperate, clutching at escape. "Think about your eternal soul. The Betty Ann thing was an accident. But this is cold-blooded murder!"

"I made a deal with the devil, Max," he countered. "I gave up my soul two years ago."

Frank grabbed the chain around my neck. He pulled it taut. The chain scissored into my flesh, garroting me. Then it broke. The ring popped off, it made a plinking sound as it struck the terraza. It rolled across the tiles.

Frank whirled around, chased the ring as it careened in drunken swirls on the bumpy stones.

A truckload full of federales pulled up beside the reservoir. I thought that somebody had summoned them when they saw Frank and I struggling at the top of the tower. Then I realized that didn't make sense. There hadn't been time.

The federales poured out of the back of the truck. They fanned out across the courtyard, stopping at tables, questioning people.

Frank had the ring in his hand. He raised the other hand, the one with the hickory stick, and came for me.

A sonic boom went off. The tower rocked. Frank fell back. People down below were screaming.

Frank scrambled to his feet. He and I both looked over the tower turrets to the scene of mayhem below.

The bomb had gone off in the crowded outdoor café just at the foot of the tower. The tables were tossed in all directions, chairs lay on their sides. Slicks of blood oozed across the patio. People were stretched out on the ground like shaken sleepers, and sitting in broken heaps, some of them crying and screaming. A couple of them were staring, mute. One man stood and looked around, the side of his skull open, a blotch of red and gray. The headless body of a woman in a polka-dot dress, seaping a black pool of blood from its neck, thick and glistening like petroleum.

Another explosion erupted, its report bounced off the hills surrounding the lake. This one was closer. It rocked the tower, more violently than the first blast. I was thrown onto my knees. I wrapped my arms around my head, covering my ears. I was screaming.

Frank would not be knocked down.

When the second blast hit, it sent him dancing on the stone tile, glissading after his footing like a man on a ship's deck. He lost his bearings, the backs of his legs slammed into the short turret wall, and he jackknifed backwards over it. I heard him enter the water with a splash.

I crawled to the wall and pulled myself up, barely able to lift my chin over the top of it. I desperately scanned the black lake, white flashes of moonlight reflected in its choppy, agitated waters. Frank bobbed to the water's surface. He was swimming. He reached the piers at the head of the weir. He threw his arms around one of them, inched his way along the blades, and then pulled himself up to the railing of the bridge.

A couple of federales peeled off from the detail. They headed toward Frank. They nearly got to him.

I staggered to my feet, blood pouring down my face from where Frank had struck me. My ears buzzing, I pressed my hand to my right ear, pulled it away, and saw it was covered in blood. Something glinted on the stones in the moonlight. I fell down onto my hands and knees, crawled to the shining object. It was Ah Ho's ring.

I slipped the ring into my pocket, ran down the tower steps. I weaved through the horrors of the destroyed café. My boot skidded on the blood pooled around the overturned tables. Broken plates shone white in the moonlight. Beans and rice and carne congealed in human blood. A foot lay beside an overturned chair. People were crying, running.

I looked over toward the bridge where Frank was pulling himself out of the water. He got onto the bridge, started to run across it. Two more federales saw him, yelled out to him. *"Alto, alto!"*

Frank wouldn't stop. The federales ran after him. They swung their Kalashnikovs forward and aimed at him.

Another explosion ripped the stones apart from under their feet. Frank disappeared.

The gangsters had meant to knock out the bridge, probably hoping to release the reservoir waters into the neighborhood below. They'd only managed to destroy a chunk of the dam—it just happened to be along Frank Kelly's escape route.

The federales who had been accosting Frank were down. One was on his knees, his palms pressed against his ears. The other two were rolling on the ground, their faces turned up toward the moon.

A ghastly smear of blood stood on the stone road a few feet away from them.

I raced down the tower steps, reached the rupture in the bridge. There was no sign of Frank, only the trail of blood where he had been standing. I ran to the other side of the bridge, looked down over the steep brick cliff that carried the sifted reservoir water from the lake to the canal that coursed through the city.

There, caught on a jutting keystone, lay Frank Kelly's corpse. His leg was bent backward at the knee, his ankle touching his ear. The water washed over him, rippling him like there wasn't a bone in his body.

52

"You went underground."

It was Ray. He was standing on the back verandah wearing a sweater vest, shoveling up sand from a tall pile into a wheelbarrow with a garden trowel.

"I'm resting," I told him. I eased into the garden chair with a cup of coffee.

"Performance," he said, eyeing the bandage on my forehead. "Takes a lot out of you."

He trundled off, pushing his wheelbarrow. I heard him calling out to the workers in his flat, broken Spanish.

A small green bird flitted overhead, poking in and out of the poinsettia blossoms. She hovered in the sunlight, gleaming emerald. A hummingbird.

I got dressed, slipped the tiny gold ring onto a chain and hung it around my neck. I ventured out of Ray and Happy's compound for the first time in several days.

The town was quieter. Subdued. But it wasn't just the aftermath of the bloody bombings. Thirteen people had been killed. Perhaps a dozen more injured. I thought about the phrase. How often do you hear news reports of incidents such as these, and the announcer always reads the words "And a dozen more injured"?

Despite all that, people didn't seem afraid, or even ruffled. It had happened. They had dealt with it. Now it was over. Another Mexican tragedy. Death comes every day in Mexico. Sometimes, it comes and raises hell.

The outdoor markets were busy, but not harried. Housewives, their straw shopping bags over their arms, patiently perused pyramids of oranges and tomatoes and pineapples. They congregated on corners and at benches beside fountains, chatting.

The streets seemed broader. And I realized that the tourists, with few exceptions, were gone.

I walked clear across town and plodded up a hill to the Museo de las Mumias. I reckoned that Ah Ho's age would have made her a likely candidate to be among the exhumed that were on display there.

I paid my hundred pesos and went in.

The walls were heliotrope colored, a purple blush like a bruise that was taking a long time to heal. The lights were dialed down low. The first display in the entry hall was a skull perched in the bowl of a pelvis. They had it behind glass and I could see my own face reflected beside the naked skull.

I proceeded into the exhibit chambers. The walls were lined with floor-to-ceiling glass cases. Corpses stood senseless in them.

Some of them were naked, their skin dried, brown like desert dirt, and collapsed into folds onto their bones. Some were clothed, and all their apparel had faded to the same colors—dusty gray and yellowed linen.

Many of them were exposed with their jaws dropped wide, in twisted Edvard Munch screams. And their eyelids were closed, caved in over their sockets, like a cloth draped over an empty basket. Hair sprouted in ragged tufts from their brown, brittle heads.

I started to feel ill. A group of Mexicans, a couple with two small children, entered the chamber. The two parents each held up a child, holding the little girls close to the display glass so they could peer into the faces of the corpses. The children were mesmerized by the expressions on the dead faces, the open mouths full of dust. One of the girls asked her father what the dead people were saying. He told her that the dead cannot speak.

I continued on through the museum. One chamber fed into another in a long series of passages, each of them lined with corpses.

The dead were suspended, held up by brackets at their backs. Their feet floated just above the floor of the cases. Some of the feet were bare. Their toenails had continued to grow after their demise. These dead talons were long, so long they curled or splayed, and yellowed.

I inspected the feet of the women. I had supposed that I wouldn't be able to recognize Ah Ho just by her mummified remains. Surely she would have assimilated into the culture—started dressing her hair in the local fashion, worn the popular styles of the day. Even her features may have been—in death—not too distinguishable from the indigenous women's. The Mexicans are, after all, descended from Asian immigrants that came to the New World eons before the Europeans.

It occurred to me that if I found Ah Ho, I would be stymied by the glass casing. I hadn't expected that when I set out on my quest.

A sign at the entry to a wide central chamber described how the museum had been renovated the previous year. For decades the mummies had stood in the open, arranged in perversely prosaic tableaus—sitting in a rocking chair or standing by a table set for tea.

The displays had been rather free-form, and the visitors could wander through and literally brush elbows with the dead as they stood about with their gaping mouths. Visitors enjoyed this happy arrangement for years. Then a few bad apples spoiled it all. The official signage described how "nosy" people had gone about the museum handling the corpses, even going so far as to filch pieces of their clothing, or their pemincen-like flesh, sometimes cracking off the occasional digit to take home as a souvenir.

I was overcome with a mounting despair. Ah Ho was nowhere to be found. And if I did find her, I couldn't get at her through the glass.

I entered the last chamber, a small room housing only two bodies. They lay down—stretched out in state in glass cases against the wall. They reminded me of train passengers asleep in their berths. The first corpse was a man, well-dressed in a vest and a swallowtail coat, and spats on his boots that once would have been polished to a very high shine.

Beyond him lay a woman. She was small. She wore a faded dress that would have been brilliant emerald green. A fancy beadwork belt was cinched around her tiny waist. It was covered in freshwater pearls. Her coiffure survived intact—ripples of black hair held in elaborate buttresses by cleverly placed enameled sticks.

My heart raced. Surely, this was Ah Ho. I walked to the end of the case to inspect her feet. The curators had taken off her little silken boots and laid them beside her in the case. They had put her bare feet on full display, so as to reveal the full barbarity of the ancient Mandarin foot-binding custom. Her feet had been broken across the top of the arch, snapped up and folded so the ball of the foot touched the underside of the heel. They would have crippled her in this way when she was a very small child, then kept the feet wrapped up in damp cloth so they would remain as tiny hooves.

It was Ah Ho. Now, I was certain.

I ran my fingers along the seams of the glass case. They were sealed tight. I felt along the top of the case. There were no openings there either.

"*Lo siento,*" I said to Ah Ho.

And I thought my heart would break.

I left the museum, with the gold ring.

I decided to walk back to my house. I started up over the hill, reached a peak that afforded a good view of the city—its gaily painted houses arranged in jumbly stacks of ocher and cobalt and pink children's blocks tossed up across the town's hills.

I descended and came to a T in the road. The left road led back to the center of town. The right forged on toward the cemetery.

I turned right.

I walked along the cemetery's tall, formidable stone wall until I reached the entrance to the necropolis.

The inward face of the tall wall was lined with plaques. It was six feet thick, deep enough to hold the bodies stacked up four stories high. These bodies in the wall lay, I assumed, with their heads pointed toward the rest of the dead, parsed in patchwork plots.

The grounds were run through with uneven grids of streets and avenues along which the dead resided in their simple graves and elaborate mausoleums. They dwelled in death much as they had in life—the poor housed next to the rich, squalor and opulence in unquestioning harmony.

I walked down some steps into a separate walled area. It was spacious, made regal by wide promenades lined with tall trees wafting in the wind. I set out on one of the graveled walkways, and ambled past a grove of lofty elms, their trunks painted white to repel hoarding insects. Their upraised branches waved high overhead. A flock of large black birds occupied the arbors. The avian spectators watched me with black, unblinking eyes. A couple of crows pushed off their aerie, sailed silently to treetops at the other end of the parkway.

In here too, the walls housed the dead. There were so many of them, all so compactly fitted in, they reminded me of the small, deep-drawered compartments of a Chinese apothecary cabinet.

A woman sat on a bench at the far end of the park. The breeze picked up snatches of her long loose hair, then laid it down again along the back of her beaded, garnet-colored sweater.

"*Buenos dias,*" I said to her.

"You're still here," she told me.

"Would you like one?" She offered me a Coronet de Luna. "These are what you like, yes?"

I thanked her. She asked me to sit beside her on the bench. I told her I was impressed she remembered me.

"I have a confession," she said. "I recognized you when you came to the shop. You are Max Bravo. But I didn't want to be embarrassing."

She told me she'd come to *Akhnaten.*

"Did you enjoy it?"

"Yes," she said. "It was very beautiful. You were magnificent."

"The story is quite marvelous," I said. "It's all true too, you know."

"So few stories are true," she said, smiling. "It's good they tell it. Because people keep telling Akhnaten's story, that makes him live. Forever."

A group of schoolchildren came marching down the pebbled path. They passed in front of us. The children were arranged in twos. They held hands with their partners.

"Are you visiting a relative?" I asked her.

"Yes," she said. She smiled and pointed to a plaque on the wall. "I bring flowers to my great-grandmother."

She had brought fresh marigolds. They barely fit in the green-patina copper funerary vase anchored into the stone.

The inscription on the plaque read: ANNA GONZALES—LOVING WIFE, MOTHER, GRANDMOTHER—DIED 1986.

She looked at me and smiled. Her cheeks were round and smooth and bright in the autumn sunlight. I looked into her eyes—copper flecked with green.

"Your grandmother," I said. "What was her maiden name? Was she from here?"

"Not originally," she told me. "My grandmother is actually an interesting story. She was born in China. She immigrated first to San Francisco, then came to Guanajuato."

I released the clasp of my necklace, let the ring slip off the gold links and drop into my palm.

"A man I know found this in San Francisco," I said. "It was your grandmother's—from when she lived there. He asked me to return it to her."

"But she is dead."

"Not really," I said. "She's not dead. Not if you wear the ring for her."

53

It was raining hard when I landed in San Francisco. I was glad. I'd had enough of Mexico's white-hot skies.

I didn't tell anyone that I was home for several weeks. My tenants, Glen and Glenda, knew I was back—they heard me pattering around in my bamboo house slippers after the cab brought me home at 2 A.M.

I went upstairs to fetch Dixie the next morning. They seemed almost reluctant to release her back to me, as if their priggish foster care provided a more stable home for the dog than my flamboyant lifestyle.

"She looks fat," I told Glen when he handed me the pug.

"We've been feeding her liver and smoked oysters," he informed me.

"Yes," I said, tucking the dog under my arm like a parcel from the butcher shop, "it will be such a hardship for her to go back to grass-fed steaks and free-range chicken."

I pounded down the steps. Dixie squirmed in the crook of my arm, craned her neck around to cast an imploring last glance at Glen and Glenda. They stood on the landing, waving at her.

"You see them every goddamn day," I told her.

She sniffed around the plate of cubed lamb and carrots I'd pan-fried for her, then she tore into it as if she'd just gone over the fence from a fasting spa. I made myself a carafe of strong coffee and began reviewing my telephone and e-mail messages. I had assiduously blocked all San Francisco contact while in Mexico.

Now all the local psychodrama came in a deluge.

Claudia Fantiani e-mailed me that she had run into Ashley Banks. She was with her son, Dante, and her new husband, Teddy Argent. She sent Claudia photos she'd taken in South America.

Dante and Teddy were dressed alike, in Wilkes Bashford slacks and sweaters. Claudia reported that the boy told her how his new dad was taking them all to Aspen so he could learn how to ski.

"Check out what clever bastards those Venezuelan surgeons are," Claudia wrote. I opened the attachment with the photograph.

I stared hard at Ashley's photo, not sure if it actually was her. I enlarged the image. Her scar was gone. And her face was now perfectly symmetrical. She had become, once again, the stunning beauty that Frank Kelly and I had met at Claudia's party many years ago. Dante stood beside Ashley in the shot. He looked taller, thinner. He looked more like Frank than ever.

I went through my mail, found a movie I'd ordered before going to Mexico. It was *San Francisco*. Clark Gable. And the love of my life, Jeanette MacDonald.

Clark is a dastardly Barbary Coast gadabout. He owns a seedy dive. It's called the Paradise. Jeanette, the daughter of a minister, is a gifted soprano. Fate conspires. She ends up singing at the Paradise. She falls in love with Clark, aptly named Blackie Norton.

The penultimate scene played. Jeanette sang the signature ballad, "San Francisco," to a very mixed crowd of high- and lowlifes in a bid to help Blackie win the cash prize that he means to donate to local urchins. The kids are the bastard offcasts born of Barbary sins. Blackie cared for them. And Jeanette cared for Blackie, because of it.

I started crying.

Jeanette, her long beautiful arms swinging, rouses the audience to sing along. They joined in the chorus: "San Francisco, open your golden gate, you let no stranger wait outside your door."

I too sang. I sang with Jeanette. I sang with San Francisco, my people. My eyes brimmed with tears. Goddamn it.

This city—this crazy, dysfunctional city—took everybody in. It was true then. It is true now.

And just as Jeanette roused her ballad to its finale, and the crowd along with it, the theater shook.

The 1906 earthquake struck. The chandeliers swayed. The walls came down. And the next thing I saw was Blackie Norton—oh God, how much like Duffy Fallon he was—wandering the streets, his tuxedo in tatters, finding scenes of heroism and vandalism and hope amid the ruins. He was reduced to desolation looking for her. I too longed to find her. My Jeanette. My hope. My love.

And, finally, Blackie saw her. Jeanette was just where she needed to be, helping the displaced and the injured; she was among the refugees camped out in the high ground of the army presidio, the city burning in the background. There she was, amid the valiant, resilient people camped out in tents. Surviving.

Blackie went to her. Jeanette. She was wrapped in the crowd, helping a minister and the mother of a dead child. She sang. And her rising soprano brought hope, and I cried even more.

Someone called out. The fire had been extinguished.

The news carried. It was a clarion call through the encampment. The fire was out. Death was not final. Catastrophe was never the end. It was just a prelude to the end.

The fire is out.

The refugees, the immigrants—the brave people who had come to San Francisco from Europe and South America and Asia and Africa—raised their heads. The fire is out.

The fire is out. Let's rebuild her. Let's rebuild San Francisco, better than ever.

I wept.

Because I knew that they were right. This was not the end. Eternity was not just an idea. It was a real thing, carved in hope, and love. And there was no varmint so dastardly that eternity was beyond his reach.

A few hours later, I was on my favorite bar stool in the Sans Souci.

It was just Johnny and I. He poured me another setup; a tequila shot with a beer sidecar.

"Nice painting," I said, saluting the seascape hanging over the scarlet-flocked wallpaper above the cigarette machine. I asked him, "Is it new?"

"Just put it up there," Johnny said. "Blashky brought it in."

"Where'd he get it."

"He painted it," Johnny told me. "He's good."

"I didn't know he painted seascapes."

It was a ship plying through a heavy sea.

I got up and took my beer with me to inspect Blashky's work. I leaned in close so I could study the brushstrokes. It was very painterly, the oils applied thick and masculine. Impasto.

I could see each hair of the brush, the texture being just as important as the color. It looked like he used his painter's knife as much as his brush to get oils on the canvas.

I inspected it, closer. And I saw more. There was a thinner, luminescent layer beneath the dense, seemingly opaque surface. Between the gnashing gray waves it shone soft and yellow.

I put on my glasses, I could make out very precise figures drawn in steady ink pen: a sturgeon, old as the world, wearing wire-rim spectacles. A beautiful woman, half her face obscured. A large, powerful woman, her frilly nightie open to reveal a pair of massive breasts, rode a bull down a dark corridor. And two dark-haired men twisted around to face each other. They were smiling.

I returned to my bar seat.

"It's good," I said.

"Another?" Johnny asked.

"Just one." I thanked him. "I'll need to get home. I have to make dinner for Dixie."

Outside, the rain came. It slammed hard into the sidewalk. A dirty torrent rushed along the gutter and escaped down the sewer grates—into the dark labyrinth that twined beneath the city streets.

Get ready

for more outrageous adventures with opera singer extraordinaire Max Bravo!

"A rollicking romp."
—Publishers Weekly

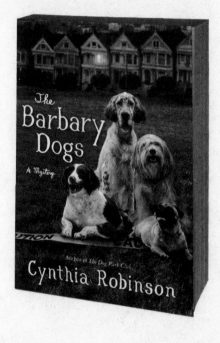

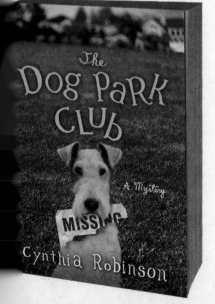

"An amusing dark comedy."
—Kirkus Reviews
(starred review)